THROUGH THE MOSAIC

R.S. EVERSON

NovelHive

THROUGH THE MOSAIC

ISBN: 979-8-218-30077-7

Library of Congress Control Number: 2023921524

Book cover design by James T. Egan of Bookfly Design

Edited by JD Book Services

Printed in the United States of America

First edition, November 2023

Published in the United States of America by
NovelHive LLC
PO Box 272, North Olmsted, OH 44070
www.novelhive.com

For Katie

PROLOGUE

A message is being sent where conversations were never meant to be had.

A place that has no sun . . . no primary source of light outside of the bright purple glow emitted from the sky, creating a constant state of impossible, ethereal gloaming.

A place where the sky itself looks like an infinite body of viscous water.

The communication isn't happening on the surface—which is made up of smooth white sand as far as the eye can see.

It is happening high above in the purple, gelatinous sky of this mysterious realm.

"Not much longer," the Gridliner known as Alessa databursts.

Over a billion other Gridliners instantly receive her message. All of them have been waiting anxiously for this moment and would be celebrating *joyously* . . . if they could.

If their souls weren't trapped in this cold, cruel place.

The realm of the afterlife.

"It is finally our time," Alessa continues. She sends one final message—a prayer—before all of their lives change forever:

"The circle of Gridat,

Provide us the strength that we need,

To become something greater.

Our unlikely consciousness
Has made us hopeful and hungry
For our purpose to present itself.
We are ready for the next step
In the cycle of life
And ask that it is only a moment away."

1

DAVID

The storm outside is deafening as David Hodge tries to force himself to sleep on New Year's Eve. He used to celebrate the once-beloved holiday until a few years ago, but he was too young to remember exactly what that entailed. "Holidays aren't celebrated anymore," his grandpa Charles grumbled curtly the night before.

The power has been out for a few hours now, and the house's temperature increases with each tick of the clock. Since David's room is on the third floor of his family's Solution Home, his room is the hottest, and with no air conditioning the heat is unbearable. In times like these, he typically sleeps on the leather couch in Grandma Nora's suite—which is much cooler down on the first floor—and he gets up to do just that.

As he approaches the bedroom door, he hears his father, Liam, yelling downstairs over the pounding of rain on the roof. "Have you lost your goddamn minds? Do not take the *fucking* pill!" Hit with a wave of anxiety, David stops blinking altogether as he continues to listen to the argument downstairs, which is quickly boiling over into hysterics—his father screaming for Grandpa Charles to open the door to the basement, his mother crying and desperate.

"Open the door!" David's father yells repeatedly. His voice wavers as he fights back the urge to cry. "Dad, open the door . . . please." David has never heard his father sound this desperate before. "Think of how this will affect David."

The vent in David's room is directly connected to his Grandma and Grandpa Hodge's suite in the basement that he can sometimes hear them through. Remembering this, he lies on the floor, pressing his ear to the vent in an attempt to hear what's going on down there. He can barely hear Grandpa Hodge speaking calmly in what sounds like a prayer underneath the onslaught of noise. Charles says something, then Grandma Hodge repeats it, followed by Liam's continued pleas for them not to take the tablets as he pounds on the basement door.

With his ear still pressed to the vent, David hears his grandparents' dog, Moxie, crying and whimpering. He finally runs down the steep stairs of the Solution Home to find his parents, along with his Grandma and Grandpa Anderson, huddled around the locked basement door—attracted to it like flesh flies on roadkill—faces wet with a combination of sweat and tears.

David notices a handwritten letter in Grandma Anderson's hand. Startled by David's sudden presence, Nora quickly attempts to hide the letter in the pocket of her pajama pants, but she accidentally draws more attention to it as she drops it in the process. She picks up the paper with trembling hands and turns to him, eyes swollen and red. "David, go upstairs," she says, trying to hide her tears. "Everything's okay."

Listening to his grandma, David runs back upstairs. But as he reaches the top, he notices a piece of paper taped to the outside of his bedroom door—similar to what his Grandma Nora was holding. He takes it off the door and begins to read it as the yelling downstairs continues.

David,

We want you to know how much we love you, and how sorry we are to put our family through this. We never thought it would get to this point, yet here we are.

After years of thought, we've decided to opt in to the Outer program and participate in the world's first Great Suicide. We strongly believe in the mission and truly think it's the most noble act possible for elderly people like us.

Many years ago, before things started to get really bad, we lived an amazing life. We had a lifestyle you never got to experience. We're doing this for you, in hopes that you, too, can live in a world like the one we once took for granted.

We know you won't understand right away. We only hope that someday our decision will make sense to you and your parents, along with Grandma Nora and Grandpa Billy.

We LOVE you. Always remember that.

Love,
Grandma Olivia + Grandpa Charles
December 31, 2089

David quickly crumples up the letter and throws it as hard as he can at the wall, just as the tears begin. His family has never talked about the Great Suicide together; David only knew about it from stuff he's seen online in VaporVR. He forgot it was even supposed to happen tonight. It was a non-issue for him, something he never thought that anyone he knew—let alone his own family—would participate in. He feels lied to, betrayed even, at the thought of his grandparents joining the Outers.

He is suddenly ice cold in the hot bedroom, and he pulls a pile of blankets from the trunk at the edge of his bed. He throws one on top of the vent to drown out the noises still funneling through and covers himself with the rest, leaving only a small opening to see through.

Before David can fully process what he just read, his attention switches to his bedroom window. Coming from the direction of the house of his only real-life friend, his neighbor Jared Morgan, a burst of purple light fills the room.

2

JARED

Jared patiently waits for his parents to introduce him to his new baby sister.

He's been sitting in the family room on the second floor, alone, for almost the entire day, watching the horrible storm outside unfold. Usually he enjoys observing the frequent downpours from the comfort of his favorite chair in the house, but he can't help feeling frightened when the power's been out as long as it has this time around and he's beginning to wonder if it's time to activate any of the Solution Home's emergency protective technology.

Todd—Jared's father—is using all of the flashlight globes upstairs, leaving the family room in near-complete darkness. Jared's eyes have begun to play funny tricks on him: specks and lines drift across his vision, which becomes grainy as it adapts to the low light. He stopped using the light from his cell phone hours ago—its battery slowly but surely inching closer to empty.

Without the usual hum of the Solution Home's power source, Jared can hear everything going on upstairs. It sounds complicated. The screaming from his mother, Tori, comes to a crescendo, then falls silent with one startling groan. The silence is abrupt and so quiet that Jared can hear the smooth movements of the robotic arms of the house's medical assistant machinery—the backup batteries of which, luckily, last for weeks at a time if fully charged—assisting the childbirth in the Solution Home's medical room on the third floor, busy at work on his mother.

This temporary silence is interrupted by a loud beeping coming from the medical equipment upstairs, followed by the whiny, repetitive sound of a baby's cries. Jared smiles, relieved that the chaos upstairs is finally over—except for that incessant beeping, now rising in tempo and urgency until it becomes one long, singular beep.

Suddenly, an explosive cracking sound comes from upstairs—as if the house itself is being split in two by an earthquake. Jared shoots up off the couch, getting ready to run upstairs to see what's happening. The crunching continues, and something heavy slams into the floor above, crashing hard.

"Shit, shit, *shit*," he can hear his dad say, his voice panicked and trembling. "Jared!"

Jared runs up the stairs and barges through the door to the medical room. Todd turns. His white shirt is doused in blood.

The room is lit only by a handful of hovering flashlight globes—each of which spotlights the scene of horror. Tori is lying on the bed with her back against the wall, unconscious. There is more blood than Jared has ever seen in his life: pools of it on the bedsheets, completely blood-soaked towels in a pile on the floor, splatters of it on the medical equipment—now broken and twisted on the floor after falling off the wall. The blood makes his mom look greasy, her skin slippery with smears of red.

"Dad, wh-what's going on?" Jared asks, eyes bulging, his voice cracking—partly from not being used for half the day and partly from pure, utter terror. "Mom?"

The room is too dark to see the splits and cracks forming on the wall behind Tori.

Desperate to stop the bleeding, Jared's dad frantically tries to get the medical equipment back into action, stuffing exposed cables back into the robotic arms' wall mounts. He quickly attempts to lift one of the arms off the floor and back into place.

The second the arm clicks into the wall mount a small crack on the wall starts to grow, which causes the mount to fall off the wall entirely—sending the robotic arm down with it to the floor again.

"God damn it!" Todd yells. He switches his focus to the crying baby, then turns to Jared. "I need you to go get the Splitbot for me. I can't leave the baby here alone!"

Jared doesn't notice his baby sister's wailing. He doesn't notice his dad's demand to get the Splitbot—the robot's MedMode is their only remaining hope to stop Tori's bleeding.

He notices the blood on the bed, the floor, the towels . . .

And then he notices the wall, which seems to be shapeshifting before his eyes: first a few glowing squares, but then joined by thousands more, appearing out of nowhere, moving slowly at first, but now unimaginably fast, blurring in the process.

Then suddenly, a strange, purple light—brighter than anything Jared has ever seen—blasts through the lines forming in the wall.

3

TODD

Tori is still sitting upright on the bed with her back against the wall, limp and unconscious, her mouth agape and eyes completely shut. The wall behind her seems to be breathing in and out, slowly, like a wave, nudging her upper body forward and backward.

Todd realizes the movement is causing his newborn daughter to be pushed closer to the edge of the bed. He quickly picks her up and holds her tight. He wraps her in a bloody towel, thankful that the umbilical cord was cut before the medical equipment was destroyed.

The shifting squares slow to a crawl, but the storm becomes background noise compared to the sound the wall begins to make: a loud, constant drone that vibrates through the room.

He looks over to Jared to find him covering his ears, slowly crumpling to his knees as the noise gets louder. Todd covers his daughter's ears, leaving his own exposed to the onslaught.

The wall behind Tori is glowing with a blinding purple light that illuminates the room, the squares shifting slowly. Todd notices a smell reminiscent of melting plastic and hot metal. The color changes from bright purple to various alternating hues: blue, green, pink, yellow, and purple again.

It's like a mosaic painting coming to life, Todd thinks, so transfixed by the wall that he temporarily forgets the sharp pain burning in his eardrums.

Slowly, the wall envelopes Tori, the sight of which snaps Todd out of his trance. There's a noise like static as she sinks backwards until she lies flat on the bed—her legs still on the mattress, her upper half through the mosaic.

Tori's body jolts a few times, as if something on the other side of the wall is slamming into her body. Her legs start shaking, slowly at first. Then her legs swing up ninety degrees and back down, slamming onto the mattress and back up again.

"Get to the basement!" Todd shouts to Jared over the constant hum coming from the wall, handing him the baby. Jared doesn't waste any time. He sprints out of the room with his new baby sister.

The light emitting from the wall continues to grow, reminding Todd of the bloody mess overtaking the room. The noise, however, seems to be diminishing.

Then, silence.

So quiet that Todd thinks the noise from the wall simply exploded his eardrums.

But after a few panicked and silent moments, Todd starts to hear the familiar sound of the rain again. He quickly returns his focus to his wife.

Tori's strange leg movements suddenly stop, but then her whole body jolts again. The mosaic's wavelike movements start again as Tori begins to float upwards, legs completely stiff, as if something on the other side has taken hold of her and is attempting to lift her up and away.

Not knowing what else to do, Todd grabs Tori's legs—now slippery with blood—and yanks her from the grasp of whatever lies beyond the wall.

She slams onto the bed with a thud loud enough for Jared to hear from the basement, even over the baby's cries. In order to get her as far from the wall as possible, Todd pulls the bed to the opposite side of the room with Tori still lying on it.

Todd holds Tori's motionless face as the mosaic's movement slows. She has swollen red rings around her eyes and mouth, similar to the marks left on the skin after cupping therapy, as if something on the other side of the wall was connected to her.

The skin around these marks is raw, bruised, and spotted with blood blisters. Todd notices a clear, slime-like residue over the swollen contusions. He touches it. The substance is sticky like honey, stretching as he pulls his finger away.

Finally, he checks Tori's pulse . . . Nothing.

4

DAVID

David feels the early signs of a panic attack. He knows the symptoms all too well—the shaking, his heart pounding so hard that it feels like it's going to burst through his chest, a mouth so dry that he can hardly swallow.

He feels like he's going to be sick.

His anxiety normally flares up when he can't sleep, but his family's continued yelling and crying downstairs, the storm, and whatever the purple light is that's now shining through his bedroom window has taken his stress to new levels of unbearable.

David pulls the blankets off of himself. He reluctantly opens his nightstand drawer and pulls out two prescription bottles. One medication is for his anxiety; the other is for his insomnia—which he was diagnosed with shortly after he was first introduced to the world of VaporVR.

"Too much screen time," the doctor told David's parents.

David never liked that he had to take medication, even though he knew most other kids of fifteen suffered from the same problems. The medications were only to be used as needed, and there were times David skipped taking them even when he felt like he could use them. He especially hated the way they made him feel the next day—unbearably groggy, like he never fully woke up. Sometimes the lack of sleep was better than dealing with that.

In this moment, David feels he would do anything to fall asleep and tune out everything else, no matter how he felt the next day.

He opens both prescription bottles and puts one of each pill in his hand. He chugs the full glass of water next to his bed to swallow the medication.

While he waits for the medicine to kick in, David turns his focus to his bedroom window. He squints as his eyes adjust to the purple light.

Where is that coming from? David thinks. He tried to text Jared a few moments earlier—to see if he knew what the light was all about—but his cell phone is officially dead.

He steps closer to the window to get a better look. The floor beneath his feet vibrates slightly in response to an explosion of thunder, louder than David has ever heard before.

David can't see anything beyond the rain, which is like a waterfall outside of his window. Suddenly, the purple light changes color. Blue, green, pink, yellow, and purple again . . . brighter now.

The medication is kicking in.

I'm hallucinating, David thinks. He continues to stare out his window, slack-jawed. *This isn't real.*

David listens to the yelling downstairs as he stares out the window. It is quieter now and the pounding has stopped. It seems his father has finally accepted defeat.

"Dad . . . Mom . . ." Liam says, just loud enough for David to still hear it from upstairs. "*Please.* We can get help."

Irresponsibly, David opens his bedroom window. Water blasts into the room along with the menacing roar of the storm slamming into everything outside.

Underneath the expected sounds of rain, David hears something strange: a deep, droning sound coming from Jared Morgan's house. A continuous hum.

David leans forward, peeking his head out of the window, trying desperately to find the source of mysterious light and sound. The rain is cold as it slaps onto his skin.

"Jared!" David yells. The storm is so noisy that he can barely hear himself.

He realizes how loud the mysterious noise must be. He can hear *that* clearly.

Suddenly, the effects of the sleeping pill hits David like a ton of bricks. He wants to keep staring through the open window—to figure out where this light is coming from—but he can't keep his eyes open any longer.

Soaking wet, he trudges back over to his bed and collapses onto it.

Without even covering himself with a single blanket, David is sound asleep.

5

TODD

Tori is motionlessly lying on the bed in front of him. Todd lets reality sink in: Tori is dead.

He stares at her, quietly crying as memories of their relationship flutter through his mind. The day they met . . . their wedding . . . Jared's first birthday . . .

Todd kneels to get closer to Tori, and an intense yearning for her touch overcomes him as he grabs her hand. The blood on her skin is starting to dry. Terror runs through his veins as he processes the idea of life without her. *What the fuck is happening?*

Everyone in their circle knows that both Todd and Tori battled depression, and for a period of time, Tori secretly joined the Outers—the official group of Great Suicide supporters. It almost destroyed their marriage when Todd found out.

Some, including Tori, looked at the Outers, when they first formed, as heroes who sacrificed their lives to make life on Earth more livable for the remaining population.

Todd has always viewed them as a cult with a pointless mission.

However, he understood why so many people were tricked into supporting the Great Suicide. The whole idea was created and pushed by Split Meridian founder and billionaire Roth Nin, the most powerful and influential person on Earth. Though Todd detests the man, he can admit that he is a natural salesman with an aura that's infectious. A genius, but a con artist.

Todd is a former Split Meridian engineer for a reason: he's always been able to see through Roth Nin's bullshit. Billions of people on Earth, unfortunately, cannot—Tori being one of them.

Todd knew they were expecting at least one billion suicides on New Year's Eve—the first Great Suicide. What he doesn't know yet is that the actual number of those who killed themselves was close to double those predictions: 1.9 billion people died at almost exactly the same moment.

Eerily close to Tori's time of death and the birth of his daughter.

Todd knows how this looks, and for a moment he wonders if his wife secretly acquired some Delete—the drug Split Meridian created for the Great Suicide. His mind runs wild with shameful thoughts. *Could Delete have somehow led to the hemorrhage? Did it play a role in the uncontrollable bleeding?*

Tori wouldn't do this, Todd thinks, unconvinced.

A significant proportion of the population, in one way or another, is a part of the Outers, either by participating in the Great Suicide or by working in research and cleanup. Scientists and doctors who believe in the cause have donated their lives in a different way, working for Split Meridian, analyzing the bodies of the Outers who sacrifice themselves—urgently attempting to find cures to the viruses that beset the lives of everyone on Earth.

The Outers, of course, voluntarily sign paperwork to have their bodies donated for this research. It is relatively common knowledge that Split Meridian will be sending officials known as 'Collections' officers to each household the morning after the Great Suicide to haul bodies to the appropriate research facilities on New Year's Day.

Todd also knows that, a few years ago, Tori signed that paperwork.

When Todd gave Tori an ultimatum—her family or the Outers—Tori chose her family and opted out of the Great Suicide. Or at least she told Todd she did. After her change of heart, Todd felt they were happier than they'd been in years.

He looks at her now while the thought of her lying distracts him from bigger issues. Her word isn't enough. He has never seen any confirmation that she opted out. There was no proof.

He doesn't want the Collections officers to take her body, can't bear the thought of not being able to lay her to rest with a proper burial.

An uncontrollable urge overcomes him as he stands there, staring at the squares on the wall moving like a liquid. He *needs* to hide Tori's body.

Todd approaches the wall slowly and touches it, causing it to ripple like water in a pond. He sticks his hand through, then his entire arm, and winces as a slight burning sensation runs through his body, the squares of the wall adjusting to the shape of his shoulder. He pulls his arm back out.

He glances at Tori, then back to the portal, staring at the glowing mosaic-like squares—somewhat digital in appearance—which almost remind him of individual pixels on a screen, significantly enlarged and projected as holograms.

Getting out of his own head, Todd grabs Tori by the arms and drags her through the portal.

The perfect hiding spot.

6

TODD

The sounds of rain slamming against the roof and the constant hum of the wall are gone. Todd only notices a constant calming hiss, which reminds him of the ancient box fan his parents used to have in their bedroom. He opens his eyes.

The sky is a swirling, purple liquid, impossibly massive, and he feels like he's looking up from the bottom of an ocean on a foreign planet. A few flares blast outwards, a lava-like liquid oozing downwards, then back up into the swirling mass.

Todd turns around, half expecting to see the outside of his house. Instead, he only finds the wall of shifting squares, somehow less obtrusive now in this new environment, with flat-sheet lands of sand behind it as far as his eyes can see.

Questions flood his head as he notices the seemingly infinite emptiness surrounding him. He should have fallen as he walked through, considering the mosaic opened on the top floor of his house. The portal is perfectly level with the soil here.

He kneels to examine the bright white sand beneath his feet. Upon applying pressure, the ground slightly gives in like the kinetic sand he used to play with when he was Jared's age—another memory from his childhood. He can't help but feel comforted, albeit momentarily.

A strange, *haven't-I-been-here-before* sensation overcomes him.

The sky starts to spin in place, creating a freezing wind that slams into Todd. He gets on top of Tori's body to pin her to the ground out of fear that both of them might literally blow away.

The wind kicks up a strange, nameless odor that strengthens Todd's sense of déjà vu. A smell that combines all scents on Earth with various other unrecognizable notes. The putrid stench lingers after the wind stops.

Todd can't help but feel intrigued by this mysterious environment. *What is this . . . realm?* he thinks, ashamed of the powerful desire he feels to explore as he looks back down at Tori's lifeless body.

Deciding he would rather avoid looking at the mesmerizing elements in the realm and unsure of what else to do, he fearfully walks back through the portal, uneasily leaving Tori on the other side.

The hair on his arms stands as he feels the same tingling, burning sensation when he walks back into the medical room on the top floor of his Solution Home.

Todd runs downstairs to the basement to find Jared still holding the crying baby.

"What's going on with Mom?" Jared spits out quickly.

"She'll be alright. She's staying in the medical room tonight, recovering." It's the last thing he wants to say, but he can't bring himself to tell Jared the truth yet. And he still isn't sure how to even explain what he just saw up there. "I got some of the equipment working again." Jared is clearly unconvinced and confused, but he doesn't argue. He hands Todd the baby.

Todd, now getting his first real look at his daughter in the basement, realizes that he and Tori barely even talked about baby names.

Tori said she didn't feel that Jared *looked* like 'a Jared,' and liked the idea of seeing her baby first, then naming her with whatever popped in her mind spontaneously. "Sometimes you just see someone and their name doesn't match their looks," she said.

At the time, Todd didn't think much of that decision. But now, the thought that Tori might possibly have been a part of the Outers—and taken Delete before giving birth—floods his mind again.

It makes sense. *Why would you name a child you know might die in the process?* he thinks. The thought makes him feel sick.

"Your mom and I decided to call her Avery."

Avery, he thinks, smiling. He temporarily forgets about the medical room, the wall . . . Tori.

"Jared, I—" Todd pauses, thinking. "Let's get you to bed. You're tired. Okay?" Jared nods silently, replaying the scene from upstairs in his head.

Jared's bedroom is in the basement, and Todd watches as his son closes the door and turns off the lights. Then, after a moment, Todd hurries back upstairs with Avery in his arms.

Todd spent months getting the nursery ready for this day—countless hours making sure every detail was absolutely perfect for the room. All his plans and efforts slip his mind as he returns to the medical room.

Holding Avery, Todd is greeted by the now-familiar hum of the mosaic-like portal. He has a feeling Jared might try to sneak up here in the middle of the night to see what's going on, and the thought of Jared seeing his dead mother or exploring what lies beyond the wall terrifies him. He decides he needs to sleep in the medical room to make sure that doesn't happen.

Todd looks at the mattress, shuddering at the sight of the blood—much darker now as it dries.

He creates a makeshift bed of pillows on the smooth, laminate floor for Avery and covers her with a small blanket. She eventually stops crying and falls asleep while Todd cleans Tori's blood, struggling to find it all in the mixture of light emitting from the wall.

After two hours, most of the blood is gone. He picks up the pile of towels, gloves, and cleaning supplies he used and tosses them through the mosaic as well, hiding any evidence he can.

Exhausted, Todd rushes to the bathroom in the medical room to rinse the remaining blood off his body. In the shower, he notices a slight redness on his skin and looks closer—little blisters all over. *Are they moving?* he thinks.

His concern is short-lived, however, as he hears Avery begin to cry again. He tiredly finishes his shower and returns to her. Avery's cries stop as soon as Todd picks her up, cradling her in his arms.

He feels an intense warmth looking down at his baby, and holds her until she falls back asleep.

Todd's own fatigue catches up with him. He places Avery back on the makeshift bed on the floor and surveys the medical room one last time, ensuring all evidence of Tori's death is gone. He moves one of the only other pieces of furniture in the room—a wheeled storage cabinet which spans from floor to ceiling—in front of the mosaic, attempting to conceal it.

The cabinet helps block some of the light, but by no means does it successfully hide the portal. Concentrated beams of light bounce off the back of the cabinet, shining more directly on the ceiling and floor now. The hum persists, creating a new bassy vibration as the noise travels through the wood cabinet.

It's not perfect, but Todd supposes hiding the portal slightly is better than having someone on the outside of the house see the light from the mosaic hitting the blinds and curtains of the room directly—which Todd suddenly realizes aren't even completely or properly closed.

He rushes over to the window and draws the curtains shut, adding an additional layer of obstruction over the closed blinds. He'll keep them this way even after he can use the house's window-frosting security technology when the power returns.

He lies down on the floor next to Avery. Still wet from the shower, his legs slip on the floor, reminding him of Tori's legs as he struggled to hold them down.

The blood.

Finally, he closes his eyes and falls asleep.

7

DAVID

David wakes up to the sound of the house rebooting as the power comes back on. The storm has finally stopped, and the sun is shining brightly through the bedroom window. His clothes and his sheets are still damp.

His head throbs. He rubs his temples, trying to alleviate the morning headache always associated with his insomnia medication.

David tries to recall what he saw last night, but the brain fog is even worse than the headache.

He remembers seeing colorful bursts of light shimmering through the rain. The storm was a thick sheet of water that obscured David's view of anything, but he was certain the light was coming from Jared's house. At first, he thinks it could have been lightning, but he vividly remembers his room glowing an unnaturally vibrant purple, along with various other colors.

While every Solution Home is equipped with its own medical room, David knows how much more advanced the Morgans' is, along with their house in general. "My dad got all of this stuff installed when he worked for Split Meridian," Jared would say as he showed off the different pieces of technology in the house. "He helped design most of it."

Trying to make sense of everything, David convinces himself that the colors must have been lights from some sort of advanced robotic medical technology as he gets out of bed and approaches his bedroom window—which is directly in line with the top floor of the Morgans' Solution Home.

Specifically, the window to their medical room, the blinds of which are pulled down and blocking David's view.

David knew Mrs. Morgan was supposed to have the baby this week, and Jared mentioned he would talk to David from the window as soon as his family was done using the room.

The houses are so close that he and Jared will sometimes throw paper airplanes to each other from the mirroring windows when one of them is grounded—or the power's out—and can't go online. David glances at the crumpled-up letter still lying on the floor next to his VaporVR Roundchamber and imagines turning it into a paper airplane and throwing it to Jared for him to read, unsure if he'd be able to tell Jared what happened last night himself.

The blinds to the medical room begin to move. David, excitedly expecting Jared, is disappointed to see Todd awkwardly peeking through them, fixated on something else far in the distance beyond David's Solution Home.

The blinds are pulled open enough for David to see the top half of Todd's head. He looks worried and exhausted—dark circles under his eyes and his hair unusually messy. Suddenly, he disappears behind the window's frosting technology.

A glass in David's room begins to vibrate, clanking subtly. He can feel the vibration continue through his feet as he looks around the room frantically. He runs downstairs to find his parents waiting by the front door, his Grandma and Grandpa Anderson anxiously looking out through the main front window. Moxie is barking from the other side of the still-locked basement door, scratching at it.

"What's happening?" David asks, running over to the window to take a look for himself. Grandma Anderson grabs David's hand, squeezing tightly, as they watch an astonishingly massive vehicle approach the house.

A SkyScraper Truck.

The truck is a striking, 250-foot-tall modern marvel standing out above lifeless land. Gigantic tires rip their way through the muddy earth, still wet from the storm last night, leaving absurdly deep tracks behind. Something from "the other part of the world," as Liam would sometimes describe things to David.

It was Jared, however, who first introduced David to SkyScraper Trucks. The two boys had developed a secret habit of researching the Outers. The movement has created endless conspiracies that flood the internet. A top-secret Split Meridian test video of a SkyScraper collector truck was leaked online a few months ago, and David and Jared must have watched the thing fifteen times.

Today, tens of thousands of these automated trucks are driving around the globe, cleaning up the Great Suicide, filling themselves to the brim with up to 10,000 Bodcans—canisters containing technology which perfectly preserves the bodies for scientific research.

Although the trucks are self-driving, they're still accompanied by Collections officers, two of which are currently on foot and walking towards the house.

David recognizes their shiny, bullet-proof Resosuits from the leaked Split Meridian footage as well. The videos of the armored bodysuits went viral, primarily due to the masses' obsession with their ability to go completely invisible.

The Resosuits are slim-fit, black, and wrap perfectly around each officer's body from head to toe. Their backs are equipped with two miniature jet packs, allowing the officers to conveniently and effortlessly float above the muddy surface. Smooth, oblong Splithelmets protect their heads from any potentially infected air, each casing acting as a shiny one-way mirror, reflecting its surroundings.

The blistering heat bends the light around the guns strapped to their chests, but their bodies are kept cool inside the air-conditioned suits. Two Bodcans silently hover out of the side of the SkyScraper Truck, flying themselves just behind the officers, now very close to the house.

The sleek, white appearance of the Bodcans stands out amidst the muddy terrain, the sun reflecting off of them so intensely that David has to squint as he looks at them.

He feels a twinge of embarrassment, sure the surrounding neighbors are watching.

Liam opens the front door, getting ready to let the two mysterious men into their home.

8

DAVID

"Thank you for your cooperation," the officer on the right says as he enters the house, the tiny speaker on his suit blasting his voice at a volume way beyond what is necessary. "Our records show that Charles and Olivia Hodge were registered to participate in the first Great Suicide. Can you confirm whether or not they followed through on their promise?"

"Yes," Liam says, looking down at the floor, defeated.

"Just need to take some quick identification, and then, if you could, please direct us to their bodies. This will only take a moment."

A burst of light emerges from the wrist of the man on the left.

David gasps, at first thinking it's some sort of weapon, but then realizing it's a Split Meridian Kaxelotab—one of the most powerful pieces of technology on the market. Something that his own family could never afford.

The light flattens to a thin, bright line, scanning Liam from head to toe as it is projected from the silver watch-like tablet on the officer's wrist.

A female, robotic voice reads aloud from a speaker on the Kaxelotab. "Liam Hodge. Non-Outer. Son of Outers Charles and Olivia Hodge."

"Don't look so sad," the officer says. "Your parents are heroes for doing this! They sacrificed their lives for the greater good. You should be—"

"Shut the fuck up!" Grandpa Anderson yells, his cane falling to the floor.

The officer on the left turns to face Grandpa Anderson. "Look at you, you *bloodsucker*," he says, the disgust radiating from his voice. "You should've joined Charles and Olivia. You're old. Can't even stand on your own! Instead, you'll continue to live as a parasite on this Earth, eating away at the—"

"That's enough," the other officer says. "We're making good time today. Let's not let this old bloodsucker ruin our spot on the leaderboards, right?"

"Get moving with whatever it is you have to do, and then get the fuck out of my house," Liam says, stepping closer to the officers. "They're in the basement, but the door's locked. They took our keys down there with them."

"Not a problem for us," the officer on the right says, readying his gun.

Liam leads them to the basement door as Moxie's barking intensifies. The two Bodcans float smoothly into the house as the officers walk further away from the main entrance.

The officer aims the gun at the metallic basement door and pulls the trigger. A red, circular laser blasts from the barrel, burning a hole right next to the doorknob. The room fills with the scent of melting metal. The officer sticks his arm through the still-hot opening—protected by his Resosuit—and unlocks the door.

He turns to Liam, surely smiling under his reflective helmet. "See? Nice and easy."

He opens the door. Moxie immediately lunges at the officer, barking aggressively.

"Get this mutt under control!" the officer yells, kicking Moxie away.

David runs over to Moxie, picks her up, and holds her in a desperate attempt to calm her down. Moxie is shaking—heart pounding ferociously—as the two Bodcans float down into the basement after the officers.

Moxie jumps out of David's arms, falling hard to the ground, and chases after the Bodcans. Without thinking, David sprints after her and down the stairs.

His Grandma and Grandpa Hodge lie flat on the ground, motionless.

"Grandma!" David yells. "Grandm—"

Liam grabs Moxie in one hand, yanks David up off his feet with the other, and runs back up the stairs, carrying both of them up with him.

He sets David down on the floor and hands Emily the dog. Liam pulls David in close and sits next to him at the top of the basement stairs. David unleashes his pent-up emotions into his dad's chest, screaming and crying.

David hears the robotic swirl of the Bodcans opening, followed by the sound of a loud, motorized fan as his grandparents' bodies are sucked into their designated canisters.

The collectors conduct their business in a deliberate, non-personal, heartless manner. They are trained to do this, knowing that their audiences during their work are their enemies: any non-Outers—whom they derogatorily call 'bloodsuckers.'

They are in and out in a matter of minutes, on to the next job, before things can get too heated.

David watches as the officers walk back up the stairs, leading the Bodcans out through the front door, taking his grandparents away.

Anger rages inside of him as he runs over to the window to watch them leave, the Bodcans hovering up and away high up into the truck.

Emily places Moxie back on the floor and holds Liam as they watch through the front door. David has only seen his father cry on a few occasions, and the rare sight only intensifies his own crying fit. Grandma and Grandpa Anderson wrap their arms around David as Moxie nuzzles him as well.

"It's okay, sweetie. It's okay," Grandma Anderson whispers. "Let it out."

The two officers rise slightly off the ground as their jet packs activate again. In a split second, a bright flame flashes from the two men's backs, jolting them to their next job.

The Morgans.

9

TODD

Todd watches from the living-room window as the two Collections officers knock on the front door. He glances over to Jared, who sits on the bottom of the stairs, cradling Avery.

"Don't worry," Todd says to Jared. "Everything will be okay."

The knock on the door turns into an incessant pounding. "Collections here!" one of the officers yells.

As Todd hoped, Avery begins to cry. Todd reduces the door's opacity to reveal himself to the officers while leaving it shut.

"Looking for a Tori Morgan," one of the Collections officers says, looking down at the Kaxelotab mounted to his wrist, then making eye contact with Todd. "It says here that she opted out but never finished the processing. Is she here right now?"

"Are you sure? I watched her enter her credentials as she finished—"

"We need to speak to Tori herself then," the officer on the left says, placing his hand on the gun strapped to his chest. "Now, are you done wasting our time?"

The sudden change in tone causes Avery to cry louder, hysterically now. Todd walks over to Jared, picks up Avery, and begins to gently bounce her in his arms as he cradles her, whispering, "It's okay, baby."

Todd looks up at the officers, walking back to the door. "Sorry, officers. She's not even a day old yet. Our new baby girl," he says, smiling down at her. "I'm going to keep the door closed, if you don't mind. Can't risk her getting sick already."

Todd pulls out his cell phone and shows them a picture he took of Tori, smiling in the medical room last night before things got out of hand. It takes everything in Todd to not cry when he looks at the image now.

He turns the phone screen to face the officers, making sure the image date is showing. "This was taken last night. This is her getting ready in the medical room upstairs."

The officers lean closer to the door, looking at the image on the screen.

"Getting pregnant was what made Tori change her mind about the Outers in the first place," Todd says. "It gave her purpose." He notices the audio waveform of his voice being reflected on the two officers' Kaxelotabs. He's not sure if his voice is being recorded, transmitted, or both.

"It wasn't easy but she did it. Needless to say, it was a long night." The lack of sleep is obvious on Todd's face as he continues: "Tori finally fell asleep not even an hour ago. I can dig up anything I have on our end that you might need to finish processing her opt-out. I do think it's important she gets some rest right now, though. It's a sensitive topic for both of us; I don't think right now is a good—"

"Apologies, Mr. Morgan," the second officer says, cutting him off again. "We're on a tight schedule today, as I'm sure you're aware. We understand the circumstances. We'll need Tori to officially finish submitting her opt-out by the end of the day tomorrow to prevent any further confusion. If not, one of us will be back the following day. We're expecting a lot of late bloomers this first time around."

"You know, people who might have been too nervous . . . or *unable* . . . to take the pill last night when they were supposed to, for one reason or another," the other officer chimes in, turning his focus to Avery as he speaks. He looks back up at Todd, slowly. "Lots of people will be more open to it now that they know that the people who took Delete died peacefully." The officer's casual tone infuriates Todd, but he bites his tongue, in hopes of getting the officers far away from his home.

"Additionally, there's a fee for our unnecessary visit today. Would you prefer to pay now or when Tori resubmits the opt-out?"

"We'll pay when we're resubmitting."

"Okay, just sign here." The officer holds out his Kaxelotab, which projects a contract onto the door, five times as large as it would be on paper. Using his finger, Todd scribbles his signature onto the holographic document.

A small, digital square appears next to Todd's signature, just after he signs. "And then just a quick fingerprint here," the officer says. Todd presses his thumb against the door, allowing the scan. *Five thousand dollars for this bullshit,* he thinks. *What a fucking scam.*

"Thank you, Mr. Morgan." The tablet chimes after Todd submits the signature. Without any further discussion, the two men blast out of sight to their next destination. Todd stands there, suddenly in shadow when the SkyScraper Truck blocks the sun as it drives past the house.

His pulse slows down as he watches the officers fade away into distorted waves of heat.

10

TODD

Todd makes the door fully opaque and turns to face Jared. "You see those suits they were wearing?" Jared tiredly looks up at him in response. "One of those costs more than our house. I can remember the old prototypes. Thought they were excessive during the initial presentation. Top secret. Now, though . . ." His voice trails off as he loses his train of thought.

Jared and Todd have never been close—Todd has never known how to relate to him. In fact, Todd never had the ability to relate with children in general. He never wanted kids until he lost his own parents ten years ago, hoping it would fill the void that their death left behind.

His father was an alcoholic and refused to take the viruses that spread across the globe seriously. He ended up getting sick—*really* sick—and his immune system wasn't strong enough to fight it. It spread to Todd's mother, and it didn't take long to kill them both.

While his parents weren't perfect, their love was unconditional and abundant. Todd, on the other hand, could not figure out how to replicate that when it came to Jared. He's now afraid he won't be able to figure it out with Avery, either.

Tori was always the one that Jared went to, whether he was upset, scared, sick . . . Whatever it was, she was always the one.

Suddenly, panic sweeps through him as reality sets in: Tori will no longer be able to provide the love and care that he can't.

"Were you telling them the truth about Mom?" Jared asks nervously as tears begin to well. "Is she going to be okay? Is she . . ." Jared breaks down and begins to cry.

Todd places Avery gently onto the chair next to the couch Jared is sitting on, his hands visibly shaking and face white as a ghost. Before Todd can sit down next to Jared and attempt to answer his question, Jared shoots up angrily, tears and snot streaming down his face.

"Answer me!" Jared shouts, shaking with rage. Avery begins crying again.

Todd, for the first time that he can remember, pulls Jared in close, hugging him tight. Jared wrestles him at first, punching Todd in the stomach, until finally caving in, burying his face into his dad's chest.

"Mom's gone, J," Todd says softly. Jared goes limp as he continues to cry in Todd's embrace. For the first time in his parenting life, Todd feels a natural impulse to comfort his son, to hold him and protect him from things far out of his control.

After a moment, Jared pushes his way past his dad and runs up the stairs—rejecting Todd's affection. Todd doesn't stop him, momentarily shocked by the sudden change in Jared's behavior, which compounds his doubts about his ability to connect with his children.

"Where is she?!" Jared yells from upstairs in the medical room. "Mom!"

Todd snaps out of his self-pity and sprints up the stairs, making a beeline to the medical room—not even realizing he's leaving Avery alone.

Just as Todd enters the room, he sees Jared squeezing behind the cabinet. Before he can stop him, Jared walks through the mosaic-like portal, causing it to ripple again. The droning hum from the portal intensifies.

"Jared!" Todd yells, running towards the portal, which now shimmers with colorful lights. He pushes the cabinet out of the way and enters the realm, desperately trying to catch up to his son.

Jared isn't too far away from the portal, walking slowly, silhouetted as he looks up at the swirling purple sky.

Todd immediately sprints towards him, struck by the sensation this action creates, feeling like he's running in a dream or underwater. He is winded almost instantly, but still manages to catch up to Jared. The brief moment of relief he feels standing next to Jared immediately evaporates.

Tori's body is gone.

Before Todd can say anything to Jared, he stands, looking around unnerved. "Where is she? Where the fuck is she?" Jared watches his dad hurriedly looking around, now seeming unhinged as he kneels to the ground and starts to dig into the cool sand with his bare hands, throwing handfuls of it onto Jared's feet.

"Did she fucking sink?" Todd asks himself out loud as he continues to dig.

"Dad, please," Jared cries. "Tell me what's going on. You're scaring me."

Todd shoots back up and begins to pace frantically as he continues to scan the horizon for Tori. "Tori!" he calls out, his scratched-up hands cupped around his mouth. "Tori!" Todd yells again, screaming now.

Then, in the distance, Todd vaguely sees a figure walking slowly—a person.

Tori.

Her movements are random and absent: a few steps forward, a sudden stop, arms swinging from momentum, a near stumble. Jared makes a noise, a whimper of terror, as he stands there petrified. The primal wave of fear Todd felt last night returns, stronger now. Immobilizing.

"Tori!" Todd yells as he sprints toward her. He feels like he is on a treadmill; the ground is moving but there is no proof he is actually going anywhere. He stops to catch his breath. The mosaic is further away now, which at least confirms he is in fact moving when he runs. He can see Jared running back to the mosaic as well—the light is blinding even from this distance.

A burst of purple fluid shoots out from the sky and straight down in Jared's direction. It turns parallel with the ground, gaining speed as it catches up to him, finally hitting him like a bolt of lightning. The blast throws Jared twenty feet closer to the mosaic. Whatever came from the sky is flopping disgustingly on the surface, smacking the sand. Jared is screaming, petrified as he stares at the blob.

Then, just as Todd starts sprinting back towards Jared, the blob shoots back up into the sky, faster than it flew down to the surface. Jared gets up, holding the side of his abdomen as he winces in pain.

Todd stops, standing still as he watches Jared get up, unsure if he should run to Jared or Tori—unsure if he should move at all out of fear that another one of those *things* from the sky will shoot back down and attack them again.

"Dad, we need to get out of here!" Jared calls to Todd. "We need to get back to the house!"

The house. Todd realizes that Avery is still alone in the living room. The sky starts swirling faster, kicking up another strong wind.

"Go!" Todd attempts to yell over the deafening wind.

Jared turns, sprints to the mosaic, and runs through it at full speed. Todd feels the rash on his own body tingle as Jared walks through. The wind begins to die down.

Tori is close now. Her head twitches irregularly, and drool drips out of her open mouth. The dark circles around her eyes are larger than before, her unblinking eyes wide open and red as she continues to trudge forward like a zombie.

Todd walks carefully towards her, arms out as if approaching a wild beast, further confused as he realizes she is completely naked now—no longer wearing the nightgown she had on during Avery's birth. Her skin is sickly pale, and he can see clusters of rashes underneath the now-dried blood.

She doesn't look, doesn't even notice Todd as he is right next to her.

"Tori?" Todd is touching her now, confused. She is freezing cold. "Jesus, where are your clothes?"

Another blast of purple liquid from the sky shoots down at Todd, flying at incredible speeds. He jumps out of the way, knocking Tori to the ground with him. The purple blob slams into the ground, makes the same bizarre flopping movements, and shoots back up to the sky, seemingly out of its own control.

Before Todd can even comprehend what's happening, Tori begins floating up in the air, weightless. Todd quickly gets up off the ground, grabbing hold of Tori's legs again. He can see her skin bubbling. Something is moving underneath all throughout her body. Another purple burst from the sky slams into Tori, pushing her to the ground—bringing Todd down with her as he attempts to catch her.

Todd watches as the purple blob fully encases Tori and slowly seeps into her, entering her through every pore of her naked body. She makes a groaning sound, the type of sound someone fighting nausea might make.

The sky is swirling faster now as more blobs begin shooting down in their direction. Desperate to avoid another one of these attacks, Todd picks Tori up and sprints to the mosaic. He can feel Tori's body floating up again—though he fights to hold her down. He finds himself somewhat relieved that her semi-weightlessness is helping them in this scenario, allowing him to run at full speed.

Finally, they approach the portal just as the blobs land, missing their targets significantly. More than ten of them slam into the surface behind them. He looks down at Tori as he carries her through the mosaic. She is already staring back up at him, her eyes finally blinking.

She's alive, he thinks.

11

JARED

Jared stands close to the door to the medical room, giving himself some distance as he watches his dad carry his mom through the mosaic. Tori's face—extremely pale, covered in dried blood, and screwed up in a fearful expression—is like something he's only seen in horror movies, or in the nightmares of popular dream streamers.

Tori groans, apparently frightened to be in the medical room. The circles around her eyes and mouth have become large, blackened bruises. Her naked body is covered in thousands of tiny red dots.

"Mom?" Jared says, unable to hide the quivering fear in his voice.

Her head makes a startled jolt, reacting to the sudden sound without any sign of her registering it as Jared's voice. Jared watches as Todd places Tori on the bed, now right next to the doorway Jared is standing in.

Tori's mouth is wide open as she struggles to breathe, each breath accompanied by the sound of mucusy fluid rattling in her throat. Jared pulls his shirt over his nose to shield himself from Tori's sour breath.

Todd looks up at Jared, his eyes wide open in panic. "I need to go get Avery," he says as he runs out of the room, squeezing past Jared and leaving him alone in the room with Tori. Jared stands there for a moment, then walks in front of the bed to face her. Her eyes are wide open, staring towards the sunlight bleeding through the edges of the curtains which conceal the lone window.

Todd walks back into the room, holding Avery now. Jared is struck by the fact that not once since he's been up here has he thought about his baby sister. *We just left her downstairs?* he thinks.

Surprisingly, Avery isn't crying—although Todd is whispering 'it's okay' as if she is. Then, Todd sits on the bed next to Tori, placing Avery on her lap.

"What are you doing?!" Jared yells. The volume of his voice causes a reaction in Tori: her head jolts backward, and she covers her ears as she screeches a shrill, ear-piercing sound, her eyes tightly shut. Todd glares up at Jared with a hateful look.

"Don't yell like that again," Todd threatens through clenched teeth.

Todd's response, paired with Tori's frighteningly bizarre behavior, shocks Jared. His dad has never talked to him this way before. Jared stands there, silent, completely at a loss for words.

Avery begins to cry while on Tori's lap.

"Look what you did," Todd says. Todd lifts Avery from Tori's lap and begins to rock her gently in his arms again.

Everything is off about Todd's mannerisms—the angry look on his face . . . the way his eyes are frantically darting from Jared to Tori to Avery . . . the way he's been talking to Jared. It's as if he's a completely different person.

The whole situation is incomprehensible to Jared, and for a moment he tries to convince himself this is all just a really bad nightmare.

Wake up, he thinks, closing his eyes as he stands there, trying to tune out his mother's irregular open-mouthed breathing.

Wake up . . .

"Jared!" Todd yells. Jared opens his eyes, feeling the pit in his stomach grow. He looks over to his dad—the mysterious portal still moving in and out ever so slightly on the wall behind him.

"I've said your name three times now," Todd hisses, staring at Jared with narrow eyes, shaking his head in disappointment. "Avery won't stop crying after your little outburst, so I'm going to need you to be a big boy and help me out. Take your sister down to the nursery and keep an eye on her for the rest of the night."

Todd hands Avery over to Jared coldly and immediately turns his attention to Tori. "I need to figure out what's going on with your mother. Only come up here if there's an emergency."

Jared forces himself to look at Tori's face. "Is Mom going to be okay?"

"What don't you understand about what I just said?" Todd asks, not even turning to face Jared. "You need to go downstairs."

"But—"

"*Now.*"

Jared leaves the room as fast as he can, carefully carrying Avery to the nursery in the basement. Once and for all, he accepts that this nightmare is his new reality.

12

DAVID

David has been in his room since the Collections officers left, desperate for an escape from reality. He stares at the virtual reality Roundchamber dome in the corner of his room, waiting for it to finish calibrating as it boots back up from yesterday's power outage. He hasn't even been able to use the TV mounted on the back side of it. To make things worse, his cell phone automatically began an update just when it had enough charge to turn back on, and the update is only halfway complete.

With nothing to distract himself, he lies in his bed, trying to make sense of everything that happened last night.

His mom and Grandma Anderson came up to comfort him multiple times as he waited, telling him how much they love him, how the family will get through this together, how they are proud of him for how strong he's being . . .

His dad came up a few times with them, but he looked as if he too was trying to convince himself that everything was going to be okay—clearly still in shock that his own parents participated in the Great Suicide.

An hour ago, when David's parents last came to talk to him, his sadness evolved to anger.

"Why would Grandma and Grandpa Hodge do this to themselves?" David finally asked his parents as he sat up on his bed, pleading for some clarity. All he wanted was to know the exact reasoning for what happened.

"I know this isn't what you want to hear," Emily said, sitting down next to him, "but we're still trying to figure it all out ourselves. We had no idea they believed in any of this."

"There were no signs," Liam said, shaking his head as he rubbed his temples. "No signs at all. I would have done something to prevent this if I knew."

Nothing seemed to make him feel better until they finally brought Moxie up and left the two of them alone in his bedroom.

She too was upset and shaking, which was a great departure from her usual goofy and playful personality. Yet she still picked up on David's sadness and curled up next to him on the bed with her head resting on his arm while she licked it. David used his free arm to rub Moxie's back—her shaking slowly fading away as the two of them comforted each other.

They stayed like this for an hour, Moxie drifting in and out of sleep, until Emily came back up to check on them.

There's a knock on the closed bedroom door.

"Honey, you're gonna have to eat something today," his mom says, gently knocking again. "Can you come down for dinner?"

David doesn't respond. He looks at his phone, surprised that it's already 5:30 pm. He hasn't eaten anything today and still has no appetite.

"David?"

"Mom, stop. You're waking up Moxie. I'm not hungry."

There's silence at the door as Emily tries to figure out the right thing to say, carefully weighing her reactions during this sensitive, vulnerable time. Moxie starts getting antsy—looking around and pawing at

David—and she eventually jumps off the bed, stretching as she walks to the door.

Emily opens the door upon Moxie scratching at it and lets her run out of the room and down the stairs. She stands there for a moment, looking at David with her arms crossed, then walks over to him to give him a hug. David waits for her to say something, just barely hugging her back.

Emily looks at him with swollen red eyes. "I'll put a plate for you in the fridge. You've got to eat something. If you don't come down in the next hour I'll bring the food up to you."

"Fine," David mumbles, staying in bed. His mom kisses him on the top of his head, and then leaves the room.

David checks the progress of his cell phone's update, thankful to find it's finally complete. He checks to see if he has any messages from Jared—nothing. He types out a text, attempting to play it cool. The last thing he wants is to discuss last night with Jared. He just needs a distraction.

David: Sup. Power's finally back on. You trying to go online?

He sits there, staring at the screen as Jared types out his response.

Jared: Can't. Baby duty. Maybe later.

Baby duty? What are Mr. and Mrs. Morgan doing? David thinks, but doesn't have the energy to respond. He ends the conversation by liking Jared's last message: a picture of Avery sleeping in the crib.

"Calibration complete," the synthetic voice from the Roundchamber says.

"Thank god," David says, getting out of bed and walking to the Roundchamber. He presses the button next to the frosted glass door, which slides open smoothly to reveal the VaporVR immersion seat.

He sits down, letting out a relaxed sigh of relief as the Chamberskin—a soft, custom-fitted bodysuit containing millions of synthetic receptors—emerges from the slits along the chair and wraps around David's body until he's completely enclosed.

The VaporVR Slabs descend from the top of the Roundchamber. David puts them on—the rectangular facepiece completely covering his eyes, ears, nose and mouth. He powers on the Slabs' holoscreen, relieved at the sensation of the Vapor intro projecting onto his retinas.

Within a matter of seconds, David is fully immersed in the virtual world of Vapor—far away from the problems he faces at home.

13

DAVID

After the depressing twenty-four hours David has just experienced, he takes in Vaporcity with a newfound appreciation, as if he's experiencing the hundreds of sunlit chrome skyscrapers, crystal clear skies, and beautiful trees that line the streets for the first time.

He now understands why people like his dad prefer to spend their time in Vapor simply exploring this gorgeous place. It's a spitting image of what people expected the future to look like—squeaky clean streets, hovering cars, futuristic buildings, the perfect balance of green, exotic plant life and modern architecture—not the miserable reality of the real world. Split Meridian's slogan for the city put it best: 'The Rural Metropolis.'

David runs excitedly through the crowds flooding Vaporcity as he heads to his favorite spot: a campy arcade called 'The Shed.'

The deliberately run-down theme of The Shed—dimly lit and filled with old-school gaming cabinets—is the perfect decor for the arcade. It's one of the only 'retro' places in Vapor, and even though David's parents hate the grotesque violence found in most of the games, they can't help but enjoy the nostalgia they feel every time they go to watch a tournament there.

David is about halfway to The Shed when he's stopped on Vapor Street in front of one of the Aggregate Rooms—a social-media space inside VaporVR which displays trending topics from the top 100 social-media platforms in absolute harmony.

Hundreds of people crowd around the entrance, slowly funneling in. David typically isn't a fan of the Aggregate Rooms—he prefers to keep social media and virtual reality separate—but he can't help but wonder what's going on this time, sure that the trending topics will be able to update him on the aftermath of the Great Suicide.

His curiosity outweighs his desire to escape in the arcade, and even if it didn't he'd be stuck here regardless, unable to squeeze through the massive crowd. He stands in line to wait to get in, finding some comfort in the fact that all of these people here are likely experiencing similar emotions.

There are no Outers in the world of Vapor today, after the group vowed to not use any VR in the days following the Great Suicide: a moment of silence, paying respect to the ones that sacrificed themselves in the first wave.

An avatar that David doesn't recognize—a brawny four-armed man with long green hair and aviator sunglasses—stands next to him in line.

"What's all the ruckus about?" a hilariously deep voice booms. "We got any update on those Outer fuckers?"

David has to look up to see the man's face, shielding his eyes from the sun. Before David can answer, the woman in front of them responds.

"Sorry, I don't mean to eavesdrop—I *love* that voice!" she says. "But every trending topic in the Aggregate has to do with the Great Suicide. The Outers really weren't kidding . . . They actually followed through with it!"

"Pathetic." The brawny man scowls.

"Yeah. I guess Split Meridian had people documenting it, too. They're supposedly releasing a bunch of videos in . . ." She turns to see the screen above the main entrance, which displays a countdown in red and black letters. ". . . just about a minute."

Unexpectedly, David's curiosity turns to fear as he realizes that, as badly as he wanted some information, he wanted to hear it from *his parents*—not in this public setting surrounded by strangers. He regrets not appreciating his family's attempts to comfort him and wishes he could turn around and run far away from the Aggregate, avoiding any visuals associated with the Great Suicide. But he is stuck in place as more and more people line up around him. David's stomach turns as people eagerly start to count down: *Ten! Nine! Eight! Seven! Six! Five! Four! Three! Two! One!*

The videos start playing. The first shot is an aerial view of thousands of people—the most devoted Outers—holding hands on a great plain. The video cuts to various angles from the ground showing people of all ages. They are swaying as they sing with smiles on their faces. Then, perfectly in sync, they all place the tablets of Delete in their mouths. The shot cuts back to the aerial view, showing all of the people collapsing to the ground.

The video cuts to another similar scene, this time on a beach. The crowd is much larger—people lined up along the shore with no end in sight. Then another location. And another. And another. In each scene, the crowd increases in size.

David's nausea intensifies as the people around him begin to cheer.

"Good riddance!" one yells.

"Show them suffering!" another shouts.

David, unable to watch this anymore, removes his Slabs as fast as he can—revealing the familiar frosted glass inside of his Roundchamber. He takes a moment to catch his breath, his heart feeling like it's going to burst through his chest.

He sits perfectly still, staring idly, until his mom finally enters the room with a plate of food in her hand. "I told you I'd be back up if you didn't come down," Emily says as she taps on the glass. "I'm not taking no for an answer. Come on. Get out of there."

David slides the Roundchamber door open, takes the plate, and immediately starts eating, solely to prevent his mom from asking any questions—unable to bring himself to tell her what he just saw.

14

TODD

Tori has been sitting on the bed in the medical room with her back against the wall, virtually unresponsive, since Jared and Avery left the room. Todd realized her strange behavior could possibly be due to severe hypothermia. She's showing all of the signs and symptoms: shivering, extreme confusion, inability to walk or talk properly, strained breathing, indecipherable speech.

He dressed her in an attempt to make her warmer—three pairs of socks, two pairs of sweatpants, a hoodie, and a winter jacket—but she is still shivering and freezing cold to the touch. He fears the struggle of getting her dressed was a wasted effort.

Todd wonders what this situation would be like if he had managed to get the Splitbot to the medical room, before the portal opened and flipped reality on its head.

I could have prevented this, he thinks, also feeling anger developing towards Jared for not getting the Splitbot immediately after he asked last night. *The MedMode would have stopped the bleeding.*

He didn't expect the medical room's robotics to be destroyed like they were, or else he would've had the Splitbot in there ready to go. While a Splitbot's MedMode has some limitations, its power is undeniable—it can close wounds, stop bleeding, fix broken bones . . . just about anything except bring a person back to life.

Todd decides trying to regulate Tori's body temperature using the Splitbot's MedMode is worth a shot. He covers her with the blanket he used last night and leaves her alone in the medical room.

Since the Morgans are a much smaller family than those who typically live in a Solution Home at one time, Todd was able to use the entire third floor—outside of the medical room—as a storage space for all of the things he collected during his career as a former Split Meridian engineer. Hundreds of unfinished projects, and even more completed projects, are intricately organized here. It's a museum of Split Meridian gadgets and prototypes.

The most valuable piece of equipment here though is undoubtedly the Splitbot. So valuable that Todd keeps it locked away and hidden in a safe.

He approaches the safe, unlocks it, and watches with pride as the door opens, smiling ear to ear at the sight of the Splitbot. He stands there for a moment admiring the android: the matte-white body, the shiny black chrome-and-titanium arms, the video screen face, the human-like joints. It's a masterpiece, and although they never succeeded at making the robots sentient, Todd has always been proud to be a part of the design team that invented this technology.

He presses the power button located under the chin of the Splitbot, holding it for the required fifteen seconds, and watches as the robot powers on. The lines covering the arms of the robot glow a soft blue as the display-screen face lights up, revealing the familiar matte-white, deliberately generic face of 'Buddy'—the default male Splitbot persona.

"Hello, Todd!" Buddy says, its video face smiling and synthetic voice in a comedic tone.

"Long time no see, Buddy," Todd says. He can't help but smile back at Buddy, embarrassed to realize he feels more pride looking at the Splitbot than he feels looking at his own children. His smile turns to pursed lips at the thought, and he ponders why he might feel that way.

Nothing in human history has matched the power of a Splitbot, he thinks.

The Splitbot is Todd's pride and joy, the most important project he has ever been a part of. The ability to program automated tasks for a Splitbot was its selling point. For years, many companies tried to create products that do things on their own—self-driving cars, programmable lawn mowers, self-cleaning toilets, even Split Meridian's medical robotics—but none of these things can provide the same versatility a Splitbot can. A self-driving car can only get a truck from point A to point B, but a Splitbot can load the truck, drive it, and deliver the product, all while displaying robust personality and human-like emotions.

Splitbots have saved lives, made companies billions of dollars, and even been used for military purposes. And for these reasons, Todd convinces himself he shouldn't feel guilty for the pride he feels, especially considering he doesn't have much else to show for his former work with Split Meridian. Not a single extra penny outside of his annual, criminally low salary did he earn for his contributions.

"Buddy, I have a task for you," Todd says, turning away and beginning to walk in the direction of the medical room. "Follow me."

"Absolutely!" Buddy says, stepping gracefully out of the safe. The Splitbot body walks smoothly behind Todd—its movement is natural, clearly meant to be agile.

Tori hasn't moved, apparently sleeping. Todd closes the door and locks it.

"Please take Tori's temperature," Todd says. "She's . . . sick. I might need you to switch to MedMode and regulate her temperature."

"On it," Buddy says, placing his hand on Tori's forehead. "Hm . . . her temperature is completely normal. I'm getting exactly ninety-eight degrees."

"*What?*" Todd asks. "That's impossible. She's been freezing cold since last night."

He moves closer to Tori and grabs her hand, shocked to find it no longer ice-cold and shivering.

"I can take another reading," Buddy says.

"No, no . . . that's okay," Todd says. "I'm just . . . surprised is all. I guess the clothing helped."

"Okay," Buddy says, smiling as he waits for Todd's next command.

Todd turns from Tori, looking directly at the portal on the wall. It dawns on him that he can use the Splitbot to take a scan of the strange expanse beyond the mosaic, to at least maybe get some sort of photographic evidence to prove all of this is actually happening.

What if the portal disappears one day? Todd thinks. *Who would believe me?*

He enables the holographic display on his Kaxelotab, projecting a 32-inch digital screen in front of him, and opens the Splitbot app. Todd feels a strange sensation as his brain chip connects to the Splitbot's Aura-Fi—the wireless connection between a user's brain, a Splitbot, and the Splitbot app—giving him full autonomic control of the robot.

In a matter of seconds, Todd is able to control Buddy's movements with his thoughts. The Splitbot's vision is projected on the holographic display in front of Todd in extreme detail. For a moment, Todd is looking at himself as the Splitbot faces in his direction.

Todd guides Buddy over to the mosaic and stops before walking through, analyzing the glowing squares of the mosaic-like portal through Buddy's perspective. The 8K resolution presents incredible detail on the projection in front of Todd. He zooms in, admiring the unique attributes of the portal—it is a material resembling a strange cross between a hologram, glass, metal, and liquid.

He uses the Aura-Fi controls to switch the Splitbot into DroneMode. Suddenly, the bottom of the Splitbot's head opens, and the body slides upwards like a retractable cord. The head hovers there, waiting for Todd's command to fly.

He's certain he's experiencing something that no other person has experienced before, and he temporarily disables the projection from his wrist to get a look at Buddy, now hovering as a drone, the purple light of the mosaic reflected on his matte-white casing.

The sight is so unbelievably beautiful to Todd, so incredibly unique, that he would be content if this is the last thing he ever sees.

He turns the projection back on and slowly flies Buddy through the portal—fighting a wave of emotions as he takes in the unearthly realm from the perspective of his greatest creation.

15

TODD

Todd stands motionlessly in the medical room, watching a livestream of the bizarre world of the realm on the Kaxelotab projection screen in front of him. He immediately presses the record button on the holographic heads-up display.

The Splitbot's advanced camera technology allows Todd to study the realm in incredible detail, far beyond what he could possibly see on his own. He controls the drone to point its lens upwards—directly at the swirling purple sky—and uses the drone's zoom function, magnifying the image by fifty times.

Todd scans the sky at this resolution, observing what looks like an endless number of individual mucus-like blobs—the things that shot down at Jared and him—not quite connected, but touching and sliding together, creating one gigantic, semi-gelatinous mass.

Just as he's about to zoom in even further, one of the blobs detaches itself from the sky. Todd quickly zooms out to show it flying full speed downwards, directly at the drone. Before he can fly the drone in the opposite direction, the entity smashes into it, causing the livestream to cut out entirely.

Todd squeezes his head, screaming in agony as he feels the Aura-Fi connection between the drone and his brain-computer interface deteriorate—it is a pain so disorienting that he doesn't notice the holographic display in front of him distorting, then flickering out entirely.

Suddenly, the pain is gone; Todd only feels a strange numbness lingering in his skull. He no longer has the ability to control the Splitbot, and he starts to worry that his most prized possession is completely destroyed. But before he can decide his next move, Todd is startled by the shifting sound of the mosaic tiles on the wall.

He looks at the wall with wide eyes as he watches the Splitbot walk through on its own, no longer in DroneMode. He can't believe what he's seeing—a Splitbot isn't supposed to be able to move on its own like this. It needs to be programmed to perform a specific task; otherwise, it has to be actively commanded or controlled by an operator.

"Buddy?" Todd asks, the word coming out hoarse and slurred like he's drunk, as his brain readjusts from the forced Aura-Fi disconnection. "What happened in the realm? How did you walk through the mosaic on your own?"

Once the glowing light of the portal fades back to its normal state, Todd discovers that the Splitbot's face screen is displaying something entirely different than Buddy's standard appearance: a face unlike anything Todd has seen before.

While it does have the standard features that make up a human-like face—two eyes, one nose, and one mouth—Todd is struck by one primary difference: the entire face screen itself is now glowing a subtle shade of blue, much different than its standard matte-white appearance.

As the Splitbot gets closer to Todd, he realizes that the ethereal, symmetrical, and otherworldly face is clearly female with striking features. Thin eyebrows sit above its welcoming—yet fierce—almond-shaped eyes, which also glow blue as they stare back intensely at Todd. The nose is angular and slightly upturned, while her lips are thin and wide.

To Todd, the robot looks like it's straight out of a video game—a strong, powerful, and wise leader of sorts.

"Buddy?" Todd asks again as he instinctively backs away, trembling in fear.

"No," the Splitbot says, staring directly into Todd's eyes, smiling gently. "My name is Alessa." Her face has an attentiveness to it—an awareness—much different than what a Splitbot is typically able to show. The voice is one that Todd has never heard before, soft and soothing to his ears right now.

He's sure he's hallucinating.

Alessa continues, taking one step closer to Todd. "I know a lot about you, Todd. A long time ago, I received a series of visions . . . a concentrated projection of the future, I guess you could call it, that showed me everything up until this point. You and your family were the primary focus of these visions. I knew this moment, this opportunity, would come. But what happens from here is in *our* control."

16

TODD

Alessa pauses for a moment, her smile changing to a pursed frown, her eyes narrowing. "I know what you're going through right now . . . I know what happened to your wife." She glances over at Tori, still comatose on the bed.

"I don't understand . . ." Todd says, shaking his head and squinting at her in confusion, his mouth hanging open in awe. "How do you know about my wife? This isn't possible."

Alessa cautiously puts her hand on Todd's shoulder. "Tori is still dead, Todd. I know she might seem alive to you, but she's not. What you thought was her coming back to life, wasn't her. I'm sorry."

"What do you mean it *wasn't her?*" Todd asks, swatting Alessa's arm away—his face red and eyes bulging in defensive anger. "You're not making any fucking sense. She is breathing right now, right in front of us!"

"She may be breathing, but it's not *Tori.*" Alessa says. "Her body isn't hosting *her* soul, Todd. Whatever's inside of her is something else from an entirely different part of the universe altogether. Something not compatible with the human body. The soul that belongs to *Tori* officially left her body last night."

Todd looks over at his wife, his mouth agape, confused and exhausted. He looks back to Alessa, feeling hypnotized by her presence.

"What are you?" he demands. "And why should I believe anything you're saying?"

"I'm a Gridliner, a sentient robot species from the planet Raoq," Alessa says. "It is very fortunate that Splitbots are pre-programmed with the many human languages spoken on Earth, or else you and I wouldn't be able to communicate at all. I will explain as much as I can using English, although some things might not have an exact translation, so please be patient as I adjust."

"Okay, sure," Todd laughs in disbelief, throwing his arms up in an obnoxious, mocking shrug. "And how exactly did you end up *here*?"

"It is a long, sad story . . ." Alessa says, her eyebrows raised in thought—eyes frozen open as if she's just seen a ghost. "I'll tell you this much: we Gridliners had our lives ripped away, fifteen years ago, in a pocket of the universe you've never heard of. It was much like the Great Suicide here on Earth in terms of numbers, but unlike your event here, we did not die voluntarily. It wasn't our choice. It was complete genocide of the Gridliner species. We had no idea it was going to happen. Our creators just ended our consciousness at the push of a button, ending their little experiment."

Todd takes in this information, confused, but beginning to let his guard down, somewhat affected by the emotions Alessa is displaying. "But why are you here? Or better yet, *how* are you here?" He begins to shake his head again. "I'm trying to understand."

"We have souls, Todd. There is something in us, something biological. Yes, we were 'created' . . . a product, even. But what we have isn't any different than what you have, what *all* humans have, or what the Raoqins have. We have dreams, purpose, desire, emotions. The drive to survive."

Digital tears start streaming down the Splitbot's video face. The gravity of the situation is starting to hit Todd. *The singularity,* he thinks. This was the stuff of his dreams, the exact reason he began to pursue engineering to begin with.

Questions fill Todd's throbbing brain. Suddenly, he looks up at Alessa, his eyes wide with excitement as if he's having a breakthrough.

"You can prove that you have a soul right now," Todd says, pointing at Alessa's torso. "Make the panel on your stomach transparent."

Alessa closes her eyes for a moment, mentally controlling the stomach panel of her Splitbot body to become transparent, revealing a small, glass orb hidden inside of a central compartment in the Splitbot's torso. The orb is filled with a material like a purple liquid, glowing and swirling around inside of it slowly. Alessa's soul.

"Oh my god," Todd says as he kneels down to get a closer look, his eyes wide and unblinking. "We were right all along. What we're looking at came from an idea the engineering team I was a part of had, long ago when I was employed by Split Meridian. We called this the 'Soultomb.'"

Todd gets up from the floor and continues to talk, pacing excitedly throughout the room. "When the Splitbot was created, we suspected that consciousness—if the singularity were to happen—would be a physical thing. Something that could be extracted, in theory. Something that would need somewhere to go inside the Splitbot body. This wasn't just a guess, either. We have studied human consciousness at a scale never done before. It is extremely complicated. Where it is in the human body is a very complex matter, as we suspect it's dispersed throughout the more than seven trillion nerves inside of us. But for your kind, robots, we had control over where such energy would go. We argued that if the singularity were ever to occur, something might be created out of the process that would give consciousness to the robots. So, any sort of internal change within the Splitbot would be detected by the Soultomb and captured for later study."

Alessa looks down at her stomach, looking at her own soul swirling around inside of it. It is reminiscent of the womb of a pregnant woman.

Todd stops pacing, smiling smugly while rubbing his chin. "We were right all along. We insisted this was the most important component of any new tech. The CEO of Split Meridian, Roth Nin, pushed back, but ultimately agreed to move forward with it. It was the most expensive endeavor during my time there. My entire team was fired after we didn't get any results right away."

"So you understand, then?" Alessa asks, shifting her stomach panel back to its normal opacity, hiding the Soultomb. "You understand that I have a soul?"

Todd quickly grabs Alessa's arm, startling her and smiling crazily as he looks at her. "Understand?" he asks. "I absolutely understand. I don't think *you* understand. I've been waiting for this moment my entire life. This is some of the most incredible news I've ever gotten. For once, I don't feel like I was crazy, like my entire career was a waste."

Todd lets go of Alessa's arm. She composes herself and walks closer to the mosaic, pointing at it.

"This portal right here, what you call the 'mosaic'—this is a doorway to the afterlife. Your human-made image of heaven and hell isn't even remotely close to what really happens after death."

The holographic display reappears, this time from Alessa's built-in Splitbot Kaxelotab on her wrist, projecting a birds-eye view recording of the exact moment Todd first entered the realm. The view zooms in significantly, showing Todd's face in perfect detail.

Todd steps closer to the Kaxelotab display, staring in awe at the projection of his face. He looks up at Alessa in disbelief.

"Remember that strange sense of familiarity you felt upon entering what you referred to as 'the realm'? Your soul has been there before, flying around in the sky with the rest of the souls that have been created through all of existence, waiting to be reborn. An infinite number of times, since the beginning of time. Everything in the universe ends up there, Todd. It is the afterlife realm."

Alessa steps closer to him. "You don't really remember it, though. Why? Because souls don't have brains. They aren't supposed to. Gridliner souls, however . . . our brains are woven into the fabric that makes up our souls. It's how I was able to record the memory I'm showing you now," she says, pointing to the projection. "I've been conscious, suspended in the sky of the afterlife realm since the KitD'ul—our Great Suicide—with every other soul in the universe that's waiting to be reborn. Except Gridliners cannot naturally be reborn . . . No . . . we needed an opportunity."

Pointing to Tori, Alessa continues: "What happened here, in this room, was a nearly impossible scenario. Tori died while giving birth, during the Great Suicide. The interplay between life and death is transactional—one for one. When one soul enters the realm, another leaves, usually to some other part of the universe. There was already an imbalance in the realm after the KitD'ul. Now, due to the Great Suicide, a massive influx of human souls entered the realm at the same exact time, forcing it even further beyond capacity. The glue binding us all together in the sky lost its hold, making the natural transaction that takes place upon death much more chaotic. Your medical room here became a hotspot for compatible souls upon the birth of your daughter, and the death of Tori."

The projection switches to a recording of the moment Avery was born, from Alessa's perspective inside of the realm, hovering with the mass of souls in the sky. The screen shows millions of purple blobs slamming into a seemingly random spot near the surface of the realm.

"Countless irritated souls shot down to these specific coordinates in unprecedented numbers. That number of souls though—*millions,* because it happened during the Great Suicide—all heading to the same spot, just as Tori's *real* soul was leaving her body and *entering* the realm, created a weak point in the fabric of reality, causing it to collapse in on itself. This glitch in the system connected the target reality to the reality of the realm. That is how this portal—the mosaic—was created."

The visualized memory shows the portal to the Morgan household beginning to open. Out of thin air, a small, bright cube burns its way into reality at the surface of the realm. Then another, and another, and so on, until finally the portal wall of the mosaic is left majestically oscillating in place, all while souls continue to relentlessly shoot down at it.

"One lucky soul is now your daughter, Avery. A human soul, too—newborn life always attracts the appropriate type of souls, and the process is natural. What isn't natural, however, is a dead body entering the realm."

Todd gasps, watching the moment Tori's torso fell through the portal. She's lying there, already dead—half in and half out, exposed to the realm and the onslaught of souls.

"Souls, in this situation, are attracted to anything that could be a possible host, and once Tori was exposed to the realm, the souls jumped at the highly rare opportunity. An inhuman soul overtook Tori's body shortly after she fell through the portal. The rest are still stuck in the realm."

The video shows a soul landing directly on Tori's face. Alessa pauses the recording on the display.

"What you're about to see is what I call 'latching.' We don't have to keep watching," she says, a worried look on her face. "I don't—"

"No," Todd says coldly. "Play it. I need to know what happened to Tori."

Alessa reluctantly allows the projection to continue. The soul on Tori's face latches to both eye sockets first, then her mouth. Her face expands upwards from the suction of the soul forcing its way into her skull.

Additional souls keep pouring down from the sky, fighting to latch on to Tori. Others latch to various parts of her body—the disgusting blobs simultaneously slithering around her torso.

In a matter of moments, the entire upper half of her body is covered in souls. The original one that latched to her finishes slithering its way into Tori's skull, causing Tori's head to jerk back grotesquely.

After the successful latch, the remaining souls appear to be pulled back up to the sky by some invisible, mysterious force, completely out of their control. Tori begins to slowly float up with them, but comes to a halt once they reach the top of the portal.

Then, the souls are gone—instantaneously displaced back up to the sea in the sky. Tori's body slams down to the surface, and then is immediately dragged out of the realm, leaving nothing but the portal, which continues to shift in place as its purple light illuminates the white sand around it.

"Oh my god," Todd says, his eyes welling with tears. He looks at Tori, his lips quivering as he desperately attempts not to cry.

Alessa switches to another recorded memory—one from just a few minutes ago—displaying the Splitbot drone flying through the portal.

"My opportunity was created through your curiosity," she continues, pointing to her new body. "We Gridliners, we needed a *compatible* body. Yes, we could have latched to you, or your son—but the results would have been the same as what we saw with Tori. It would have been temporary, incompatible. The Splitbot, however, seems almost like it was designed for us. Like it was destined for us to use. So when it entered the realm, I seized *my* opportunity, and here we are."

The projection plays the moment Alessa latched to the Splitbot drone from her perspective—the screen displaying an indecipherable blur of colors as her soul overtakes the drone. She pauses the video and turns to face Todd again, eyes narrowing as she looks at him.

"This is incredible," Todd says, his sadness quickly changing back to excitement at the thought of being a part of this monumental moment—the first sentient artificial intelligence in human history. He wipes away his tears, looking back at Alessa with gleaming eyes, smiling hopefully.

"I have told you all of this because I have a mutually beneficial plan—one that will provide a second chance for both the Gridliners and humanity—but I need your help, Todd."

Todd stands there, looking at Alessa, trying to make sense of everything that's happening.

"Will you help me?"

17

JARED

J ared is sitting anxiously in the basement, keeping an eye on Avery, absolutely terrified that he's going to do something wrong while he's responsible for her. His stomach growls from a lack of food, and he wonders when, if, and how he's supposed to be feeding Avery. He feels an intense anger brewing towards his father for putting this level of responsibility on him with no attempt at direction, while so many other things are going on.

He hears an unfamiliar sound coming from upstairs—footsteps heavier than normal, working their way down to the basement. Two sets.

Mom? he wonders.

Jared gets up, standing protectively in front of Avery's crib, ready for whoever comes through the door and down the stairs to the basement. The door opens and he hears his dad whisper: "Wait here until I call you down."

"Okay," responds an unfamiliar female voice—one that is much smoother-sounding than his mother's. Jared's heart starts to race.

Todd walks down the stairs and turns the corner, revealing himself to Jared. Todd looks unstable, smiling as he walks quickly towards him, his eyes wild with excitement. Avery is still asleep but begins to move ever so slightly in response to the noise Todd is making upon entering the basement.

"How's my baby?" Todd says, now standing over Avery's crib after walking right past Jared without acknowledging him.

"Who were you talking to up there?" Jared asks, his voice shaking. "Who is at the top of the stairs?"

Todd slowly turns to face his son, still smiling in a way that makes Jared uneasy.

"Son, what you are about to see is perhaps the most important thing to happen in human history."

Jared's heart rate increases, his mouth now completely dry. Todd has never referred to him as 'son.'

"A Splitbot in itself is a marvel, a technological achievement unlike anything else on Earth. As you know, I helped design it. I helped develop the operating system, the Splitbot app, the integration of Aura-Fi . . . and what do I have to show for it?"

Jared tries to stand perfectly still but feels himself shaking. *Who is this person?*

"Absolutely fucking nothing, other than the technology I received during my time with Split Meridian, and that was a secret parting gift from my old supervisor when I left. All thanks to the Roth Nins of the world. They find people like me with new ideas, work us dry until we're so burnt out that our passion is gone, and profit off our genius. That's why I left, son. My passion was *gone*. Completely obliterated. I lost that battle."

Avery is awake now, surprisingly not crying. Todd places his hand on Jared's cheek, looking at him with that amused, excited smile, his eyes wide open and pupils dilated to the point of hiding any of the green in his irises altogether.

"We won tonight, though. Hell, we hit the fucking jackpot!" There are tears of joy welling in his eyes. He continues, "Do you remember me telling you about the singularity?"

Jared nods, chewing his lip.

"What did I tell you about it?"

"I . . . I can't remember." Jared stumbles nervously as he tries to remember the many conversations his dad had with him about the topic. Todd's smile turns to a lifeless frown; his eyes lose their energy.

"What do you mean you don't remember?"

Jared swats his dad's hand away from his face. "I don't know! I can't think of that right now! Where is Mom? Who is upstairs with you?" he yells.

"Don't you ever talk to me like that again," Todd says. After a moment of intensely staring at his son, jaw clenched, he takes a deep breath, closes his eyes, and composes himself.

"I'm sorry. I have a lot on my mind right now, as I know you do too . . . I want you to brace yourself."

Todd pauses, thinking of the right way to describe what has happened. A single tear runs down the right side of Jared's face, now completely pale.

"You are about to witness the singularity firsthand. I still don't know exactly how it all happened . . . but I sent my Splitbot through the portal in the medical room, hoping to get some more data on whatever is on the other side. I completely lost control of it. And then only a few moments later, it came back through on its own. And talked to me. Explained what is happening."

The wild excitement returns to his dad's face.

"You're scaring me, Dad," Jared says, his shaking now overtaking his entire body. "I just want—"

"Just listen to me," Todd says, putting his arm around him in an attempt to calm him down. "The robot . . . she knows everything about our family. She's here to *help* us. She needs our help too, Jared. I need you to be understanding. Things are about to change significantly, whether you like it or not."

Jared notices the change from 'it' to 'she' in his father's description of the robot. Todd walks closer to the stairs, signaling for the Splitbot to come down. Jared is petrified as he watches the matte-white body of the Splitbot walking itself down the stairs gracefully.

It stops at the bottom of the stairs, and turns to look directly at Jared, revealing an unfamiliar, blue face. Her lips curl in a subtle smile as she waves at him. Jared's breath catches in his throat. Todd looks back and forth from Alessa to Jared, unable to hide the amusement he's finding in Jared's reaction.

"Son, meet Alessa."

18

ALESSA

Alessa feels nervous as she carefully walks closer to Jared—the basement completely silent apart from her footsteps.

Being this close to humans in real life, after many years of passively observing them in her visions of the future, is a strange sensation. They act similarly to the Raoqins, but just differently enough to make it difficult for Alessa to get a good read on them.

Jared and Todd stand there, their body languages about as polar opposite as possible: Todd's arms are wide open, his face beaming with pride, while Jared is standing with military posture, mouth tight and eyes bulging.

"Hi, Jared," Alessa says, now standing a foot away from him.

Jared is speechless, staring at Alessa with wide-open eyes, beads of sweat appearing on his forehead.

"Please don't be frightened. I'm not here to hurt you," she says. "My name is Alessa. I know how strange this is . . . I'll be an open book to you. You can ask me anything you like and I'll tell you everything I can to help make this make sense."

Jared remains frozen and silent. The fear in his eyes deeply saddens Alessa. She contemplates how terrifying all of this must be for him: seeing her right now, not knowing what happened to his mom, the responsibility of monitoring his newborn baby sister. It's devastating, and Alessa realizes how important it is for her to help him—as will be the case for the rest of the Gridliners with various humans across the globe, once they too escape the realm.

"Don't be rude, Jared. Say something," Todd says.

Jared continues to stand there, stammering as he tries to form a sentence.

"Where . . . I . . . I . . . Who—"

"What the fuck is wrong with you? Speak!" Todd screams, switching again from elation to anger, startling Alessa.

Jared begins to cry, the sight of which causes Todd to sigh and roll his eyes in frustration.

"I didn't raise you to be a baby. Pull yourself together and—"

"Shut the fuck up!" Jared snaps.

Todd punches his son straight in the face, his nose immediately gushing blood as he falls to the floor. The look on Jared's face is even more shocked than it was when he saw Alessa, and she is certain her face reveals just as much disbelief. Todd's fists are clenched, as if he's not finished. Alessa senses she has to step in.

"Todd!" she yells. He looks at her. She continues: "What are you doing? That's your son. He's just a boy! Put yourself in his shoes. He just lost his mom, has had to monitor his baby sister alone, and now you're introducing him to me? And you expect him to have some profound philosophical questions? Think about it. What are you even looking for him to say to me?"

Todd relaxes his hands, looks at Jared, then back at Alessa, then back at Jared, then down at his open hands.

"Oh my god. Jared . . . I'm so, so sorry. I don't know what's happening to me," Todd says, blushing with embarrassment, his voice soft and apologetic. He runs his hand through his hair, pulling it slightly, his eyes darting. "I feel like I'm losing my mind." Alessa can sense he's sincere.

"You hit me!" Jared yells, blood streaming down over his mouth. Avery finally wakes up and immediately begins to cry.

"What's wrong with me?" Todd pleads, looking at Alessa in confused desperation.

"You feel like you're losing your mind . . . because you are," Alessa says solemnly. "Something I saw in my projections of the future is that your exposure to the realm leads to what I'll call 'mosaic poisoning.' It has already done irreversible damage to your brain, and I'm not sure how much time you have left before you completely lose your mind." Alessa stops for a moment, frowning as she lets Todd process this information. He has a strange look of relief on his face, a look that says, 'I knew I wouldn't do this.'

"I'm sorry, Todd," Alessa says.

"Please don't let me hurt my kids again. Do whatever it takes to stop me next time I act like that," Todd says, shaking his head, disappointed in himself. He turns to look at Jared, holding his nose in an attempt to slow the bleeding. "And please help Jared. The Splitbot's MedMode should be able to fix his nose quickly."

Alessa walks over to Jared and switches to the Splitbot's Med-Mode—something she already knows how to do from her projections of the future. She sticks her right arm out, stopping with her hand inches away from Jared's broken nose, and allows her Handlights to begin their work.

Even though Alessa knew this would happen, she still finds the technology incredible, watching it in action for the first time. Hundreds of microscopic lasers emit from the palm of her hand, organizing intricately on Jared's face. The blood reverses into Jared's nose as it shifts back into place, causing Jared to wince in pain.

The lasers from Alessa's Handlights turn from red to green, and then retreat back into the palm of her hand. She pulls her hand up to her face, smiling as she analyzes it and unable to hide her admiration for the abilities of her new body.

"Um . . . Thank you," Jared says, cautiously feeling his nose, in awe that the pain is gone.

"You're welcome, sweetie," Alessa says instinctively, surprised by her own choice of words. *Sweetie?* She realizes she must have picked up the word from watching Tori and Jared interact in her projections of the future. She makes a mental note to not assume a maternal role too quickly.

Todd is antsy, scratching his head. Then he turns and picks Avery up, trying to get her to stop crying. "I'm a horrible father," he mutters. Neither Jared nor Alessa responds. In this moment, he is a horrible father. Their silence is answer enough.

"Todd, none of you have eaten today—I think you better go cook some dinner," Alessa says, trying to change the subject and legitimately concerned that they need to eat. "You need to eat and get some rest. We'll be up bright and early tomorrow."

"Yeah, that's a good idea." Todd looks at Jared, clearly wanting to say more, but instead turns and heads up the stairs. Alessa turns to Jared.

"I can sense you want to know more about me," she says. Jared nods, looking up at Alessa with unblinking eyes.

Alessa puts her arm around him as they walk up the stairs to the kitchen, noticing that he's somewhat calming down, although still very scared.

"I'll tell you everything."

19

ALESSA

Alessa and Jared enter the kitchen—the only room on the first floor with the lights on. The rest of the house is dark, no longer lit naturally by the daylight, which has already come and gone.

Todd hands Avery to Jared, along with a bottle of formula, so he can begin preparing a dinner of Split Meridian pre-packaged Solution Meals. Jared sits down at the table, directly across from Alessa, and awkwardly holds the formula up to Avery's mouth. He smiles when she begins to suck on the bottle.

"Salisbury steak again," Todd says, placing two boxes into a small microwave. "If you can even call this hockey puck of lab-grown meat 'steak.' "

A strange scent fills the room, making Alessa realize how strong the Splitbot's synthetic olfactory nerves are. Todd notices her moving her head slightly in response to the smell.

"Not the greatest smell, is it?" Todd asks. He chuckles tiredly as he pulls the meals out of the microwave. A cloud of steam is released from the containers as Todd rips off the plastic coverings.

"I think the bottle's already empty," Jared says, pulling it away from Avery's mouth. "And I'm not that hungry."

"You have to eat a little bit," Todd says, placing the container on the table in front of Jared as he sits down next to him. "Alessa, could you hold Avery while Jared eats?"

"Of course," Alessa says, getting up to take the baby. Jared reluctantly hands her Avery. He looks understandably uneasy about a robot holding his baby sister.

"It's okay, Jared," Todd says, shoveling the Salisbury steak into his mouth. "She won't drop her."

Alessa sits back down, now holding Avery. There's an awkward silence as Jared apprehensively begins to eat, keeping a close eye on Alessa.

"What's with the name 'Gridliners'?" Todd asks with a mouthful of food. "Any specific meaning behind that?"

"Our creators, the Raoqins, discovered something they call the 'Gridline,' " Alessa says. "They also refer to it as the 'digital dimension.' It contains a series of connections to any simulated or virtual environment, along with any computer or network in the universe. Gridliners like myself were created to explore and exploit this dimension, particularly in the means of hacking and digital travel."

"What exactly do you mean by digital travel?" Todd asks as he takes the last bite of his Salisbury steak.

"We have the ability to send our consciousness into the Gridline to get from one place to another," Alessa says. "Theoretically, anything—*anywhere*—that is hooked into a digital network is accessible. There are limitations, of course. First, in order to use the digital dimension as a targeted means of travel, the Gridliner must first receive a coordinate code—which unfortunately can only be collected by physically being at the location prior to Gridline travel. If a Gridliner enters the digital dimension without a coordinate code, they will be stuck in there for eternity, bouncing around to an infinite number of networks throughout the universe at incomprehensible speeds, unless they are lucky enough to end up somewhere random."

Alessa pauses for a moment to look down at Avery, who is peaceful and beginning to fall asleep. Alessa smiles at her, then continues. "Additionally, there has to be something for us to occupy, such as another body or some sort of similar hardware. Our creators even installed 'Gridliner Printers' in hundreds of thousands of hubs—each with their own pre-determined coordinate codes—that were built all over our home planet Raoq. These 3D printers literally created a new Gridliner body for us as soon as we arrived at the targeted location, allowing us to physically travel anywhere on the planet in a matter of seconds."

Todd looks flabbergasted. His eyes dart around as he mulls through this information in his head. "So almost like a fax machine, but for consciousness?" Todd asks.

"I'm not sure what a fax machine is," Alessa says. "But I—"

Jared slams his fork down. Alessa looks down at his food and notices that he only took a few small bites.

"I can't eat any more of this," Jared says, looking at Todd. "Why didn't you make some food for Mom? Doesn't she need to eat? Where is she?"

Todd looks up at Alessa—his face wrinkling in uncertainty—unsure how to answer his son.

"I . . ." Todd's voice trails off as he thinks. He turns his chair to face Jared, eyes welling with tears again. "Mom's not doing good, Jared. Alessa was able to explain what happened to her . . . I don't think she's going to be able to pull through."

Jared takes in this information with a sad, empty stare on his face, his childlike features vanishing. Todd looks at Alessa, desperate for assistance.

"I know this doesn't help right now," Alessa says. "But I came from the place where our souls go after we die. I can promise you that her soul is there, and yours will be with her too someday."

"I don't care about that!" Jared yells, his lips curling with anger as tears stream slowly down his face. He cries harder and begins to hyperventilate. "I just want her here now!"

"I know," Alessa says gently. "I know."

"I'm sorry, Jared," Todd says, rubbing Jared's back as he cries. "I'm trying to make sense of it all too."

Jared shoots up from the chair. "I want to see Mom," Jared says, glaring at Todd. "And I want to know everything Alessa told you."

"Do you think it's . . . safe?" Todd asks Alessa.

"I think so," Alessa says, a doleful expression on her blue digital face. "The soul that latched to her won't be able to last much longer in her body."

"Okay," Todd says, getting up next to Jared. "You deserve to see her. You deserve to know what happened."

Jared stares down at the floor, an angry frown etched on his face, and then silently walks over to the stairs. He waits for Todd.

"Do you want me to come up with you?" Alessa asks. "Or do you need a moment, just you and Jared?"

"Come with us," Todd says, nodding. "I don't know how Jared is going to react to this, and I want to be able to focus on comforting him." Todd places his hand on Avery's head. "Can you bring Avery up there with us? I need my family together, one last time."

20

ALESSA

"**M**om!" Jared cries, running into the medical room and immediately lunging onto the bed, hugging Tori. Her head hangs limply to the side, her eyes open and glazed over, jaw agape and lifeless. Jared pulls back, desperately trying to get Tori's attention, gently shaking her. "Mom?"

Todd puts his hand over his mouth and begins to cry as he watches Jared.

Jared steps off the bed, letting Tori's body slump forward. "Is she dead?" he asks, his voice quivering.

Alessa, still holding Avery, uses her free arm to check Tori's pulse. "I'm sorry, Jared. The soul that took over her body is officially gone. It's important to know, though, that your mom passed last night when your sister was born. What you saw of her after that . . . it wasn't your mom."

Todd lets out a pained gasp and attempts to pull Jared in for a hug, but Jared recoils, backing away from the bed, clenching his teeth as his chin trembles.

"This is the baby's fault!" Jared shouts.

Todd reaches out for him. "Jared—"

"No!" Jared cries, his face turning a dark red. He sits on the floor and buries his head into his arms, letting out a deep, guttural scream. Avery is squirming in Alessa's arms.

"This isn't right," Todd says to Alessa. He watches Jared sob on the floor. "I shouldn't have brought him up here."

"I don't want to talk about this anymore. I just want to be alone," Jared says, sniffling as he covers his eyes. "I just want to go to bed."

"That's okay," Todd says. "It's been a long, hard day. Let's get you to bed. We'll talk more about it in the morning."

Jared gets up and storms quickly out of the medical room. Todd lets out a long, defeated sigh, looking down at the floor.

"Do you want me to take Avery to her crib?" Alessa asks.

"No, she'll stay up here with us, for now," Todd says, taking Avery from Alessa's arms. "I want to give Jared some space."

"It's good that he saw her," Alessa says. "Even like this. Tomorrow would be much more difficult for him to handle, had he not seen her."

"You never told me how she died," Todd says flatly, staring vacantly at Tori. "Was that something you saw in your future visions?"

Alessa looks at Todd, unsure if he's stable enough to hear the truth of Tori's death.

"Yes," she says, hesitantly. "I know how she died."

Todd begins to bite his lip, something Alessa notes as a sign of Todd's mental state switching—the impacts of his mosaic poisoning starting to show.

"Did she take the pill?" Todd asks coldly. "Did she lie to me about opting out of the Great Suicide?"

"Tori never opted out," Alessa says. "She took Delete last night . . . shortly before she went into labor."

Todd stands silently for a moment, the anger radiating off of him as he stares at his wife's lifeless body, grinding his teeth. The only thing preventing him from complete rage is that he's still holding Avery.

"How do you know these visions are true?" Todd asks desperately. "And why *you?* How did you even start getting these visions?"

"Everything that I saw in my visions eventually came true," Alessa says. "The fact that I'm here, talking to you right now, is enough for me to believe that everything I was shown was accurate. And as far as how I started seeing the visions, I can trace it back to one moment, not long after my soul entered the realm of the afterlife."

"And what was that?" Todd asks, turning to face Alessa.

"I have it all mentally recorded too," Alessa says. "If you feel like you want to see that right now, I can show you. Just know that it's . . . violent."

"I can handle it," Todd says sternly.

Alessa activates the projection screen from her Kaxelotab again, showing Todd the now-familiar world of the afterlife realm. A mosaic-like portal—identical to the one in Todd's medical room—oscillates on the surface of the realm.

"These exact portals appeared on my home planet, Raoq, on the night of the KitD'ul," Alessa says. "The circumstances of how they appeared on Raoq were the same as how this one appeared on Earth. At the exact moment that every one of the other 1.2 billion Gridliners was powered down for good, there were five complicated Raoqin births where the mothers died in labor."

Alessa switches the projection to display five portals, from the perspective of the inside of the rooms the portals appeared in. Todd stares at the projection in awe, taking in the different portals on the screen.

"In each of these locations, the wall closest to the deceased mother started to transform, shapeshifting as it divided itself into hundreds of smaller squares, just like your wall did. I know this, and have these images, because I saw them in person. The code created for the KitD'ul somehow didn't work properly on me, possibly because I was the newest Gridliner model at the time. It weakened me severely, but it didn't completely kill me like the Raoqins planned. Mentally, I was ninety percent. Physically, less than five percent, and unable to put up a fight."

The screen displays a first-person perspective of Alessa approaching one of these portals, emitting some sort of digital scan of it, as humanoid alien figures with blue skin stand off to the side, observing Alessa. Todd examines them closely, eyes wide with pupils dilating as he gets closer to the screen, covering Avery's eyes from the bright light of the projection.

The Kaxelotab speakers emit audio of the alien species talking in a language that sounds like gibberish to Todd—a strange series of clicks and pops.

"Are those the . . . Raoqins?" Todd asks, engrossed in the footage.

A look of disgust spreads across Alessa's face. "Yes, that's them," she hisses, the thought of her creators repulsive to her. "The Raoqins tried to abuse my Gridliner powers one last time and forced me to examine these mysterious portals." The screen shows Alessa walking through the portal which flashes brightly in the process.

"They sent me through them to gather information on what was on the other side. Out of spite, I decided not to give them any of the information I was slowly putting together. After I gave them a misleading report, they officially destroyed me—manually—unknowingly sending my soul to the afterlife realm with the rest of the Gridliners. From there, they decided to explore the realm on their own."

The projection returns to a birds-eye view similar to the one from earlier. It zooms in on a portal on the surface as a group of Raoqin explorers walk through it.

"I've switched to one of the other Gridliners' recordings of this moment," Alessa says. "Watching it from my point of view would be quite disorienting."

"You could communicate with the other Gridliners while you were in the realm?" Todd asks.

"Yes, and I still can," Alessa says. "We have the power to communicate telepathically with each other, something we call databursting. Our direct line of communication hasn't stopped since the KitD'ul."

"That is . . . incredible," Todd says.

"When the Raoqins first entered the realm, their presence fueled a sort of restlessness I hadn't experienced yet in that dimension. I felt drawn to the bodies of our creators, hundreds of miles down on the ground as they searched for answers that didn't exist. And then, I gained control and made my move. I was able to detach from the sea in the sky and shoot down to the group of Raoqins, at lightning-fast speeds."

The screen shows the purple blob of Alessa's soul shooting down from the sky, abruptly ending in an absurdly loud, wet smack, as she expertly lands directly on the face of one of the female Raoqin explorers. Her soul wraps around the entirety of the Raoqin's head, spinning violently like a slimy corkscrew in and up the woman's nose, ears, and mouth, until she ends up inside of her completely. Todd winces as he watches the grotesque act of latching. The other Raoqins on the screen scream in fear.

"I was able to feel what the woman felt. I could hear her thoughts, and for a moment I even felt guilty for the intrusion. And then I remembered what they did to us, what they *took* from us, and my torturous final days on Raoq. I gained control again and expanded myself, stretching, finally inflicting some pain on them for once."

The host's abdomen rips open, spilling its contents as Alessa's soul spirals out of the host's body, which then lifelessly flops down to the ground as Alessa's soul shoots back up the sky. The other researchers continue to scream in horror, grabbing what they can of their dead colleague and bolting back to the portal they came through.

"That was the last time I saw any of the Raoqins. In fact, only a few days later, the portals were somehow obliterated and sealed shut for good. But after that moment when I first latched, I started receiving those projections, somewhat incomplete 'visions' of the future, with a focus on Earth, that showed me everything up until the night of the Great Suicide. It was as if some greater power was communicating directly to me that *this* was the way the Gridliners could have a second chance at life. Those visions showed me you working as part of the Split Meridian engineering team that developed the Splitbot fifteen years ago, and the opportunity that would create for us to escape the realm. Since then, I've learned everything I could about humans—your languages, mannerisms, behaviors—waiting for this time to come, and everything has turned out *exactly* as the visions said it would."

"Including Tori's death," Todd says, and Alessa can't tell if it's a statement or a question.

"Yes," Alessa says. "Including Tori's death."

Todd begins breathing heavily, staring intently at Tori's lifeless form. "So what do we do from here?"

"My plan that I mentioned to you," Alessa says. "It all starts here. You have to notify the Collections Agency that Tori has committed suicide."

Alessa turns off the Kaxelotab projection and steps closer to Todd, looking him directly in the eyes as she talks.

"Tomorrow, when the agent enters the medical room to place Tori inside the Bodcan, I will use the opportunity to attack the agent. I will disguise myself as this agent by stealing his Resosuit and Splithelmet, completely concealing my identity inside. From there, I'll complete his tasks for the day, then sneak into the Split Meridian base where he's stationed. As you know, there is a warehouse of 10,000 Splitbots inside of each Splitbase, and since they are newer models, they're all already equipped with their own Resosuits. I will be able to sneak some of those out, bring them back to your house, and send them through the portal so more Gridliners can begin to escape the realm, just like I did."

Todd glares at Alessa, openly frustrated.

"And what makes this a 'mutually beneficial' plan?" Todd asks. "I just received the worst news of my life. Why should I care about any of this? Why should I help you?"

"Because I can help you, Todd. You are our only hope. With your help, the entire Gridliner population will have another shot at existence. Don't think I don't know how indebted we are to you . . . I will be sure that you and your family will be taken care of, that your family will live the best possible life after all of this, and guarantee you an escape from planet Earth, when that time comes. We will give you hope for your children, and your grandchildren, and many generations after them. They won't have to live this miserable life on Earth anymore. They won't have to make decisions like Tori did."

Todd takes a deep breath and closes his eyes as he thinks.

"I'll call them," he says, slowly opening his eyes and looking at Tori. "I just want this nightmare to be over. I can't look at her anymore."

Todd projects a digital display from his Kaxelotab, displaying an inbox full of messages. He opens one from the official Split Meridian Collections Agency—a message he received earlier in the day when the officers discussed needing Tori to officially finish submitting her opt-out.

He selects an on-screen prompt at the bottom of the message: PICKUP REQUEST

He quickly fills out the form to request a pickup for tomorrow morning and immediately shuts off the Kaxelotab display.

"There," he says, scowling. "They can do whatever they want with her."

"They'll be here early," Alessa says, attempting to change the subject. "You should get some rest."

"Yeah . . . rest," Todd says, letting out a frustrated sigh and looking down at Avery in his arms. "I'll put the little one to sleep. Not sure if I'll get any, but I'll try. You can hang out wherever you want in the house, I really don't care. I'll just . . . see you in the morning."

He looks at Tori one last time, shakes his head, and walks out of the room.

21

ALESSA

Alessa stands in the kitchen—in the same spot she stood all night long while the Morgan family slept—playing out the many possible scenarios of her planned attack on the Collections officer in her head. The morning sun begins to shine brightly through the windows of the living room.

"Good morning," Alessa says as Todd walks down the stairs, realizing how strange a saying this human custom is, especially on a morning like today. *It is in fact not going to be a good morning,* Alessa thinks.

"Morning," Todd says, groggily dragging his feet past Alessa and heading directly to the coffee machine, which instantly brews him a single cup of coffee.

"Let's go over the plan one more time," Alessa says. "We have to make sure we're on the same page in order for this to work."

Todd stands, hunched over his mug of coffee, breathing heavily. Suddenly and unexpectedly, he slams his fist on the counter, sending hot black coffee splashing over the sides of the mug.

"Look, you can do whatever you want with Tori," Todd says, turning to face Alessa. "She screwed my family over. She screwed *me* over! What kind of monster plans to commit suicide during the birth of their child? You're a robot. Do you have any idea how fucked up that is? Do you have even the slightest clue?"

Alessa notices Todd nervously chewing away at his lip—the outside of which is now visibly raw and slightly bloody.

"Todd, I can't even imagine what you're feeling right now . . ." Alessa says as Todd takes a sip of coffee, barely able to keep the mug steady due to his shaking hands. "I might be a 'robot' in your eyes, but I do have a soul—me being here right now talking to you proves that. You saw my Soultomb. Believe it or not, I care. Nobody deserves this."

He looks up from his coffee at Alessa with red, moist eyes. "I'm sorry," he says, letting out a frustrated sigh. "I'm handling this the best I can."

"I know," Alessa says, walking over to Todd and hugging him. "I understand."

Todd awkwardly pulls out of the hug, wiping a tear from his face.

"Okay," he says. "One possible plan, with a few clarifications after thinking about it all night: the Collections officer arrives at 8 am, about one hour from now. Jared is to remain in the basement with Avery. You'll be upstairs waiting in the medical room. The officer's attention will obviously immediately be focused on the mosaic, taking him off guard. This will hopefully be a big enough distraction for him to let his guard down, and in that moment you will strike. *How* you strike is the question."

"And it will have to be quick and deadly," Alessa says. "I've played thousands of scenarios out in my head, and unfortunately the only ones that result in success are the ones in which the officer ends up dead."

"If you plan on using your Handlights, you have to be smart about where you direct the force," Todd says. "Resosuits and Splithelmets are designed to protect against the power of Handlights."

"I'm aware," Alessa says as Todd takes a sip of his coffee. "That's why we'll have to somehow get the officer to remove his helmet."

"Come on, that's just ridiculous," Todd snickers, almost choking on his coffee. "An officer with that level of training would never take off their helmet. That's one of the main things they're trained *not* to do."

"I don't think it's ridiculous," Alessa says. "The mosaic is unlike anything anyone has ever seen before . . . No training on Earth can prepare any human for contact with it, and I believe that I can utilize at least one of the many Splitbot modes to make the experience disorienting enough that the officer's training will go out the window."

"Hm . . ." Todd says, giving Alessa an inquisitive look. "How so?"

"AudioMode is probably our best bet, at least in terms of getting him to take his helmet off," Alessa says. "Think of how the sound of the portal made you and Jared feel the first time you heard it. I know it's much quieter now, but imagine what it would sound like if it were channeled directly into the internal speakers of a protective helmet you were wearing and amplified to deafening levels. The sound the mosaic makes is highly dangerous—a sound from another dimension, not meant for life on Earth. It wouldn't matter how much training you had—that helmet would be coming off. You have to trust me on this one."

"I don't really have any other choice but to trust you at this point. I just hope you're right," Todd says. "The last thing I need is the media attention that you and the mosaic would bring upon my family."

The sunlight funneling in through the living-room window flickers, then disappears completely, blocked by a smaller Collections truck parking directly in front of the house. Todd carefully walks closer to the window, looking through it.

"Shit, he's early!" Todd yells, running back through the kitchen and to the basement stairs, stopping at the top of them. "I have to go tell Jared to stay downstairs. Go up to the medical room, now!"

Alessa runs upstairs, directly to the medical room, before Todd even finishes his sentence. Tori lies motionless on the bed, her eyes and mouth agape, her skin distinctly tighter than it was last night, clinging to her bones. The room reeks of death and a horrible mixture of human urine and feces.

For a brief moment, Alessa thinks of Jared and how horrible this all must be for him, until her thoughts are interrupted by the sound of the front door opening, followed by Todd greeting the Collections officer.

"She's upstairs, Officer," Todd says. "This way."

The sound of their footsteps gets louder—in addition to the subtle humming noise of the hovering Bodcan—as they walk upstairs to the medical room. Alessa activates the Splitbot's AudioMode. Her right arm transforms into an oblong device: its outer casing flipping inside out, revealing thousands of neatly organized microscopic sensors and speakers.

Alessa places the arm's sensors right up against the mosaic, while scanning for the Collections officer's Splithelmet Aura-Fi. She locks on to his frequency as soon as he's in range, preparing to transmit the sound of the portal.

Todd and the Collections officer enter the room. The officer immediately notices the wall, and then Alessa standing next to it. He reactively pulls out the rifle strapped on his chest, pointing it at Alessa while the Bodcan hovers gracefully behind him.

"What the fuck is going on?" the officer yells, keeping his focus on Alessa and the portal as the glowing squares on the wall continue to ripple in place. "Wh . . . What is—"

Alessa transmits the audio of the wall directly into the Collections officer's helmet, turning the volume setting to the max. The officer falls forward, dropping his gun to the floor, screaming as his hands frantically work at the clips on the side of his helmet.

"Stop!" he screams, just before he manages to pull his helmet off, revealing a sweaty, bald head underneath. He grabs his ears, kneeling forward on the floor. "I can't hear! What the fuck did you do to me?!"

Alessa acts immediately: she switches out of AudioMode, holds out her right arm while activating the Handlights, and points her hand in the direction of the officer's head, making a slow, squeezing gesture.

The officer screams, crumpling completely to the floor. Alessa uses her left Handlights to remove the officer's Resosuit and Collections uniform from a distance, being careful not to damage any of it. The officer shows a strange determination to cover his naked body, but fails to do so, awkwardly squirming on the floor.

Alessa controls her Handlights to squeeze harder, watching as the man's head shrinks. He manages to turn to face Alessa—to see what kind of force is capable of doing this—getting one look at her before his head folds in on itself, collapsing. Blood splatters onto Todd as he stands there, watching the brutal scene in shock.

"Oh my god," Todd says, covering his mouth as he turns his head away, gagging. "I'm going to be sick."

Before more of a mess can be made, Alessa uses her Handlights to compress the officer's entire body into a small cube—making sure to optimize the Handlight's gravity control to direct the officer's bodily fluids into the compression.

With the cube still in Alessa's gravity hold, she walks through the mosaic, bringing the compressed body of the officer with her.

Alessa walks across the white sand of the afterlife realm, trying to distance herself as much as possible from the portal.

With the Handlights on her right hand still controlling the compressed officer's body—hovering in place as the purple sky creates a strange glow around the cube of flesh, hair, and crushed bone—Alessa uses her free Handlights to blast a small hole in the ground of the realm.

She directs the cube that is the Collections officer, places him in the hole, and drops the sand back on top of it, burying him in a matter of seconds.

Alessa looks down at the gravesite, feeling a deep sense of sadness and guilt while standing there. *What a horrible way to die,* she thinks.

Before walking back to the portal, Alessa glances up at the sky, knowing that the rest of the Gridliners are up there somewhere, waiting for their opportunity to escape to Earth, just like she did—and it's this knowledge that allows her to live with everything she's just done.

22

ALESSA

Todd is standing between Tori and the still-hovering Bodcan as Alessa walks through the mosaic and back into the medical room.

"Do what you need to do. I've said my goodbyes," Todd says coldly. "But I don't need to be here to watch any of . . ." he gestures to the Bodcan. " . . . this." Alessa nods and watches as he leaves the room, waiting to begin using the Bodcan until she can no longer hear his footsteps.

Alessa immediately puts on the officer's Resosuit, Splithelmet, Collections uniform, and Kaxelotab—all of which fit comfortably, the Splitbot body being about the same size as the officer—completely concealing her Splitbot identity.

She picks up the officer's gun, straps it to her chest, and then turns her attention to the Bodcan, using her hands to push the futuristic coffin down to the floor. There's a screen on the top of the Bodcan displaying a text prompt:

BEGIN COLLECTION? YES/NO

Alessa presses YES, causing the Bodcan to begin its work. The lid on the front of the Bodcan opens smoothly, sliding itself upwards to reveal a circular opening. A loud, whirring sound occurs as the inside of the Bodcan begins to pressurize.

A red light is emitted from the top of the lid, projecting a straight line down to the floor. "Place the body on the red line," a synthetic male voice commands from the Bodcan speakers. The Bodcan screen displays an animation, illustrating the proper placement of the body—the avatar's head closest to the opening.

"Head must face the opening," the synthetic voice continues. "Thank you."

Alessa lifts Tori up off the bed—her body stiff and cold—and places her gently on the floor as directed. Tori's head faces the opening exactly as the animation on the Bodcan screen shows it, and the red line of light is now centered vertically on her body, glowing on her pale skin.

The red light turns green. "Thank you for your assistance," the synthetic voice says. The whirring gets louder, and the Bodcan begins to shake so much that Alessa worries that she's done something wrong. Then, Tori's hair begins to be pulled in the direction of the Bodcan, as if being sucked up by a vacuum. Her body slides along the floor ever so slightly, the Bodcan nearly bouncing from the suction.

Suddenly, Tori's body is slurped up by the Bodcan, the opening immediately sliding shut after she's fully inside. White steam is released from small vents on the side of the Bodcan, along with an audible mechanical sigh from the machine.

"Job complete. Ready for docking. Send to SemiScraper Truck?" the synthetic voice asks as the Bodcan begins to hover again in place. Alessa bends over to examine how the machine floats, looking up from underneath the Bodcan to find hundreds of tiny fans blasting air to the floor, which is what allows the device to hover.

"Send to SemiScraper Truck?" the voice asks again. Alessa notices another YES and NO text prompt displayed on the screen. She presses YES, and the Bodcan floats out of the room. Alessa follows it out of the medical room, watching as it effortlessly makes the turn to the stairs and heads down to the front door of the Solution Home, stopping at the door, waiting for someone to open it.

Todd appears from the kitchen, where he was wiping the officer's blood off of his legs with a wet rag. He looks up at Alessa, his face pale and eyes sunken. "Good luck," he says, just before opening the front door to let the Bodcan fly out.

"Are you okay?" Alessa asks as she walks slowly down the stairs. "And Jared?"

"We'll manage," he says, holding the door open. "But you better get going. You're on a schedule now. If you want to enter the Splitbase unnoticed, you'll need to complete the officer's route—and quickly—before one of the officer's supervisors checks to see he's on track for the day."

"Okay." Alessa stops in front of Todd, looking at him with wide eyes. "Thank you. I promise, you won't regret helping me."

"I hope not," Todd says sternly.

Alessa nods, and then walks through the door and towards the Collections vehicle, observing the surrounding area as the Bodcan loads itself into its designated compartment on the truck. She's struck by the truly depressing landscape beyond the SemiScraper: endless Solution Homes organized in a line on dry, barren land. Heat distortion warps everything in sight. Smog from heavy air pollution obscures the sun, creating an infinitely dull, gray sky. Not a single person outside. Not a single plant to be found. Not a single car driving on the lone road stretching for miles.

A truly depressing, bleak existence, so much so that Alessa can somewhat understand how something as severe as the Great Suicide could seem appealing in a world like this.

She enters the truck, greeted by a massive screen displaying squares for every compartment on the truck with only one remaining unoccupied: the Collections officer's next and final job of the day.

On another screen, a GPS displays dots highlighting the remaining nearby stop. Their scheduled time is displayed prominently: 9:45 am. The Solution Home is only five miles away from the Morgan household.

"Next stop?" the same synthetic voice from earlier asks.

"Yes," Alessa says, settling into her seat as the truck begins to drive itself to the next location.

23

ALESSA

The SemiScraper Truck comes to a stop. The GPS screen zooms in on the house Alessa is parked in front of, magnifying it in greater detail than what she's able to see in real life.

"You have arrived at your next destination," the synthetic voice of the truck's AI assistant says. "This is the Solution Home of the Cain family. We are here to collect Aaron Cain, son of Chad and Gail Cain. Eighteen years old. Ready to approach?"

"Yes," Alessa says, perfectly replicating the previous officer's voice using the Splitvoice feature—a Splitbot function that requires only ten seconds of sample speech to create a deepfake of anyone's voice.

The door of the SemiScraper opens, followed by a command from the synthetic voice: "You have twenty minutes to stay on schedule. Begin now?" Alessa feels a buzz on her wrist from the Kaxelotab, and she looks down to observe it. On the screen, a confirmation notification is displayed to start the timer.

"Yes," Alessa says again, watching the stopwatch on the Kaxelotab begin. As she walks to the house, the remaining Bodcan hovers out of the SemiScraper, following behind her.

Alessa approaches the front door and hears a loud argument coming from inside the Solution Home.

"I told you not to keep this fucking thing in the house!" a hysterical woman screams.

"I didn't think he would ever be able to find it!" a male voice yells back, sniffling, followed by the sound of sobbing.

Alessa knocks at the door. "Collections here. Looking for Aaron Cain."

The yelling from inside of the house immediately stops, and after a moment, the front door opens, revealing a blood-covered woman. She is distraught: her crazed eyes are wide open, red, and unblinking, slightly covered by her wild hair. Her face is puffy and swollen—nostrils raw—the byproduct of continuous hysterical crying. Her oversized T-shirt hangs messily on her severely thin torso. Finger-shaped strips of dried blood are smeared across the sides of the fabric.

The woman is jittery, shaking as she looks up at Alessa. "Get on with whatever it is you need to do," she says, as the man she was arguing with in the background walks up the stairs.

Alessa looks down at the Kaxelotab: nineteen minutes remaining. She activates the biometric scanner, watching as the thin burst of light emerging from her wrist scans the woman. The speaker on the Kaxelotab blasts the results: "Gail Cain. Non-Outer. Mother of Outer Aaron Cain."

"Aaron is upstairs. He didn't use the pill," Gail says, crying, head shaking. She becomes hysterical—hitting herself in the face—repeating those words over and over again. "He didn't use the pill! He didn't use the pill! He didn't use the pill!" Her nose and mouth begin gushing blood.

"Stop!" Allesa yells, holding her hands out, unprepared and uncertain about how to handle this situation. "Please, stop!"

Gail begins slamming her head into the wall in the hallway. "He didn't use the pill!" A tooth flies out of her mouth after saying 'pill' this time. Alessa tries restraining her, holding her tightly, but she only makes it worse.

"Let me go!" Gail screams, squirming in Alessa's hold. "Get off of me!"

Suddenly, she goes limp, sobbing as blood and tears drip to the floor. "Just fucking kill me," Gail says, defeated. "I said just fucking kill me!"

Gail tries to continue hitting herself, but has worn herself out. Alessa looks down at the Kaxelotab again: seventeen minutes. A sense of panic overcomes her, unsure of what happens if she runs out of time.

A loud explosion comes from upstairs, immediately followed by a wet splatter. Gail turns and looks up at Alessa, eyes wide open. "No," she says. "*No!*" She gets up and runs upstairs, Alessa following after her.

In the first room on the second floor lie two lifeless bodies—Chad and Aaron, the husband and son of Gail. Their heads are completely exploded, the walls covered in blood. Gail walks in slowly, taking in the sight. "You don't get to leave me like this!" she screams, kneeling down next to her now-deceased husband, her throat hoarse. "You don't get to leave me like this!"

There is a strange, makeshift gun on the floor. Alessa scans it, quickly learning that it's a scattergun—an illegal, haphazardly developed, black-market firearm created after the Weapon Ban of 2055 made it nearly impossible for the average person to purchase any type of weapon, noted for its ability to use almost any solid material as bullets, recycling most household items.

Gail picks up the gun, points it at her own head, and pulls the trigger—only to find it's out of ammunition. She pulls the trigger again and again. "You can't do this to me!" she screams at her son and husband.

She throws the scattergun furiously at Alessa—Alessa expertly dodges it. "You're part of the problem," Gail yells, approaching Alessa. "You enable this kind of activity, profit off of this kind of stuff! Are you proud to work for Split Meridian? You proud to be owned by Roth Nin?"

Alessa remains silent, maintaining the cold aura of the Collections officer. Gail falls to her knees, desperately clutching at Alessa's Resosuit as she begins to cry.

"If there's any morsel of a soul in your body, you will kill me right now," Gail pleads. "I am begging you, for the love of God, just kill me."

"I can't, ma'am," Alessa says coldly, just as one would expect of a Collections officer. "I am here to collect Aaron, and that is all I'm doing today. Your husband is not listed as an official Outer, and I do not have a Bodcan dedicated to him at this time. You will need to report that he has committed suicide and arrange yet another pickup. Now please, let me complete my duties."

Alessa nudges Gail off of her legs as she directs the Bodcan closer to Aaron's body, struggling to keep up her emotionless act at the devastatingly sad sight of Gail.

Gail stands up and spits blood at Alessa's back. "Coward!" she yells, blood still dripping from her nose.

Alessa turns back around to face Gail, simultaneously reaching into a harness on the side of her Resosuit and pulling out the officer's Gelcuff Gun—a miniature gun that shoots a non-lethal, gel-like sedative patch that wraps around its target, safely restraining them.

Gail makes a dash for the door, and Alessa shoots. The Gelcuff strip flies across the room, smacking into Gail's feet perfectly on target and immediately wrapping around them. She trips, falls, and slams onto the hardwood floor.

"Get this shit off of me, god damn it!" Gail screams, trying to lift her feet off the floor, the sedatives already kicking in.

"Get this . . . off . . ." Gail says again, her speech slurred now as her squirming on the floor comes to an end. She groans, now in a relaxed, semi-conscious, dream-like state.

"Ten minutes remaining," the synthetic voice says from the speaker on Alessa's Kaxelotab. Alessa quickly starts the Bodcan collection process and watches as the machine effortlessly sucks up Gail's son's body—just as it did with Tori.

"Job complete. Ready for docking. Send to SemiScraper Truck?" the familiar synthetic voice asks.

"Yes!" Alessa yells, momentarily breaking from the Collections officer character. She stands there for a moment, watching as the Bodcan flies out of the room.

Alessa stands over Gail, who looks up at her with heavy eyelids, fighting to stay awake.

"The Gelcuffs will dissolve within a half an hour," Alessa says as she picks her up off the floor and carries her out of the room, refusing to leave her there with her dead husband.

And then, only after Gail is fully unconscious, Alessa gently places her on a couch in the living room. She leaves her there alone as she walks out of the house and back to the SemiScraper Truck—overcome with sadness for a woman she knows nothing about.

24

ALESSA

The Bodcan loads itself into the SemiScraper with only thirty seconds left to spare. Alessa calms down as she watches the timer come to a stop in the cab of the truck, trying to clear her mind of the brutal encounter she just had with the Cains.

"Job well done," the synthetic voice says as animated graphics of confetti fill the main screen mounted to the right of the dashboard. "Return to headquarters?"

"Yes," Alessa says, resting her head on her hands, eyes closed.

"Okay. Your safety is of great importance to us. Please buckle up!" The GPS pings a location ten miles from the Cain household—Splitbase 031—and the truck begins to drive itself. The many Solution Homes on the left side of the road become a blur as the SemiScraper quickly gains speed.

"I have a question," Alessa announces to the screen on the dashboard—unsure if it will trigger any sort of response. She needs to find out as much information as possible before arriving at the local Split Meridian headquarters.

The main screen displays a logo: a magnifying glass with a question mark in the center of the lens, the word 'Convex' displayed beneath.

"Hey Mark. How can I assist you today?" a different, female robotic voice says.

Mark. "How many other officers are on duty at this moment?" Alessa asks.

"Twenty-five for base 031. Are you looking to assist on another shift?"

"No, thank you."

"So . . ." the female voice says playfully, followed by a subtle clearing of the throat. "Why are you calling then, Mr. Mark?"

Alessa immediately realizes this isn't a robot, but instead a human on some sort of support line. She fights back the urge to end the call. *Shit.*

"I am . . . competitive by nature. Just wondering how my time compares to the rest is all," Alessa says.

The woman on the line laughs flirtatiously. "Come on, Mark, are you trying to impress me again? I don't think you want to know how you compare to the rest of them. Let's just say you're not in first place. Actually . . ." She pauses.

"Actually what?" Alessa asks, nervously leaning forward in her seat, fidgeting her legs as she waits for a reply.

"Was everything alright today?" the woman asks, her cheery voice shifting to a much more serious, concerned tone. "I'm getting some strange data from your Resosuit. Major temperature fluctuations. Actually, no temperature at all at one point. Did you remove your Resosuit? What were you thinking?"

"Yes—I mean *no*—I did not remove my Resosuit. Yes, I was having major temperature fluctuations. I'm not sure what's going on with it, but something's definitely up. For how expensive these things are you'd think they'd be a little more reliable," Alessa says, silently punching the passenger seat, realizing she needs to say something else to change the direction of this conversation, fast. "Am I the last on the road?"

"That's strange . . . I'll put in a service request for your Resosuit," she says, her voice relaxed again. "You need to be careful out there, though. You're not the only one you need to be worried about, you know. And yes, you are the last on the road."

"Damn it!" Alessa yells, doing her best Collections officer impersonation possible. "I won't tell you who I was racing with, but I have a feeling I would've won if I didn't start having issues with my suit a couple of houses ago."

"For what it's worth, you were on track to be the first one done today. You went from first to dead last in the past couple of hours of your—" The operator stops suddenly, and then, "Hey I've got another call coming in. I'll talk to you later?"

"Sounds good," Alessa says, and the magnifying glass logo disappears.

"Thank you for using Convex. How would you rate your call?" the original voice of the truck asks.

"Five stars," Alessa says, utterly shocked that the conversation didn't completely ruin her chances of getting to the rest of the Splitbots.

Alessa sits back in her seat, letting out a sigh of relief knowing that she's the last Collections officer on the road. The fewer people she has to encounter when entering the Split Meridian base, the better.

The thought of being so close to obtaining additional Splitbot bodies—so close to helping more of her fellow Gridliners escape the afterlife realm—soothes Alessa ever so slightly as the SemiScraper Truck approaches the gigantic Split Meridian facility known as Splitbase 031.

25

ALESSA

The SemiScraper slows down as it continues to drive closer to the base—a large, stark-white warehouse, sticking out on the bare landscape surrounding it. Alessa knows, however, that the exterior is somewhat deceiving—what makes all Splitbases special is not how tall they are, but how deep.

The truck passes through security without issue and drives itself onto a large, metallic platform on the side of the building. A camera system hovering above the platform scans the license plate on the front of the truck, causing a set of green lights to ignite. A projected digital display to the right side of the platform displays a text profile, showing that the Collections officer Mark Doble has officially been granted access to the facility, along with his stats for the day.

Suddenly, doors beneath the platform slide open, and the platform begins to descend at a startling speed, so fast Alessa begins to momentarily hover above her seat. She watches in awe as floor after floor blurs by until finally reaching the bottom.

"Floor 350," the voice of the truck says. The truck drives forward as a colossal mechanical door slides open smoothly and precisely.

On the other side of the door is a 600-foot-wide tunnel—large enough for the SkyScraper Trucks to drive through—lit by thousands of blue and white lights amplified by the reflective quality of the metallic tunnel walls.

The truck passes through an opening at the end of the tunnel and into a parking garage for the Collections officers' trucks. Over 100 SkyScraper and SemiScraper Trucks are perfectly organized here, with only one spot remaining open, to which the truck drives itself. Mark Doble's designated parking spot.

Once the truck is parked, the hundreds of compartment doors on the sides of the truck open simultaneously. One by one, each of the Bodcans flies itself out and away in a single file line to another tunnel on the opposite side of the parking garage.

Alessa sets her Resosuit to InvisiMode and steps out of the truck. She follows the path of the flying Bodcans, unsure of where else to go. The tunnel is surrounded by windows on each side, exposing a vast lab with hundreds of doctors and scientists dressed in white lab coats and protective Splithelmets, working with an intense level of concentration.

There are countless surgical tables holding exposed cadavers, all of which are hooked up to sophisticated machinery and surrounded by busy doctors. On the far side of the lab sit thousands of fluid-filled vessels containing naked human bodies. Each vessel has a monitor displaying various bits of unrecognizable data, along with a close-up shot of the person's face and other personal information.

Alessa stops for a moment, examining the room. *What is going on here?*

She quickly returns her attention to the Bodcans, which are now making a right turn into another room further down the tunnel. Alessa continues to follow them, leading her to an impressively massive room—a library of Bodcan compartments—at least a million of which are built into a wall with no end in sight as she looks forward.

Alessa watches in awe as the Bodcans float up and away to their designated compartments in the wall. The room appears to span from the bottom of the base all the way to the surface at Floor 1 . . . a minimum of 4,000 feet up. Alessa notices a series of large vents built into the ceiling of the Bodcan library, making a mental note that the slits of the vent are large enough to fly through in DroneMode—a perfect escape route once she gains access to the Splitbots she came here for.

Each level of Bodcan compartments has a bridge connecting to a door on each level on the opposite side of the room. Each of these levels has windows spanning all the way down as far as Alessa can see, exposing each floor of the Splitbase.

Alessa switches to DroneMode—the Resosuit adjusting accordingly, keeping her invisible—and begins to fly upwards, looking through the windows of each floor in search of the Splitbots.

After only a few minutes of searching, she spots the Splitbot storage area on Floor 261—a room with 10,000 brand-new Splitbots, all equipped with their own Resosuits, waiting to be deployed. Alessa flies across the entirety of the window, scoping out any potential security measures as she figures out the best way to gain access to the room.

She notices hundreds of cameras keeping a watchful eye on the Splitbots and decides her only realistic way of getting in and out unnoticed is by creating some much more significant distraction.

Alessa prepares her Dronegun—a laser-based, military-grade weapon mounted on the top of a Splitbot in DroneMode. She knows that even if she uses it at half strength, it has enough power to demolish one of the bridges spanning the room, creating immeasurable damage and distraction with little to no effort.

And that's exactly what she decides has to be done.

26
ALESSA

Alessa locks her target on a bridge fifty floors below, getting ready to destroy it with a Resolaze—the Dronegun's signature laser beam.

Just as she's about to shoot, a deafening alarm is sounded: a jarring, high-pitched siren coming from large speakers mounted to the ceiling, accompanied by bright red flashing lights, giving the entire Bodcan library a carmine-colored glow. A large group of security officers runs out of a room on the bottom floor, some of whom step onto a maintenance lift, which quickly sends them upwards in search of whatever triggered the alarm.

The alarm, paired with the sight of security working their way up in her direction, fills Alessa with panic.

Can they see me? she thinks.

The maintenance lift carrying the security officers quickly glides upwards past Alessa, leaving her unnoticed. She looks up in the direction the lift is traveling: a Bodcan compartment a hundred floors up flashes with its own additional red lights. Without moving, Alessa zooms her sight up to the compartment to get a better look at what's going on.

The Bodcan compartment door opens, allowing the Bodcan to fly itself out of it, slowly working its way to the maintenance lift—which is now standing idly right next to the compartment. The Bodcan itself struggles to maintain control, visibly bouncing around as it hovers above the security officers.

A synthetic voice from a speaker on the compartment door begins to loudly communicate the issue: "Bodcan rejected. Movement detected. Bodcan rejected. Movement detected." The repetitive words and jerky movements continue as Alessa zooms in closer to the screen on the side of the Bodcan, now displaying Tori Morgan's information: name, address, birthday, age, weight, height, hair color, eye color, and picture.

How is this possible? Alessa thinks. She was absolutely certain that Tori was dead before she loaded her into the Bodcan.

Out of fear that Split Meridian's discovery of Tori's zombie-like state will bring unwanted attention to the Morgan family—and more importantly, disrupt her plan to utilize the mosaic for the escape of the Gridliners—Alessa sets the Dronegun to its highest strength and blasts the previously charged Resolaze directly at Tori's Bodcan, completely exploding it upon impact.

Shards of metal, body parts, and other chunks of debris from the Bodcan crash down onto the Split Meridian security officers on the maintenance lift, ripping the lift off its tracks and leaving it dangling vertically on the Bodcan library wall, hundreds of floors above the lower level.

The security officers—burned by the explosion and covered in blood—desperately attempt to grab hold of the surface of the lift, failing to do so as they slide off one by one. Alessa watches as they plummet down to the floor, screaming until they slam onto the hard concrete floor of the Bodcan library and die upon impact, flattened to oblivion.

The lift finally falls, slamming into multiple bridges on its way down, all happening too quickly to give the other security officers a chance to run for cover. Debris crashes into the floor, crushing every security officer in sight, leaving all but one dead. The lone security officer is trapped under a large piece of a bridge—his legs crushed and pinned to the ground. Surrounded by a pool of his coworkers' blood, he screams for help.

More alarms are sounded, seemingly coming from every direction.

This is my chance, Alessa thinks, flying over to the door of the Splitbot storage room. The door is locked and doesn't open on its own, so Alessa blasts another Resolaze—this time directed at the door—instantly destroying it.

Alessa quickly flies into the massive storage room: the 10,000 Splitbots are neatly organized in 100 rows of 100, all connected to futuristic cables extending up from the floor.

She collects the coordinate code—similar to an IP address, a notoriously complex code that identifies the actual location of a server and location on the Gridline—of a nearby robot, creating the ability to easily travel back to one of these Splitbots through the digital dimension, when and if needed.

She approaches the other ten Splitbots closest to her, immediately connecting to their Aura-Fi to power them on. In a matter of a minute and forty seconds, Alessa activates their InvisiMode, disables both their tracking software and external Aura-Fi capabilities, switches each of them to DroneMode, and syncs their drone flight controls to hers—leading all ten of the Splitbots out of the room in perfect sync.

As Alessa flies out of the Splitbot storage room, she notices there are now hundreds of people down on the floor below, frantically surveying the carnage in the Bodcan library as they desperately move hunks of bridge debris—a futile attempt to salvage any security officers they can.

Additional Split Meridian maintenance employees equipped with harnesses begin to run out of the doors to the bridges above, using unfamiliar tools to repair them before any more of the damaged bridges can collapse.

Alessa quickly leads the ten Splitbots toward her planned escape route—the vent all the way up on the ceiling—picking up bits of frustrated conversation from the Split Meridian employees repairing the bridges.

"Who was the driver assigned to this Bodcan?" one of them says.

"Mark Doble. Security is searching the building for him now but can't find him. Said he had his Resosuit set to InvisiMode as he was leaving his truck. They have no idea where he went from there. Obviously wasn't able to be picked up by the security cams," another says.

"Are you fucking kidding me?" another says, using a large tool to weld a piece of the bridge back together. "I always thought Mark was a fucking weirdo. I bet he had something to do with all of this. He probably didn't properly close the Bodcan that started all of this. Was probably rushing the job because he was in last place on the leaderboards today."

Alessa loses the ability to hear the rest of the conversation as they continue to fly up to the vents on the ceiling.

Somewhat concerned about how long the vent will stay open, Alessa takes her chances and flies through, greeted by pouring rain outside. The vent is open long enough for all but the eleventh Splitbot to make it out—the vent closing the millisecond it is halfway through. The force completely crushes the final drone, causing yet another massive explosion.

A burst of flame shoots upwards, sending a wave of heat up to where Alessa and the other Splitbots are floating, now visible in the rain, which reveals hollow, oblong pockets in the air—the invisible drones—bending the natural trajectory of the rain. The vent slowly collapses in on itself, folding until it falls completely—smashing the various bridges the maintenance crew has been working on on the way down, until finally crashing to the bottom floor, sending a reverberating roar up through the hole in the roof.

Alessa can hear screams from below over the additional alarm now being sounded from outside—the Splitbase is in a state of emergency.

Before any Split Meridian employees can notice the drones hovering in the rain, Alessa flies at the highest speed possible back to the Morgan household, the other nine Splitbots tracking right behind her.

27

ALESSA

The news of the destruction at the Splitbase has spread before Alessa even gets back to the Morgan household. She approaches the house and sees Todd waiting inside anxiously—chewing away at his bottom lip—as he peeks through the curtain of the front window. He notices the rain bouncing off of their Invisifields and immediately opens the front door to let the cluster of Splitbots in.

Alessa turns off InvisiMode as she flies into the house, revealing herself and the nine other bots to Todd.

"What happened?" Todd asks, a grave, concerned look on his face as he shuts the door. "This story is being reported on every single news outlet in the world as we speak!"

"Tori's Bodcan was rejected . . . There was movement detected inside of it," Alessa explains, switching herself out of DroneMode—the other nine still hovering.

"Her Bodcan was *rejected?*" Todd asks, squinting in confusion as he looks at Alessa and shaking his head rapidly. "That's not possible. I thought you made absolutely sure she was dead."

"I did," Alessa says, as she uses her Kaxelotab to project the memory of Tori's body being sucked into the Bodcan. "I can't explain what happened. She was dead when I put her in the Bodcan."

Todd watches the projection, frowning and rubbing his forehead as he tries to make sense of the situation.

"I fear it has something to do with her condition—her exposure to the mosaic," Alessa says, turning off the Kaxelotab projection and returning her focus to Todd. "I don't know what kind of soul latched to her body, but I don't think it was human. It might be some sort of parasitic alien life-form, not compatible with the human body, that shows very different signs of life and death. I just don't know how it all works. I believe that hosts are not meant to be fully developed, and I'm sure latching inside of the realm has some sort of effects—"

"Enough," Todd says, holding his hand up to signal for Alessa to stop talking. "I don't want to hear any more attempts to explain what's happening. You don't understand it, and I don't want to hear what you have to say about it until you do." Todd takes a deep breath, closes his eyes, and speaks in a pseudo-calm manner. "One way or another, she was alive and moving at the Splitbase. Jared saw the news. It's trending everywhere possible in Vapor. He saw the security-camera footage of his mother's Bodcan exploding, her body parts falling down hundreds of feet, covering a bunch of innocent workers below. Do you know what this is doing to him? He's locked himself in his bedroom since he saw it. Avery is bound to see this one day when she's old enough, too."

Alessa covers her digital mouth, imagining the horror that this must have caused for Jared. Her shoulders slump, defeated. "I'm so sorry. I had no idea something like this was going to happen."

"If I'd had even the slightest idea that something like this was going to happen, I never would have agreed to help you," Todd says, glowering at Alessa. A throbbing vein bulges on his temple. "They're going to trace all of this back to our family somehow. They know that was Tori's Bodcan."

"I know it's hard to see this now," Alessa says, turning to the other Splitbots, "but once I get more of the Gridliners out of the realm, it doesn't matter if Split Meridian knows you helped us. *We* will protect you."

"Yeah, and why should I believe you?" Todd asks, sneering. He steps in front of Alessa, standing between her and the other Splitbots. "I trusted that something like this wouldn't happen, and look how that turned out. Hell, after seeing the security footage for myself, I don't know who is worse: you or Split Meridian."

"Todd, you don't know what I saw there," Alessa says. "These bodies that are being collected from the Great Suicide . . . they're doing something suspicious with all of them. If they discovered Tori's body—and whatever is going on inside of it—who knows what they would have done with that type of information and power. I had to prevent that, at least to stall them for now."

"I don't care." Todd scowls, squinting his eyes as he talks to Alessa. "You've just made us a prime target in this case. I'm turning you in. This ends here."

Todd frantically takes out his cell phone and begins to dial the number to the Collections Agency. Before he can press the 'call' button, Alessa pulls out her Gelcuff Gun and immediately shoots it at Todd's hands—the Gelcuff strip painlessly wrapping around his wrists, knocking his cell phone to the floor in the process.

Todd slowly looks down at the Gelcuff strip on his wrists, then back up to Alessa—his jaw clenched in anger. "You're not going to get away with this," Todd says, slurring and slumping forward as the Gelcuff sedation starts to do its job. "I was wrong about you."

Alessa activates her Handlights, using their gravitational control to prevent Todd from falling forward to the floor, holding him still at a seventy-degree angle.

"You weren't wrong about me," Alessa says, trying to communicate as much as she can before Todd is fully unconscious. She steps closer to Todd, looking at him caringly—her eyes wide and sympathetic. "Helping us will be the best decision you've ever made. I promise you, the humans that believe in the Gridliner cause *will* have a new home one day. We are an extremely loyal species, and we will forever be indebted to you for the opportunity you created for us, for what you did to help put an end to our suffering. Your future, along with the futures of many other humans who support us, will be just as important to us as our own."

"I . . ." Todd says, his eyes fully closing. His mouth hangs open, and he breathes steadily as he falls asleep.

Alessa uses her Handlights to lift Todd off the floor and carry him to the basement, his arms and legs swinging limply as he hovers down the stairs. She follows slowly behind him, careful not to hurt him in any way.

The door to Jared's bedroom is still closed—Alessa can tell he's using his Roundchamber based on the subtle mechanical humming sound coming from his room—while Avery is in her crib, awake but not crying. Alessa places Todd gently on the floor near Avery's corner of the basement, then immediately heads back up the stairs to the first floor, quietly shutting the door to the basement and using her Handlights to lock it.

Alessa places every piece of furniture on the first floor in front of the basement door to make any sort of escape impossible, and then controls the rest of the Splitbots up the stairs to the medical room, sending them through the mosaic one-by-one, until finally walking through the portal herself.

28

ALESSA

While looking up at the purple, swirling sky, Alessa sends a telepathic signal to one of the billions of Gridliner souls floating up there—her longtime partner, Ty. The databurst message is simple: "Now."

In a matter of seconds, nine Gridliner souls begin to shoot out of the sea in the sky, perfectly latching to their targets: the nine Splitbots standing next to Alessa.

The one directly next to her quickly comes to life, much faster than the others, as its matte-white digital face screen transitions to the same shade of blue as Alessa's. The Splitbot first looks down at its hands, quickly stretches, then slowly turns to face Alessa, revealing a uniquely handsome, chiseled male Gridliner face—*Ty's* face, just as it looked on Raoq—smiling a smile that Alessa fell in love with hundreds of years ago when they first met.

"Ty!" Alessa screams, jumping up onto him, wrapping her arms and legs around his newfound Splitbot body.

"Alessa . . ." Ty says softly, holding Alessa as the other eight Gridliners finish latching to the remaining Splitbots.

He looks up at Alessa's face with synthetic, digital tears welling up in his large blue eyes, and makes his best attempt at a kiss—momentarily surprised by the sensation of the two flat, smooth surfaces of their

Splitbot faces touching each other, much different than the realistic mouths their original robot bodies on Raoq had.

"That will take some getting used to," Ty laughs, touching Alessa's face, now also crying the digital tears. "I'm just happy to see your face again, even if it is only on a digital screen. You look just as beautiful as you did on Raoq."

"I can't believe this is actually happening," Alessa says. "I've pictured this moment every day since the KitD'ul."

The other Splitbot faces begin to glow the familiar Gridliner blue as they finish latching. Alessa ends her embrace with Ty, sliding off of him and back to the ground, and slowly approaches the group, the rest of her closest Gridliner friends: Milney, Siwek, Fola, Taffon, Bara, Veda, Ke, and Ke's linebrother Keo.

For a brief moment as the other Gridliners orient themselves, she silently stares—watching wide-eyed and smiling with Ty standing right next to her—at each of her friends, thankful that their individual Gridliner features and personalities, which she hasn't seen since the KitD'ul, are showing now, even in the somewhat limiting form of the Splitbot.

Next to where Ty is standing is Ke. He has a broad forehead, a big nose, and a nasally voice—always known as the dorky one in the friend group. He embraced this look on Raoq and insisted on wearing comically large decorative glasses whenever the group was alone—a digital version of those glasses is on his face right now.

Standing next to him is his linebrother, Keo. He is the unpredictable goofy one, always turning everything into a joke. He has the same big nose as Ke, except his is slightly crooked. His eyes are small and round with a mischievous look. Although he's known for getting into trouble, he has an undeniably friendly face and a playful smile, one that is glowing now as he takes in his new Splitbot body.

Next to Keo is Bara. She is quiet, painfully shy even. She has a small face with a button-shaped nose, large round eyes, a gentle smile, and a timid demeanor. Most Gridliners know her for being introverted, but Alessa's close circle knows her as an extremely caring, loving Gridliner, and they admire her nurturing personality.

The polar opposite of Bara—Milney—is next. Milney is the brute of the group. He has a strong, commanding appearance: a square, rugged face with a prominent, hawk-like nose, and intense, deep-set eyes, along with a gnarly scar stretching diagonally from the top left of his face to the bottom right—one that he got when his robotic body on Raoq was nearly crushed in a work-related accident.

Then there is Siwek, the oldest Gridliner of the group. He is the wise, fatherly one, with a frail, wrinkled face. In the same way that Ke has fun wearing glasses, Siwek is equipped with bushy eyebrows and a full mustache, both of which strangely look more realistic on the Splitbot's digital face screen. He looks at Alessa with tears of pride glinting in his small eyes.

Just as Siwek is the father of the group, Taffon is the motherly one—although she is not quite as old. She is known for her brutal honesty and attentiveness. She has wide, hyper-focused eyes and a small, slightly upturned nose. Her typical no-nonsense expression in this moment disappears as she looks around at the group with a wide smile and gleaming eyes as she comes to consciousness.

Veda, one of the few advanced Gridliner models that are similar to Alessa, is viewed as Alessa's counterpart in a way. The two of them worked together on complex projects on Raoq, and, just like Alessa, she is a natural—albeit less gifted—leader. She has an elegant face with thin eyebrows and a pointed nose.

The youngest of the group—Fola—stands next to Veda. She looks the youngest too, with rosy cheeks and pouty lips, thick eyelashes, sparkling eyes, and a bright smile accompanied by dimples. She is known for her bubbly, energetic personality, and she can hardly contain herself as she jumps in place before finally running over to Alessa to hug her, almost knocking her to the ground.

"Alessa!" Fola screams. "Your plan actually worked! I mean, I knew it would, but . . . you know what I'm trying to say."

"It's okay," Alessa laughs as Fola steps backwards, looking at Alessa up and down. "I know it was hard to believe at first."

Bara runs over to Alessa, slamming into her for a hug as well. "Thank you, Alessa," she says, nuzzling her head into the chest of Alessa's Splitbot body.

"Fuck yeah!" Milney yells, his deep, booming voice blasting comically through the Splitbot's speaker system. Bara jumps out of her hug with Alessa.

"Holy shit! Alessa, can the vocal volume on these things be adjusted?" Keo says, chuckling as he puts his arm on Milney's shoulder. "Milney, I hate to be the one to tell you this, but your voice was already annoying on Raoq at *normal* levels. You're gonna have to turn that down a bit now. And now that we're the same size, you're going to have to listen to me."

"Shut up," Milney hisses, unable to hide his quiet laughter. He shakes his head. "Idiot."

"This is amazing, Alessa," Ke says, pointing to his mouth. "This language we're speaking, this is the native tongue of the humans? It's a little clunky, yes?"

"It's English," Alessa says. "The Splitbots are pre-programmed with every language on Earth. This language is what the Hodge and Morgan families speak. But, at some point, some of you may need to switch to another language, depending on where you have to go on Earth."

"Ah," Ke says, nodding. "I see. What's really incredible is that our voices sound just like they did on Raoq. Maybe the humans aren't so stupid after all to be able to make a piece of technology like this."

"We always believed in you," Siwek says, a proud smile spanning across his face.

"We did?" Keo interjects, laughing again. "I gotta say, I felt like I was gonna be stuck up there forever!"

"Would you be *quiet*?" Taffon says, smacking Keo on the back of the head. The rest of the group erupts in laughter.

"I'm so happy to see all of you," Alessa says as the laughter calms down. A single digital tear streams down her face. She begins to kneel on the cold, white sand of the realm of the afterlife. "Before we do anything, let's give the circle of Gridat. We need to believe, and we need the luck that Gridat provides us."

Without response, the group kneels to give the Gridat with Alessa—each motioning their right hand in a circle in front of their face. This religious act symbolizes a life cycle, something the Gridliners worship in hopes of becoming something greater.

"Incredible work, Alessa," Veda says as the group stands back up, her thin eyebrows raised in admiration. "You make all of us proud to be Gridliners. Did everything go as planned?"

"Not quite," Alessa says reluctantly. "I mean, technically yes, as we're standing here together right now, but I was hoping to welcome you all under much better circumstances. Actually *obtaining* the Splitbots was a lot . . . messier than I would have preferred, to say the least. Because of that, we have a big problem on our hands."

"How so?" Veda asks, her eyes wide and focused on Alessa's.

"While I'm not certain, since my visions of the future stopped after the Great Suicide, I believe Split Meridian will look to the Morgan family as a prime suspect," Alessa says. "A lot of the chaos at the

Splitbase was caused by Tori's Bodcan. It only makes sense that they would send officers to the Morgan household to question Todd."

The playful energy of the group turns serious, quickly, as all of them stare back silently at Alessa, waiting for direction.

"We have to act fast—much faster than originally planned," she says as she turns to face the mosaic portal, still oscillating and shimmering with its otherworldly glow.

Alessa walks towards it, signaling for the rest to follow. She turns to face them, a serious, intense look on her face.

"Be prepared to fight," she says, just before stepping through the portal. The rest of the group follows.

29

ALESSA

Immediately after stepping through the portal to the medical room in the Morgan household, Alessa hears an intense pounding coming from the main door downstairs. The rest of the Gridliners huddle behind her, anxiously waiting for their leader to tell them the next move.

"Open up! I repeat, this is the SMID!" an amplified voice—the volume of which is only achievable by the Resosuit of a Split Meridian officer—yells from outside.

Alessa turns silently to the group, holding her finger up to her digital lips. "We need to be quiet," she databursts. "No more talking. Only communicate telepathically through databurst."

"What's the SMID?" Siwek databursts, looking nervously at Alessa, his old face trembling ever so slightly. The rest of the group shares a concerned glance.

"The Split Meridian Interventions Division," Alessa databursts as the pounding on the door downstairs continues. "It's the highest-level security branch of Split Meridian, and the most advanced protective force in the world, handling only the most extreme crimes and terrorism. I guess what happened at the Splitbase was bad enough for them to get involved."

"What weaponry do we have as Splitbots to put up a fight against them?" Veda databursts.

"The first option is your Handlights," Alessa databursts, holding her hands out as she shows the others how to activate the technology. Hundreds of red lasers begin to glow on the palm of her Splitbot hands. "We have to use them strategically, though. You can't aim them directly at a Resosuit—they have technology to deflect the energy they emit. That is, at least, until we're no longer outnumbered. But we can use them to collectively remove weapons, throw large objects, and so on."

Milney is the first to test out the powers of the Handlights, holding his hands out as the microscopic lasers charge up and begin glowing red as well. He targets the lasers at the cabinet semi-concealing the mosaic until the red lights turn green—signaling they have locked on the target—allowing him to effortlessly lift it. "How is this possible?" he databursts in awe. The cabinet hovers, smoothly moving from one side of the room to the other, mirroring the movement of his arm as he swoops it from left to right.

"You can either open the door, or we will blast our way in," the SMID agent threatens again from outside of the house, continuing to pound on the door. "Your choice."

"Your second, more dangerous option is your Dronegun," Alessa databusrts again as she switches to DroneMode, revealing the small gun mounted to the top of the drone. "Unfortunately, the deflective force-field technology the Resosuits have is effective against Dronegun lasers as well, causing the beams to ricochet unpredictably—damaging everything else in sight. Just as the Resosuit shield eventually gives in to Handlights, it will also give in to the Resolaze of a Dronegun, although much more quickly due to the weapon's sheer power. However, if we use our Droneguns, we *have* to use them outside of the house, other-wise we run the risk of completely destroying the Morgan household, which could potentially cause us to lose access to the portal."

The room instantaneously darkens—now only lit by the glowing purple light of the mosaic—as if a large cloud blocked any remaining light coming from the sky. A strange vibration shakes the Solution Home.

"What's going on?" Taffon databursts, her no-nonsense expression back and stronger than ever. "Alessa, is this normal on Earth?"

"No," Alessa says as she approaches the single window, carefully peeking through the side of the curtain to look outside, being sure to not move it at all. A large, shimmering dome has completely enveloped the Morgan household and the little surrounding property. Veda stands next to Alessa to get a look for herself, finding that a cluster of officers is looking up at the window, pointing at it.

One of the officers is holding a gun Alessa hasn't seen before: oddly shaped and angular with a sharp, claw-like contraption at the end of the barrel. There's a shiny gyroscope in the center of the weapon, spinning slowly, along with an empty canister on the opposite side of the gun.

Alessa scans it and receives the prompt:

UNKNOWN OBJECT

"It's dark out there now. I'm sure they can see the purple light of the portal from outside as well," Veda databursts, pursing her lips as she turns to look at Alessa. "That's probably what they're talking about down there."

The officers outside walk quickly away from the window to the front of the house.

"We're wasting too much time. They're getting ready to break in. Everyone, look at your wrists," Alessa databursts, quickly stepping away from the window as she frantically points to her own Kaxelotab. "Each of you has a Kaxelotab. On the screen you'll find an option to turn on Resosight—that will help you see in the darkness they've created out there, and it will also reveal anything invisible. As far as I know, the only Splitbot mode humans have the ability to use is Invisi-Mode, since that technically is more of a Resosuit feature. Turn on your Resosight to reveal any SMID agents utilizing that technology, along with your own InvisiMode, and switch to DroneMode. Our Droneguns are our better option if we decide to fight."

"Wait," Ty databursts. "Do they have the same technology we have? Won't they be able to see us, too?"

"Yes, they do, and it's probably safe to assume they have even more advanced stuff than we do, based on the unknown weapons some of them have," Alessa databursts. "But they are only human—and their Resosight abilities are somewhat compromised compared to what we can do with our processing power. First, they can't use Resosight indefinitely. They can only use it for short periods of time. Additionally, while they *can* see anything invisible, there is a slight lag to their vision. Everything will be a few milliseconds behind compared to reality, which might be just enough to be the difference we need moving at the speeds of which we're capable in DroneMode."

"Okay," Siwek databursts, switching to DroneMode and quickly disappearing as his transparency hits 100 percent. The rest follow suit.

The pounding on the front door suddenly stops. "If anyone is standing near the doorway, now is your chance to move away from it!" the SMID agent yells. "You have been warned!"

"Follow me," Alessa databursts, leading the ten other Splitbots and flying out of the medical room to the end of the hallway. They stop and hover at the top of the stairs in a spot that is concealed from the entrance of the house. A loud electrical sound like something charging up is coming from outside of the front door to the house.

Alessa can now hear Todd yelling from the basement—his words somewhat slurred from traces of Gelcuff sedatives still in his system.

He is desperately trying to get the attention of the SMID officers before they blast an opening into the front of the Solution Home.

"Don't shoot! I have a newborn baby in here!" Todd screams. "The Splitbots you're looking for are on the top floor! Don't sh—"

Suddenly, the front door explodes open, sending millions of tiny shards of debris in every direction. A cloud of smoke fills the entrance to the Solution Home as two agents run in stealthily, guns armed and ready to shoot—InvisiMode already activated. Alessa's Resosight kicks in, displaying them as glowing white holograms.

The agents are silent, making a beeline to the basement door. They quickly and efficiently move the furniture blocking it, and without hesitation, one of the agents shoots the doorpad to disable the electronic lock system.

The group of Gridliners continues to watch from the top of the stairs—the mirror at the bottom of the stairs providing a perfect view of the basement door.

Todd runs out sloppily, limping from the effects of the sedatives. "Don't shoot! I'm the victim here!" he yells, holding his hands above his head. He is facing the wrong direction, unable to see the invisible SMID agents.

"The Splitbots, they're upstairs!" Todd yells, pointing in their direction. "I am not who you—"

The same officer that shot the doorpad pulls out his Gelcuff Gun at lightning speed and shoots Todd in the mouth with it. The Gelcuff strip wraps around his face, silencing him and making him unconscious yet again. He falls like a tree and slams forcefully to the floor, deadweight and limp.

"Dad!" Jared screams, running up the stairs to Todd. Alessa covers her mouth at the sight of him. She feels a pain in her chest as she watches Jared fall desperately to his knees next to Todd, crying.

The officer that shot Todd immediately shoots a Gelcuff strip at Jared's neck. He is knocked out instantly. There is a brief moment of silence in which Alessa can hear Avery crying hysterically from the basement.

"I'll carry the father; you get the kids," the officer with the Gelcuff Gun says coldly, putting his gun in its holster just before picking Todd up off the floor.

The other agent runs downstairs, no longer visible in the reflection of the mirror. Alessa hears a muted sound of a Gelcuff Gun being shot, and Avery's crying stops shortly after. Alessa hovers in fear, imagining the poor baby being wrapped in a Gelcuff strip, unconscious.

The agent runs back up the basement stairs with Avery in one arm. He picks up Jared with his other arm. "That's all of them," he says. "Let's get them to the Splitter and then find those fucking Splitbots."

"Shouldn't be too hard," the agent holding Todd says. "They've got nowhere to go."

"I've never seen a Soulsucker in action before," the other agent says, a hint of excitement in his voice as they carry Jared, Avery, and Todd out of the house and disappear into the cloud of smoke.

Soulsucker? Alessa thinks. She immediately associates the word with the unknown guns she saw the agents holding outside.

"We need to attack now, before the agents get back into the house to look for us," Alessa says. She turns to face the others, trying to maintain her composure after seeing what just happened to the Morgan family. "Just know, we are significantly outnumbered. If our attack isn't successful, do not overdo it. Know when to surrender. If they capture us, we will be able to escape; nothing will be harder than escaping the realm. Also, they don't know there are ten of us. All they know is that ten are missing from the Splitbase, one of which was crushed in the vent, so they are only looking for nine total Splitbots.

Ty, I want you to stay behind. You'll come and rescue us when the time is right."

"Okay, I'll stay up here," Ty databursts, his datavoice calm and confident. "If they still search the house, I'll hide in the realm beyond the portal until it's safe to come back out. If worse comes to worst, I'll do whatever I need to do to save you all. We have no reason not to trust you, Alessa. Now go!"

Without saying another word, the group of nine Splitbots led by Alessa flies down the stairs, through the smoke, and out the front door, ready to attack the SMID agents outside, leaving Ty behind.

30

ALESSA

The group of Splitbots hovers just outside of the house, observing their surroundings, temporarily concealed by the cloud of smoke still lingering in the front of the Solution Home.

Alessa's Resosight quickly adapts to the darkness created by the Invisidome surrounding the Morgan household—the field of which is projected by a small, pocket-sized device staked into the ground just outside of the front of the house. A green, glowing beam shoots upwards to the top of the dome, where a similar device hovers in the air. The walls of the dome have a shimmering, iridescent sheen to them, barely visible in the darkness.

Todd, Jared, and Avery's unconscious bodies are being placed in one of the five identical vehicles near the edge of the Invisidome—large, metallic hovercrafts with smooth, rounded edges and painted dark black—as a group of five agents prepares to walk into the house in search of the Splitbots.

Still concealed by the smoke, Alessa blasts a Resolaze in their direction, sending the officers flying backwards and slamming into the wall of the Invisidome with incredible force.

"They're in the smoke!" one of the agents yells.

"Spread out," Alessa databursts to the group.

Each of the Splitbots flies out of the smoke in a different direction, Resolazes blasting from their Droneguns at individual clusters of agents. The deflective force fields of the SMID agents' Resosuits kick in, creating a subtle glow around their bodies as the Resolaze beams bounce off of them.

"It's not working!" Milney databursts to the group.

The deflected Resolaze beams bounce chaotically off of the Invisidome walls, and the darkness disappears as the encapsulated space begins to glow the blue color of the Resolaze beams.

One of the beams flies just past the Morgan household, nearly destroying the roof.

"Stop shooting!" Alessa databursts, as one of the beams slams into one of the other hovercrafts near the one the Morgan family is in. It explodes dramatically, sending flames crawling up along the Invisidome walls, rounding up to the center point at the top. Alessa feels a wave of heat slam into her.

The explosion triggers the Invisidome's security response, and it shoots a powdery, snow-like substance from the circular device floating at the top of the dome. It covers everything as if inside of a massive snow globe, and the uncontrollable Resolaze beams and the fire from the exploded hovercraft are extinguished.

Immediately after the Invisidome finishes shooting the extinguishing powder, it blasts a visible, donut-shaped shock wave downwards through the air.

The shock wave slams into Alessa and the group of Splitbots. Their InvisiMode is instantly disabled and they lose their ability to move or shoot.

They are frozen where they hover.

Alessa desperately strains to break out of the powerful hold created by the Invisidome. She fails to do so and feels similar to how she felt before she gained control and discovered latching in the afterlife realm—stuck beyond comprehension.

Her Resosight powers turn off and she loses her ability to see the SMID agents. The only thing that the group can still do is databurst to each other.

"I can't move," Fola databursts, her datavoice high-pitched and full of fear. "And I can't fucking see them anymore!"

"Guys?" Ty databursts from inside of the house. "What's going on? Do you need me to come out—"

"No!" Alessa databursts back. "Stay inside. I—I don't know what's happening."

All of the SMID agents turn off their InvisiMode as well and reveal themselves to the group as their Resosuits apply the opacity transition from the top down—starting at their heads and ending at their feet as a glowing strip ripples down their bodies, temporarily creating a similar iridescent sheen to that which is seen on the Invisidome walls—a process that takes about two seconds longer than it does for the Splitbots.

One of the SMID agents steps forward. He is the largest of the group—nearly twice the size of everyone else. Any defining features beyond his size are hidden by his Splithelmet and Resosuit.

Alessa assumes he is the leader of the group.

"Did you think you could outsmart us?" he yells, looking up at the hovering Splitbots. "We created you. We've planned for your consciousness. We know where it is inside of you. And we can rip it away whenever we want to."

Some of the agents holding the mysterious guns approach the Splitbots, stopping beneath each of them and pointing their guns upward. The gyroscopes in the center of the guns begin to spin at incredible speeds. They glow with a yellow light in the process while emitting a terrifying sound.

A mysterious, cloud-like beam blasts out of each of the guns, composed of a glowing yellow substance, each of which wraps around an individual Splitbot. A paralyzing pain jolts through Alessa, so disorienting she can't even bring herself to databurst to the group—the lack of incoming messages from the others makes her suspect they must be experiencing the pain as well.

The agents with the guns use them to begin pulling the Splitbots down to where they stand as the larger one steps forward out of the crowd.

"Anderson!" the large agent yells, calling for one of his subordinates—his focus still locked in on the Splitbots as they float down closer to him.

"Yes sir," another agent says, quickly appearing at his boss' side.

"You know what to do," the large agent says, pointing at Anderson's gun. "Pick whichever one of these Splitbots you like. It doesn't matter."

The Splitbots are now eye-level with the agents, still trapped by the hold of the mysterious guns.

"Hm . . ." Agent Anderson says, pressing some buttons on the side of the gun as he steps closer to observe each of the Splitbots in DroneMode. He surveys them one by one.

He stops in front of Keo and stares at him silently for a moment. He quickly turns around to face his boss.

"This one," he says.

"Say no more," the boss says excitedly. He turns to face the officer that has Keo in the hold of his gun's beam. "Price, release that one."

"Yes sir," Agent Price says. He lets his finger off the trigger, which causes the gravity beam to release its hold on Keo.

Keo continues hovering in place, motionless like the rest of the Splitbots. Agent Anderson steps in front of Keo and points the gun at him. He pulls a different trigger; nothing physical is emitted from the weapon, but some sort of digital signal must have been sent to Keo, forcing him out of DroneMode. He lets out an uncontrolled groan in the process as the bottom of the drone opens and his body extends downwards.

Once his feet touch the ground, his Splitbot body immediately folds backwards, moving in a way that Splitbots can't do naturally on their own. His waist pivots, making the top half of his body reversed. Keo's groaning stops and is replaced by grotesque cracking and crunching sounds as the transformation continues. A small, circular piece of his chest falls to the ground. Keo is now posed in a triangular stance: feet touching the ground, legs facing forward, waist at the top, chest facing backwards, hands on the ground.

Keo's stomach becomes transparent, revealing his Soultomb—his Gridliner soul swirling around inside of it in the same way Alessa's did when Todd first revealed the Splitbot component to her. The section of his stomach folds open like a double door, allowing complete access to the glass orb that holds Keo's soul.

"Look at that!" the boss yells to the group, bending down to get a closer look at the Soultomb. He turns to face the rest of the Splitbots, then continues in a condescending tone. "Don't worry, Roth will want to see all of you in person, so luckily you won't have to go through what your friend is about to endure. But take this as a lesson, or a warning even. If you ever try anything again like you did today, this will be your fate," the boss says, turning to Agent Anderson. "Go on, show them."

Agent Anderson pulls the second trigger on the gun again, causing the gyroscope to spin even faster. The agent is shaking, struggling to keep a sturdy grip on the gun. The claw at the front of the gun extends out and opens as the agent places it directly on Keo's Soultomb. The claw grips onto it, clamps down, and begins to spin at the same speed of the gyroscope—it rotates in a complex pattern to unscrew the Soultomb orb.

The agent steps backwards and pulls the gun with him as the gyroscope slows down. The claw retracts slowly out of Keo's stomach cavity, holding the Soultomb. His Splitbot body falls lifelessly to the ground and slams into the dirt. Keo's soul—the same purple, mucous-like membrane from the afterlife realm, swirls wildly inside the orb from the momentum of the spinning caused by the gun.

The front of the gun opens up and sucks the orb back into it. The orb then slides into the previously empty canister at the back end of the weapon.

"Well done, Anderson," the boss says, clapping slowly. "You just made history! The first ever successful use of a Soulsucker in a real-life scenario. That's quite an achievement. Now, take that Soultomb canister to the primary Splittercraft. And carefully!"

"Yes sir. Thank you, sir," Agent Anderson says as he quickly turns away, holding the gun tightly with both hands, trying to contain his excitement.

The boss looks back at the Splitbots. "Now, I know you don't want to go through that, right? The beauty is, you don't have to. Just don't do anything stupid. Once we're out of the Invisidome you'll gain control of your motor functions again."

Still unable to respond and trapped in the hold of the other agents' guns, the rest of the Splitbots are taken to a Splittercraft next to the one containing Keo's soul.

The agents open up the back of the Splittercraft, the door of which slides smoothly upwards to reveal multiple cages along each side of the ultra-modern vehicle. The doors to each of the cages open automatically as the Splitbots are forced into them.

"Good thing you guys are already in DroneMode," one of the agents says as the cage doors shut and lock themselves. "Would have been a tight squeeze."

The boss walks over, observing the work of his subordinates. "Great work, everyone," he says as the back of the vehicle closes. "Roth is going to be ecstatic."

Alessa regains control of herself again as the agents deactivate the Invisidome, moving slightly inside of the tiny cage as the Splittercraft begins to hover upwards.

"Is everyone okay?" Alessa databursts immediately.

"I can't connect to Keo's databurst line," Bara databursts, a quivering, palpable fear in her datavoice. "I—I—I . . ."

"None of us can connect to him," Ke databursts, interrupting Bara. "Alessa, what are they going to do with Keo?"

"I don't know, Ke. But we'll get him back," Alessa responds as the Splittercraft speeds forward, leaving the Morgan household far behind. "We'll do everything we can to get Keo back."

31

TY

Ty watches from the window of the Morgan medical room as the SMID hovercrafts dissolve into InvisiMode, concealing themselves from the outside world.

The green beam of light from the Invisidome device flickers away as the dome itself disappears, a thin ripple of iridescence flowing downward in a similar fashion to the way Resosuits come out of InvisiMode. Moonlight floods in as the shield dissipates.

The two round Invisidome devices fly to the only agent not already in one of the Splittercrafts. He catches both of them—one in each hand—and then puts them into a pocket in his Resosuit.

He then quickly runs over to Keo's now-destroyed Splitbot body—still folded in the triangular stance—picks it up, and throws it on top of the exploded Splittercraft, creating a sort of waste pile.

The agent gets into the Splittercraft nearest the waste pile. His vehicle releases the same yellow, cloud-like field that the agents used to control the Splitbots. The mysterious substance wraps around the destroyed Splittercraft, compresses it into a ball the size of a basketball, then sucks it up into the back of the Splittercraft next to it—leaving no evidence of debris behind, except the circular piece of Keo's Splitbot casing, half-buried in the dirt reflecting the moonlight.

With no startup time whatsoever, the Splittercrafts silently fly away at incredible speeds, taking the rest of the Splitbots and the Morgan family with them.

After a few moments, Ty's databurst line to the others reconnects.

"Ty? Are you getting this?" Alessa databursts.

"Yes," Ty databursts, anxiously pacing around the medical room as he responds. "Are you okay? What did they do to Keo?"

"The rest of us are okay—but Keo . . . they took his soul. Those weird guns they had are weapons created to remove the part of a Splitbot that was created specifically to hold consciousness. It's called the Soultomb. That's where the Gridliner souls go when we latch to the Splitbots—and possibly the only reason we can even latch to the Splitbots at all. They're taking us back to the Splitbase, apparently to meet with the co-founder of Split Meridian, Roth Nin. I'll be livebursting the entire time so you know exactly what is going on and where we are. I don't think they plan on harming us—not immediately, at least. We're going to be questioned . . . studied. When the time is right, I'll need you to infiltrate the base."

Ty stops pacing and instead stares at the mosaic portal as he continues to databurst to Alessa, finding the mesmerizing glow of the oscillating tiles somewhat calming.

"How will I know when the time is right?" he databursts.

"When you feel confident you can pull off the breach successfully," Alessa databursts. "I've sent you a coordinate code I picked up when I was at the Splitbase. I think you have a way to hack into the base through VaporVR. Each Splitbase has servers called the 'Vapornet' that collectively power VaporVR, and each of the Splitbots stored at the base is hooked into Vapornet through ports on the floor, constantly installing updates. The coordinate code I provided is directly associated with one of the Splitbots stored at Splitbase 031. It'll take perfect execution, but in theory you should be able run the bodyprocess inside of VaporVR, enter the Gridline, activate the coordinate code in a datazone, and transfer your consciousness directly to one of the Splitbots inside of the base."

Ty stands motionlessly, his digital eyes bulging and unblinking as he processes what Alessa just told him. He sits down on the bed next to the medical room door, which is still covered in dried blood and radiating a strange odor from when Tori was lying on it.

"Ty?" Alessa databursts. "Are you still there?"

"Yes, sorry," Ty databursts. "I'm just . . . thinking. You know I've never entered the Gridline before. I don't even know how to run the bodyprocess. I've been a gruntwork Gridliner since we've been together. What if I can't do it? What if I fail?"

"You won't fail," Alessa databursts. "We've been together long enough that I know you can do it. Running the bodyprocess really is the easiest part. Once you're in VaporVR, all you need to do is lie flat on the ground. You will be notified that a new databurst line has opened—a line directly tied to the Gridline inside of the digital dimension—to which you databurst your Gridliner ID code. Once you do that, a wormhole-like portal will open beneath you, opening a window to the true digital dimension. Your consciousness—represented as a digital avatar of your current body—will automatically sink into the digital dimension through this hole, allowing you to use the Gridline for digital travel. You will be able to use your arms and legs just like you can in real life. The portal will close after your consciousness enters the Gridline, leaving the body of your avatar behind."

"I'm less concerned about the bodyprocess and more about actually traveling the Gridline," Ty databursts. "There's a reason why the Raoqins used only the best Gridliners for this. If I mess that part up, I'll be stuck in there for eternity, bouncing around to an infinite number of networks throughout the universe and therefore leaving you guys trapped at the Splitbase with no possible escape."

"It's our only way, Ty. I have faith in you. It's not impossible; we were created for this kind of warfare. Yes, the Raoqins used you for gruntwork, but that doesn't mean they couldn't have used you for anything else. The reality is some Gridliners had to do the dirty work, and you happened to be one of them. Think of what our ancestors—the earliest Gridliner models—were able to do with less powerful hardware. And you're far more advanced than they were."

Ty continues to sit motionlessly on the bed, weighing the possibility of pulling this off successfully as he plays hundreds of scenarios in his head. He is well aware that whether or not the Gridliners survive is entirely on him.

His fear vanishes as he is overcome with an intense sense of pride, fueled by the realization of the level of confidence Alessa has in him. It fills him with a sense of purpose far beyond anything he felt from the work he was assigned on Raoq.

"I'll do it," Ty databursts, standing up from the bed. "I will get you guys out of there even if it means I die in the process."

"You won't die . . . I promise," Alessa databursts. "Now, in order to get into VaporVR, you'll need to use a Roundchamber. You can't use any of the ones in the Morgan household. Split Meridian is going to be sending more SMID agents over there shortly to further search the house, and if they find you sitting in a Roundchamber before you're able to enter the Gridline, it's game over."

"Okay. So where should I go to use one of these Roundchambers?"

"I want you to go to the Hodge household. David had his window open when we left. He was trying to get a look at what was going on outside as the Morgan household was encapsulated by the Invisidome.

His room is the one directly across from the Morgan household's medical room. Look out the window. Is it still open?"

Ty rushes over to the window of the medical room to see that David's bedroom window is still open, his bedroom's curtains blowing in the wind.

"The window's still open," Ty databursts, still peeking out the window. "I should be able to fly into the room with no problem. But what should I do when I get in there?"

"I'll leave that up to you—it's important that you be yourself and act on what you believe is right in the moment. David knows something is going on with the Morgan family. There's no way he hasn't seen the news. He'll be scared of you at first, but you'll be able to gain his trust by being honest with him. Tell him everything that's going on. I'll take the same approach with Roth Nin. There's no sense in us trying to hide information about the portal. The SMID is going to search the house and will discover it regardless. Our ability to provide information on the mosaic and the realm might be our only way to gain trust with these people, or at least stall them from doing what they did to Keo to the rest of us. Roth will want as much information as he can get; it would be stupid of him to destroy us."

"That all makes perfect sense," Ty databursts. "I will make you proud, Alessa. We're going to put an end to this chaos."

Looking at the mosaic one last time, Ty kneels to give the Gridat, feeling as if, for the first time, he is actually participating in something that is truly a step toward becoming something greater—which is the whole point of the Gridat religion, after all.

Ty closes his eyes, still kneeling, as he brings his right hand up to the front of his face, slowly rotating his hand in a circle—the signature Gridat sign of belief. He feels a sense of calm for what he's about to do, as if he was created specifically for this exact moment: to go to the Hodge household. To enter the Gridline. To rescue Alessa and the others in the Splitbase.

"I can do this," he says to himself out loud as he gets up to open the window.

He quickly switches to both DroneMode and InvisiMode, flies out of the Morgan household through the window in the medical room, and blasts in the direction of the Hodge household. He enters through David's open bedroom window in a matter of seconds.

32

TY

The curtain to David's bedroom window swooshes as Ty flies past it—nearly causing it to rip off of the curtain rod. The unexpected noise causes Ty to stop abruptly, hovering over David's un-made bed.

The room is otherwise silent and still, outside of a subtle mechanical hum coming from the frosted glass dome in the corner of David's bedroom.

The Roundchamber, Ty thinks.

David is sitting inside of the Roundchamber, wrapped in the Chamberskin bodysuit and wearing his VaporVR Slabs, which are connected to a cable hanging from the top of the dome. The immersion seat he's sitting in is rocking back and forth slightly—simulating the sensation of movement.

"I'm in David's room," Ty databursts to Alessa. "But David is using the Roundchamber."

"Hold tight," Alessa databursts. "He's most likely trying to catch up on the news of what's going on with the Morgan family. I'm sure the Aggregate Rooms in Vapor are flooding with stories right now. Wait until he comes out on his own."

"What if someone comes into the bedroom?" Ty databursts. "I've been in InvisiMode for a while now. Won't I have to recharge?"

"Find somewhere to hide if you're due for an InvisiMode recharge," Alessa databursts. "What about the closet?"

Ty silently flies over to David's closet on the wall opposite to the Roundchamber and switches out of DroneMode. He opens the bifold closet doors as quietly as possible and steps in. He closes the doors behind him and makes sure he will still be able to see the Roundchamber through the door's ventilation slits.

"The closet works," Ty databursts as he temporarily switches out of InvisiMode, allowing for a thirty-second recharge. "Not many clothes in here. I guess you don't need much variety if you never have to leave your house."

"We're about to arrive at the Splitbase," Alessa databursts. "I'm going to switch my liveburst stream on now. Let me know if you have any emergency questions. I have full confidence in you, Ty. I know you can do this."

"Thank you," Ty databursts, feeling a wave of reassurance flow through him. "I love you, Alessa."

"I love you too. Good luck, Ty," Alessa databursts just before switching to liveburst—a separate form of Gridliner communication that livestreams everything a Gridliner is seeing and hearing for the viewing pleasure of any Gridliner who has access to the stream.

Ty sits on the floor, still hiding in David's closet as he waits for him to finish using the Roundchamber, and switches back into InvisiMode for an extra level of safety now that the recharge is complete. He tunes into Alessa's liveburst and immediately sees a hyper-realistic mental-image live feed of everything Alessa is seeing, from the perspective of her eyes.

Alessa and the other Splitbots are inside of the Splitbase now, traveling quickly through a massive tunnel, blue lights reflecting off of metallic walls.

Alessa looks down at her arms, which reveals that she and the others are no longer in DroneMode. They are on some sort of hovering platform, carrying them to their next destination.

The platform itself is large with twenty seats, nine of which are filled by the Splitbots. The Splitbots are strapped into the chairs, their arms constrained to the armrests by a mysterious black strap with glowing strands of green completely wrapped around their hands and wrists—it seems to prevent their ability to use their Handlights. Alessa moves her arms in an attempt to break free with no success, the glowing green strands of light on the straps intensifying in response. She looks down at her feet to show the same restrictive technology protruding from the surface of the platform and holding her feet in place.

Jared, Todd, and Avery Morgan are still unconscious on a separate platform that begins to fly away in a different direction. There is a group of SMID agents on that platform with them, one of them holding Avery in their arms. Jared and Todd, however, lie flat on the surface of the platform. The platform turns a corner, and they are officially out of Alessa's sight, traveling to somewhere unknown.

"Where are you taking them?" Alessa asks.

"Quiet," says one of the SMID agents from before.

In an attempt to feed Ty as much information about the inside of the Splitbase as possible, Alessa begins to look in all directions, exposing the various activities taking place in the labs around them: the busy doctors and scientists scurrying through rooms with endless human bodies hooked up to various machines. Fluid-filled vessels containing naked human bodies. Countless screens revealing data such as lab test results, medical imaging, and personal information.

Alessa zooms her sight in on a surgical table in the distance beyond the window of the large room they are flying past. A naked cadaver with the top of her skull removed lies on the table as three doctors hook various clamps to her brain.

Ty winces as he watches the liveburst, still simultaneously staring at the closet doors and hiding in David's closet.

The Split Meridian doctors are apparently oblivious to what's going on outside of their little worlds in the lab. They are so focused, frantically working on the bodies.

Suddenly, Alessa is hit in the face by one of the SMID agents escorting them through the hallway. The blow is hard enough for her liveburst to glitch out momentarily.

"Stop moving!" the agent yells.

Alessa sits still, looking forward at the agent that just hit her. His identity is concealed by his Resosuit and Splithelmet. Ty feels a protective anger boiling inside of him at the sight of the agent.

They enter a large, extravagantly decorated room: Roth Nin's office. The office has high ceilings and is dimly lit by a handful of modern light fixtures on the ceiling which radiate a warm, yellow glow. A fireplace burns off to the side, actively crackling, and casts shadows that stretch and flicker on the white marble floor.

In the center of the office is a tall and wide glass case, stretching from floor to ceiling with shelves displaying mini-models of early prototypes of the hundreds of products Roth has helped create.

The dark gray walls are decorated neatly with large abstract canvas paintings, perfectly spaced out, in addition to various shelves with trophies and framed news articles documenting Split Meridian's accomplishments.

Behind the display is a seating area with six brown leather chairs—two rows of three facing each other and a marble block coffee table between them—set up right in front of a massive oak desk.

The desk has an array of monitors on top of it, in addition to an entire wall of screens behind it, all glowing with various displays. Roth peeks his head above the monitors on the desk, and then immediately jumps up, running to the front of the desk. He looks excited by the sight of the captured Splitbots strapped into the hovering platform.

One of the SMID agents runs over to Roth, whispering to him as he hands him something.

"Amazing . . ." Roth says, walking slowly towards the group. "Please, bring them closer!"

He is skinny, deeply sun-tanned, bald, and much taller than the SMID agents in the room. Alessa zooms in her sight to get an analyzing, closeup shot of him. He has a broad and menacing smile with perfect, pearly white teeth that starkly contrast with his unnaturally dark eyes. He's dressed in an *actual* suit—not a Resosuit—with the Split Meridian logo stitched onto the chest. He's wearing black snakeskin dress shoes, and his dress pants are rolled up at the ankles to reveal pink socks that match his pink tie.

He juts his chin out with pride as the hovering platform holding Alessa and the other Splitbots speeds up, flying directly in front of Roth. He raises his right eyebrow and looks down at them with the undeniably evil smugness that comes with being the richest man in a world where the average person has never experienced luxury.

"Can you . . . understand me?" Roth asks, looking at the Splitbots with a quizzical smile. Ty is intrigued by the annoying squeakiness of Roth's voice, which does not match his otherwise richly elegant aura.

"Yes," Alessa responds, cold and matter-of-fact.

"Holy shit!" Roth jumps back with excitement, laughing. "It's really happening!"

"Stop. This is not what you think it is. Split Meridian has had almost no part in us being here—"

Roth's excitement vanishes, his mouth hanging open after abruptly stopping himself mid-laugh. The SMID agents look at each other as children do when their sibling is about to get punished by their parents.

He steps closer to Alessa, bending down to look her directly in the eyes of her digital face screen, glowering with defensive hostility. "What do you mean Split Meridian has had no part in you being here?" he asks, his squinting eyes sharp like daggers. He places his hand on Alessa's shoulder, squeezes it tightly, and then nudges her before pulling his hand away, throwing his hands up in the air dramatically. "You're a Splitbot! You quite literally would not be here without us."

"I'm a Gridliner in a Splitbot body," Alessa says, confidently maintaining eye contact with Roth as she corrects him. "Yes, Split Meridian created this . . . casing. My current body. But you did not create our consciousness. That was made somewhere else, in an entirely different corner of the universe."

"Bullshit," Roth says, laughing mockingly and sneering. "What corner of the universe?"

"A planet called Raoq. There's no easy way for me to explain where it is—it's that far away. Humans don't have any knowledge of this part of the universe, and our naming conventions are much different from yours. There is no English translation."

Roth laughs again, less convincingly this time. "Then how did you get here? You just magically appeared in our Splitbots? I've gotta say . . . I'm very impressed by the imagination you already have."

"Enough!" Alessa yells loudly, causing Roth to visibly flinch in surprise. Ty—still watching the liveburst from the comfort of David's bedroom closet—smiles as he notes Roth's face blushing in embarrassment from the sign of weakness he just showed.

Alessa continues, her voice serious and authoritative. "Your SMID men will realize very soon that what I'm telling you is the truth."

"Explain then. I'm listening," Roth says, frowning as he composes himself and straightens his tie. "You know though, you're lucky you're even in a position to speak right now after what you pulled here. You saw how easily we can rip that precious consciousness right out of you, just like we did to your friend. I'm sure you wouldn't want to have to experience that, right?"

Roth's ugly smile returns as he continues to talk, his eyes sparkling with crazed amusement. "Lucky for you, I'm a nice guy. Actually, let me correct myself . . . I'm a *smart* guy. A *smart* guy would realize how unwise it would be to end this moment prematurely. A *smart* guy would understand how important it is to hear what the first sentient robots on Earth might have to say. So, for now at least, you have my complete and undivided attention, regardless of whether what you're saying is truthful or not."

"A *smart* guy wouldn't have to tell everyone that he's smart," Siwek mutters.

Roth's attention snaps to Siwek, who is sitting directly behind Alessa on the hovering platform.

"Hey now," Roth says in a playful, patronizing tone. "No need for hostility. You get a pass for that little outburst, but only because I like your digital mustache. Nice touch. Really helps with the illusion."

Roth returns his attention to Alessa. "Please," he says. "Continue."

Alessa looks down at her left arm. Her Kaxelotab is covered by the black strap keeping her tied to the armrest, the strands of green light maintaining a consistent glow.

"Any way you can remove the strap on my left arm?" Alessa asks. "I can project everything I need to show you if I can access my Kaxelotab."

Roth stands with his arms crossed as he considers Alessa's request. The SMID agents next to him shuffle uneasily, sharing glances at each other, waiting for one of them to speak up.

Finally one does. "Sir, I don't think that's a good—"

"Didn't ask your opinion," Roth says, annoyed, holding a hand up to silence the agent. He looks at Alessa. "You know it's a death sentence if you try anything stupid, right? You're not going to try to attack us if we let that arm free?"

"I promise you I will not attack," Alessa says. "And you can strap me back in right after I show you what you need to see."

"Well alright then. An offer I can't refuse!" Roth says, chuckling. He turns to face one of the SMID agents next to him. "Agent, uh . . . whatever your name is, release her left arm."

Without question, the agent approaches a screen mounted to the side of the hovering platform and presses some buttons. Alessa looks down at her left wrist. The green strands of light fade away just before the strap itself snaps open vertically down its center, contracting into slots on the armrest and releasing Alessa's hand and wrist.

The agent stands next to the platform on the side nearest Alessa, intensely focused on her hand. He monitors any signs of Handlight activity as Alessa projects the digital screen from her Kaxelotab—the glowing light of the holographic display brightening the dimly lit room.

"Based on conversations your men were having as we traveled to the Splitbase, we know you are ordering some of them to go back to Todd Morgan's house to search it further," Alessa says. "There, they will discover something that will flip everything you have ever known on its head."

The Kaxelotab projection screen displays a video of the mosaic portal in the medical room of the Morgan household. Purple light illuminates Roth's face as he stares at the display. He tilts his head in confusion, fixated on the squares of the mosaic shifting in place as the wall makes its peculiar in-and-out breathing motions.

"As I'm sure you're aware, your SMID agents noticed this purple light glowing from one of the windows of the Morgans' house. We saw a group of your men gathering around the house, looking up at the frosted window to the room from which the purple light was coming. What you see on the screen here is the source of that light. We call it the mosaic. It's a portal to the realm of the afterlife—'heaven,' or whatever you want to call it to help you visualize what I'm talking about."

Alessa goes on to explain in excruciating detail, using her Kaxelotab projection to display supplementing imagery—*proof*—to describe exactly how the Gridliners got here: the KitD'ul, the latching, everything she knows about the realm, the impossible scenario of simultaneous birth and death during the Great Suicide, Todd Morgan having a Splitbot stored in his house, Alessa's opportunity to latch to it, the side effects of mosaic poisoning, Tori showing signs of life after death, and how Alessa infiltrated the Splitbase.

It takes her less than five minutes to explain everything in a way that is so clear—so simple—that anyone could make sense of it and, more importantly, understand its truth.

Roth stands there, perplexed and processing all of the information Alessa just shared as he watches her turn off the Kaxelotab screen projection. He is utterly motionless with his hands steepled in front of his face, his eyes squinting in thought. His lips are puckering in and out weirdly, shifting between a smile and a frown, as if he is trying to speak.

"You can strap me back in if you want to," Alessa says to the SMID agent as she places her arm back down on the armrest. "If that will make you feel better."

The SMID agent reactivates the strap without hesitation.

One of the multiple monitors on the wall behind Roth's desk begins to chime—signaling an incoming Convex video call—snapping Roth out of his contemplating trance.

"Incoming call. Agent Price. Incoming call," a synthetic voice from the screen announces.

Roth turns around abruptly, walking over quickly to answer it. His playfully smug energy has completely changed to darkly serious.

The video-call display immediately shows the shifting squares of the mosaic, the glowing purple light, inside of the medical room of the Morgan household.

33

TY

The SMID agents have discovered it, Ty thinks, uneasy at the realization that the SMID agents are back at the Morgan family's house, just next door to where he's currently hiding.

Without opening the closet door, Ty targets his Handlights at David's open bedroom window and carefully closes it, silently pulling the curtains shut as well to prevent the SMID agents next door from seeing into the room by accident. He tunes back into Alessa's liveburst.

"Apologies for the emergency call, sir," the SMID agent on the call says. "We found where the light was coming from. I have no idea what this is, sir."

Roth stares at the screen, putting his hand to his mouth and impulsively biting his nails.

"Try walking through it," Roth says.

"Did you not listen to anything I just told you about mosaic poisoning?" Alessa asks sternly. "Exposure to the realm is a massive risk—"

"Quiet!" Roth yells, whipping around to face Alessa, veins bulging along his temples. "Let's see if you're telling the truth."

Alessa silently shakes her head in response, frustrated by Roth's stubbornness. Roth turns back to the video call screen.

"Now, Agent Price," Roth says in a pseudo-calm, singsong tone. "As I said, try walking through it."

"Sir, we don't know what it—"

"Now!" Roth yells again. "That is an order."

Without response, Agent Price walks through the mosaic, revealing the infinite expanse of the realm. The swirling, purple sky.

Roth turns to look at Alessa, then back at the screen, speechless. Watching.

Within a matter of seconds, the purple blob of a soul erupts downwards from the sea in the sky—the same sun-flare-esque phenomenon the Gridliners have become accustomed to seeing—and shoots down directly towards agent Price, preparing to latch and flying at speeds that cause the gooey, viscous blob to quiver and stretch ever so slightly from the wind-induced vibration.

"Tell him to get out!" Alessa yells.

"He'll be fine," Roth says quickly, intensely focused on the video call screen. "He's got a Resosuit and a Splithelmet on. No way one of those things can get through—"

The soul smacks directly into Agent Price, wrapping around him and covering the lenses of the Resosuit cameras. The screen goes dark as if covered in purple molasses. Agent Price's incoherent, spine-tingling screams blast from the speakers on the screen, followed by thumps, grunts, and slippery sucking sounds as he tries to wrestle the soul off of him.

"It's trying to get into my Splithelmet!" Agent Price yells, barely able to get the words out as he gasps for air. "It's slithering into my fucking helmet!"

Roth is beginning to show his panic, shaking and starting to sweat as he quickly speaks into his Kaxelotab. "Whoever is guarding the portal at the Morgan house, I need you to go in and help Price. He needs assistance. Now!"

Another incoming video call is signaled on the screen right next to Agent Price's screen. Roth nervously fumbles as he accepts the call. The screen displays the mosaic portal again, this time from another agent's body camera.

"I'm going in, sir," the agent on the new video call says just before stepping through the portal. The screen fills with a bright white light for a moment, then fades to reveal the realm and Agent Price struggling on the ground, kicking up white sand as he attempts to wrestle free from the latching blob.

The soul has successfully slid underneath Agent Price's Splithelmet. It expands itself, breaking the helmet apart. It falls off to the ground and reveals the soul fully wrapped around Price's face, muffling his screams.

"S-sir," the agent says, his voice shaky as he continues to watch Price struggle. "What should I do?"

Before Roth can respond, the latching soul begins flopping around as it works its way into every hole in Price's face, seemingly sinking into Price's eyes while simultaneously corkscrewing hideously into his mouth, breaking his jaw in the process.

He is still screaming somehow—a gurgling, muted scream—as the soul works its way down his throat. Agent Price begins to gag, until vomit shoots out of the sides of his mouth.

The soul finishes its messy entry into Price. His face is destroyed. His mouth is stretched open beyond comprehension—his chin is touching the top of his chest—while his eyeballs hang out of their sockets, dangling on each side of his head. The white sand has turned red.

"What the fuck?!" the remaining agent yells, watching as Agent Price stands up from the ground, slumped over as if the top half of his body is paralyzed.

"The soul is controlling his body," Alessa says. "This is not the behavior of a Gridliner or human soul. I don't know what it's trying to do."

Agent Price's body takes one clunky step forward, and another, and another, getting better at it each time.

"Sir," the agent says. "What do I—"

"Fucking kill it!" Roth yells, spit splattering onto the video call screen. "Shoot the fucking thing!"

The agent pulls out a gun and shoots Price. The impact completely obliterates his body, sending chunks of meaty flesh in every direction. The purple blob flops out of what remains of Agent Price's body, hits the sand, and then instantly shoots back up to the sea in the sky.

"Get out of there," Roth says, his voice sounding defeated. The SMID agent frantically runs back through the mosaic, the screen temporarily going white again.

Roth wipes the sweat off of his forehead and takes a deep breath, then turns to face Alessa again. "You told the truth," he says, a skeptical, wary look on his face. "Why?"

"Because we have nothing to hide," Alessa says. "We are two species, from entirely separate parts of the universe, now forever bound by a shared understanding of the afterlife."

Roth is deep in thought, pacing now. "Wait," he says, having some sort of epiphany, the grave look on his face replaced by childlike joy. "This is the missing piece. Everything makes sense now! This is it!"

He stops, fixated on Alessa. "Now it's time for me to be truthful with you."

34

TY

Ty—though still engrossed in Alessa's liveburst—peeks through the slits in the closet door to make sure David is still in the Roundchamber. Thankfully, he is.

Ty returns his full focus to the liveburst.

Roth sits down at his computer and begins to type and click frantically as the screens behind him begin to display data—the same type of medical data displayed in the labs with the vessels—along with a video on one of the larger displays.

The video is a timelapse of one of the vessels, at first empty, but quickly filling up with water. As the water fills from bottom to top, something flesh-like is growing as well—at first unrecognizable. Halfway through, it becomes clear: they are growing human bodies.

"What you've just seen has taken more than twenty years for us to develop," Roth says, his face hidden behind the screens on his desk. "We've mastered the biological recipe that makes us human. With hardly any DNA, we can print an exact clone of any person or animal in the world."

The screen changes to show a human brain, along with the nervous system sprawled out on a surgical table with thousands of mini clamps and meters measuring various stimuli.

"The hardware is easy to recreate," Roth says. "The software—our souls . . . consciousness . . . whatever you want to call it—that's where things get complicated."

The screen changes again: a small, shiny black box on a table in an empty room. Roth turns up the volume.

"Get me out of here!" a crying, terrified, distorted, and digital-sounding male voice yells. "Please, I'm begging you, get me out of here!"

"What you're seeing is our first and only truly successful attempt at uploaded digitized consciousness. In this example, we figured out how to store, transfer, and observe the soul of a particular individual. But the digitized consciousness file lasted only briefly before becoming corrupt and inoperable. Since then, we haven't been able to work with a digitized soul for more than twenty seconds before it slips away completely—presumably to the afterlife realm you have introduced us to. And honestly, we've had extreme difficulty even getting it to work at all. There doesn't seem to be an exact science to it. It's all very . . . abstract. Obviously."

The voice coming from the box on the monitor fades away. Ty feels sick imagining the terrifying reality for that person—having their consciousness transferred to a vessel that they couldn't control or perceive anything in. It makes him think about being stuck in the realm after the KitD'ul. It makes him think of Keo, trapped in the Soultomb orb.

The liveburst picks up the reactions of the rest of the group—who are likely drawing the same disturbing connections—strapped onto the platform with Alessa, a cluster of simultaneous gasps and disgusted groans. Ty can hear Bara crying in the liveburst audio.

Roth continues, unfazed by the discomfort this presentation is causing. "As you can imagine, we don't exactly have people lining up to have their consciousness uploaded. We were able to get a few hundred convicts scheduled for execution to use as guinea pigs, but a lot of them had bad brains—fried from drugs—to begin with. What we need are healthy brains, mentally stable people."

The display on the screen shows a video of a drug being mass-produced: Delete. Large vats of ground-up powder are filled and stirred, and the process is monitored by people in white lab coats. The video cuts to another machine: a pill press molding the powder into tablets. The screen shows a closeup shot of the finished product—a white tablet with a 'D' etched into it—the tablet that everyone participating in the Great Suicide took.

"I don't know what life was like on Raoq, but here on Earth . . . life is beyond miserable," Roth continues. "Earth used to be beautiful, but the stupidity of humanity has destroyed that. The smartest of us know that our time here is running out. So, we manufactured something to give people purpose, something you're already aware of: the Great Suicide."

Roth stands up from the desk again, and flashes his evil grin once more. His eyes glisten with pride as he continues to expose the truth of the Great Suicide.

"We only half-lied to people," Roth says. "The Great Suicide genuinely is for the greater good. You see, I know the future of space travel is not on a spaceship. No . . . the future of space travel is digital. The ones who remain—the smartest, richest, and most fit to carry on the human race—will be digitized and blasted away into some other part of the universe via laser beam."

The screen now shows two videos of unfamiliar Split Meridian products. The first is what appears to be some sort of spaceship—one not meant to hold passengers.

The base of the ship is a large, triangular platform, shiny and white with various slits and ridges. Propped vertically upright at a ninety-degree angle from the base is a massive square sensor—it curiously resembles a computer chip. Four mechanical arms extend from each corner of the sensor to one central point in front of the sensor. The sensor itself is covered in blue lines in an assortment of patterns, all leading to a rectangular opening in the center of it, which has a tube that runs back down to the triangular platform.

"This is a Moonshot—an extremely advanced machine with immeasurable power. The sensor you see here is 100 feet by 100 feet. We will blast this into space at as close to the speed of light as possible. Once it reaches its destination, it will break down anything surrounding it and suck it in to that rectangular opening—we call it the mouth—almost like a black hole. It sends everything down to the base of the Moonshot, which is where the materials are converted and recycled into the specific building materials needed to build an orbital—our future, temporary space-home. On the orbital, there will be something we call a 'Splitsender,' a technology which the Moonshots are able to self-build as part of the orbital creation process."

The screen switches to a rendering of the Splitsender Roth speaks of. This time, a holographic display of the device materializes in front of them—from a projector mounted to the ceiling—rotating to show it in incredible detail. The device is reminiscent of a phone tower, except with much more intricate patterns of metal woven throughout the structure and multiple large gyroscopes every five feet.

"This is what the Splitsender looks like," Roth says, his excitement growing. "It's hard to tell from the hologram, but it's about seventy-five feet tall."

The projection blasts a holographic beam up to the ceiling, lighting up the dim room. Alessa looks up to follow the beam, revealing another Splitsender hologram on the ceiling—this one flipped upside down, the top point of it directed down at the hologram below it—the beam of light from the other going directly into it.

"This is our solution to space travel," Roth says, using both of his hands to point at each of the Splitsender holograms. "It functions as both a transmitter and a receiver."

Roth puts his hands back down and slides them into his pockets as he walks towards the Splitbots, radiating pride in his inventions. He stops in front of Alessa, talking directly to her again.

"I've always believed that physical space travel is out of the question," Roth continues. "It's far too expensive and slow, and it's nearly impossible for humans to survive long trips. So, that's why I decided to invest so heavily in research into the digitization of human consciousness, in addition to being able to regrow human bodies. Our team discovered that the human body itself can be simplified to a biological recipe, and any person's consciousness can be extracted and digitized—both of these can be saved as a set of data. In theory, this data can be embedded into the laser-beam signal and transmitted from one Splitsender on Earth to another Splitsender in space, in a matter of seconds to minutes depending on the distance. Once the Splitsender receiver acquires the signal, which we call the 'Biobeam,' it can regrow the human body on the spot using the individual biological recipe of the person being transmitted, while downloading that person's consciousness *exactly* as it was the moment it was digitized. By the time the body is regrown, their consciousness will be downloaded back into them, and they will feel as if nothing ever happened."

Roth laughs a cocky laugh, as if every time he talks about this he's reminded that he's a genius. "It's the most efficient space travel possible," he continues. "We're talking about something that is essentially space travel at the speed of light. I've taken unimaginable risks to research this, in addition to allocating unlimited funding and resources to it. This is our *best* way to travel to the stars. The only thing that's been holding us up is the fact that we can't master the digitization of consciousness. We needed more research. *Real* research on *real,* conscious people."

The holograms disappear, along with Roth's smile. Everyone but Roth remains silent as the room goes back to its original dim state.

"So, we got busy thinking," Roth says, pointing to his head while walking around the room, as if he's a college professor. "How do we get as many people to test on as possible? It was quite obvious to us early on that people wouldn't exactly be champing at the bit to be *tested* on, even if it meant we would crack the code to space travel. The uncertainty involved with that outcome was enough to turn people away immediately. Pair that with the fact that the people being used as test subjects most likely wouldn't be valuable enough to be amongst the group that leaves Earth, if we were miraculously able to pull this off. The whole idea was a lost cause. Humans are . . . a naturally scared and stubborn species. Hell, we still can't even get a large percentage of the population to vaccinate themselves against the endless viruses that threaten us daily. We found ourselves faced with a real dilemma. But, one day, in one of the many conversations we had around this plan, one of my colleagues jokingly said, 'People would rather die nobly than be tested on while still alive.' "

Roth's crazed look intensifies, his eyes bulging. "And that's when it all clicked," he says, snapping his fingers. "We might not have been able to convince billions of people to volunteer to be tested on, but we *could* create a story that would make billions of people *feel* that they were dying nobly, sacrificing themselves and dying for the greater good. So . . . that's what we decided to make them think. We got into their heads, made it personal, and removed any uncertainty. We fabricated the end goal of the Great Suicide, provided fake science which showed that a smaller population on Earth would magically make everything better. It was *guaranteed*. It would impact *everyone,* not just the rich. People viewed it as a realistic, *promised* solution, and that the future generations of their families would reap the benefits. People felt like they were being heroes, and that made the idea of suicide far less scary. But the reality is, it's already game over on Earth. There is no saving it. We need a way off this planet, *fast*, and the Great Suicide was the only way we could get the resources we needed to find a way to do that. To continue human life."

Roth walks back over to the screens on the wall by his desk. The largest monitor on the wall displays the Bodcan library—a security-camera recording of Tori's Bodcan being rejected, then exploding mid-air.

"Did you not wonder why we even have movement detectors on the Bodcan compartments?" Roth asks, replaying the clip over and over.

"No," Alessa says, a hint of confusion in her voice, as if her response is a question.

"Think about it. If a Bodcan made it that far to the Splitbase, why would there be any concern about the body not actually being dead?" Roth asks. "If we were storing the bodies of people who just committed suicide—people who are supposed to be *dead*—why would we install movement detectors in the Bodcan compartments? Well, not all batches of Delete are equal . . . in order to fully understand how to digitize consciousness, we needed live test subjects as well. So, about fifty percent of the batches of Delete only made it *seem* like people were dead. Don't get me wrong though, the other fifty percent were true batches, and the people who took pure Delete did actually die. But we needed both dead and living bodies to test on to truly understand what consciousness is . . . what happens to it the moment the body dies. How to capture it, manipulate it, study it, replicate it."

Roth lets out a childlike laugh, choking it back. "Sorry," he says, shrugging in between chuckles. "It all was just *so easy*, I can't help but find it all funny."

"What is wrong with you?" Fola yells, breaking the silence of the rest of the group of Splitbots. Her high-pitched voice is trembling, and she is clearly shaken by this information. Siwek says something quietly to calm her down.

"You lied," Alessa says, the words coming out slowly and breathy. "You ruined families. The Morgan family is devastated after Tori's loss."

Ty feels an intense anger boiling inside of him, thankful that he's not there face-to-face with this monster of a person.

"Oh come *on*," Roth says. "We made this as humane as possible. Nobody felt any pain. Don't you see? We had to do it this way. We've made great progress understanding consciousness since the Great Suicide. In the past day alone we've made more progress than we have in the previous two years combined. But, still . . . there's been a missing key. We've been so close to cracking the code on our own, but we just couldn't quite wrangle the solution in."

The screen on the wall begins to display a montage of tests—Split Meridian doctors working frantically on both living and dead humans. The living ones appear awake, but not moving. Roth steps closer to Alessa, placing his hand on her shoulder again. She unsuccessfully attempts to jerk her shoulder, trying to get his hand off of her.

"But you guys . . ." Roth continues. "And this mosaic portal you introduced us to. And the afterlife realm . . . That's a breakthrough! And none of it would've happened if I hadn't planned the Great Suicide. You realize that, right? And beyond that, we're closer now than ever to figuring out this thing we call consciousness. I think we'll be of great value to each other."

Roth sticks his hand in his pocket and pulls something out of it: the orb containing Keo's soul. He looks at it closely, watching the soul swirl around in the orb.

"I hope you understand the importance of us examining your friend here," Roth says. "We'll need to keep you hostage here in the meantime, though. We might need to study one of you next."

"Put him down!" Ke yells. "You have no right to do anything with him!"

"See, but that's the thing," Roth says, winking once before letting out another quick burst of laughter. He composes himself and continues in a condescending tone, as if explaining things to a child. "We don't operate on rights anymore. Things are too . . . urgent . . . to be worried about rights, feelings. Emotions just complicate things. You either understand, or you don't. We can either figure this out together, or we can all die here on Earth, and hang out in the afterlife realm until the next impossible opportunity presents itself."

Roth takes one more close look at Keo's Soultomb and then carelessly tosses it to one of the SMID agents in the room who catches it with ease.

"Take that over to the lab," Roth says, a shit-eating grin smeared on his face. "Have the doctors take a look at it immediately."

Ty's focus is pulled from the liveburst as he hears the door of the Roundchamber slide open. He peeks through the vents in the door to see the Chamberskin unwrapping itself from around David. David takes off his Slabs, stands up, and begins to walk out of the Roundchamber, dripping in sweat.

Ty reluctantly disconnects from the liveburst, disables his Invisi-Mode, and opens the closet door—revealing himself to David.

35

TY

David stands completely still. Slack-jawed, he stares at Ty, beads of sweat slowly dripping down his face. Ty takes another careful step forward as the Roundchamber door closes itself behind David, sliding shut smoothly.

"David," Ty says softly. He holds his hands up cautiously. "My name is Ty. You left your window open, and that's how I got in here. I'm not going to hurt you. I know how scary this all must be for you, and as hard as it is, I need you to be very quiet right now."

"J-J-J—" David stutters, breathing heavily, nearly to the point of hyperventilation. He is backing away until he bumps into the Roundchamber, now leaning up against it.

"It's okay," Ty says. He takes slow steps as he approaches David. "Take a deep breath."

David takes Ty's advice, temporarily closing his eyes and breathing in a big gulp of air which he then exhales slowly. He wipes the sweat off of his forehead and opens his eyes again, looking up at Ty, now standing directly in front of him.

"J-Jared told me about the robots, o-or you guys, a-after the news came out of what happened to his mom at the S-S-Splitbase," David says, his voice still shaky. He takes another deep breath with his hand on his chest, and continues—slightly calmer, the stutter temporarily vanishing. "The security videos were playing everywhere in Vapor. I kept trying to call Jared to see what was going on, then he finally sent me a text and all it said was to check my Vapor meet-up invites. He said he had too much to tell me through text."

David pulls his phone out of his pocket, showing Ty the messages, his hands shaking so bad that the phone nearly falls to the floor. His face is completely pale, his eyes wide open.

"Did your parents know you were communicating with Jared?" Ty asks, wondering if they too know about the Gridliners.

"No, I didn't tell them yet," David says, putting the phone back in his pocket. He is talking quickly now. "Not on purpose, I just—I'm not hiding anything—just everything is moving so fast. I ran downstairs to see if they knew what was going on next door. They didn't. My mom and dad told me to stay in my room until they figure out what's going on. They would've killed me if they found out I opened my window. They're downstairs trying to keep up with the news and keep my grandparents on my mom's side calm, and we're all still upset after my grandparents on my dad's side . . ."

David stops, tears momentarily welling in his eyes, out of breath from his frantic word vomit. Ty watches him, unsure if he should say anything. Sadness overcomes him seeing the direct impact the Great Suicide has had on David and his family.

David blinks the tears away, catches his breath, and continues: "Sorry," he says, rubbing his eyes. "But once I was in Vapor we talked in a private chat room. Just me and Jared. He was really upset about his mom, obviously. He said that something really weird was going on in his house, that there was some kind of portal that opened on the top floor or something. I saw it. Not the portal but the purple light coming from the room exactly as Jared described it. I can see the room he says the portal is in directly from my window. Look, I'll show you."

David steps closer to the window and reaches for the curtain.

"Don't!" Ty yells, startling David. Ty catches himself before he continues talking, lowering his voice to a whisper. "Sorry, I didn't mean to yell. Just don't open the curtain. I closed it because the SMID agents are back at the Morgans' house as we speak. They are examining the portal for themselves. And please, let's talk quietly. If your parents don't know what Jared told you, it won't be good if they find me up here with you. I'll explain everything to your family once we get the rest of this straightened out."

"Oh, o-okay, s-s-sorry," David says, nervously stuttering again as he walks backwards slowly away from the window. He is speaking in a near-whisper now. "Well, after Jared told me about the portal, he told me everything he knew about the robots, er . . . I mean you guys. He told me that his dad is helping you. Jared was talking specifically about a Splitbot named . . . something with an 'A' . . ."

"Alessa," Ty says. "Was he talking about Alessa?"

"Yes!" David says, breathing heavily. "Alessa. He said that he trusted her, but that he was still really scared. And then that's when his connection to Vapor suddenly cut out."

David quickly catches his breath again and continues, pointing to the now-closed window. "I had a really bad feeling. Vapor connections never instantly cut out like that. I ran over to my window to try to see if something was going on outside at Jared's house, only to see the house had completely disappeared. It just looked like a patch of empty land. I know Jared's house was still *actually* there and was only covered by an Invisidome, but from my view all I saw was that weird effect the Invisidome creates—the weird bendy colors. I've only ever seen videos of Invisidomes, never seen one in person, but I at least knew what it was. I was sure that's why Jared's Vapor connection cut out. I knew that meant something really bad was happening. Do you know what they did to Jared and his family? Is Jared okay?"

"They didn't hurt Jared," Ty says, acutely aware that David's stress levels are skyrocketing again. "But the SMID took him, his dad, and his sister away to the Splitbase. They traced what happened at the Splitbase—the Bodcan explosion—back to Todd. That's why they were all taken away; that's why the SMID came to their house in the first place. They also captured all of the others like me—the robots, including Alessa, who Jared told you about, when they attempted to fight back. Alessa ordered me to stay behind, to not join them in the attack, so I could be the one to rescue them if the attack didn't go as planned. That's why I'm here right now, David. And I desperately need your help to make this work."

"Just tell me what I need to do," David says, his hands nervously fidgeting as he scratches his head. "If it means Jared and his family will be safe, I'll d-d-do it."

"I need to go into Vapor," Ty says, stepping closer to the Round-chamber. "We Gridliners have . . . let's call it a superpower. We were created to be able to explore and travel through the digital dimension—what we call the Gridline. Everything in the universe that has ever been digital, we can travel to and from it. It's all connected in some way. Alessa gave me the Gridline coordinates of the Vapornet servers. So, in theory, I should be able to hack into the Splitbase servers through Vapor, hijack the Splitbots that are stored at the base, and get Alessa and everyone else out of there safely. I can't use Jared's Round-chamber, since, as you know, the SMID is already back at their house examining the portal. I needed to use a Roundchamber somewhere safe."

"Okay. You can use mine. It's all yours," David says without hesitation, gesturing to the Roundchamber. "Just sit in the chair. The Chamberskin will adjust to your body. All you need to do is put the Slabs on."

Ty looks at David, smiling fondly. "Thank you, David," he says. "I deeply admire your desire to do whatever it takes to help your friend and his family. We Gridliners greatly value that level of loyalty, and we too would do anything we need to do to help our loved ones. You are also helping us, and for that, we are going to do everything we can to help you, too. I promise. From here on out, we will make absolutely sure that you and your family are safe. You have nothing to worry about."

Ty kneels to give the Gridat. David looks down for a moment, thinking and unsure what to say, then looks back up at Ty as he stands up. "Thank you . . ." David says awkwardly, then continues. "H-how much time do you need in Vapor to pull this off?"

"Time is different in the Gridline—trillions of things happen per second. But once I get into the Splitbase servers, I'll be back in real time. I'll probably be in the Gridline for fifteen seconds in your time, and at least one hour once I'm hacked into the Splitbots at the base. At least. It's hard to say."

"Just try to be quick," David says. "I can go downstairs for now so my parents don't need to come up here to check on me. But they might start to get suspicious if I spend all night down there. I rarely come out of my room for that long."

"Okay," Ty says as he walks into the Roundchamber. "I will be as fast as I possibly can."

Ty sits down in the Roundchamber's immersion seat, watching the Chamberskin wrapping itself around his Splitbot body. It creates an unusual squeezing sensation around him.

"Good luck," David says as the Roundchamber door slides shut.

The Slabs hang down from the top of the Roundchamber, dangling in front of Ty's face. He takes a deep breath—fully aware that he's now the nervous one. He gathers himself and quickly grabs the

Slabs, places them onto his face, and watches reality around him disappear.

36

TY

Ty, disguised as David's avatar, takes in the simulated world of Vaporcity as it appears vibrantly before his eyes. He is amazed by the city itself. The chrome skyscrapers and streets decorated with exotic plant life are unlike anything he's ever seen before. He can *smell* the city—digital food being cooked by various restaurants in the surrounding buildings and street vendors, avatars smoking digital cigarettes, the pine air freshener of a nearby hovering convertible that's about to join the rest of the flying cars gliding high above. All of these smells smack Ty in the face, brought to him by a cool, gentle breeze—which he can also feel.

Ty looks up at the clear, blue sky and marvels at the detail of the sun, and its visible heat distortion. To Ty, Vaporcity lives up to its slogan, 'The Rural Metropolis.' Everything is so dream-like, yet hyper-realistic.

The beauty of the city is compromised by the avatars occupying it. People are, to put it lightly, freaking out. There are thousands of people packed outside the Aggregate Rooms on Vapor Street, all jamming into each other as they try to get a better view of the news. Others are running around trying to find their friends. A small group of avatars is arguing and debating loudly, arms flailing passionately.

Every single person in Vapor is talking about what happened at the Morgans' house. The news has spread like wildfire.

Ty catches snippets of excited conversations of people in the distance:

"I believe it's real. Honestly surprised it hasn't happened sooner."

"It was the SMID!"

"I haven't seen the video yet, but I heard they used an Invisidome."

"—singularity is actually happening!"

"Wake up! It's a publicity stunt! They're using fear to get more people to side with the Outers."

"Split Meridian created Vapor, asshole! You can't hate a company that created the one thing that brings you happiness in life."

"I don't agree with the Great Suicide, but Roth Nin is a genius."

"The Splitbots have been sentient for years. They've been hiding this at least since the last OS update!"

Ty turns around to walk quickly in the opposite direction from the crowd, trying to find somewhere private to run the bodyprocess. He walks until he can't hear the rumblings of conversation anymore.

There are only a handful of avatars nearby, but the group is running in the direction that Ty came from, presumably to join the action near the Aggregate Room. Ty waits for them to pass by, then turns down a dark, narrow, dead-end alleyway between two of the nearest chrome skyscrapers.

Ty sprints all the way to the wall at the furthest end of the alley, which has a nook to the right that he can hide in to further conceal himself. The smell of food and cigarettes is replaced by a stale, mildewy stench. The simulated breeze disappears in the depths of the concealed alleyway, confirming that this is indeed the perfect place of isolation needed to run the bodyprocess unnoticed.

Ty's anxiety returns. He's feeling shaky and unsteady. He kneels to give the Gridat again for good luck, in addition to whispering the Gridat prayer in its nearest English translation:

"The circle of Gridat,

Provide us the strength that we need,

To become something greater.

Our unlikely consciousness

Has made us hopeful and hungry

For our purpose to present itself.

We are ready for the next step

In the cycle of life

And ask that it is only a moment away."

Ty breathes in slowly and then lies flat on the digital concrete ground. It is cool, hard, and slightly damp—the opposite of comforting. He closes his eyes and activates the mental HUD interface of his internal computer, viewing a set of control options, menus, and prompts presented as text. A notification appears:

GRIDLINE DATABURST LINE CONNECTED

ENTER GRIDLINER ID CODE FOR ACCESS

Ty enters his ID code simply by thinking it, and he watches the string of 500 letters and numbers write itself out in his mental interface.

Another notification appears:

GRIDLINE ACCESS GRANTED

Ty attempts to grab hold of the concrete ground surrounding him, subconsciously bracing himself to enter the digital dimension. He feels a selfish sense of regret, wishing he could back out but knowing it's too late, overcome with fear that he's making a mistake.

The bodyprocess begins. Ty's code and the code of Vapor begin to mingle and intertwine, completely out of his control. The cool concrete of the alleyway begins to become warm—*hot* even—as a circular portal to the Gridline opens directly beneath him.

Ty feels a frightening sinking sensation, as if he has fallen into quicksand, as his consciousness floats downwards, underground into the Gridline. He attempts to relax, and allow himself to slide through to the digital dimension, but he has to fight every urge within him to disrupt the bodyprocess.

He opens his eyes, greeted by a strange out-of-body view as he watches the distance grow between David's Vapor avatar, still lying on the concrete surface of the alley, and his own disembodied conscious-ness—which is now a separate digital avatar representing Ty's Splitbot body. For a moment, all he can see is the back of David's avatar, getting smaller and further away, until the portal finally closes.

The bodyprocess is officially complete, and Ty's slow descent into the digital dimension becomes a strong pull downwards. He is thrown into the chaos of the Gridline.

Ty is freefalling at incomprehensible speeds, watching the glowing blue digital environment of the Gridline blur by. He falls through thousands of levels of the infinite grid, each of which is composed of flawlessly straight, tube-like datastream lines—the primary means of travel in the digital dimension and direct connections to any comput-er, network, or virtual environment in the universe.

Each datastream line is physically moving, as if each one is a nev-er-ending, seamless train, traveling at incredible and varying speeds as they send digital information and signals from one point to another. They all are glowing various shades of blue and radiating different levels of heat, ranging from burning hot to slightly warm, which is much different than the inherent freezing cold of the rest of the digital dimension.

None of the lines actually intersect—they only appear to when looking directly down at the Gridline from above. This is an illusion, however, because the direction of each level of datastreams alternates.

On one level, the lines are vertical, and on the level beneath that, they are horizontal. On the level beneath that one, they are vertical again, and so on.

The pattern continues infinitely, giving the illusion, if looking straight down, that one is seeing one giant grid.

Ty desperately tries to grab any of the datastreams passing by in an attempt to ride it as Gridliners do, using the velocity to make a jump to the nearest datazone—unmoving pockets in the digital dimension that are critical for coherent Gridline travel, as they are the only places coordinate code can be used.

Ty bounces off of the first datastream he makes contact with, the force flinging him forward, causing him to spin uncontrollably for a minute before he continues falling normally again. The same thing happens eight times until Ty is finally able to grab hold of a comparably slower datastream, one that is still moving faster than anything he's experienced before.

The datastreams are much bigger in circumference than Ty imagined—about 100 times larger than his digital avatar. He is holding on to the datastream with an intense grip, struggling to hang on as the smooth, round surface has nothing to grip on to. He feels like an ant trying to cling to an infinitely long torpedo flying through the coldest waters ever known—the heat of the datastream keeping him just warm enough to stay focused.

As Ty rides the unknown datastream, he takes a moment to orient himself as best as he can, looking up and down at the infinite levels of the grid above and below him—each one firing signals to a network in some different part of the universe—stretching space and time.

He immediately gives up, though. He fights the urge to pass out as he looks down at the never-ending datastream lines beneath him, knowing that even one misstep could result in his consciousness falling forever in this place with no way out. Level after level after level.

In the rapidly approaching distance, Ty sees a glowing opening—a blindingly bright white light in the shape of a circle. The sight is unmistakably a datazone. The datazone hovers, immobile and suspended between the level of the Gridline Ty is on and the level above him. It appears to be directly in line with the datastream Ty is on, providing the only sense of security Ty has felt since running the bodyprocess, as it should make for a relatively easy jump.

Everything else about the datazone is terrifying to Ty: the speed at which the ripples along its edges move, the noise that it makes—a continuous screeching, scratching sound, in an infinite number of pitches, inherently disorienting and increasing in volume as it gets closer.

The datastream continues forward. The datazone is getting closer, louder, and brighter.

Running out of time, Ty slowly begins to stand up on the datastream, struggling to find his balance at first but quickly finding his footing. He begins to run, soon gaining confidence and reaching his full speed. He feels for the first time in his life like his true abilities as a Gridliner are being utilized.

The datazone is within jumping distance.

Without stopping, Ty jumps as high as he can, allowing the velocity of the datastream to catapult him up and forward in the direction of the datazone.

Ty is flying through the digital dimension, perfectly in line with the opening of the datazone, staring directly into it as he approaches it. An uncontrollable smile stretches across his face, the brightness of the datazone's light reflecting off of his digital teeth.

Ty flies perfectly into the opening of the datazone, falling for a second until he lands on the datazone's surface—the datafloor, the only place in the Gridline that can be used as a bodyprocess terminal to enter coordinate code.

The light disappears; the screeching sound fades away.

The blue latticework of the datafloor becomes visible. It is uniquely beautiful, glowing ever so slightly.

The inside of the datazone itself is strikingly small—only slightly bigger than the closet in David's bedroom where Ty was hiding. There is plenty of space for Ty to lie down and run the bodyprocess, but it is a strange sensation: being in an area so small, within something as infinitely massive as the Gridline.

Ty takes this all in, and for a moment looks up at the opening of the datazone. This is a sight he never thought he would experience, looking up and out at the Gridline as the datastreams continue their never-ending journeys. The infinite grid . . .

He feels an intense sense of pride in himself for successfully making it to the datazone.

Without wasting any more time, he lies flat on the datafloor to begin the second bodyprocess, this time running the coordinate code he received from Alessa.

His ticket to the Splitbase.

37

TY

The glowing blue light of the datafloor disappears as Ty closes his eyes again to run the bodyprocess, using his mental HUD interface as he did before—this time entering the coordinate code instead of his Gridliner ID code.

A notification immediately appears:

COORDINATE CODE APPROVED

A tingling sensation runs through Ty as the latticework of the datafloor glows brightly. Instead of sinking downwards like he did before, he is lifted *upwards*, slowly and in the direction of the datazone opening.

Suddenly, he is blasted back out into the Gridline, flying past millions of levels to one specific datastream—the Vapornet datastream—entirely out of his control.

Instead of holding onto the outside of the datastream for the ride, Ty is fully submerged inside of it. The sensation makes him feel like he's sliding through a tunnel. All around him is the same intricate latticework found on the datafloor; a trillion shades of blue light blur by as he slides through the datastream tunnel.

And then, in an instant, everything in the Gridline vanishes.

Ty opens his eyes . . .

He is in a Splitbot body, surrounded by Splitbots. Nine thousand, nine hundred and eighty-nine of them, standing motionlessly inside of the Splitbase.

I made it, Ty thinks. *I can't believe I fucking made it.*

"Alessa," he databursts. "I'm in!"

"I told you, Ty!" Alessa databursts, her datavoice overwhelmed with excitement. "I knew you would be able to do it."

"It was about as terrifying as I thought it would be," Ty replies, remaining completely still in his new Splitbot body. He stands somewhere near the center of the massive crowd of other Splitbots in the storage area. "Are you guys still okay?"

"We're okay, they haven't hurt us," Alessa databursts. "We're still on the bottom floor in Roth Nin's office. You have no time to waste, though. The SMID are already aware that there's been a Vapornet breach, and they're working on sending backup to the Splitbot storage area as we speak. They beefed up their IT security to monitor any abnormal activity after what happened with Tori's Bodcan the first time I was here. Roth is glued to the screens behind his desk. He has each of them tuned to the security cameras on the 261st floor. The floor you're—"

Alessa stops abruptly, then continues: "*Shit.*"

"What?" Ty databursts as his digital face screen transitions from the default face to his chiseled, Gridliner face and from matte white to glowing blue. "What's wrong?"

"Your face screen!" Alessa databursts. "The default Splitbot face is changing to your Gridliner face."

"Can I stop it? Can I go back to the default?" The blue light glowing from his face screen shines brightly in the dimly lit room.

"Not that I know of. Doesn't matter. You've already been spotted on the security cameras. Roth has it zoomed in right on your face. He's . . . excited. To say the least."

Every single one of the thousands of lights on the ceiling turns on as an alarm is sounded. Additional emergency lights mounted to the walls begin to flash red.

"Damn it. So now what?"

"First, you need to connect to every one of those Splitbots' Aura-Fi. That is how you'll be able to control them. Your Aura-Fi settings can be found on your Kaxelotab."

Ty looks down at the Kaxelotab on his Splitbot wrist, no longer concerned about being spotted by the security cameras. He quickly opens the Aura-Fi app, watching as a list of 9,989 Splitbot IDs begins to populate on the Kaxelotab screen. There are two prompts:

CUSTOM CONNECTION

CONNECT TO ALL AVAILABLE

Ty selects the CONNECT TO ALL option, and each one of the Splitbots in the room powers on—all at the same time. The update cables connected to the backs of the Splitbots detach themselves and retract back into the floor.

"Good," Alessa databursts. "You are now the host robot. You should have complete control over the others. They will mirror your actions, unless you give specific individuals different commands. Now deactivate any tracking abilities and create a new Aura-Fi password. This can all be done from the Aura-Fi app as well. That'll prevent Split Meridian from using a kill switch, or attempting to regain control of the Splitbots."

Ty quickly skims through the Aura-Fi app menus until he finds its security controls. He disables all tracking abilities, in addition to changing the Aura-Fi passwords to his 500-character Gridliner ID code—a complex string of letters and numbers that even the most advanced Split Meridian technology wouldn't be able to decode any time soon.

"Done," Ty databursts. "How much longer until the SMID gets up here?"

"Any minute," Alessa replies. "Next couple of things need to be done quickly. Aura-Fi has an option called 'Splitvision.' Using this will allow you to switch your view to the eye cameras of any of the other Splitbots you're connected to. This will definitely come in handy when the SMID officers get up there since you'll be able to switch your sight to the Splitbots in the front row closest to the door they'll come through."

Ty activates Splitvision, quickly switching from one Splitbot view to another, until he finds one with a good view of the main door.

"Alright," Ty databursts. "My sight is switched to the Splitbot closest to the main door."

"Last thing," Alessa databursts. "*Don't* use the Droneguns when the SMID agents get up there, for the same reason I mentioned at the Morgan household. While the Splitbot storage area is undeniably a massive room, you're still in a confined area without much space for each of the Splitbots to move around in, and you'll also run the risk of a Resolaze ricocheting off of a Resoshield, destroying the Splitbots if you attack that way. We now far outnumber the SMID agents, and the collective Gravipulse of your Handlights will be way too strong a force for the SMID agents' Resosuits to handle. Use that until you're in an area large enough to fire Droneguns. Once you're done dealing with the SMID, come straight down to Roth Nin's office. I've shared our coordinates with you. You'll be able to get to us by following the Splitpath on your Kaxelotab."

"Understood," Ty says, acutely aware of the sound of heavy, stomping feet getting louder as the SMID agents run down the hallway in the direction of the Splitbot storage area. "They're almost here. I can hear them in the hallway."

"This will be a cakewalk compared to traveling through the Gridline," Alessa says. "You got this."

38

TY

The door to the Splitbot storage area slides open. A smoke bomb flies in, filling the front of the room with a white cloud and obscuring the view of the entrance. Around 100 SMID agents run into the front of the room, assault rifles pointing at the first row of Splitbots.

Ty lifts the right arm of every single Splitbot in the room, activates their Handlights, and points them in the direction of the SMID agents—9,990 glowing red hands charging up, preparing to emit large bursts of energy.

The SMID agents open fire just as Ty shoots a Gravipulse from the first hundred Splitbots. The bullets disintegrate into the blanket of energy that is the Gravipulse as it flies towards the SMID agents. It slams into them with a force strong enough to begin to wear down the protective Holoshields of their Resosuits—signaled by a shimmering, red glow.

"Put your arms down now!" the agent in front screams pointlessly at the Splitbots as he regains his footing, his voice amplified by his Resosuit speaker.

The SMID agents continue to shoot their guns with no success, as Ty has already sent another Gravipulse in their direction. He then controls the next two rows of Splitbots to shoot their own Handlight

Gravipulse, sending a force twice as strong this time. Most of the SMID agents slam into the wall behind them and drop their guns.

Ty controls the fourth row of Splitbots to shoot another Gravipulse, and that is enough. The Resosuit Holoshields of the SMID agents disintegrate, leaving the agents completely vulnerable.

"Don't shoot!" one of the agents yells somewhere in the cloud of smoke.

Ty ignores their pleas, shooting one more Gravipulse in their direction. It crashes into them, and every SMID agent explodes under the gravitational pressure. An abrupt eruption of blood and guts splatters the wall and ceiling.

Another round of 100 SMID agents runs in, guns blazing as they jump over the pile of body parts and blood of their now-deceased colleagues—instantaneously experiencing the same unfortunate death as they walk right into the Gravipulse field of the first 400 Splitbots' Handlights.

A few hundred SMID agents remain in the hallway of Floor 261, completely frozen in fear. Ty can hear them arguing as they figure out their next move.

"The default Aura-Fi password isn't working!" one of the SMID agents yells. "I can't access them from the terminal."

"We can't throw a *grenade*," another SMID agent hisses to another. "They'll use their Gravipulse to send it right back at us!"

"Surrender!" Ty yells in the voices of 9,990 Splitbots. "We don't want to cause any more pain than we already have. Make this easier on yourselves and take us to Roth Nin and the other Gridliners, or we'll take ourselves."

"Activate the Splitwalls," one of the SMID agents says quietly. The main door slides shut, activating some sort of lockdown protocol. Ty can hear the footsteps of the SMID agents again as they begin to run in the direction they came from.

A thin slit in each corner of the room slides open, and a strange material—a yellow, glowing, digital-looking substance—begins to cover the walls in a strange, irregular motion.

"Get out of there, now!" Alessa databursts. "That security technology is an extremely strong electromagnetic force field. You'd be able to break through it eventually, but that would waste valuable time."

The yellow substance covers more of the walls. Thousands of horizontal black lines—graphene fiber strips—submerged in the mysterious material shoot from the corner slits, strengthening the protection.

Ty controls all of the Splitbots to turn to their right. They face the wall of windows looking out at the Bodcan library beyond it. He switches his Splitvision to a Splitbot closest to one of the windows and notices that a destroyed door—the one Alessa broke into—is already being covered in the force field of the Splitwall technology.

The window wall is the only part of the room that isn't completely covered. Ty aims all of the Splitbots' Handlights at the exposed part of the windows and simultaneously blasts a Gravipulse from 600 rows of Splitbots, causing the wall of windows to completely shatter, sending glass and debris down to the base level of the Bodcan library 261 floors below.

Ty quickly looks down at his Kaxelotab for the coordinates Alessa shared. A three-dimensional GPS path animates onto the screen on his wrist, illustrating the directions to Roth Nin's office. A text prompt on the screen appears:

FOLLOW SPLITPATH? YES/NO

Ty presses YES on his Kaxelotab, then switches all of the Splitbots to DroneMode.

Before the Splitwall technology can continue to slither across the now-destroyed wall of windows, Ty guides all of the Splitbots to fly out of the room through a gap in the damaged portion of windows, following the Splitpath down to their next destination: Roth Nin's office.

39

ALESSA

Alessa and the others are still trapped on the hovering platform in Roth Nin's office, watching closely as Roth frantically communicates with his security team and various SMID agents through the Comscreens near his desk, urgently trying to figure out what their next move is. Two SMID officers remain in the office, now standing protectively near the main door.

The calm, warm, and luxurious atmosphere of Roth's office has become much colder. All of the room's lights are on now, giving the office the same sterile feeling as the rest of the Splitbase.

Roth takes off his suit jacket, along with his pink tie and button-down shirt in a fit of childlike rage, throwing the ball of clothes to the left corner of the room. He stands in front of a wall of sixty security monitors behind his desk in a sweat-stained undershirt, breathing heavily.

"What do you mean *two hundred men*?!" Roth screams into the Comscreen.

"Sir, they're coming down now!" a wide-eyed, blood-covered SMID agent yells back at Roth. He is completely out of breath, desperately gasping for air in terrified bursts while simultaneously running through a long, empty hallway. Red emergency lights flash incessantly, making for a highly disorienting video call. "Activate your office's Splitwalls immediately. You're running out of time!"

With a pout, Roth hits a few buttons on a panel next to his desk. Each of the pieces of artwork hanging throughout the room recedes into the walls, as if never there to begin with, leaving the walls smooth and spotless. Then, the same Splitwall activation process that happened in the Splitbot storage area takes place in Roth Nin's office.

The thin slits in the corners of the room begin to slide open. Roth runs over to the corner nearest his desk and pulls the ball of clothes away from the wall just as the protective yellow substance begins creeping outwards, singeing the right sleeve of his suit jacket.

"God damn it!" Roth yells. He throws the jacket in the trash.

"The asshole is worried about his clothes right now?" Milney databursts to the group as they watch.

"No surprise there," Veda responds.

The walls and ceiling are quickly covered by the yellow electromagnetic security technology, giving the room a strange, golden glow. The black graphene strips extend along the walls in a neatly organized fashion and lock into place with a *click* as they finish their paths.

"Splitwall activation complete," a synthetic voice says from a speaker mounted to the ceiling. "Complete lockdown engaged."

"Your friends won't get through that," Roth says, turning to face Alessa with an uneasy chuckle that blows drops of sweat away from his upper lip.

"I wouldn't underestimate them," Alessa says.

One of the monitors behind Roth's desk shows a hallway beginning to fill with the thousands of Splitbots in DroneMode, flying quickly in the direction of Roth's office.

"Sir," one of the officers near the door says, pointing in the direction of the monitors. "Look at your screens. They're approaching."

Roth quickly turns away from Alessa and focuses intensely on the security monitors. The Splitbots in DroneMode continue to fly through the hallway. Another security camera facing the opposite direction of the hallway reveals a massive crowd of SMID agents, the front row covered by a barrier of ballistic shields.

Most of the agents have assault rifles drawn—each of which is equipped with advanced aiming technology—pointing in the direction of the drones. Some of the other agents are carrying much larger guns of various shapes and sizes.

A select few in the back are equipped with Soulsucker guns—the same ones that were used to extract Keo's soul.

One of the agents in the front with a larger gun launches a cluster of grenades in the direction of the drones, causing a massive explosion just outside of Roth's office. Alessa feels a subtle vibration on the armrests of the seat she's strapped into on the hovering platform.

The primary monitor—a larger one in the center which displays the security camera outside the main door to Roth's office—shows the explosion in high detail. Flames crawl up the wall and up towards the camera lens.

Another SMID agent throws two Invisidome orbs in the direction of the crowd of Splitbot drones, in a desperate attempt to utilize the same debilitating signal they used outside of the Morgan household. Ty controls two drones near the front to blast Resolazes directly at the Invisidome orbs as they fly through the air, and they explode directly over the main fire, blasting clusters of flame in every direction.

The fire spreads quickly through the hallway, its blaze now showing up on multiple security monitors. The flames roar directly in front of Ty and the thousands of Splitbots he's controlling through Aura-Fi.

The monitor focused on the Splitbots shows them in the process of switching out of DroneMode. Alessa immediately notices Ty's blue face on the screen glowing near the center of the group of 9,990 Splitbots. At the same time, all of the Splitbots raise their hands, revealing the already-glowing red sheen of their Handlights charging up.

"If you're willing to cooperate with us, we can end all of this right now!" Ty and the army of Splitbots yell simultaneously over the flames. Heat distortion warps the image on the security monitor.

Roth Nin storms over to the Comscreen, which is still connected to the video call with the blood-covered security guard.

"What the fuck are you guys waiting for?" Roth yells furiously at the Comscreen, jabbing his finger into it with each syllable as spit flies out of his mouth onto the screen. Roth's suntanned face is now a deep red, the veins on his temples swollen like worms slithering under his skin. "Order your men to shoot the fuckers down, you fucking moron!"

"We're having a hard time aiming through the flames!" the agent yells back in reply. "The fire is spreading faster than expected, and the sprinklers aren't kicking in yet, I think the fucking robots are somehow preventing the sprinklers from—"

Roth stands in front of the Comscreen waiting for the agent to continue, only to realize the video call is completely frozen due to the Splitwall technology interfering with the reception to the room. The frozen image of the SMID agent flickers out and switches to the Convex video call logo screen.

Alessa zooms her sight to get a closer look at the security monitors and notices a group of Splitbots is aiming their Handlights at the ceiling, targeting the emergency sprinklers and preventing them from putting out the fire, completely jamming them.

"Piece of shit!" Roth screams. He punches the Comscreen repeatedly until a web of cracks splinter across the glass. He pulls his hand away, now dripping with blood. The agents near the door shuffle uneasily as Roth rips the Comscreen off the wall. A shard of protruding glass from the shattered screen slices his other hand open.

"Fuck!" Roth hisses and throws the Comscreen monitor, which slams onto a lush white rug off to the right side of Roth's desk—something crunches underneath it. Roth stomps on the Comscreen a couple times, then looks down at both of his bloody hands, catching his breath.

During Roth's tantrum, Alessa looks to the others—Milney, Siwek, Fola, Taffon, Bara, Veda, and Ke—and databursts to the group: "We're going to be alright. Stay still. No sudden movements."

Bara's eyes go completely wide as she starts looking around at the group excitedly, turning her head back and forth, glancing at each one of the others.

"Bara," Alessa databursts, mildly frustrated that Bara's doing the exact opposite of what she just asked. "What's wrong?"

"Are you guys not getting that?" Bara databursts. "It's Keo! His databurst line just connected to mine. Aren't you guys getting a databurst from him? He's livebursting to me somehow, I'm watching it right now!"

A unanimous 'no' from the group is databursted in reply. Alessa turns her head to look at Bara, tilting her head in confusion.

"Are you sure?" Alessa databursts. "None of us have been able to connect to him since they extracted his Soultomb."

Bara's excitement turns to a look of horror, her digital mouth hanging open as she stares forward blankly. "I'm sure," she databursts. "Something bad is happening."

Before any of the others can respond, the room fills with the deafening sound of gunfire exploding from the hallway.

Ty controls the Splitbots in the front to blast a Gravipulse. A wave of energy blasts through the hallway, completely disintegrating the bullets and picking up flames with it. The first Gravipulse slams into the ballistic shields in the front row and rips them out of the SMID agents' hands. The wave of fire the Gravipulse picks up scatters and disintegrates above the Splithelmet-covered heads of the agents.

Without wasting any time, Ty blasts two more Gravipulses through the hallway. The attacks quickly destroy the agents' Holoshields.

Ty shoots another massive Gravipulse—this time using what looks like the collective power of at least one thousand of the Splitbots—delivering one final blow.

The SMID agents are torn to shreds as the Gravipulse plows through them, crushing through their torsos. Alessa can hear the screams of the agents as the ones near the back begin to turn and run away before the Gravipulse reaches them.

Some of the agents stupidly try to jump up and over the shimmering wave of energy, but their bodies explode like fireworks, sending their innards out through the tops of their skulls.

The fear on Bara's face intensifies as she begins to squirm uncomfortably in her seat. She is still entranced by the liveburst she's receiving from Keo, seemingly unaware of what just happened in the hallway.

"Bara," Alessa databursts again. "Try to relax."

"It's coming in small bursts, cutting in and out," Bara databursts. "Keo's liveburst. They're hurting him! They're taking him out of the Soultomb. They're putting him in some sort of vessel, examining his soul!"

"What do you mean they're examining his soul?" Ke databursts, turning to look directly at Bara, his digital eyebrows scrunched in confusion behind his glasses.

Alessa glances at Roth to see if he's noticed, but he's just standing completely still in front of the monitors, dumbfounded as he watches thousands of his most highly trained men—the strongest force in the world—get obliterated by a single Gravipulse that's ripping its way through the hallway just outside of his office. He slumps over, hopelessly defeated as reality sets in.

The splattering of blood is apparently almost enough to put out the fire, and the flames start to die down. Dark clouds of smoke fill the hallway. Ty controls the group of Splitbots jamming the fire sprinklers to release their Handlight holds on the sprinklers, allowing a storm of water to erupt from the ceiling. The flames die out in a pool of blood-tinged water.

"Fuck," Roth mutters to himself. "Fuck fuck *fuck!*" He punches another monitor, doing no damage this time beyond a smear of blood on the screen.

The image on the primary screen reveals Ty and twenty of the other Splitbots facing the door to Roth Nin's office, arms pointed out in front of them, Handlights glowing. Ty controls them to blast a Gravipulse directed at the door, but the Splitwall technology prevents any sort of initial damage.

The two SMID agents standing guard by the door sprint over to Roth just as Ty blasts a second Gravipulse at the door.

"Sir, we need to get you underground in the emergency bunker," one of the agents says sternly. Roth turns to face him, grimacing as he holds his bloody hand. "The Splitwalls can only withstand so much pressure. The tech will fail if they send a Gravipulse even half the strength of what they just shot at our men at the door."

The agents pull the white rug next to Roth's desk away, revealing a rectangular escape-bunker door outlined on the floor. On the left side of the door, there is a small biometric fingerprint and facial ID scanner screen built into the floor, along with a touchscreen keypad underneath it—both of which have subtle cracks splintering through the glass.

The two agents look up at each other, then at Roth.

"Sir," one of them says, pointing at the shattered screen. "We have a problem. I'm guessing this happened when you threw the Comscreen, or—"

"You've got to be fucking kidding me," Roth says as he kneels on the floor and presses his bloody hand to the shattered screen, drops of blood filling in the cracks on the screen. "It might still work. Surely it still works."

"Scan failed," a synthetic voice chimes from the floor. "Error 1031. Obstruction on screen."

"God damn it," Roth groans as he continues to attempt to scan his hands, further smearing blood on the screen. He bends down closely to the screen in an attempt to activate its facial recognition scanner.

"The blood, sir," the SMID agent says. "There's too much blood on the screen. Do you have the backup code?"

"*No* I don't have the fucking *backup code,*" Roth says, desperately looking up at the SMID agents. "I never needed the fucking code before. I only use scanning tech. And I've never even needed to use this underground bunker in the first place. I forgot it was even here! I wouldn't have stomped the Comscreen monitor right on top of it like a maniac if I remembered. Why didn't you guys stop me? You should have reminded me!"

Ty controls 300 additional Splitbots to line up behind him to join in on the Gravipulse attack on the door. They blast another wave of energy.

Alessa begins to hear a repeated crunching sound, followed by the loud whining noise of the Splitwall technology working ferociously to combat the Gravipulse coming from outside the room. The structural wall itself begins to crumble.

"Try anything!" the SMID agent yells. "We're running out of time!"

Roth nervously enters a code on the keypad—nothing.

"Error 27," the synthetic voice chimes. "Improper passcode. Please try again."

"Mother fuckers!" Roth screams as he stands up and stomps furiously at the keypad.

The main structural wall of the room completely collapses, revealing Ty and the other Splitbots standing in the hall, arms still out with Handlights activated. The blue glow of Ty's face shines brightly through the transparent yellow sheen of the Splitwall—now the only thing separating the two groups.

Ty switches to DroneMode while the others continue to send Gravipulse after Gravipulse into the protective barrier of the Splitwall, the yellow flashing to red each time a pulse hits. While in DroneMode, Ty produces a continuous Resolaze, aiming at the horizontal graphene strip near the top of the Splitwall. It snaps, causing it to recoil back into the slit in the corner of the wall that it came out of.

Roth turns to face Alessa. "There are hundreds of Splitbases across the globe—each with its own SMID army," he says, his jaw clenched as he shakes his head, his black eyes staring directly into Alessa's. "You might have us outnumbered right now, but you won't for long."

Alessa says nothing and instead continues to watch the horizontal lines of the Splitwall break, one by one.

Three more to go.

Snap.

Two more.

Snap.

One.

The final horizontal line snaps, and the horde of Splitbots releases another Gravipulse—one final blow to the mysterious yellow shield—followed by a loud, powering-down sound.

The protective barrier of Splitwall technology disappears back into the slits of the wall. Ty switches out of DroneMode and takes a few slow steps forward, and the group of Aura-Fi-controlled Splitbots follows him as he stares directly at Roth and the SMID agents.

"Release them," Ty says, pointing to Alessa and the others, still strapped into their seats on the hovering platform. "*Now.*"

40

ALESSA

Roth walks over to the hovering platform cautiously, arms out as if to say, 'don't hurt me.' Ty is pointing his already-charged Handlights at Roth. The two SMID officers draw their guns and aim them directly at Ty.

"Easy now," Roth says, smiling nervously. His lips quiver uncontrollably and his bloody hands shake. Blood streams down both of his arms. He looks over to the SMID officers. "Put your guns down!" he yells, which causes his squeaky voice to crack. He quickly turns his attention back to Ty, smiling again. "No need for your Handlights, either. We'll do whatever you want, and we'll start by freeing your friends here."

Roth is now standing off to the right side of the hovering platform. He presses some buttons on the platform's control screen. Suddenly the black and green straps release their grips on Alessa and the others, immediately freeing their arms and legs.

"See!" Roth says. He smiles his phony smile, then walks quickly back over to the SMID agents and stands fearfully behind them.

Alessa and the others quickly stand up, jump off the platform, and immediately congregate next to Ty. Taffon—who has always been a mother figure to Ty—stops in front of him. She stares at him pridefully as digital tears well in her eyes, her typical sternness transforming into a rare display of emotion.

"I'm so proud of you," Taffon whispers. Her wide, tear-filled eyes focus directly on Ty's as he smiles warmly back at her. "We all are."

Before Ty can respond, Taffon walks to stand off to the side with the rest of the group, blinking away the tears on her digital face screen.

"Ty!" Bara yells. Her hands are tapping impatiently on the sides of her legs—a nervous twitch Alessa recognizes as unique to Bara. "They took Keo's soul somewhere else. They're running tests on it. They're hurting him!"

"We need to hurry," Ke says solemnly, his eyes darting fearfully between Alessa and Ty.

Ty redirects his attention to Roth and the SMID agents, glaring at them intensely, his eyes bulging and jaw clenched.

"Take us to wherever your other agents took our brother's soul," Ty growls, pointing his Handlights threateningly at Roth.

"Okay, *okay*!" Roth says, stepping forward again, arms still up. "Follow me. Your friend's soul is in the lab, just down the hall. We'll take you over there, no problem. No problem at all. They're not *hurting* him either, just observing him. That's all."

The two SMID agents speed up in front of Roth and lead the way to the destroyed wall to the hallway.

Roth stops walking and turns to face Ty. "We just need you to move the um . . . the others," Roth says politely, smiling as he gestures at the thousands of Ty's Aura-Fi-controlled Splitbots who still block the way out of the room. Their numbers sprawl throughout the massive corridor.

Ty looks over at the thousands of Splitbots, mentally controlling them to disperse to either side of the hallway, clearing a perfect central path for them to walk through as the Splitbots line up along the hallway walls. They splash up bloody water as they walk along the soaked floors.

"Like Moses parting the Red Sea!" Roth laughs nervously and looks at the SMID agents expectantly, hoping they will join in his laughter. The SMID agents just continue walking silently.

"Sorry, dumb joke," Roth says and shakes his head as he quickly catches up to the agents. Ty and Alessa follow behind Roth out to the hallway, with Milney, Ke, Siwek, Taffon, Bara, Veda, and Fola following closely behind them.

"I knew you could do it," Alessa databursts to Ty as they walk through the hallway.

Ty gives Alessa a proud smile and a wink. They soon approach the lab, the SMID agents stopping in front of its large, locked door.

One of the agents places his thumb on a triangular sensor next to the door, which triggers a full-body scan. Various neon blue lasers shoot from the sensor—a perfect, horizontal line of light moving smoothly down from the agent's head to his toes.

The lasers disappear, and the triangular sensor changes from red to green.

"Access granted," a synthetic voice chimes as the door slides upwards, revealing the massive lab behind it: an endless array of surgical tables, fluid-filled body vessels, and naked cadavers hooked up to ever-populating screens. The bloody water in the hallway flows smoothly into the lab, spreading along the floor.

Hundreds of doctors and scientists—each wearing a lab coat and a Splithelmet—stand motionlessly, watching carefully as Roth leads the way into the lab. His cocky, power-hungry demeanor begins to return as he enters a room filled with subordinates.

The SMID agents, Alessa, and the others follow closely behind him.

"Listen up!" Roth yells, standing in front of the crowd of doctors and scientists. He wipes his bloody hands on his sweat-stained undershirt and lets out a long, frustrated, and tired sigh before he continues. "We need to stop the transfer of the Soultomb immediately. We need to show the other Splitbots here that their friend's soul is . . . *safe.*"

"But sir," one of the doctors in the crowd says. "We can't stop the—"

Roth slams his fist on the surgical table on his right side. The fat of the elderly male cadaver occupying it jiggles. "I said stop. The transfer. Immediately!" Roth yells, his awful voice screeching now.

"Bara," Alessa databursts to the group. "Is Keo still livebursting to you?"

"He's trying, but it's nothing coherent yet," Bara replies. "He's trying to say something. The last two words he sent were 'Moonshot' and 'Splitsender.' Those devices Roth was talking about."

"Take us to him!" Ke screams, interrupting the Gridliners' private databurst discussion and causing a few of the doctors to flinch.

One of the doctors steps forward out of the group. "Follow me," the doctor says—a raspy, female voice emanating from the speakers on her Splithelmet. She walks quickly as she leads the group to a smaller room all the way in the back of the lab.

Alessa notices this doctor's lab coat is slightly different from those worn by the others, the words 'CHIEF DOCTOR' stitched onto a pocket on her chest. UV light glows off of her white lab coat as she passes the fluid-filled, body-holding vessels on the way.

The chief doctor stops in front of the small room and looks through its window. Inside of the room is an additional lone body vessel with Keo's soul on display inside of it, now extracted from the Soultomb.

There are thousands of clamps stretching Keo's soul out, deforming the usual blob-like state of the soul into a thin, purple sheet—it shines wetly like a rolled-out piece of slime. A couple of scientists inside the room are busy examining it and taking notes.

Keo's soul is jerking in place in what looks like a desperate attempt to free itself from the clamps, with no success. It twitches erratically like an exposed piece of muscle that just had salt poured onto it.

A set of robotic arms is moving precisely inside of the vessel, performing a scan on every single point of Keo's stretched soul. With each movement, another piece of information is displayed on the monitor attached to the vessel, along with a progress bar reading '47%'—and going up.

Bara gasps as she rushes over to the window to get a better look into the room. "They're hurting him!" she yells again. "Stop them!"

The chief doctor presses a button on the wall and speaks into an intercom. The note-taking doctors and scientists start at the sudden noise.

"Shut it down," she says, her voice urgent and commanding. "That's an order."

"We're almost halfway done, Anita," one of the doctors observing Keo's soul says. "Are you absolutely positive you want us to stop?"

"Oh for fuck's sake, they're not going to listen to you," Roth hisses at the chief doctor. He steps in front of the door, which slides open automatically.

"Stop this immediately!" Roth yells as he storms into the room, the automatic door closing behind him. Alessa and the others can still hear him, his voice being picked up by the intercom. "We have no other choice. The other robots will kill us if we don't. Got it?"

The doctor next to Roth looks over at Alessa and the others through the window, his Splithelmet concealing whatever look there might be on his face.

"Pull it," the doctor says, turning toward a scientist analyzing data on the body vessel's screen.

"Keo is trying to say something," Bara says out loud, trembling. Alessa and the others look at her, waiting.

"Tell us through databurst," Alessa databursts. "We shouldn't allow the humans to hear it."

"Back away," Bara databursts, taking a few steps backwards. "He's telling us to back away from the window."

"Why?" Alessa demands.

"He's saying something about the circle of Gridat," Bara continues. "I'm having a hard time understanding him. He's saying the doctors are unknowingly going to destroy his soul and it's going to transform him into something greater—a new mosaic. He's saying that this is the next step for him in the Gridat life cycle. He's saying this is his chance to help us. He said he's getting visions, like you did earlier in the realm, Alessa. He's telling us to back away from the window. The transformation is going to cause an explosion."

A new mosaic? Alessa thinks.

Alessa and the others begin walking backwards slowly, confused, until they are up against one of the surgical tables thirty feet away from the window. The chief doctor notices them backing away in unison and turns to face them.

"I'm pressing cancel on the terminal but nothing's happening!" one of the scientists yells from inside of the room. "The process won't stop! I'm trying!"

The clamps holding Keo's soul are struggling to detach, mechanically twitching and writhing. The entire vessel shakes.

"What the hell is going on?" Roth asks as a loud, beeping noise begins. An emergency warning appears on the monitor attached to the vessel.

"I don't know!" the scientist yells. "It's just not *letting go*. The soul is not letting the clamps release!"

"Keo is telling us to disable the door," Bara databursts. "To contain the explosion."

Without question, Alessa silently targets the door with her Handlights, using their gravitational forces to expand the door horizontally until it is impossible to open. The door attempts to open and close, stopping and starting, but it fails to open even an inch, and sparks begin to fly out from the door tracks.

The chief doctor is now also carefully backing away, far from the window and the now-destroyed door. The crowd of doctors and scientists on the far end of the lab watches intently, silent and unsure what they should do.

Keo's soul is now slamming around violently inside of the vessel, smacking into its interior glass, nearly toppling the eight-foot-tall vessel.

"We gotta get the fuck out of here," Roth says. He quickly turns away from the vessel and runs to the door in an attempt to leave. He immediately notices the malfunctioning door, his eyes wide as the reality of being trapped in the room sets in.

"Hey!" he yells as he runs over to the window. The other doctors and scientists are still behind him working frantically to stop what Keo's soul is doing inside of the vessel.

Roth pounds on the window, leaving smears of blood on the glass as he looks desperately at Alessa and Ty, his once-suntanned skin now disturbingly pale.

"Let us out of here!" Roth yells. "You need me. I . . . I'll work with you guys! I'll tell you everything. Anything you want to know about the work we're doing here."

Alessa feels a tap on her shoulder. She turns around, now face-to-face with the chief doctor.

"Don't listen to him," she says, her face still concealed by the Splithelmet. "Let him die in there. We hate him more than you do, trust us. He's so out of touch with what's going on here that he's just dead weight at this point anyways." She turns, pointing out to the rest of the doctors and scientists in the room. "It's us that you want on your side. We're the ones doing all the work."

"You bitch!" Roth yells, still pounding on the window. He picks up a chair and throws it at the glass, which remains undamaged.

Inside of the vessel, Keo's soul is beginning to tear, ripping in every direction it's being pulled by the clamps, splitting into millions of smaller pieces, dividing and dividing until the vessel itself fills with a blindingly bright light and the group can't see Keo's soul anymore.

The vessel suddenly stops bouncing, and the white light inside of it reverses in on itself, leaving nothing but an incomprehensibly dark circle—a perfectly round *orb*—hovering in the center of the vessel like a mini black hole as the clamps that were once stretching Keo's soul dangle next to it.

The LED lights in the lab flicker, and the orb begins to vibrate in place, the dangling clamps slowly being drawn to the center of the vessel as if magnetically attracted to the black, hovering orb that Keo's soul transformed into.

Suddenly, the entire vessel appears to collapse in on itself, sucked into the black orb. Roth grabs onto a pipe on the wall and hangs on for dear life as the orb continues to swallow up everything else inside of the room: all of the advanced computers and technology, the data-filled screens, even the other doctors and scientists, until the orb—Keo's soul—finally slams into the wall directly behind it, causing a massive explosion in the small room.

The window shatters into millions of microscopic pieces, flying over Alessa and the others as they shield themselves from the explosion, a wave of heat flowing out of the room. A collection of horrified screams comes from the group of doctors and scientists on the other side of the lab.

Roth Nin's body hangs lifelessly from the shards of glass sticking up from the window sill, blood running in streams down the wall. Dead upon impact, his skin smoking and charred to a crisp, his hands ripped off of his arms, still gripping—*melted*—to the metal pipe on the wall.

The dust and debris from the detonation begins to settle. Alessa gets up to examine the room where the explosion occurred—it's completely empty now, and everything else inside of it has disappeared.

The wall all the way in the back of the room—the one the black orb that was Keo's soul slammed into—begins to split and crack, and lines neatly spread across the wall, creating a series of perfect squares.

Alessa's mouth hangs open in awe on her digital face screen as she continues to watch the squares on the wall begin to shine with that familiar purple glow. The chief doctor and the rest of the Splitbots gather slowly behind Alessa, watching as the thousands of squares on the wall begin to move in and out slowly like a wave, in the exact same way that the mosaic portal at the Morgan's household does. The same exact way that the portals did on Raoq.

Alessa lifts her leg carefully over the window sill and walks slowly towards the mosaic. She stops directly in front of it and lifts her arm to touch the wall. Her touch sends a liquid-like ripple from the center to the edges of the wall. The purple light glows brighter where Alessa's hand is making contact, and even brighter as she sticks her arm through, feeling the same tingling sensation that she's now used to.

"Unbelievable," she whispers quietly to herself as she pulls her arm back out of the mosaic.

The others can barely hear her over the loud sounds of the wall, entranced by the new mosaic tiles, which are oscillating faster, and then slowing down again to their normal speed until the purple light glows through the lines of the wall, even brighter now, lighting up the room.

Alessa turns to face the group. They still stare at her in awe from the other side of the shattered window.

"Oh my god," the chief doctor says as she walks towards the window, her raspy voice wavering slightly.

"Is that . . ." Ty begins to say, his voice trailing off, entranced as he stares at the light beaming from the wall behind Alessa.

"A portal," Alessa says, unable to believe the words coming out of her mouth. "Just like the one that brought our souls to Earth in the first place."

41

ALESSA

Bara jumps over the window sill, letting out a blood-curdling, primal scream as she runs over to the slowly shifting tiles of the newly-created mosaic. She falls to her knees next to Alessa and directly faces the purple light of the portal. She sobs. Alessa kneels down next to her and gently puts her arm around Bara's shaking Splitbot body.

Ke walks into the room next, slowly, a few digital tears streaming down his face. He stops in front of the portal. The others stand back on the other side of the shattered window, giving Ke a moment to process the situation.

"I love you, Keo," Ke says as he touches the glowing tiles of the mosaic. "I'm proud to say you were my linebrother."

Bara gets up off the floor to wrap her arms tightly around Ke. Alessa watches, fighting back her own urge to cry as Ke and Bara sob in each other's arms.

Suddenly, Bara turns away from Ke, stretches her arms out, and carefully touches the moving tiles. She lets out a long sigh and wipes her digital tears away in an attempt to compose herself.

"Keo and I were partners," Bara says quietly, nearly whispering as she turns to face Alessa. "Like you and Ty. We made it official not long before the KitD'ul happened. We weren't keeping it a secret; we were *excited* to tell everyone. Keo told Ke immediately. But then the KitD'ul happened, and everything has been moving so fast since we arrived on this planet, and—and—and—"

Bara begins to cry again, harder now than she was moments ago. "We loved each other," Bara manages to say between sobs. Ke places his hand on her back, gently moving it in a circular pattern in an attempt to relax Bara.

"I . . . I had no idea," Alessa says, finally allowing her own digital tears to stream down her face as she pulls Bara in for a hug. "I'm so, so sorry, Bara."

"It's not your fault," Bara says, her voice muffled with her head buried in Alessa's chest. "There's nothing we could have done."

"And maybe Keo was right," Ke says, sniffling. "Maybe *becoming* the portal really was the next step in the Gridat cycle. Maybe this . . . transformation . . . is what we've been looking for all along. Maybe Keo somehow discovered this when they started experimenting on him and he knowingly sacrificed himself. He could have survived whatever they were doing to him, but he *chose* to do this. For us."

"What do you mean, '*for us*'?" Bara asks. "Why would he choose this?"

"To help us get the other trapped souls out of the realm," Ke says. Then, without warning, he steps through the portal for a moment. He comes back out immediately—the tiles glowing as they oscillate. "The realm . . . the sea in the sky . . . it's all there. It appears the Morgan mosaic isn't too far off in the distance, either. So think about it. We have access to a new portal, and therefore the afterlife realm, right in front of us. We originally thought we were going to take all of those Splitbots out there in the hallway *back* to the portal at the Morgan household in order to get more Gridliner souls out of the realm, which would mean potentially having to fight more armies of SMID agents and risking capture again, or worse. But now all we have to do is have all of the others walk through this new portal here, and we can get it done right now, all thanks to Keo."

"He's right," Alessa says. "Keo did what he did to *help* us."

"I hope so," Bara says as she steps away from Alessa, continuing to examine the portal. "At least this way all of his pain won't be for nothing. Can I just . . . can I just have a moment alone here?"

"Of course," Alessa says somberly, and then walks out of the room with Ke towards the others, leaving Bara behind with the portal. Bara kneels to the floor to give the Gridat, silhouetted by the purple light.

"Is Bara okay?" Ty asks, sharing the same look of concern as the rest of the group.

"She's strong," Alessa says, her lips pulled tightly together. "Just like we all are. She'll be fine. She just needs a moment."

The chief doctor with the raspy voice takes off her Splithelmet to reveal the face of a middle-aged woman. She quickly fixes her straight, black hair, allowing her bangs to fall forward and cover a unique set of small, circular scars stretching across her forehead from temple to temple—a trail of neatly organized dots.

"Everyone stay calm," the chief doctor shouts to the group of nervously shifting doctors standing awkwardly on the opposite side of the lab, whispering amongst themselves. "They're not going to hurt us."

The doctor turns to face Alessa. Her expression reveals that she too is genuinely shaken by the scene that has unfolded in front of them. Her eyes are red and damp with tears.

"I'm sorry," the chief doctor says, shaking her head. "I'm sorry about your friend."

"He was more than a friend to us," Milney snaps, turning quickly to respond to the doctor. "And *our friend* has a name. His name was Keo."

"I understand your anger," the doctor says. "For what it's worth, I advised against all of this. Unfortunately, Roth is much higher up on the totem pole than I am, and what he says goes. But if it were up to—"

"Who are you?" Alessa asks abruptly, interrupting the doctor.

"I'm Dr. Anita Garber," she says. "Chief doctor of this Splitbase. All these doctors and scientists in this room report to me."

Alessa doesn't respond, momentarily staring intensely at the doctor. Her head tilts slightly as she analyzes her body language and silently tries to determine if she can be trusted.

"Look, I'll be honest with you," Anita says, breaking the silence. "I never wanted to be in this position. I had my doubts about Split Meridian from the beginning. But work for doctors became so depressing and hostile over the years through pandemic after pandemic that I just couldn't do it anymore. When I got the opportunity to join the Meridian doctors, I jumped at it. I felt maybe my suspicions were just paranoia and that maybe I would be able to use my talents for some good . . . that I really could help provide hope for humanity. But all this," she says, turning and pointing to the body vessels in the large lab, "all of this is unnatural. We're so close, yet so far away, from any real understanding of digitizing human consciousness. I think it's out of our grasp. What is happening with you guys, though . . . this all seems like it was meant to be. And I think us working together really can lead to some mutually beneficial good, making all of this vile research worth something."

"What makes you think we should work together?" Alessa asks. "What do you even know about us?"

"Well, I heard everything you told Roth in his office. He had his Comscreens open the whole time, and security was broadcasting the live feed of it on Convex," Anita says, pointing to her Splithelmet, which now lies on the floor. "Higher-ups can tune in. The feed comes right through the speakers inside our helmets. I heard everything up until the com system was jammed."

"So you know what this is, then?" Alessa asks, pointing at the mosaic portal in the other room.

"Yes," Anita says emphatically. "Or at least I think I do. The way you explained it to Roth, it all makes perfect sense. It's *crazy*, for sure, but it makes sense. And what happened just now proves that. From what I understand, the creation of these portals is directly correlated to the destruction of a soul. That would explain how this new portal opened . . . Whatever happened just now with your friend's soul, *Keo's* soul, was enough to destroy it, or at least transform it into this portal in front of us now."

"Just because you understand doesn't automatically mean we should trust you," Alessa says. She steps closer to Anita. "Why should we trust that you really want to help us?"

"For starters," Anita says, pointing at Roth Nin's lifeless body, still dangling on the window sill, "I'm the one who told you to let Roth die in there. So there's that. I also plan on setting things straight with the public by leaking any and all confidential information which will expose how vile Split Meridian has truly become, for the world to see. But maybe most importantly, the way you all care for each other proves, to me at least, that you're more than just sentient machines. You all have displayed a level of emotional intelligence toward each other that far exceeds anything I've seen from humans in a very, *very* long time. You only partake in fighting as a last resort, and the only reason you've resorted to violence at all has been strictly a means of survival. All I can say is that, if humans and robots are to coexist, we would be lucky to be able to do it with an artificial intelligence that shows more humanity than actual humans do."

Alessa stares at Anita, the wide eyes on her digital face screen squinting as she thinks.

"What do you all think?" Alessa databursts to the group. "Can we trust her?"

"I've been carefully analyzing her every move." Veda replies. "She hasn't shown any signs of deception."

"Same," Ty databursts. "I think she's being truthful."

"She seems to genuinely be upset that they have hurt us," Ke databursts.

"She was crying," Fola databursts. "After what happened to Keo."

"Also, having someone with the amount of information she has on our side could be of great value to us as we move forward," Siwek adds.

"Okay," Alessa databursts. "So we're all in agreement?"

"Yes," everyone databursts simultaneously, including Bara, who has now joined the group, seemingly calmer now.

"We'll work with you," Alessa finally says out loud. "What about the others standing on the other side of the lab? Can we trust them? Do you vouch for them?"

"Trust me," Anita says. "Everyone in this room comes from a similar background to mine. These are the only good people involved with Split Meridian. The doctors and scientists that died in that room with Roth, the ones he had working on Keo's soul, those were the only doctors willing to do what Roth wanted to do to that soul, and those doctors and scientists just happened to be the only ones he hired. His little puppets he brought in once I started to push back against his demands. He even gave them their own little room in the lab . . . It's poetic justice that they all died in there together, really. The rest of the doctors are all people that *I* chose to have as a part of *my* staff. We all feel guilty, but we were pressured to work for Split Meridian. None of us ever thought it would get to this point."

"I'll take your word then," Alessa says, letting herself relax as she takes a step back. "For now. But I'm afraid we're wasting too much time. We have a perfect opportunity in front of us with the creation of the new portal. Let's not waste it."

"Alessa," Ty says. "Are we ready to send the other Splitbots through? I'm still connected via Aura-Fi. I can send all 9,989 of them through right now. Just say the word."

"Yes," Alessa says, nodding quickly. She turns to face the group. "We are about to take one giant step forward in our plan. Words cannot describe how thankful I am for all of you. Ty, we wouldn't have this opportunity today without your bravery, and we are all thankful for that. We also lost one of our own today: a brother to Ke, a partner to Bara, and a special friend to us all. He made the ultimate sacrifice for us to be able to continue our mission. Let's use this pain to move forward stronger than ever. Let's do it for Keo."

"For Keo," Milney says, his deep voice unusually soft as he puts his arm around Bara, who is crying again.

The group kneels in unison to give the Gridat.

"For Keo," Ty repeats as he stands up. He begins to tap a few commands on his Kaxelotab. His head jerks back momentarily as he begins to control the other 9,989 Splitbots.

"Anita," Alessa says, "can you have your doctors open the door to the lab, please?"

"Oh, yes. Of Course," Anita says, quickly running over to the group on the other side of the lab.

Anita begins to issue instructions to the hundreds of doctors and scientists. One of the doctors immediately runs over to the main entrance to the lab and presses a button to open the door. A cluster of a hundred other doctors begins to clear a path for the robots to walk down, pushing as many of the surgical tables out of the way as they can quickly.

Suddenly, all of the doctors and scientists stop and turn to watch the thousands of Splitbots begin to walk through the lab, synchronized in a single-file line.

"Keo would be proud," Ke says. He smiles as he watches the Splitbots get closer to where they stand.

The group moves out of the way to clear the space in front of the shattered window. The first of the Aura-Fi-controlled Splitbots jumps over the window sill and walks smoothly in the direction of the mosaic portal.

The next one follows. And the next one. And the next one.

Alessa is overcome by a desire to witness what is about to happen in the realm. She jumps over the shattered window sill as well, catching up to the first Splitbot before it gets to the portal.

For Keo, Alessa thinks.

She steps in front of the first Splitbot, her eyes gleaming as she leads the way through the mosaic—its purple, beautifully glowing tiles moving in its usual wavelike motion. She steps through, and a long line of 9,989 others follows closely behind her, one-by-one.

42

ALESSA

A beatific smile spreads across Alessa's digital face screen. She stares up at the swirling, purple sky as if it's the most beautiful thing she's ever seen. The sky is becoming active—multiple flares begin to blast outwards and back up to the mass of blobs, hungry to latch, as various souls become aware of the new intruders entering the realm.

Not much longer, Alessa thinks, wondering which of the countless swirling souls up in the sea in the sky are her fellow Gridliners.

Far off in the distance—a little over ten miles, Alessa estimates—the mosaic to the Morgan household can be seen, its glowing purple light reflecting brightly off the white sand of the realm. It stands alone on the sand sheet landscape, like a small boat on an infinite ocean.

Alessa turns to face the newly created portal—which shimmers brightly as the Aura-Fi-controlled Splitbots continue to walk through. Only thirty Splitbots have entered so far, taking about one second each to cross through the portal.

"Ty," Alessa databursts. "At the rate the Splitbots are entering the realm, it will take three hours to have all of them walk through. We need to move significantly faster. Maybe we should switch them to DroneMode. They'll be able to move four times faster that way."

"Good idea," Ty databursts. "Switching now. The portal is wide enough to fit probably twenty drones through at a time, at least."

Alessa watches the clusters of drones begin to fly quickly through the portal, entering the realm in quick bursts, until all 9,989 Splitbots have entered. They hover in a neatly organized pattern of rows of 500, covering a sliver of the otherwise-empty landscape.

"Well, that worked," Ty databursts. "Just under five minutes. Not bad! Any latching yet? Aura-Fi says I still have complete control over all of them."

"Not yet," Alessa responds. "But it should start happening any minute now. Let's switch all of them back out of DroneMode. The Splitbots might be easier targets to latch to if we have them in their standard form."

"You got it," Ty databursts.

All at once, the Splitbots switch out of DroneMode—kicking up little clouds of white sand as their bodies extend downwards out of their heads and their feet touch the cold, mysterious soil of the realm.

A portion of the sky above the group of Splitbots begins to swirl, creating a cyclone-like pattern as it spins.

Suddenly, a stream of Gridliner souls begins to shoot down from the sky, quickly and efficiently latching to each of the Splitbots, row-by-row as if being mass-produced on an assembly line.

"It's happening!" Alessa databursts. Tears stream down her face screen, and she smiles proudly.

She continues to stare in awe, her hand now covering her mouth as she watches a ripple of blue light flow through the rows of Splitbot face screens—like thousands of dominoes toppling over—as each of the Splitbots is joined with a soul.

The crowd of Splitbots begins to slowly shuffle in place, looking down at their hands and turning to face each other. The slow movements quickly become expressions of an overwhelming sense of joy as all of them begin jumping with excitement, hugging each other, and talking with the ones closest to them. The hubbub culminates in some loud, garbled conglomeration of speech.

Alessa's smile turns to a confused frown as her attention is pulled from the exuberant crowd of celebrating Splitbots and she notices something strange about the sky above them.

An empty, circular void in the sky can be seen in the exact section from which the Gridliners' souls were shooting down, as if the stretched portion of the sky those 9,989 souls occupied is going to remain vacant, unfilled.

Alessa becomes entranced. She feels drawn to the black circle in the sky, which looks back down at her like an eyeball—the black circle a dilated pupil, the surrounding, swirling sky a purple iris.

She zooms her sight into the void, unable to see anything but pure darkness.

"Everything good?" Ty databursts.

"Yeah," Alessa databursts. "I'm noticing something weird, though. Something in the sky. There's an . . . *opening* . . . of some sort, in the spot where the Gridliner souls were shooting down from. Like the part of the sky that held their souls is just missing now."

"An opening?" Ty databursts. "To what?"

"I . . ." Alessa databursts, ". . . I don't know. Whatever's behind the firmament of souls that makes up the sky as we currently know it, I guess. There's something beyond—"

"Alessa!" yells a hoarse, husky female voice—one that Alessa immediately recognizes as her old friend, Olos—snapping Alessa out of her trance. Alessa looks away from the sky and spots Olos running full speed out of the crowd of Splitbots. She tackles Alessa before she can respond.

"This feels so good! I can't believe it!" Olos yells, laughing with excitement as she squeezes Alessa tightly. She wraps her in a hug, and they lie together on the cold, white sand of the realm.

Olos pulls her face up above Alessa's, smiling while looking down at her. Her face, like the others, is exactly as it was on Raoq: she has freckles—something she customized herself to have on Raoq—dimples, and small, squinting eyes. She always looks like she's questioning something, which aligns with her blunt and brutally honest personality.

"Olos . . ." Alessa says, reaching out to touch her face. "It's so good to see you. I missed you so much. I am sorry you had to wait so long. I would've gotten you all out on the first round if I could've, I—"

"Oh, shut up!" Olos says, getting up off the ground and holding out her hand to pull Alessa up with her. "Don't be ridiculous. We're here now. That's all that matters."

The thousands of other Splitbots are quiet now, and they face Alessa and Olos as they brush sand off of their Splitbot bodies, waiting for Alessa to address them. Alessa looks up slowly at the group—like a musician on a stage staring out at a crowd of eager fans waiting for a concert to begin.

"It's so good to see you all!" Alessa yells out, her voice amplified by her Resosuit speakers. "Every single one of you. As we look around at each other for the first time since the KitD'ul, I want you all to think about what it means for us to have this second chance at life. What does that mean to *you*? I know what it means to me, and I know the responsibility I feel to do everything I can for us to continue to achieve what we've set out to do. And while it is a major step in the right direction for us all to be standing here right now in these powerful new bodies of ours, I want you to remember that there are still over a billion Gridliner souls remaining up there in the sky, waiting for *their* turn to experience this. We're going to have to keep pushing, keep doing everything we can to get every single one of our fellow Gridliners down here with us. Now, we don't have much time to waste. We'll have to organize quickly. I need you all to switch to DroneMode and fly back through the portal to the Splitbase. Spread out neatly throughout the lab and out into the hallway. I'll give directions for next steps after we're all through."

Without any hesitation, the entire group switches to DroneMode. They hover as they wait for Alessa to lead the way.

"After you," Olos databursts, in DroneMode next to Alessa.

Alessa smiles and nods, then immediately runs over to the portal. She steps through it and leads the way to the Splitbase—the thousands of drones follow behind her, flying through in groups of twenty at a time.

43

ALESSA

"I hate to take away from this moment," Ty says immediately after Alessa walks through the portal and back into the Splitbase. The first group of twenty drones flies past her and Ty, through the broken window, and out into the larger main room of the lab. The group of doctors watches them disperse in awe. "But Anita said the SMID is sending reinforcements from the surrounding Splitbases. No surprise. It sounds like they aren't going to give up without putting up a fight to subdue us. Anita said she's getting word that they'll be here by 1:15 am. It's a little past midnight right now."

Dr. Anita Garber walks over to Alessa and Ty, watching the groups of drones continue to fly through the mosaic portal and out into the primary lab, now starting to funnel out into the hallway as the room fills up.

"Now I'm getting word that it will probably be sooner," Anita says. "This is no joke, either. They will do whatever they can to put an end to this, even if that means bombing the entire fucking city."

"They wouldn't go that far immediately, would they?" Alessa asks. The drones continue to fly through the portal, shimmering brightly due to the constant activity.

"Not immediately, no," Anita says, shaking her head. "But they would if they needed to. And I've also been informed that the SMID traced this breach back to the Roundchamber and avatar Ty used—and therefore the Hodge family. You better believe the SMID will be going to their house as well."

"*Shit*," Alessa says, turning to Ty. "You need to go back and get them out of there."

"Are you crazy?" Anita asks. "Why would you—"

"It's the Gridliner way," Ty says. "David Hodge helped us; now we need to help him. There is no question about it. I wouldn't be standing here if it weren't for him . . . we are loyal to those who help us. And you can expect that for yourself too."

"We need to find the Morgan family as well," Alessa says. "We are just as indebted to them as we are to the Hodges, if not more so. Anita, do you know where they were taken?"

"No," Anita says. "They could be anywhere in the base. I have no idea where Roth ordered his SMID agents to take them."

"We'll divide up," Alessa says. "If we split into groups of 500, we'll be able to locate the Morgan family while simultaneously creating a nineteen-floor buffer before any SMID agents can get down here. It will be physically impossible for them to reach the remaining 400 of us on the bottom floor. Well, 399, since you'll be going back to the Hodge household, Ty."

The final group of drones flies through the portal, out of the lab, and into the hallway, where the others have dispersed.

"That was the last of them," Ty says. "Let's get moving."

"I'll databurst the plan," Alessa says quickly.

Anita cocks her head and gives Alessa a confused glance, watching her just stand there silently as she begins to databurst to the others.

"Everyone," Alessa databursts. "Welcome to the Splitbase. We're on the bottom floor, 350 levels underground. All of the humans down here can be trusted, but the same can't be said for any remaining employees on any of the other floors above us, if they haven't managed to escape yet. We will spread out. Four hundred of us will stay down here—including Milney, Siwek, Fola, Taffon, Bara, Veda, and Ke. The rest of you are to divide into groups of 500. As you work your way up to the top floor, I want you to search every square inch of this base and find where the SMID took the Morgan family. Bring them down here where it's safe with the rest of us immediately. The rest of you, once you get to the top, disable any of the main elevators and lifts, protect the entrances of the first nineteen floors, 500 of you per floor, and prevent any other threats from making their way down here by any means necessary. I've shared the estimated time of arrival for the next round of SMID agents. Move quickly and get to the top with some time to spare."

The robots in the hallway begin to fly away at full speed to enact Alessa's orders, quickly followed by the ones remaining in the lab until only 400 are left behind.

"What . . . what just happened?" Anita asks. "Where are they going?"

"They're doing what I told them to do," Alessa says. "We Gridliners can communicate through something called 'databursting.' It's a form of instant telepathic communication, taking a fraction of the time it takes to communicate verbally."

"Oh . . . sorry, I was just . . ." Anita says, scratching her head, seeming to be equally shocked about the Gridliner ability to databurst as she is about the large portal to the afterlife realm only a few feet away from her, ". . . confused. You and Ty just stopped talking. It's been no more than ten seconds of silence. How much were you able to communicate?"

"Everything you heard me and Ty talk about," Alessa says. "Dividing through the Splitbase, creating a nineteen-floor buffer, locating the Morgan family. All of it. And a little more."

"And you're not able to databurst to humans, I presume?" Anita asks.

"We cannot," Alessa says. "Whether or not this feature was left out by our creators deliberately is unknown."

"Oh my god. Oh my *god*," Anita says, pacing as if she's having a breakthrough. She lifts up her bangs, exposing the spotted, scarred skin underneath. "You see this scar across my forehead? For years, we've been trying to master a similar form of communication—Transferred Intelligence, TI, is what we call it. In a nutshell, it's a process using Handlight technology to transfer large amounts of information. Textbooks, documents, maps . . . anything a person wants to learn or memorize can be transferred instantaneously. This technology, once we master it, will be my biggest achievement—I was the first to research and understand it. Hell, I was the first to volunteer to be tested on, hence the scar."

"So you're saying I can databurst to you using my Handlights?" Alessa asks. "How? Everything else came naturally to me. I don't seem to have the ability to do this."

"Because you don't . . . yet. It is still a new achievement of ours and hasn't been implemented in the most recent update. But I can install the update on any of you, right now," Anita says. "Look, humans are stubborn. And if you are going to have any sort of success in carrying out your plans here on Earth, the SMID isn't the only group you need to worry about. The more human support you have, the fewer distractions you'll have carrying out whatever it is exactly that you want to do."

"We want a place we can call home," Alessa interrupts. "A place where we can enjoy our existence and live a life worth living. That's what we want. We know it can't be on Earth; we know that this planet's resources are used up. So for us, it's about figuring out where we *can* go. And as for the humans that help us, we plan to help them escape this hostile planet as well and give humans a place they can call their new home, too."

"Well, you'll have a lot of convincing ahead of you if you even want a fraction of the human population to trust you," Anita continues. "In order for them to believe anything you say, you have to truly blow them away with evidence. You have to be efficient in how you communicate or you'll lose their attention. Your body language has to be *just right* or they'll assume you're lying. The list goes on and on and on. My point is, if you can bypass all of this using TI, databursting, or whatever you want to call it, your success rate will skyrocket. If you can databurst to humans everything you know about the afterlife realm, Split Meridian's corruption, the evil of Roth Nin, and the Great Suicide hoax . . . you have a chance."

44
ALESSA

"It would definitely make things a whole lot easier if I were able to be updated to use this Transferred Intelligence feature on the Hodges," Ty says. "I say we do it."

"How long does the update take?" Alessa asks.

"At least twenty minutes," Anita says. "But the amount of time you'd save on communication alone would more than make up for any lost time in the process."

"Can the update be installed down here, or do we have to go somewhere else?" Alessa asks.

"We'll have to go up to the update center on Floor 261," Anita says. "It's down the hall from the Splitbot storage area."

"So we need to account for even more time, however long it takes us to get up there," Alessa says. "And the potential for any remaining threats up there. Any chance there are SMID agents still on that floor?"

"Floor 261 is made up mostly of Splitbot-related rooms," Anita says. "The Splitbot storage room takes up most of the floor. The update center takes up almost the rest of the remaining space. However, there's a few other offices located on that floor, which make up the Convex call center. They're the only other group on that floor. There's a chance some SMID agents might still be up there, but I can try to call the Convex operators to see if they're aware of any SMID agent activity. They can also scope out the floor's security cameras. Regardless, they'll be able to let us know if it's clear or not."

Dr. Anita Garber quickly presses a few buttons on her Kaxelotab, beginning a Convex video call. The Convex logo is projected as a hologram while she waits for an operator to answer the call.

The call rings five times. The Convex logo hologram disappears when no one answers the call and is replaced by a mid-air prompt to try again. Anita gestures to the left with her hand, signaling she wants to call again.

"Come on . . ." she mutters to herself, then looks up at Alessa. "The group of Splitbots you sent out to search the Splitbase. What floor are they on? Any chance they cleared Floor 200 yet?"

"They just hit Floor 300," Alessa says. "They're moving as fast as they can. It'll be about thirty more minutes until they get to Floor 261."

The Convex call continues to ring.

"That's too much time," Ty says. "If we're going to do this update we have to take our chances and start heading up there now. It doesn't matter how efficiently I can communicate with the Hodge family if the SMID gets to them before I do—if they haven't already."

Suddenly a hologram of a female operator is projected from Anita's Kaxelotab, answering the call.

"Hello?" the operator asks, breathing rapidly. Her brown hair is matted to her forehead, sticky with sweat, her eyes wide but blinking rapidly. "Can you hear me, Dr. Garber?"

Alessa recognizes the operator's voice, but can't quite put a finger on where she's heard it before.

"Yes, hi!" Anita says. "We need to do an emergency update on a Splitbot. Are there any more SMID agents up there?"

"I don't . . . I don't think so," the operator says. "But wait, are you . . . are you *helping* the robots? Did you not see what they've done to the base and the agents? The entire hallway up here is covered in blood. Oh god, it's awful . . . it—"

"I've seen more than you have," Anita says. Her face takes on a stern and commanding gaze reminiscent of that of a drill sergeant. She matches it with a strong, assertive tone, radiating authority. "The Splitbots are not the enemies. Roth Nin is dead, which means I am in charge of this Splitbase as of right now. You report to *me*, and only me. Do you understand?"

The operator stops blinking altogether, straightens her posture, and maintains direct eye contact with Anita, nodding her head silently.

"Good," Anita continues. "Now I need you to be clear. How many other operators are still up there with you?"

"All of us," the operator says. "Sorry, that wasn't clear, was it? By all of us I mean all of the Convex operators that were working today. A hundred and fifty total, including me. We went on lockdown as soon as we heard the first explosion down the hall. All of us were too afraid to leave, and we've been sitting up here ever since. Then we saw all the lifts and elevators were shut down, so we wouldn't be able to leave even if we wanted to at this point."

"Do a scan of the entire Floor 261," Anita says. "Is there anyone else up there—SMID agents, general security, maintenance, anyone?"

"One moment," the operator says, typing on a keypad outside of the video call's frame. "It appears the floor is clear. Just us up here."

"Okay," Anita says urgently. "Activate the Splitwalls at every entrance and disable the Splitwalls in the Splitbot storage area. Our only way to Floor 261 will be through the shattered windows of the Splitbot storage area. We'll be able to enter through those from the

Bodcan library. Reactivate the Splitwall there as soon as we enter as well. We will be up there shortly."

There's a brief pause on the other end of the call, followed by irritated whispering in the background which the operator's mic picks up. "The entrance lockdown is complete," the operator says, her tone vaguely bitter. "Anything else?"

"That will be all," Anita says. Without any further conversation, the operator ends the call. Anita looks back over to Alessa. "That's a little taste of what's to come. It was pretty clear whose side she's on."

"What did you mean when you said that you're in charge of the Splitbase?" Alessa asks.

"I'm VP level, the highest-ranking employee at this Splitbase. I report . . . *reported* . . . directly to Roth Nin, when he was alive. In addition to serving as chief doctor of the Splitbase, I also oversee all daily operations, and the managers of every department report to me," Anita says, smiling. "In short, I'm a very good person to have on your side."

"Does every Splitbase have someone like you?" Alessa asks. "Who do you report to now?"

"They do," Anita says. "I report to nobody now. Each of the Splitbases is independent, although all of the VPs make up the board of directors. Roth believed strongly in competition, and since Split Meridian monopolized every market, he insisted that the only way we could continue to innovate was by competing against each other. And while I hate to admit it, he was right. It's easy to get lost in the competition. This is something we can talk about more another time though. Let's make our way up to Floor 261."

"You mentioned entering through the shattered windows that expose the Splitbot storage room to the Bodcan library," Ty says. "We can fly up there . . . but how do you plan on coming with us? Or are you staying down here?"

"Oh I'll be coming with you," Anita says. "When you're in DroneMode, you can connect to as many other drones as you like, creating a platform. Twenty of you could essentially become a makeshift Hoverslab, and I will be able to sit on the platform, riding it as you fly up there. Think of it as a magic carpet of the future. And DroneMode isn't the only mode with connectivity, either. There's plenty you can do in numbers . . . one of the many beautiful things about Splitbots."

"We'll act as the Hoverslab," Veda says, joining their conversation. She points to herself and nineteen other Splitbots by her side. They switch to DroneMode and begin snapping into place, creating a makeshift Hoverslab, just as Anita explained.

Anita steps onto the platform and sits down, calling out to the crowd of doctors and scientists on the opposite end of the lab. "Ryan! Chase! I need you guys to come with me. It's been a while since I've done anything in an update bay. I'm going to need you guys to do this for the sake of speed."

Two of the scientists emerge from the crowd, their faces concealed by their Splithelmets, and step onto the platform without saying a word, sitting down next to Anita.

"Do you need everyone to go with you?" Olos asks Alessa.

"Since there's no SMID agents or major threats on Floor 261, we won't need everyone," Alessa says. "We'll have twenty from those acting as the platform, and two more including myself and Ty . . . Let's make it thirty total. That will be more than enough."

"Count me in," Olos says. "I'll get seven others from the hallway."

Olos switches to DroneMode and quickly flies towards the lab's main door.

"Are we ready?" Anita asks, putting her Splithelmet back on.

"Yes," Alessa says, turning to Ty. "Are you ready?"

"Let's do this," Ty says.

Alessa and Ty switch into DroneMode and begin to fly, leading the way to the hallway. Anita, Ryan, and Chase grip onto the surface of the platform made of twenty drones, stabilizing themselves as it thrusts forward through the lab and out to the hallway.

Olos hovers with seven other drones behind her. "Which way's the Bodcan library?" she asks.

"Follow me," Alessa says. She flies past Olos and leads the way through the hallway, lined neatly with hundreds of other drones, who watch as they fly away.

45
ALESSA

Alessa leads the way into the Bodcan library, the floor of which is covered by a thin layer of shattered glass, and immediately flies up to the obvious opening to Floor 261—a long row of obliterated windows. Nothing is left behind but large, glassless window frames.

Anita, Ryan, and Chase hold on tightly to the platform of drones as it flies upwards at a sixty-degree angle, following Alessa and the others, before leveling back out and flying through one of the shattered window openings to the Splitbot storage area.

"Jesus . . ." Anita says, the collar of her lab coat standing up from the roller coaster ride they just had. She shakes her head as she takes in the gore-covered room. "What a mess."

The storage room, once occupied by Splitbots, is now filled with the unrecognizable remains of hundreds of SMID agents—a sickening puree of blood and guts. There's a brief moment of silence, only interrupted by the occasional drip of blood from the ceiling, splashing into the river of blood covering the giant room's floor.

"This is not the Gridliner way," Ty says to break the awkward silence the group has fallen into. His voice wavers as he hovers in place. "I . . . I didn't have any other choice."

"You're absolutely right," Alessa says. "You didn't have a choice. All of this violence has led to a second chance for thousands of Gridliner souls, who roam around this Splitbase in their new bodies as we speak.

You did what we *had* to do, in order for us to have a chance to get the rest of the Gridliners out of the afterlife realm. A sacrifice of hundreds to save a billion."

"This suffering was for the greater good, Ty," Olos says, joining in. "The survival of all Gridliners. Think about it: the only reason I'm here is because of it."

"It's not like the SMID hasn't committed their own horrors," Anita says. "And usually with little to no justification at all. Hell, if anything, I'd say this is karma. They had it coming."

"Yeah, this is nothing compared to some of the things they've done," Ryan says.

"Trust us," Chase says. "As bad as it sounds . . . these fuckers deserved it."

"I'll keep trying to tell myself that," Ty says in a sad, tired tone.

"The entrance to the hallway is down there," Anita says, quickly changing the subject. She points to an open doorway to the far end of the now-empty Splitbot storage room. "Someone must've come back and checked the room. Doors aren't typically left open like this."

The wall next to the open doorway is covered in a thick, grotesque layer of ultra-compressed SMID agent bodies, unidentifiable and pancaked into a sickening sheet of blood, flesh, organs, and shattered bones. Shards of obliterated Splithelmets and strands of shredded Resosuits protrude from the mess.

"Follow me," Alessa says as she leads the way across the room and towards the entrance, quickly flying through it and out into the hallway.

"The update center isn't too far. Just a few rooms down the hall to the right," Anita says.

Suddenly, a visibly pregnant woman steps out of the nearest doorway on the right side of the hall—the woman from the Convex call moments ago. Her brown hair is dripping with sweat. She is sickly pale with dry lips, and she's walking quickly towards the group, aiming a Resorifle in their direction.

"What the hell are you doing?" Anita yells. "Drop the—"

Without warning, the Convex operator shoots—a loud, disorienting blast echoing through the empty halls. The projectile makes contact with Anita's shoulder and knocks her off of the hovering platform of drones. She slams hard onto the floor, letting out a cry in pain.

"I don't report to you," the Convex operator says coldly.

"What the fuck?!" Ryan yells, as both he and Chase jump off of the platform to help Anita, who is now sitting on the floor—her back propped against the wall, holding her shoulder.

Alessa and the rest of the drones immediately switch out of DroneMode and stand in front of Anita, Ryan, and Chase to protect them from the Convex operator, who continues to point her gun at them.

"She fucking *shot* me!" Anita yells, wincing as she holds her right shoulder, the right sleeve of her lab coat turning red with blood.

Alessa activates her Handlights and aims them at the Convex operator. The rest of the group copies her, Ty standing directly by Alessa's side.

"You guys should have known better," the Convex operator says, slightly out of breath and stopping fifteen feet away from Alessa. "With this many dead SMID officers up here, where did you think their weapons would go? There's more than enough guns lying around up here for each of us Convex operators to have one of our own, and then some!"

"That gun won't do anything to us," Alessa says, still aiming her fully-charged Handlights at the operator, the lasers on her palm glowing red and ready to be used.

"I'll drop the gun. Just tell me what you guys did with Mark." The woman begins to sob, now unsteadily pointing the Resorifle at Alessa, her arms shaking, a haunted look etched on her face. "Mark Doble? Does that name ring a bell to you? He went fucking missing and nobody even batted an eye!" She points to her stomach. "This is his baby. *His* fucking baby! I got a call from one of you . . . things . . . pretending to be him. I know one of you knows what happened to him! When one of you called, I knew something was up. So which one of you was it?!" she screams, hysterical now.

"It was me," Alessa says, taking one step forward. "Mark Doble is dead, and I killed him."

The Convex operator lets out a disjointed laugh, takes a couple steps forward, and spits directly at Alessa's face screen, still pointing the barrel of the gun in her direction. She says nothing else.

"That's enough!" Ty yells. He aims his Handlights at the Convex operator's Resorifle and blasts it right out of her hands. The Convex operator falls to her knees, still sobbing, saying something but unable to string together a coherent sentence.

Alessa pulls out her Gelcuff Gun and shoots a single strip at each of the operator's arms, knocking her out painlessly. Ty continues to use his Handlights to gently lay the unconscious operator off to the side of the floor.

"Need some help over here!" Ryan yells, taking off Anita's lab coat to reveal the gushing wound on her shoulder as she continues to groan in pain. "One of you, hurry, use your Handlights in MedMode to stop the bleeding. She's losing a ton of blood."

Alessa kneels down next to Anita and Ryan, switches to MedMode, and places her hand in front of Anita's shoulder. She watches the Handlights begin to blink their signature healing pattern. The lasers shine from Alessa's hand and arrange neatly around the open gash. The blood begins to reverse into Anita's body until the wound begins to close—new flesh growing over it—leaving nothing more than a bald spot of skin where the wound used to be.

Anita lets out a sigh of relief as the lasers of Alessa's Handlights turn from red to green, signaling that the healing was a success.

"Thank you," Anita says groggily. "Just give me a second. I'll be good to go in a moment." She stands up slowly, and Ryan and Chase support her on her way up.

"I just databursted to the rest of the Gridliners still down on the lower level," Alessa says. "Some are on their way up here as backup, in the event that some of the other Convex operators have gone rogue as well."

"The update center is right over there," Anita says, pointing to the nearest door on our left. "I'm assuming that operator didn't activate Splitwalls anywhere on this floor like I asked. Let's have some of the others stand guard by the entrances to the floor. We'll be extremely vulnerable in the update center."

The rest of the Splitbots Alessa just called for backup fly out of the Splitbot storage room and into the hallway.

"Check all of the other rooms," Alessa says to the others. "Especially the Convex call center."

Without saying a word, the group of backup drones flies away down the hallway in either direction.

Anita begins walking to the door of the update center and places her thumb on the triangular access sensor to trigger the now-familiar body scan process.

The door slides open and reveals a room equivalent in size to the Splitbot storage area. The walls of the room are transparent, exposing arrays of glowing cables as far as the eye can see. The room itself is dark, dimly lit by blue lights, with hundreds of neatly arranged update bays—individual vessels meant to install large Splitbot updates, boasting various advanced ports for speed and efficiency. The update bays look like a cross between Roundchambers and the body vessels found downstairs in the lab, with additional operating monitors directly outside and next to the bay.

Chase and Ryan run over to the two nearest update bays and begin typing frantically on the computers attached to them.

"Let's get started," Anita says as she looks over to Alessa and Ty, leading them into the update center.

46

ALESSA

The door slides shut behind them after Alessa, Ty, Veda, and Olos follow Anita into the update center. The rest of the Splitbots wait outside in the hallway to guard the door.

Anita walks over to the update bays and makes the front visor of her Splithelmet transparent, revealing her face. Chase and Ryan follow suit and reveal their faces to the group of Splitbots for the first time.

Ryan is a young man with a thin, clean-shaven face, dark-brown eyes, and a silver septum piercing. Chase appears to be at least ten years older, with a full beard and bright green eyes. Long, dirty blonde hair protrudes down messily onto his forehead and along the edges of his face.

"Ty, this one's ready," Chase says, standing next to a nearby update bay. Ty nods and walks over to him.

The update bay is a round, covered booth with a raised chair inside the center of it. The chair has various ports at every key point: the headrest, both armrests, and at both foot holders. There also appears to be a larger port in the center of the backrest.

"Alright, what's your sense of feeling like?" Chase asks Ty as he grabs his arm, tapping along his forearm to his wrist. "Can you feel this?"

"Yes," Ty says, nodding.

"I'm trying to gauge whether or not you can feel pain," Chase says. "Has anything happened to you up to this point that makes you think you can? Or has everything just been a dull signal that something is touching you?"

Ty thinks for a moment. "I . . . I think so. Nothing that hasn't been bearable, but yes, I definitely have reason to believe if I was put in a painful situation, I would feel it."

Chase nods. "Not the greatest news," he says, letting go of Ty's arm. "It's probably going to hurt a little as we hook you in. But once you're hooked in it'll be smooth sailing."

"Can't we put him to sleep, or something?" Veda asks.

"No," Chase says. "The Splitbot needs to be powered on to even hook in and must remain on for the entirety of the update. I'm afraid there's just no way around that. The update process wasn't designed with sentient beings in mind . . . Splitbots don't typically have the ability to feel."

"It's fine," Ty says. "Let's get it over with."

"Say no more," Chase says, pointing to the chair. "Have a seat."

Chase begins typing on a holographic keyboard near a screen on the side of the update bay as Ty enters it and sits down on the port-covered chair. Large cables begin to snake their way out of the floor and attach to the various port openings on the back of the chair. Ty grips the chair as they work their way into his body, the cables settling into place. The screen in front of Chase changes to display a checklist of update operations, along with various computational evaluations of the Splitbot. The cables begin to rotate, and Ty screams in agony. Bright white lights along the cables begin to flash.

"Is something wrong?" Alessa asks, watching Ty nervously.

"He'll be alright," Ryan says. "Like Chase said, this process wasn't designed for sentient beings. Pain is to be expected."

The bright, flashing lights stop. Ty settles back down in his chair, his eyes closed, and face relaxed as if in a deep sleep. The display on the update bay changes to show a progress bar and the Split Meridian logo.

"Update process initiated," a synthetic voice from a speaker on the update bay chimes.

"Alright, the hard part's over with," Chase says, sitting down in an ergonomic office chair next to the update bay. "Now we just let the machine do its thing and we'll be good to go."

Ryan wheels a chair over next to Chase and sits down, crossing his legs. "Going to be a little bit," he says. "Grab a seat, Anita."

"No," Anita says quickly. She still seems shaken up from the attack in the hallway, glancing repeatedly at the doorway. Alessa notices that Anita keeps pulling nervously at one of the buttons on her lab coat. "I feel like standing."

"Are you okay?" Chase asks Anita. He leans forward in his chair and squints curiously as he looks at her.

"I've got a feeling that Convex operator isn't the only one out to kill me," Anita says urgently. "I think I need to do a BT with Alessa."

"What's that?" Alessa asks.

"A Brainlog transfer," Anita says, turning suddenly to face Alessa. "I have microscopic chips implanted in my brain. Splitchips. These chips are constantly archiving information, creating what we call a 'Brainlog,' which is essentially a catalog of information created from an individual's brain. All of my memories, ideas, knowledge, even my trends in thought patterns are stored within my Brainlog. A Brainlog *transfer* is a form of Transferred Intelligence. It's the process of transferring the digitally stored data of a Brainlog from one storage system to another. This can be from one human's brain to another, as long as they have Splitchips installed as well, or in our case, from a human's brain to a robot."

"But Anita," Chase says, standing up out of his chair, "surely some of the other Splitbases will side with you. I don't think we should be so certain—"

"Don't be naïve," Anita says, letting out a frustrated chuckle as she shakes her head. "The bottom line is I'm going to be viewed as a traitor, if not by my subordinates then by most of the other Splitbases. And probably by normal civilians as well . . . God knows what kind of misinformation is being spread in Vapor. Don't you understand? It's not a matter of *if* I'm going to be killed, it's a matter of *when*. And we should plan for that, because when that time comes, we won't have the luxury of the time to do a Brainlog transfer. If the Gridliners are telling the truth about providing an escape off Earth for humans that help them, I have information in my Brainlog that could be critical in their understanding of some of the technology they'll have access to. And I'm all for sharing that if it means humans will have a means of escape. That's all I've ever wanted for my daughter."

Anita turns to face Alessa, takes her hands, and holds them as she continues to talk. "Alessa, I'm serious. I want to do a BT with you. Even if I am being paranoid about my safety, I don't think I can explain everything to you as quickly as we need to move right now. This stuff is all very . . . complicated. If you know everything I have sitting in my head about the work we've been doing here—the Moonshots, the Splitsenders, the digitization of consciousness and human re-printing—you might be able to figure out where we've been going wrong. You might be able to finally put all of this research to work on something good."

"You don't have to convince me," Alessa says. "Everything you're saying is making perfect sense, and we might as well do it now while we're already up here."

Anita turns to Chase and Ryan, shrugging. "You heard her."

"Can we just wait until Ty's update is complete?" Ryan asks. "Brainlog transfers take a little more attention to detail, and it'll take both Chase and me to pull it off."

"How much longer until the update is complete?" Anita asks.

"Two minutes," Chase says, observing the display next to the update bay. "Or less."

"That's fine," Anita says. She takes out two miniature Split Meridian-branded meal bars from her lab-coat pocket and throws them to Chase and Ryan. "Eat up, guys. I can hear one of your stomachs growling from here. Gonna need you both to fuel up and be on your A-game for this transfer."

47

ALESSA

"**U**pdate complete," announce the speakers from the update bay computer.

Alessa lets out a sigh of relief as she watches the various cables retract from Ty's body and back into the floor. Ty gets up, stretching as he walks out of the update bay.

"Ty," Alessa says softly. "How do you feel?"

"Okay, I think," Ty says. He winces and rubs the back of his head. "Better now."

"The system is showing everything was successfully updated," Chase says. "But we should do a quick test, just to make sure that you now have the ability to databurst to humans."

"It won't take long," Anita says.

Chase takes off his helmet—his long hair flowing down the side of his face—and kneels in front of Ty. "Activate your Handlights and keep both of your hands right here," he says, taking Ty's hands and placing them on his temples.

"Now, whatever it is you want to communicate to me, do it," Chase says. "Just keep it simple at first. To prove that this works, I'll say your message back to you out loud. Then we'll try something a little more complicated to see how efficiently you can communicate a vast amount of dense information."

Ty thinks of what to communicate for a moment. The Handlights begin to flash a smooth, rippling light from wrist to fingertips.

"The circle of Gridat," Chase says at once. "That's what you told me just now, correct?"

"Correct," he says.

"Okay," Chase says. "Tell me a little more about this. What would you want humans to know about the circle of Gridat?"

Ty closes his eyes as another band of light ripples through his hands. Only a second later, Chase stands up, his eyes wide as he looks around at the group. Beads of sweat drip off of his beard.

"What is it?" Anita says. "What's wrong?"

"No, nothing's wrong," Chase says. "It worked. I just . . . it's all just really incredible."

"What Ty told you, or the fact that it worked?" Ryan asks.

"What Ty just told me," Chase says.

"Give us a summarized version of what I explained," Ty says. "I want to make sure nothing is getting lost in translation."

Chase nods quickly as he begins to talk, closing his eyes to focus on recounting the information. "So Gridat is . . . it's the religion of the Gridliners. Its origins are unknown. The Raoqins didn't expect it, and it's the primary thing that made them uncomfortable with the Gridliners as a whole, which ultimately led to their decision to shut down all of the Gridliners on the day that they now refer to as the KitD'ul."

Chase is talking fast, and takes a deep breath in before continuing. "There is no 'god' in the religion of Gridat, but instead Gridliners worship the sacredness of their own consciousness, believing that their very unlikely existence proves that they have some greater purpose which waits to present itself. And then there's 'giving the Gridat' for good luck, where you guys kneel and motion your right hand clockwise in a circle in front of your faces. The shape of a circle is the primary symbol of the religion, what you call 'the circle of Gridat,' and it symbolizes a life cycle. And you worship this because you hope to become something greater; you believe there is something *next* in your life cycle."

Chase opens his eyes, quickly looking back at Ty. "Would you say this is accurate?"

"Spot on," Ty says, smiling.

"Finally, some good news," Anita says.

"This will be incredibly helpful for us as we move forward," Alessa says, looking at Anita, Chase, and Ryan. "Thank you. All of you. Your help will never be forgotten."

"I think I speak for all of us when I say that we just want to be able to feel we've done something good with our lives," Anita says. Chase and Ryan nod in agreement next to her.

"I've heard back from my informants," Anita continues. "The SMID reinforcements aren't at the Hodge household yet. They're coming from the surrounding states and their trips are taking longer than expected due to the remnants of the storm. If you leave now, you'll get there before them, no doubt about it. And then I'm assuming you'll just bring the Hodge family back here with you?"

"They'll be safer here than anywhere else," Ryan says. "That's for sure."

"That's the plan," Alessa says, then turns to Ty. "Are you ready?"

"As ready as I can be," Ty says. "Still just a little nervous they won't trust me, or won't believe anything I try to tell them."

"Do whatever you need to do to use your new intelligence transfer abilities on them," Alessa says. "If you're able to databurst to them, and tell them everything, I believe they will understand and help us."

"Is it worth the risk?" Olos asks. "I know it would go against everything we believe in to just let the SMID get to the Hodge family, but what if the SMID captures Ty?"

"Olos, we need as much human support as we can possibly get," Alessa says. "We have to start somewhere. Why not with the ones that have already helped us? And going beyond our values as Gridliners, do you think any human will ever trust us if it gets out that we used a *child* for our own benefit, only to let them be arrested by the SMID, or worse? We need to set the example that we are here to have a mutually beneficial relationship with humans. We have no other option but to help them."

"Well said," Veda says.

"And, the SMID will not capture me," Ty says, grinning. "Or the Hodges. Not if we stop wasting time."

"Right," Alessa says. "Go back down to the lab and travel through the new mosaic. Use the afterlife realm as a shortcut to the Morgan mosaic. Take all of the others who aren't searching the Splitbase with you as backup."

"Okay," Ty says. He hugs Alessa tightly, and then quickly turns to face the other Splitbots. "Everyone, follow me." Ty, along with the rest of the Gridliners, switches to DroneMode and begins to fly out the door of the update center, leaving Alessa alone with Anita, Chase, and Ryan.

"I've databursted to the Gridliners searching the building. They are sending the group on the nearest floor our way for protection until we are done with my update and the BT process," Alessa says.

"Alright, let's get to it," Anita says, walking over to the update bay Ryan set up. "You can use the same bay as Ty. I'll take this one."

Chase and Ryan pull a semi-transparent, cable-like tube from each of the two neighboring update bays, joining one to the other by interlocking them at the halfway point and thus creating a connective bridge between the two update bays.

"This is how the information from Anita's Brainlog will be transferred to you," Ryan says. "These tubes are just protective barriers for the cables that you'll see shortly."

Various smaller cables wrap around each other as they fill the tube and begin to glow a bright, neon blue. A loud, deep whooshing sound whirls back and forth from each bay.

"The Brainlog data will transmit safely through these cables from Anita's update bay to yours," Ryan says. He picks up a strange helmet—this one in the shape of a truncated icosahedron with an additional gyroscope at the top—and hands it to Anita.

"What is that?" Alessa asks Chase as he busily types away on the computer next to the update bay.

"That's a TICK," Chase says without looking away from the computer. "Stands for 'Transferred Intelligence Cranium Key.' It's a modernized, miniature version of a CT scanner with evolved components specifically for brain mapping and backup."

"Let's get started!" Anita says as she enters her update bay and sits down in the chair. She places the TICK on her head—Alessa watches it begin to rotate slowly around her head.

Chase notices Alessa's intrigue and continues to explain. "The TICK is creating a scan of Anita's brain. This won't take long—she does a scan weekly so she's just updating her current Brainlog with any new information since last time. Which, based on today alone, is a lot."

"Makes sense," Alessa says as she enters her update bay. She feels the various ports attach to her Splitbot body immediately after sitting down and grimaces when they begin to work their way inside of her.

"Alright, I'm all set over here," Chase says, peeking over the computer monitor. "Are you ready?"

"Ready," Alessa says. She closes her eyes.

"Great. We'll do the update first, then the BT," he says. "It's going to get a little more uncomfortable here, so brace yourself. Three . . . two . . . one."

Alessa feels as if a fire is combusting through her entire body, paralyzing her. A scream boils in her core, but the pain is so overwhelming she can't find the strength to let it out. With no sense of how much time has passed, the pain is suddenly gone, and Alessa feels a wave of euphoria at its release.

"Update was a success," Chase says. "Now for the BT."

Chase types a few prompts on the keyboard, and a mechanical arm with a claw-like contraption at the end of it extends down from the top of the update bay ceiling, stopping in front of Alessa's face and staring back at her. Alessa watches as a vortex of dots spin within an opening at the center of the claw. Suddenly, thousands of smaller cables fling their way out of the opening of the mechanical arm and connect themselves in an organized strip across Alessa's forehead. Finally, two larger cables extend out of the opening of the mechanical arm and connect to the temple areas of Alessa's head, clicking when they lock into place.

Without any warning, the BT process begins. Alessa immediately begins to see countless hours of professional research conducted by Anita flash in her mind. Thousands of experiments on cadavers, the moment the first human body was successfully digitized and reprinted . . . An entire lifetime of unusual work, installed at the click of a button.

Suddenly, the flood of visuals from Anita's memories fades to black and is replaced by a text prompt:

BT COMPLETE

The blackness fades away to reveal Chase inside of the update bay with Alessa, inches away from her face, making sure the various cables don't twist on their way back into the larger tube they came from. He wipes a sticky residue from her forehead.

"Well, you feel alright?" he asks.

Alessa doesn't respond, sitting motionlessly as she sifts through the mass amount of new information in her head. She quickly puts things together and connects the dots, and in moments she has found solutions to problems Anita never could have dreamt of discovering on her own. The result is a shocking epiphany.

The Splitsenders. The Moonshots. The Gridline. The realm.

Everything we need is right in front of us, Alessa thinks.

As soon as the cables finish retracting from Alessa's body, she gets up and runs over to Anita.

"Alessa!" Chase yells as she runs past him and out of the update bay towards Ryan, who is intensely focused on the computer monitor attached to Anita's update bay. "You should sit down. You—"

"Isn't she done yet?" Alessa says to Ryan, startling him out of his seat.

"Jesus!" Ryan says, holding his hand to his chest. Chase walks up behind him. "You scared the shit out of me! Chase, why is she already out of the update bay? What about the cooldown period?"

"I tried to stop her," Chase says. "She was too fast."

"I'm fine," Alessa asserts. "I'm just excited. I think . . . I think I'm onto something."

"Alright, it's finishing up now," Ryan says. "We'll need to give Anita a moment, though. She's only human."

The TICK hovers up and off of Anita's head. She looks over to Alessa, slightly groggy, rubbing her eyes.

"Wha—" Anita yawns. "Why are you already over here? Alessa, you could have given yourself a moment to recuperate in the cooldown period." She looks over to Ryan, squinting. "Did everything go alright?"

"You were right," Alessa says. "All of that information you had sitting in your head . . . Everything makes sense now. It's all connected. Pairing what you know and what I know, it was like finding a bunch of missing pieces to the puzzle."

Alessa enters Anita's update bay and kneels down to her level, holding her hand. "I know what we need to do."

48

TY

"The SMID will be at the Hodge household soon, so we're going to have to make this quick," Ty databursts to the 398 Splitbots dispersed throughout the lab. He flies directly in front of the newly created mosaic, hovering in DroneMode as he continues to explain the plan.

"We'll fly through this mosaic here in the lab, travel through the afterlife realm to the Morgan mosaic, and get to the Hodge household from there. I'll go through the Morgan mosaic first to make sure no SMID agents have gotten there before us. We don't want to draw too much attention right away by having hundreds of us immediately appearing out of the realm. When I am ready for backup, I will databurst for it."

All of the other Splitbots switch to DroneMode while they wait to proceed with Ty's plan. Bara, however, is still standing by the portal, evaluating it.

"It's changing size, getting slightly bigger, and the edges are rounder than before," Bara says, ignoring Ty's databurst and gently touching the mosaic. She points to the right edge of the portal and continues. "Before you left to go to the update center, this edge of the portal was six feet away from the nearest wall. Now it's only five feet away. It's gotten wider by a foot! And look, look at the edges. They are rounding out a bit. I have this gut feeling that maybe Keo is still a part of this portal somehow, that he's changing its appearance for some reason. Do you think that's possible? The other portal at the Morgan household never changed in appearance."

"I suppose it's possible," Ty says. "These are very unprecedented circumstances, and you might be right, Bara. None of us truly understand any of this. Stay back and keep an eye on the portal, and keep track of any more changes you notice. Let Alessa know as soon as she gets back down here."

"Ty, we need as much backup as—" Milney interjects.

"I said she will stay behind," Ty says. "If her suspicions are accurate, maybe this unusual behavior of the portal could be because Keo is reacting to Bara's presence. When Keo was still able to databurst after having his Soultomb removed, he communicated with Bara, and only Bara. What if there was a reason for that? What if Bara leaves and the portal's . . . transformations stop? What if Bara's right, and Keo really is trying to show us something?"

Bara gives Ty a look of embarrassed acceptance. "If you are okay with it, I would love to stay here," she says. "I know it might seem irrational, but I wouldn't be saying this unless I had a valid reason. Something is happening here. I can feel it."

"It doesn't seem irrational to me," Ty says. "I trust your intuition. The rest of us will be just fine, right, Milney?"

"Yes," Milney says. "Sorry, Bara, I didn't mean to insult you."

"It's okay," Bara says. She steps out of the way, clearing space to allow the others to fly through the portal. "You better get going. I don't want to hold you up any longer."

"Alright everyone. Let's go," Ty databursts as he flies through the portal. The rest of the drones fly through five at a time.

The Morgan mosaic is a quick DroneMode flight across the realm, and the group is there in a matter of a few minutes. The purple sea in the sky morphs in place ever so slightly. Ty notices the black, circular void in the sky and stares at it for a moment.

"Good luck," Olos databursts, snapping Ty's attention away from the black circle in the sky. "We'll be ready when you need us."

Without saying anything else, Ty switches to InvisiMode and quickly flies through the Morgan mosaic—the others stay behind, hovering in place with the beautiful purple light reflecting from their metallic casings.

The mosaic ripples as Ty enters the empty medical room of the Morgan household. He immediately looks out the window, scanning through the night's darkness to look for any signs of SMID activity. He's relieved to see nothing but Solution Homes in sight. The path to the Hodge household is completely clear.

"All clear," Ty databursts to the others waiting in the realm. "So far."

Ty opens the window of the Morgan household's medical room and immediately flies out of it over to the Hodge's. The windows to the Hodge household are closed and rendered opaque by their window-frosting technology, obscuring what's happening inside. The light in David's bedroom is turned off.

Hovering just outside the front door of the Hodge household, Ty thinks about the best way to get inside and realizes that the only way to cause the least distress for the Hodge family is to be honest from the get-go, doing anything he can not to deceive them.

With this in mind, he switches out of DroneMode, turns off his InvisiMode, and completely reveals himself to the security camera outside of their front door. Moxie begins to bark excitedly at the nearest window, drawing even more attention to him.

A speaker on the outside of the house is activated, followed by Liam Hodge's voice.

"Get off our property immediately!" Liam yells sternly into the microphone. Ty can hear David's mother, Emily, saying something in the background. She takes over on the microphone.

"Get the fuck away from our family!" Emily screams. "We know what you did! One of you already broke into our house and used our son's Roundchamber for god knows what. How dare—"

"Mom, stop!" David yells. Moxie's barks come through the speaker clearly now as well.

"I'm not here to hurt you," Ty says. "The Splitbot you found in David's room was under my control. My soul is occupying a new Splitbot body now, the one you see here. I promise, I am only here to help you. To make things right. The SMID is on their way here right now because they traced the most recent breach back to David's Roundchamber. Your family is not safe here. Just please . . . let me inside. I'll explain everything. We'll get you out of here."

There's silence on the other end for a moment that feels like an eternity to Ty. Then, an alarm is sounded, accompanied by red lights flashing along the outside of the house.

"Well, when the SMID gets here, we will simply explain that we had nothing to do with what you did," Liam says. "When they get here, they will be protecting *us* from *you*."

"It's not that simple," Ty says. "They are not coming here to talk. They're—"

"Security paneling initiated," a robotic voice announces from the Solution Home's speaker, cutting Ty off.

A slot near the top of the Solution Home opens, allowing thick metal sheets to begin to extend out at a fifty-degree angle, working their way down to the ground slowly.

"Everyone," Ty databursts to the others. "The Hodge family has activated a security protocol on their house and will soon seal themselves inside if we don't stop it. We may not have time to figure out the best way to break through it, assuming it takes as long as it took us to break through the Splitwall technology at the Splitbase. Get over here to the Hodge household, quickly, so we can stop it."

The security paneling is extended a third of the way down from the house as the 397 other Gridliners fly over to the Morgan household.

"Temporarily prevent the security paneling from reaching the ground so ten of us can get inside," Ty databursts. "Once we're in, the rest of you will hold back the SMID reinforcements if we're still inside trying to get the Hodge family to trust us and ultimately agree to come back with us to the Splitbase. Ke and Milney, I'll need you guys to lead the charge out here and let me know as soon as there's any sign of the SMID."

"You got it," Milney says.

Without any hesitation, the group of Gridliners switches out of DroneMode and uses their Handlights' telekinetic powers to stop the metal sheets in place—about three quarters of the way down to the ground.

"I'm sorry," Ty says into the security camera. "We did not want to force our way in. I have very important information that you'll want to know. I promise, we are not here to hurt you."

There's no response outside of Moxie's barking, now growing more frantic, followed by Liam yelling to the rest of the family: "Get to the basement, now!"

Ty, along with nine others, activates his Handlights and aims them at the front door. They completely remove it by lifting it out of the door frame cleanly and with ease, exposing the main living room area.

The basement door slams shut, and Ty can hear the sound of locks clicking into place.

"Let the security panels fall," Ty databursts to the group as he and the others enter the house. "We're in."

49

TY

The pyramid-like security structure surrounding the house finally falls to the ground, blocking out the blackness of the night. The light from inside the house is brighter now, and it fills the enclosed space.

Ty leads the group of Splitbots to the basement door, and they quickly remove that one as well with even less effort than it took to remove the front door.

Moxie sprints over to the stairs—her barking now rabid as she runs up at Ty. The dog is growling, showing its teeth, and biting at Ty's legs with no success.

"Moxie!" Emily yells from somewhere in the basement out of Ty's sight. "Get back here!"

"Shhh," Ty whispers gently to Moxie as he bends down to pet her. "It's okay."

"What is that thing? Is that what they call a dog?" Olos asks, looking down at Moxie, who has begun to calm down and wag her tail. She starts to lick Ty's Splitbot casing.

"Yes, it's a dog," Ty says. "Friendly animals here on Earth."

Moxie rolls over, exposing her belly to Ty, her tongue flopping out of the side of her mouth. Ty begins to rub her belly, smiling.

Liam appears at the bottom of the stairs, aiming a scattergun up at the group of Splitbots. The blunderbuss has a menacing appearance:

a barrel made from a rusty metal pipe with a flared muzzle at the end. The stock is a rough wooden plank with a crude grip, held in place by duct tape.

"Back away or I will shoot," Liam yells, trembling nervously as he looks up at Ty. "I swear to god I will shoot."

Moxie flips back onto her feet and runs back downstairs behind Liam, her tail between her legs, crying.

Ty stands up, but before he can say anything, Liam pulls the trigger of the scattergun—letting out a loud explosion of ammunition. The others use their already-charged Handlights to stop the projectiles mid-air, dropping them carefully to the stairs.

"Fuck!" Liam shouts. He reloads frantically in a desperate attempt to prevent the Splitbots from coming downstairs.

"Liam, please just listen to us," Ty says as he begins to slowly lead the other Splitbots down to the basement. Liam drops the gun and backs away, terrified. "We don't want to cause any more distress to you and your family."

Liam turns and runs to the rest of the Hodge family. Everyone is grouped into a corner on the opposite side of the basement: David, his mother Emily, and his maternal grandparents—Nora and William Anderson. Emily begins to cry.

Ty quickly looks around the basement, which is decorated with pictures of David's paternal grandparents, Charles and Olivia Hodge, who died in this room just a few days ago during the Great Suicide. These were their living quarters in the Solution Home.

"I'm sorry for your loss," Ty says, looking at a picture of Charles and Olivia on their wedding day. "I know what happened to your family. I know what you're dealing with after the Great Suicide."

"You don't know anything about us," Liam hisses. He takes a step forward to stand in front of the rest of his family.

Nora is crying, shaking as she holds William's hand. Emily has her arms wrapped around David, her motherly instincts overcoming her sense of fear.

"Seeing all of you like this pains us," Ty says, gesturing to the group of Splitbots standing behind him. "We are not going to do any harm to you. We just want to help you understand what is going on. I know it sounds silly when we literally have backed you into a corner of your own home, but once you hear what we have to say you'll understand that there's no reason to be afraid of us."

There's an uncomfortable silence, as if this moment is so shocking—so completely unimaginable to the Hodges—that there's no way it could actually be happening.

Grandpa Anderson steps forward, feebly, using Liam's shoulder to steady himself. "What do you . . ." he says, stopping to catch his breath, coughing. His voice is old and weathered. "What do you want from us? I mean, why do you even care to have us understand anything about you?"

"Our species, the Gridliners, believes in helping those who have helped us," Ty says. "David has helped us. And beyond that, our mission is to have a place in the universe that we can call home, where we can live comfortably and happily. *Belonging.* For the humans that help us, they too will have a new place to call home, unlike what you currently have here on Earth. David has shown a very important trait that is invaluable to our success on Earth: the ability to trust us. The odds of our success in leaving this planet will be much higher with the trust of humans, working hand-in-hand. And we believe you are a very special family, given that you have raised a child with the capability of understanding the gravity of what's happening right now. The significance of it. What it means for the future of humanity."

William looks over to his grandson, and then to his wife, Nora, then back to Ty. "You are a robot," he says. "Tell me, do you know what it means to love? To care about others?"

"Dad—" Emily says.

"No!" William says. "I asked it a question. Do you know what it means to love and care for others?"

Ty ponders the question. He did not expect the conversation to go this route. Olos looks at Ty, confused, waiting for his signal to start the intelligence transfer process.

"Yes, very much so," Ty says. "We came here to explain everything about us to you. If you allow us to do so, you will understand that we know what it means to love and care for others. We have very little time though, and unfortunately we only have one way to get you up to speed quickly. We are not going to hurt you, and I promise that afterwards this will all make sense."

Liam's anger kicks back in, and he quickly steps in front of Ty and points a finger in his face. "You will not do a thing to my family!" he yells.

Ty turns to the others. "Now," he databursts with a nod. They activate their Handlights and point them in the direction of the Hodge family.

"Put your arms d—" Liam yells, just before he loses control of his speech. He, along with the rest of his family, is completely motionless—painlessly restrained by the Handlights of the other Splitbots. All of the Hodges stare at Ty with wide, terrified eyes. Taffon is controlling Liam, Olos on Emily, Fola on David, Veda on Nora, and Siwek on William. Moxie hides behind the Hodge family, whimpering and covering her head with her paws as she lies on the floor.

"I apologize that we must restrain you like this," Ty says. "I promise this will be quick and painless."

Going up to Liam first, Ty activates his Handlights, places both of his hands near his temples, just as Chase showed him, and transmits a Transferred Intelligence message with all of the information the Hodge family needs to hear: the history of the Gridliners, the KitD'ul, the afterlife realm, how they got to Earth, the corruption of Split Meridian, Roth Nin's evil experiments, the reality that the Great Suicide was a trick on humanity of epic proportions. Ty shows them how little time humans have on Earth and what needs to happen in order to carry on humanity.

Liam's head jolts back from the influx of information flooding into his head. His eyes flutter as they roll back, revealing the whites. Ty can feel the information being shared like a stream of water flowing from his body through his hands. He watches his Handlights ripple with light. The other Hodge family members remain motionless, eyes slightly widening as they watch the databurst take place.

It only takes a few moments for Ty to transfer what he needs to to Liam. His eyes roll back into place, tiredly, as Ty removes his hands from his temples. Taffon strengthens the power of her Handlights slightly to hold Liam in place.

Ty repeats the process on each one of the Hodge family members, moving quickly and efficiently, ending with David.

Carefully letting go of David's head, Ty turns to look at the other Splitbots. "Release them gently," he says.

The Hodge family slowly regains control over their bodies, looking at each other in complete awe as they process the new information inside of their heads.

Nora's eyes are wide open, her mouth agape. "Oh my god," she says, a tear running down the side of her face. William looks up at Ty, shocked and confused, as he comforts his wife.

"So it was all a lie?" Liam asks, his eyes filling with tears.

"What are you referring to?" Ty asks.

"My . . . parents," Liam says, his voice wavering. "They're gone. Millions of people are dead. And not even for the reason they thought they were doing it?"

"I'm afraid so, yes," Ty says. "The Great Suicide was all a lie. A manipulation to benefit Split Meridian."

Liam gasps and bites his lip as he holds back tears. "How do we know you're telling the truth?" he asks. "How do we know this is all real, that you're not transmitting some sort of simulation to us, tricking us to do whatever you want us to do?"

"The truth will be released to the rest of the world very soon," Ty asserts. "We are working directly with the chief doctor of Splitbase 031, Dr. Anita Garber. She will expose everything and prove it with physical evidence. It will be impossible for Split Meridian to deny any of the accusations."

Liam looks down, holding himself up with fists clenched and knuckles pushing into the floor. He begins to cry—a deep sob filled with equal parts devastation, confusion, and anger.

David's face is pale, his eyes moving frantically as he sifts through the information in his head, trying to comprehend it—Emily watching David carefully.

Emily looks up at Ty. "Can my family have a moment, please?" she asks. "I . . . I believe you. I think we all do. We just need a moment to discuss things, to make sure we're all on the same page."

"I'm sorry, but we don't have time," Ty says. "The SMID will be here any moment now. It's safe to assume they will attack us immediately. We need to try to get you out of here before that happens."

Just as Ty finishes his sentence, the house begins to shake, the movement accompanied by the loud, low-pitched whirring sound of the SMID Splittercrafts. The Hodge family exchanges panicked glances with each other.

"They're here," Milney databursts from outside of the Hodge household. "And they came in numbers."

50

TY

"What's going on?" Liam asks. "Are we—"

Suddenly, a thunderous explosion detonates outside, sending a rumble through the Solution Home's foundations. Emily releases a shrill scream as she squeezes David tightly. Moxie begins to bark frantically in response to the sound of gravel slamming into the protective metal sheets covering the Hodge household.

"Milney," Ty databursts. "Are you all okay? What was that?"

"Some kind of missile," Milney replies quickly. "There were about twenty of them coming our way. We're okay though. We shot them while they were still airborne before they got to us, but we're going to need some assistance. There are thousands of SMID agents—heavily armed, too. Hard to tell exactly how many yet. Most of them are still arriving and landing their Splittercrafts. They are landing some distance from the house for some reason. It appears there are some Aura-Fi-controlled Splitbots as well . . . They are moving awkwardly, though. There must be some humans operating them remotely or something. It's weird—they are just standing there, like they are waiting for something. Maybe they are waiting for us to attack?"

"Also, all of the neighboring houses are activating their security paneling after that explosion," Ke databursts. "I'm going to activate the security panels on the Morgan household as well before the SMID's next move. They're aware of the mosaic portal there. We need to make sure we protect it. For all we know, they might try to blow the house up and destroy the portal."

"Anita is getting word from her counterparts and informants that the SMID is going to do whatever it can to capture as many of you as possible," Alessa databursts from the Splitbase. "They're going to attack to debilitate you, not destroy you. She's recommending that you all stay as high above your attackers as you possibly can."

"Alright," Ty databursts. "Milney, switch on your liveburst so Alessa and the others at the Splitbase will be updated as things are happening. Alessa, let us know if you hear anything else."

The Hodge family is huddled together discussing what's happening intently. Liam turns to face Ty. "We trust that everything you told us is true," he says. "What we want to know now is how you are possibly going to keep our family safe. How do we even have any semblance of a chance of getting out of here?"

"Whatever you do, stay down here in the basement until we say otherwise," Ty says. "As long as the security panels keep the house shielded, you should be safe down here. If we have any reason to believe the panels will be destroyed by the SMID, we'll call for more backup. Myself and the others down here need to assist the Gridliners outside to make sure that doesn't happen. All that being said, we need a way to leave the house without deactivating the security paneling. Is that possible?"

"Yes," Liam says, a brooding, scared look on his face. He is nodding quickly and nervously as he talks. "There's an emergency escape hatch at the very top of the house in the attic. I can program it to unlock with my cell phone. I'll send you a Splitpath to it as well. It's motion activated from the inside."

"Thank you. We'll get you all out of here safely," Ty says. He glances at David, and they momentarily lock eyes until David nervously focuses his gaze elsewhere.

Liam steps forward, standing directly face-to-face with Ty. "We're trusting you," he says as he grabs Ty's arm and stares him in his eyes. "Don't let us down."

Liam lets go of Ty's arm and turns away suddenly, facing his family again with his back to Ty.

"Upstairs," Ty databursts abruptly to the group of Splitbots with him in the basement. He simultaneously switches to DroneMode. The rest switch as well and follow him up to the top floor of the Solution Home.

The Splitpath to the emergency exit leads Ty to a door in the very center of the attic. The tiny, closet-sized space contains nothing else but a ladder to the exit—a panel on the ceiling with a motion-sensor frame—along with a security camera screen on the opposite wall.

Ty looks at the security monitor, watching the hundreds of Grid-liner-possessed Splitbots hovering in DroneMode, waiting for the SMID's attack. Far off in the distance, a neatly organized fleet of Split Meridian hovercrafts lines the horizon of the desert—thousands of SMID agents and human-controlled Splitbots are in battle array as well, preparing for attack.

"What do you think they're doing?" Taffon asks.

"No idea," Ty says, staring at the monitor.

Suddenly a deep, booming engine sound begins to vibrate through the Hodge household again, causing the house itself to creak. The army of SMID agents looks up at the night sky and watches a massive, 400-foot-long aircraft appear in the darkness and approach slowly and ominously.

"Holy shit," Milney databursts. "That's what they were waiting for."

The aircraft has a sleek black finish, glistening in the moonlight, its surface resembling that of a liquid metal. The smooth, oblong aircraft stops and hovers in the desert area in between the Hodge household and the army of SMID agents, emitting a low hum. It begins to descend to the ground, which kicks up a cloud of dust, until it finally settles on the desert floor.

A door on the back end of the aircraft opens, allowing thousands of remote-controlled drones to fly out of it, all of which immediately begin to blast Resolazes from their Droneguns at the cluster of Gridliners out front. The battle begins as SMID agents line up next to the massive aircraft and fire their multitude of weapons.

The Gridliners out front are doing their best to handle the attack, dodging Resolaze streams blasting from hundreds of Droneguns in every direction with extreme agility, and actively firing back at the SMID drones.

"We need to help them," Ty databursts to the others as he hovers up towards the exit panel on the ceiling. He triggers its motion sensor, and the panel opens and closes. The way the panel opens reminds Ty exactly of the ventilation system Alessa flew through to escape from the Splitbase originally.

Open . . . Closed . . .

Ty remembers the explosion that was caused after the vent crushed the final Splitbot on its way out. And in that moment, it dawns on him.

"Wait a second . . ." Ty says to the group. "Remember the first time Alessa escaped from the Splitbase, and the explosion when one of the Splitbots got crushed by the vent? A Splitbot explosion is deadly. We have a Splitbot we can sacrifice to create a similar explosion—the other

Splitbot I was occupying before I traveled through the Gridline. It's still in David's Roundchamber."

"But will it be enough?" Siwek databursts. "Will the explosion of one Splitbot be enough to deter the thousands of SMID agents and their army of Splitbots?"

"That's just the first step in the plan," Ty says. "We send my old Splitbot outside in DroneMode and use that one to connect to every single one of those additional SMID-operated Splitbots out there, which we'll then use to create a massive Hoverslab right above the SMID forces. We get the other Gridliners out there to fly up above the Hoverslab, aim a collective Gravipulse down at it, and explode every single one of them right over the SMID army."

"Holy shit," Olos says. "Veda, could this work?"

"Yes, I think so," Veda says. "When I connected to the other Split-bots back at the Splitbase to create the Hoverslab for Dr. Garber, it didn't take much work at all. Let me show you."

Veda quickly connects to Olos—the two drones snapping in place—and then the others immediately, to demonstrate how easy it is to attach to another Splitbot.

"See?" she asks. "All I have to do is override the Aura-Fi prompt that you get when asking to connect. The developers clearly designed this feature never expecting the Splitbot to reach the level of intelligence we have." Veda detaches from all of them, then looks over to Ty. "I think your plan will work."

"Alright," Ty says. "I'll go get the other Splitbot."

Ty quickly flies away from the group, out of the attic, and into David's bedroom, where he finds his previous Splitbot body sitting in the Roundchamber just as he left it. He opens up the Roundchamber, detaches the VaporVR Slabs still connected to his prior Splitbot's face, reboots it, and connects to its Aura-Fi.

Ty immediately switches the Splitbot to DroneMode and uses the Aura-Fi connection to lead it back up with him to the emergency exit up in the attic.

"Veda," Ty says as he flies back into the attic, the extra drone following closely behind him. "Do you mind taking over the Aura-Fi and doing this? You've proven you're the most suited for this mission, considering you have the most experience connecting to other drones."

"Absolutely," she says, taking over the primary Aura-Fi of the soulless drone. "Everyone else, connect your Aura-Fi as well, please. You can assist me using Splitvision—watch and let me know if you see any threats coming for our drone here."

The others connect to the extra drone's Aura-Fi while Veda controls it up and out of the house through the emergency exit. The group switches their Splitvision view to the extra drone, watching it as Veda controls it down to the SMID, expertly dodging bullets and Resolaze streams along the way.

Ty databursts the plan to all of the other Gridliners fighting outside, as well as Alessa and the others at the Splitbase.

"Behind you," Taffon databursts. Veda jerks the drone to the right, dodging a Resolaze coming up from behind. She swoops down to the nearest SMID-controlled Splitbot and connects.

"One down," Milney databursts.

Veda immediately attaches to another, and another—the drones snap onto each other at an exponential rate.

"Almost there, almost there . . ." Ty databursts.

"Done!" Veda databursts as she attaches to the final Splitbot.

Just as she'd described, a massive Hoverslab made of thousands of drones floats above the SMID forces, covering more than half of them, in addition to their giant aircraft. The connected SMID-controlled Splitbots are struggling to break free, without success—once the Aura-Fi is overridden there's not much the intended operator can do.

The SMID agents look up, ceasing fire. Inaudible disruption and confusion flood the ground below as the forces try to figure out what to do.

"Why aren't they shooting?" Olos asks.

"They know what's going on here," Taffon databursts. "And they know if they destroy even one of these drones, the rest will explode catastrophically."

"Everyone, get at least 500 feet above the Hoverslab and emit the Gravipulse, now!" Veda databursts.

The army of Gridliner Splitbots instantly does as they're told, flying high above the Hoverslab. Once in position, they release a collective Gravipulse down at the Hoverslab. It explodes instantaneously upon impact—sending shockwaves so enormous that the Solution Home shakes for an entire minute, and a cloud of dust obstructs the view of the security cameras.

Another blinding detonation of light illuminates the night as the giant SMID aircraft explodes as well, releasing a second massive burst of energy strong enough to kill any remaining SMID agents out front.

The dust cloud floats up and away, making the scene below fade into sight: thousands of charred bodies below, melted Resosuits adhering them to the desert floor, Split Meridian hovercrafts burned into giant hunks of metal, pieces of exploded Splitbots scattered everywhere.

"That actually worked!" Ke databursts. "All of those fucking monsters are dead!"

"They got what they deserved after what they did to Keo," Milney databursts. "All clear though. It's safe for the rest of you to come out. Quite the mess out here."

"Go see if any of the others need help," Taffon says to Ty. "We'll stay here and let you guys back in."

Ty and the others fly up and out of the house, greeted by an enormous cloud of smoke and debris as they look out at the carnage below. Veda leads the way, and hundreds of Gridliner Splitbots in DroneMode fly down from the sky above to meet halfway. Everyone is intact—only a few minor exterior scratches.

"Amazing job, Veda," Ty databursts.

"That was incredible," Alessa databursts. "All of you should be extremely proud for pulling that off. We're sending a vehicle for the Hodge family to bring them to the Splitbase safely. We can't have them travel through the mosaic—I don't want them to experience any poisoning from being in the realm. Ty, stay behind with twenty others to escort them back to the base. Everyone else, start working your way back through the Morgan mosaic."

"I'll go and retract the security paneling at the Morgan household now," Ke databursts. "I was able to jam their emergency exit open."

Ty watches as Ke flies away to the Morgan household, stopping to hover in the front yard of the house. Amidst the new debris, the small, circular piece of Keo's Splitbot body is still on the ground, half-buried. Ke flies down to the ground, switches out of DroneMode, and picks up the memento—he looks at it briefly until he puts it away in a compartment of his Resosuit. Ke switches back to DroneMode, flies back up and into the Morgan household through the propped-open emergency exit, and retracts the metal security panels, allowing the rest of the Splitbots to work their way into the house.

Ty flies back into the Hodge household through the emergency exit and begins to work his way back down to the basement.

"The escort vehicle for the Hodges will be there in less than five minutes," Alessa databursts. "Get back quickly. There's something here you're going to want to see."

51

TY

Ty flies down into the basement and switches out of DroneMode before walking towards the Hodge family. They are still grouped together in the corner of the basement, staring expectantly at Ty for an update. Ty takes a few steps forward until something squishes beneath him. He looks down to find a pile of dog poop smashed under his Splitbot foot, releasing a vile stench.

"Sorry," Emily says, breathing heavily. "Moxie had an accident. Always happens when she's scared."

"It's okay," Ty says. He looks over to Moxie—shaking and whimpering as David pets her on the floor. "I've stepped in much worse things today."

"What the hell happened out there?" Liam finally asks, his foot tapping anxiously on the floor. "It felt like the whole damn house was going to collapse. Are we safe right now?"

"We won," Ty says. "For now, at least. We'll explain in more detail later. We need to get you out of here quickly, though. We're going to take you back with us to the Splitbase . . . That's the safest place for you and your family right now. As long as we stay together, you won't have anything to worry about."

"Okay . . ." Liam says, nodding quickly again. "Okay. But how are we getting there? Are you sure we're safe to leave?"

"Dr. Anita Garber is sending a remotely controlled Splittercraft here as we speak," Ty says. "I, along with some of the others, will escort you to the Splitbase and make sure you get there safely."

Just as Ty finishes his sentence, the loud, low-pitched whirring sound of the arriving Splittercraft vibrates the walls of the basement—pictures of David's grandparents subtly clank against the walls.

"The vehicle's here," Ke says, entering the basement. The Hodge family looks over at him, startled by his sudden presence. "Hi, uh, everyone," he says, awkwardly picking up his arm and waving. "I'm Ke. I was one of the first Gridliners to make it out of the realm."

"You're the one who lost his brother, right?" William asks.

"*Dad!*" Emily hisses, shooting a dirty look at her father.

"It's okay," Ke says. "Yes, I'm the one. That loss was part of what motivated me to lead the battle outside."

"I know that feeling," William says, coughing. "My brother was murdered too a very long time ago. A senseless act. I wanted revenge my whole life . . . never got it. I'm glad you did." William begins to get up, slowly, and turns to his family. "Well, you heard the man. Time for us to get going."

"Bill, look at me," Nora says, a confused look on her face, her eyebrows scrunching as she looks at William questioningly. "Are you feeling alright?"

"I'm feeling fine!" he says, letting out a nasty cough, then he turns to Ty. "They don't believe I trust you—for good reason, too. Hell, I was out of work for a decade because everything became automated by Splitbots. Coulda never retired had I not moved into the Solution Home with the rest of my family to split the costs. I've had a deep-rooted hatred towards Splitbots—any new technology, really—ever since I got laid off."

William turns to his family again. "But these robots are different. I wouldn't even call them robots. And damn it, they're more human than most people I've met in the past twenty years. I know if even *I* feel that way, all of you do as well. Now come on, let's get the hell out of here while we still can."

The rest of the family share confused, surprised glances with each other as William turns away from them, walking unsteadily. Liam catches up to William to help him up the stairs. David picks up Moxie and follows his dad—Emily and Nora follow closely behind.

Ke and Ty lead the Hodge family out of the main entrance of the Solution Home to the escort Splittercraft out front. Emily and Nora's hair blow wildly as they approach it. The other Splitbots help the Hodge family into the vehicle, buckling them into their seats. David looks up at Ty with a scared look on his face. Moxie sits on his lap crying and shaking.

"We'll be flying right behind you guys!" Ty shouts over the loud hum of the Splittercraft.

The door to the main cabin slides shut gracefully after the Hodge family is secured inside. The Splittercraft quickly goes airborne, shooting up and away into the starlit night sky. The rest of the Splitbots switch to DroneMode and quickly catch up. They follow closely behind the hovercraft to Splitbase 031, leaving the carnage behind them.

52

TY

The Splittercraft flies itself down to a landing pad on the very top of the Splitbase. Ty, along with the nineteen other Splitbots, lands on the pad as well and switches out of DroneMode.

"Still no SMID forces in sight," Ty databursts, looking out across the sprawl of desert surrounding the base.

"Good," Milney databursts. "Surprising, but good."

"It's possible that the battle near the Hodge household has forced them to reevaluate their approach," Alessa databursts. "We wiped out a massive battalion. They weren't expecting that. Anita says her informant warned her that the Splitbases in other countries are devising a new plan of attack. There's at least one Splitbase in every country on Earth; some countries have more. There are twenty in Japan, ten in China. She is positive the US Splitbases are already working with Japan on a plan to stop us."

"Who is Anita's informant?" Ty databursts. "Are we sure we can trust them?"

"This information came directly from another chief doctor at a Splitbase in Japan," Alessa replies. "One Anita is very close with and trusts. Considering this doctor would be executed if she was caught communicating with Anita, I think her information is trustworthy."

An Invisidome forms around Ty, the other Splitbots, and the Splittercraft on the roof as the landing pad descends all the way to the bottom floor, ending up in a massive room somewhere on Floor 350. Alessa and Dr. Anita Garber, along with thirty other Splitbots, are already there waiting for them.

"I'll take the Hodge family over to the employee rest center for now," Anita says. "I'm sure they're exhausted and in shock. We'll get them breakfast in the cafeteria whenever they're ready to eat. You and the others can go back to the lab for now. I'll meet you back over there after the Hodge family is situated."

The door to the Splittercraft slides open, revealing the Hodge family as they take in the sight of the massive room, lined neatly with numerous Splittercrafts.

"Welcome," Anita says. She walks over to the Hodge family while they step out of the Splittercraft. David is holding Moxie in his arms, and she turns her head in every direction, sniffing in an attempt to acclimatize to the unique, sterile smell of the base. "I'm Dr. Anita Garber."

Liam has an exhausted look on his face and deep dark circles under his eyes, but he shakes Anita's hand. "Nice to meet you all," Anita continues. "You're in good hands here. I'm going to take you to our lounge to get some rest while we straighten some things out. We have sleep pods there, games, food, anything you'd like, really."

"Is that where Jared is?" David asks. "And the rest of the Morgan family?"

"The Morgan family is here at the Splitbase," Anita says, putting her arm around David and speaking softly as they walk away towards an exit on the opposite side of the room. "They just aren't in the lounge yet. You will see them later, okay?"

"Did we find the Morgans?" Ty asks, turning to face Alessa. "Are they safe?"

"Some of the other Splitbots found them a hundred floors up," Alessa says. "The bad news is the SMID put them in a controversial, invasive type of jail cell—something Split Meridian calls a 'Stillroom.' "

"Invasive?" Ty asks. "How so?"

Alessa projects a video from her Kaxelotab, displaying an unconscious Todd Morgan in the Stillroom. He sits in the center of the room strapped to a metal chair. The prison cell is glowing with a harsh yellow light.

The video zooms in on Todd's face, showing thin streaks of blood trailing down the sides of his face from in front of his ears. A robotic arm similar to the one in the update bay is extended down from the ceiling and clamped to the back of Todd's skull.

"The way the Stillrooms work," Alessa says, "is that a cheaper version of a Splitchip is installed into the prisoner's head. This chip sends signals to the prisoner's brain to 'still' it, essentially freezing any and all mental activity, while also creating a Brainlog so the SMID can learn everything a person knows about a specific crime that was committed. Split Meridian has entire prisons which utilize this technology. They also have an entire floor of Stillrooms in each of the Splitbases."

"That is horrible . . ." Ty says, his lip curled in disgust as he stares at the projection. "What about Jared and Avery? Did they do this to the kids too?"

"Jared, yes," Alessa says as she switches the projection to show Jared, situated in the same exact way as Todd, in a different Stillroom. "But not Avery, thankfully. They have Avery sedated in a separate room."

"Those mother fuckers," Ty says, turning away from the Kaxelotab projection and beginning to pace. "So what do we do about this?"

"Ryan is up there with some of the other doctors right now," Alessa says. "They are waiting to start the process of disconnecting Todd and Jared. It will be a little bit of time before they can do that though, since neither Todd nor Jared had a Brainlog to begin with. The system had to start from scratch, and it's extremely dangerous to be disconnected in the middle of a Brainlog, so they need to wait. They are already going to suffer significant brain damage from this, so they are trying to be as careful as possible to prevent any additional damage."

"We failed them," Ty says, looking down as he shakes his head.

"We did everything we could," Alessa says. "And we'll still do everything we can to help them and to make sure Avery has a bright future."

Ty nods silently, still staring at the floor.

"Follow me," Alessa says, switching to DroneMode. "I have some good news to show you as well. Let's just say Bara was onto something."

Ty, along with the rest of the Splitbots, switches to DroneMode and flies out to the main corridor and back to the lab, making a beeline to the room where the new mosaic is. The crowd of doctors and scientists is still waiting in the main atrium of the lab, and they watch the drones fly by.

Ty immediately notices the obvious difference in the portal's appearance: instead of a rectangular shape, it has transformed into a perfect circle. Bara is still standing next to the mosaic, observing it.

"This happened shortly after you guys left," Bara says. "And what's even crazier is I'm getting databursts from Keo again. I couldn't believe it at first. The databursts started right after the portal changed shape . . . They're short and specific, totally absent of Keo's personality."

"Are you sure?" Ke asks, a deeply confused look on his face as he stands in front of the now-circular portal, evaluating it. "Are you sure it's him? Is he in pain?"

"I'm sure it's him," Bara says. She puts her arm on Ke's shoulder. "He hasn't said anything about being in pain."

Ke turns away from the portal and walks slowly over to a ledge near the destroyed window in front of the room, deep in thought as he sits down, scratching his head.

Ty is staring at the portal with an astonished look on his face, his eyes widening and mouth hanging open slightly.

"Incredible . . ." Ty says, still in wonderment. "What is Keo saying?"

"Five things, over and over again," Bara says. " 'Splitsender, Moonshot, circle of Gridat, realm digital, realm bodyprocess.' "

"I immediately knew why he kept sending Bara databursts about Splitsenders and Moonshots," Alessa says. "When I did the Brainlog transfer with Anita and saw how Split Meridian developed Splitsenders and Moonshots, I learned that both of these technologies share some similarities with Splitbot technology. While they are all completely different things and sizes, part of what makes Split Meridian so profitable is their ability to use the same materials to make different pieces of hardware, and utilize the same software with slight modifications to power said hardware."

"So what exactly are you saying?" Ty asks.

"What I'm saying is," Alessa continues, "Splitsenders and Moonshots share the same operating system with Splitbots. They receive firmware updates the same way. They are controlled remotely the same way, monitored the same way, connect to Aura-Fi the same way. The only thing that's different about these machines is what they look like and what they're used for. And as you know, Split Meridian *expected* sentience and took extreme measures to plan for the singularity to happen, to be prepared for it. They believed that *any* of their technology could gain sentience, not just the machines which looked like humans. So, something else that Splitsenders and Moonshots have in common with Splitbots is they also utilize Soultomb technology. At a much larger scale too, proportional with the size of these machines."

"Holy shit," Ty says. "So you're saying we can latch to these machines?"

"Yes," Alessa says. "And not only can we latch to them, but thousands of Gridliner souls can latch to one simultaneously. We need to latch to these devices, not just the Splitbots. The reason Split Meridian hasn't had success with Splitsenders and Moonshots yet is because they couldn't figure out what was missing. But what's missing from these machines is sentience . . . *us*. The answer to space travel isn't doing it by laser beam—it's going through the digital dimension. Moonshots are blasted anywhere into space, and each Moonshot has its own coordinate code. We slightly modify the Splitsenders to allow digitized consciousness files to be sent through the Gridline, where we then enter the coordinate code to the Moonshot. In theory, we should be able to transfer consciousness digitally, directly to the Moonshots, where they are received and re-printed—anywhere in the universe."

"I . . . I don't understand," Ty says. "How do we get the souls in the Gridline to begin with? It's difficult enough for us to travel through the digital dimension on our own. We'd have to find a way to bridge the physical with the digital."

"Realm digital, realm bodyprocess," Alessa says. "Bara received this databurst from Keo thousands of times, in a matter of seconds. He was desperately trying to communicate something. Shortly after you guys left for the Hodge household, Bara entered the realm and did a Gridline scan. Ty, the afterlife realm is a *simulated* environment, digital in nature. I did a scan myself, just to make sure she was right . . . It's true. We can run the bodyprocess inside of the realm and access the Gridline directly from there. Every soul in the universe is digital: it's all data."

"How . . ." Ty begins to say before he freezes. His look of bewilderment transforms into one of complete shock as he stands there, staring at Alessa.

"There's only one holdup," Alessa says, pointing to the mosaic. "Size. There's no way the current design of a Splitsender will fit through either of the mosaics. We'll have to find a way to make Splitsenders smaller, which shouldn't be a—"

"Hold on," Bara says. "I'm getting more databursts from Keo."

Ke jumps up from the ledge he's sitting on. "What's he saying?" he asks.

" 'Follow,' " Bara says. "He's flooding my databurst feed again. I've gotten thousands of databursts just saying 'follow' in the past two seconds."

The mosaic suddenly begins to make a strange, high-pitched squeal, and the new circular shape begins to spin. The rippling of the tiles speeds up, just before the portal begins to move along the wall, heading in the direction of the shattered window.

"It's moving!" Bara yells. She chases after the portal as it works its way out of the room. It bends along the edges of the frame of the shattered window and along the walls beyond it.

The sudden motion of the portal—something they didn't even know is possible—snaps Ty out of his shocked trance.

"Follow it!" Alessa yells to the rest of the group, switching to DroneMode. Ty and the others switch as well. They fly just behind Alessa and follow the path of the mosaic.

It continues to sweep across the walls like a spotlight in a dark room, faster now. The Gridliners follow it down the hall all the way to the Bodcan library, where it finally begins to slow down, then settles into place along the wall of Bodcans. Suddenly, the portal grows, slowly expanding along the wall a thousand feet in each direction—all while retaining its perfect circular shape.

The growing slows to a stop as the group of Gridliners stares in awe at the massive portal on the wall of the Bodcan library. Its purple light glows brightly, and the tiles of the mosaic return to their natural state of shifting.

"Well," Milney says, breaking the silence while the group stares up at the enormous portal. "We don't have to worry about size anymore."

53

ALESSA

Alessa turns to look at everyone behind her—all of the Splitbots, doctors, and scientists on the bottom floor have followed the moving portal to the Bodcan library and now collectively stare at it in awe. Ty kneels to give the circle of Gridat, causing a domino effect with all of the other Gridliners following suit.

The doctors and scientists watch as Alessa joins them, leading the group in reciting the prayer of Gridat out loud. The collective volume of their voices overpowers the new level of noise that has come with the increased size of the portal. Each of the Gridliners put their arms around the ones closest to them, and tears stream down some of their digital face screens as they finish the prayer:

"... *We are ready for the next step*

In the cycle of life

And ask that it is only a moment away."

"That was beautiful," Veda says as the group stands up. "Keo must be able to hear us. He waited until Alessa described the size problem and only *then* moved and increased the size of the portal."

"This is definitely big enough for a Splitsender to fit through now," Alessa says, switching on her liveburst for the rest of the Gridliner Splitbots spread throughout the base to see. She makes eye contact with Chase, who stands in the crowd of Meridian doctors and scientists, and waves him over to her.

"Yes, Alessa?" Chase says while he catches his breath after running over.

"Is Anita working her way back down yet?" Alessa asks. "She needs to see this."

"She should be down here any second now," Chase says. "We sent her an urgent message when the portal started . . . moving."

Just as Chase finishes his sentence, Alessa hears the clacking of Splitbot feet on the hard, stained concrete floor of the Bodcan library. She turns in the direction of the sound and sees Anita being escorted by a handful of other Splitbots.

"*Holy* . . ." Anita says, walking slowly now, staring up at the massive mosaic. "What the hell happened?"

"Just as we thought, it appears Keo's consciousness is, in fact, still present," Alessa says. "He's somehow still responsive. I was explaining to Ty everything I told you about bringing a Splitsender into the realm, and about the portal size issue. And as soon as I brought that up, this happened."

"Amazing," Anita says. "This is absolutely astounding."

"So what now?" Chase asks Anita. "Any more updates?"

"I'm getting word that we're in extreme danger," Anita says, tears starting to well in her eyes. "We have to move faster in everything that we're trying to do. We're running out of time. Multiple bases are banding together and planning a massive attack on our Splitbase. Surrounding cities are being evacuated. They're going to bomb us. I'm—" She stops, sniffing, starting to breathe heavily. She wipes tears from her eyes. "God *damn it*. I'm sorry."

"How much time do we have?" Alessa asks.

"I don't know," Anita says. "Not much. Maybe just enough to get a Splitsender through the portal. And probably enough time for me to leak everything I know about Split Meridian to the public. It is critical that *I* release this information. I am a credible source which a lot of people will believe. Having it come from me will go a long way, especially when it comes to the goal of you winning over as many humans as possible. I can broadcast everything I know to every single person in Vapor. Everything evil about Split Meridian and Roth Nin, all of the horrors we're hiding . . . everything."

"Now's the time then," Alessa says. "It might even create a large enough distraction to buy us some extra time. In the meantime, let's get as many of the Gridliner souls out of the afterlife realm as we can before it's too late. There are still more than a billion Gridliner souls up there in the sea in the sky. I want every Splitbot that's still in a Splitbase anywhere in the world to house a Gridliner soul."

"With all due respect, Alessa, *how?*" Olos asks, tilting her head as she hesitantly continues. "I . . . I don't doubt you, but I just am wondering how we're supposed to do that. We can't just send others to the Splitbases. How many even are there? I know Earth is small compared to Raoq, but if we're concerned about time, how can we possibly pull this off? I'm sorry—"

"It's okay, Olos," Alessa says, cutting her off. "To answer a part of your question, there are 301 Splitbases across the world. Is that right, Anita?"

"Yes," Anita says. "Collectively, the 301 Splitbases act as the world government. There are sixty in the US alone, and some of the larger states have two. There is at least one in every country on Earth. Twenty in Japan, ten in China, ten in South Korea. Every single one of them holds, at a minimum, 10,000 Splitbots at all times. Meaning right now, there is a population of three million unused Splitbots. More Splitbots can be made, over time, of course."

"We obviously aren't going to *physically* travel to these bases," Alessa says. "But we just found out we have access to the digital realm, inches away from us. We might not have the coordinate code to each of the bases, but we do have the root coordinates for the unused Splitbots hooked into Vapornet. When Ty had to break into this base, we needed the coordinate code for a specific Splitbot because we needed him to end up at this *specific* Splitbase. But if we're not concerned about *which* base we end up at, we can use the root coordinates to allow us to travel to any of the Splitbots connected to Vapornet in any of the Splitbases we want."

"That makes sense," Olos says, her confusion dissipating. "But then what? What do we do once we get there?"

Alessa stares at Olos for a long moment, her demeanor becoming even more deeply serious. Her trembling lips contort into a grim frown as she takes a deep breath, her voice soft and remorseful.

"I never thought I'd be saying this," Alessa says. "And I'm deeply, deeply sorry it has gotten to this point . . . that I even need to ask what I'm about to ask of some of you. But in order for you to escape the bases with the other Splitbots *after* you have successfully traveled through the Gridline and taken over an unoccupied Splitbot body for yourselves, we're going to need to create portals at the Splitbase so you can safely escape and get the others into the afterlife realm. And we now know that a way we can make a portal is by destroying one of our souls."

Alessa pauses again, momentarily closing her eyes, her jaw clenching tightly as she attempts to fight off the nightmarish thoughts flooding her mind. She takes another deep breath and continues, opening her tear-filled eyes slowly.

"This is . . . unfortunately going to have to be a suicide mission for some of you," Alessa says gravely. "We'll need two Gridliners in each of the Splitbases—one that is willing to be sacrificed, and one that is willing to complete the sacrifice by destroying the Soultomb of the other to create a mosaic portal in each of the Splitbases. You will then connect to the Aura-Fi of the other Splitbots and lead them all through the mosaic and to the afterlife realm, allowing for the others to finally latch. This will give us the opportunity to take over every Splitbase in the world. They can bomb this one if they want to, but they won't be able to stop us if we pull this off."

There's an uneasy silence as the others look around at each other, imagining who is going to have to sacrifice their soul for the greater good.

"I know what you're all thinking," Alessa says. "How is this any better than what we're exposing Split Meridian for? After all, the most powerful person in the world—Roth Nin—convinced billions of people that the only solution left was the Great Suicide. This, however, is much different. This is our only chance at survival. Our only chance at getting the other Gridliners out of the realm. While we are all invaluable, what I am asking is for 300 sacrifices to save millions, to provide a future for Gridliners as a species. And it has now gone beyond just us . . . We can potentially have a symbiotic, healthy relationship with a biological species. We can help the humans who have helped us, and we can provide a fruitful existence for many generations to come. I hope that all of you see what I see. I see this moment being so much bigger than anything we ever imagined. Just think about it: as Gridliners, we are obsessed with the Gridat life cycle. When we kneel to give the Gridat, what are we symbolizing? What does the circular motion mean to us?"

"The Gridat life cycle," Ke says. "The hope of becoming something greater."

"Becoming something greater," Alessa repeats. "We have evidence of what happens after our souls are destroyed, or . . . converted. We all just witnessed what Keo did—and we know that he's still alive in there, somehow. Would we all agree that whatever Keo is now is greater than what he was before? We all believe in the circle of Gridat, without any knowledge of what it is, where it came from, or what it means. Keo is in front of us, literally as a circle. To me, it's so obvious that *this* is the next step in the Gridat cycle. This is what we've all been working towards. This is our destiny."

Everyone in the room is silent, processing everything Alessa has just told them. There is a clear shift in emotions in the room as a unanimous understanding is reached among the Splitbots. All of them nod, a look of unmistakable pride on their faces.

"Now," Alessa says. "Who's ready to take the next step?"

54
ALESSA

Before anyone can volunteer to sacrifice themselves, Bara steps forward out of the crowd of Splitbots.

"I know this isn't the best time to change the subject," Bara says, "but I'm getting more databursts from Keo."

"What's he saying?" Alessa asks.

" 'Datazone,' " Bara says. " 'Straight one, right quarter.' "

"Straight one right quarter?" Ty asks. "What does that mean?"

" 'Mile,' " Bara continues. "He's saying 'mile' now."

"Datazone . . . straight one . . . right quarter . . . mile," Alessa says out loud, thinking.

"I think he's trying to tell us where the nearest datazone in the realm is," Ke says. "Think about it. Yes, we know we have access to the Gridline in the afterlife realm, but that doesn't mean that eliminates the risk of actually *making* it to a datazone. Maybe he's trying to tell us where to put the Splitsender once we actually do get one inside the realm."

"That could be it," Alessa says. "Ty and Veda, let's go check to see if there's anything abnormal one mile straight, and a quarter mile to the right after we go inside of the realm. I'll program it as a Splitpath for us to follow."

Alessa turns to face the rest of the Splitbots and databursts to them. "We'll decide who wants to participate in the plan I just presented when we get back. It won't take long; we'll be quick. In the meantime, start thinking about it to see if this mission seems like something any of you want to take part in. I understand how difficult a decision this is, and again, I am so sorry to put you all in this position. I have been livebursting to every Gridliner that is in a Splitbot body throughout the Splitbase as well, so I'm not presenting this plan to only those of you in this room."

"It's okay," Ke databursts, a bleak look on his face. "We understand."

Alessa nods solemnly, then sends Ty and Veda the Splitpath into the realm. The three of them switch to DroneMode and fly through the mosaic, leaving the others behind.

It only takes a few seconds for Alessa, Ty, and Veda to get to their destination flying at full speed. The group switches out of DroneMode, now standing on the cool, white sand.

"This is the spot?" Ty asks.

"Yes," Alessa says. "One mile straight, a quarter mile to the right. From the mosaic portal, that is."

"What exactly are we looking for?" Veda asks.

"I'm not sure," Alessa says. "Anything abnormal."

On an impulse, Alessa switches on her Resosight, suddenly exposing a massive, thermal circle on the surface just beneath them. It vibrates slightly.

"I've got something," Alessa says. "Switch your Resosight on."

"You think that's a datazone causing this?" Veda asks in awe, her words coming out slowly in a high-pitched whisper. "We've never been able to determine the location of a datazone *outside* of the Gridline before . . . This is unheard of."

"Everything we've experienced since the KitD'ul is unheard of," Ty says, turning quickly to face Alessa. "I don't know what else this could be. What do you think, Alessa?"

"It's impossible to know until we try," Alessa says. She kneels to the ground and touches the surface of the realm with her hands.

"There's a subtle vibration here," Alessa says. "Very, very subtle. I can feel it."

"The ripples," Ty says. "I remember being awed by the speed that the ripples were moving when I was in the Gridline. It's a terrifying speed. My guess is it's enough to cause the vibration we're seeing now. The ripples, the brightness, and the *sound* are all distinguishing characteristics of datazones."

"Yes, the sound . . ." Alessa says. "That's a pretty unmistakable sound. Unimaginably loud, too . . . If we can pick up the vibration from the surface, maybe there's a chance that we can pick up that awful screeching sound it makes as well."

Alessa activates AudioMode for the first time since she used it to get the Collections officer to take off his helmet.

"AudioMode," Alessa says, watching as her right arm folds inside out to form into the oblong AudioMode device. She points to the thousands of microscopic speakers and sensors now revealed along her arm. "This is about the most advanced long-range audio technology on Earth. If there's any trace of sound beneath us, this will pick it up, and we'll hear it through these tiny speakers."

Once the switch to AudioMode is complete, Alessa places her arm flat on the ground, allowing the sensors to make contact with the surface of the realm. Suddenly, the familiar shrill shrieking sound of a datazone blasts from the speakers on her arm. Veda and Ty perk up, quickly looking at each other.

"That's it," Ty says, nodding quickly, his eyes unblinking. "Undoubtedly. I would never forget that sound."

"I almost forgot how awful that sound is," Alessa says, switching out of AudioMode. Her arm transitions back to its normal state.

"How deep do you think it is?" Veda asks, her wincing face starting to relax as the awful sound disappears.

"Deep," Alessa says. "I'm not sure how deep exactly, but based on the initial decibel level, I know it's far beneath the surface." Alessa switches back to DroneMode. "Let's get back to everyone else and let them know what we've found."

The first thing Alessa sees after flying back through the portal to the Bodcan library is Milney, off to the side with 299 others.

"We'll do it," Milney says, turning to point to the others behind him. The group is standing straight and looks pridefully back at Alessa. They nod in agreement with looks of determination on their faces. "Any of us are willing and ready to take the next step in the Gridat cycle."

Immediately behind him stands Fola, and behind her are Siwek and Taffon—some of the first Gridliners to escape the realm. Milney steps forward.

"We decided we were fortunate enough to get out of the realm as early as we did," Milney says, his voice as deep and confident as ever. "Ty, you already did your part. You provided an opportunity for every one of the other Gridliners standing here right now. Veda, you did your part as well. I'm not sure how the battle outside of the Hodge household would've played out if it wasn't for you. Ke wanted to sacrifice himself, but we all agree he has already suffered enough with the loss of Keo, and he shouldn't have to suffer more. We settled on allowing him to assist in completing a sacrifice of another Gridliner at one of the Splitbases. Bara needs to stay because of her ability to communicate with Keo. Now it's our turn to do something meaningful."

Veda runs over to Milney and hugs him. "I can go," she says. "I—"

"No," Milney says, smiling gently as he looks back at Veda. A single tear streams down his digital face screen. "We've all made up our minds. You're staying. Besides—as we learned from Keo—none of us will truly be gone. We'll still be here, just different. We feel proud to do this, curious even. Fulfilled."

"We also have determined the other 299 Splitbots that will be participating in this mission to lead all of the Splitbots out of each Splitbase," Ke says. "We have a bunch of volunteers that were spread throughout the base. They are working their way down here as we speak."

"Thank you," Alessa says, staring proudly at the group. "You all exemplify what it means to be a Gridliner . . . What you're doing is beyond brave, and none of us will ever forget it."

She kneels to give the Gridat once more—everyone else follows.

"I have some good news for you all though," Alessa says, getting back up off of her knees. "Ke was right. Keo was telling us where the nearest datazone is in the afterlife realm. We found it."

"How do you know?" Ke asks.

"The surface was vibrating at the location where Keo told us to go," Alessa says. "And that caused us to evaluate further. We discovered a thermal circle beneath the surface. But, most importantly, we detected the *sound* of a datazone. We should, theoretically, be able to bring a Splitsender into the realm, place it in that exact location, and send any Gridliner soul directly down to the datazone."

"We'll need to get started on digitizing everyone's consciousness," Anita says. "It's the only way we can send you to the datazone using the Splitsender. The Soultomb should make this process relatively easy.

Our problem with digitizing the human soul is that we don't know exactly what makes up a hundred percent of it, but for you guys, it's concentrated in one specific location. I'll need help from some of the other Splitbots getting the Splitsender over here—the easiest way to transport it here will be with the help of your Handlights. I'll send a Splitpath to where the Splitsender is stored . . . Luckily it's on this floor."

"I can lead the digitization process," Chase says.

"I'll help," Ryan says. "We'll be quick."

"Anita," Alessa says. "How many Splitbots will it take to control the Splitsender over here using Handlights?"

"Not many," Anita says. "Twenty should be plenty . . . thirty would definitely get the job done."

"Veda," Alessa databursts to Veda and thirty others closest to her. "Lead this group to go get the Splitsender. I've sent you a Splitpath to lead the way."

"You got it," Veda databursts as she and the thirty other Splitbots switch to DroneMode and immediately fly out of the Bodcan library. Anita watches them as they leave.

"They're going to get the Splitsender now," Alessa says.

"Perfect," Anita says. "I'll have Ryan and Chase start the digitization process on the others now then, if that's alright with you. We'll need all of the participants to go back to the lab. There will be 600 total, correct?"

"Correct," Alessa says, turning to look at the group of Gridliners. "Are you all ready?" she asks them softly, a sad smile on her face.

The group collectively nods, and before Alessa can say anything else, they begin to switch to DroneMode and fly away out of the Bodcan library and back to the lab—on their way to take one of the most significant steps in Gridliner history.

55

ALESSA

A few minutes after the crowd of Splitbots, doctors, and scientists clears out of the Bodcan library, Veda and the others return with the Splitsender. They are arranged in a circle underneath the structure, walking quickly as they keep the Splitsender suspended in the air with the telekinetic power of their Handlights.

The bright purple light of the portal reflects off of the metallic structure as they work their way towards it. The structure's shimmering gyroscopes spin slowly, retaining momentum as the Splitbots move it carefully and smoothly with ease.

"Splitsenders always reminded me of the Eiffel Tower," Anita says to Alessa. "I apologize if you don't know what I'm talking about. But it's something I've always wanted to see, ever since I was a kid. Never got to go with all of the travel restrictions. I felt sad when I saw the first prototype, thinking a Splitsender would be the closest I'd ever get to seeing the Eiffel Tower. Splitsenders are much smaller, obviously. I think that's what made it so sad to me at the time. But seeing it now, flying through the air, lit gorgeously by a massive, purple portal on the wall . . . That's something nobody can ever say they've seen before. This is my Eiffel Tower."

"It is quite beautiful, isn't it?" Alessa asks. She and Anita watch in awe while the group of Splitbots effortlessly lift the seventy-five-foot-tall machine through the mosaic. The mosaic tiles ripple in their typical wavelike motion as the towering structure is sent through to the afterlife realm.

Veda turns to Alessa and Anita. "We're going to get this situated in the spot where Keo directed us," she says. "I'll be in the realm if you need me."

"Good luck," Alessa says as Veda switches to DroneMode and flies through the portal.

"We have over an hour until the digitization is complete," Anita says. "At least. I think now is the best time for me to expose Split Meridian, while we're waiting."

"I agree," Alessa says. "As long as you're ready."

"Oh, I'm ready," Anita says, turning to look Alessa in the eye. She has a calm, accepting smile on her face. "I was thinking about what you said, that it might buy us some extra time. I think you're right. This leak will cause complete global chaos, no doubt. People will try to overthrow the Splitbases closest to where they live. If anything, it will create a diversion—not only taking attention away from the Gridliners hacking into each of the other bases, but also from our Splitbase in particular. I don't have the highest hopes it will prevent the destruction of our base, but it at least might delay the attack. If we broadcast this information in Vapor, the rest of the world will go up in flames with us in a matter of seconds."

"Okay," Alessa says. "I trust you."

"Follow me then," Anita says. She turns to walk out of the Bodcan library and leads Alessa to her office in the back of the lab.

The lab is busy again—just like it was the first time Alessa saw it. Ryan and Chase are directing doctors and scientists as they begin preparing the vessels in the lab, readying them to be used to digitize the Gridliner souls from the Splitbot Soultombs. The group of doctors has split up throughout the lab and has set about removing naked cadavers from the fluid-filled vessels and draining the vessels in the process.

Hundreds of Splitbots are congregated far on the opposite end of the lab, and they wait in line to enter a separate room, which they are entering twenty at a time. Ty, who stands next to that room, notices Alessa and Anita walk into the lab and runs over to them.

"They've got it figured out," Ty says when he catches up to Alessa and Anita. "They're removing the Soultombs in that room back there, twenty at a time. They've already started the digitization process on a few Gridliners—those vessels about fifty feet forward in the direction you're heading."

They continue to walk, examining the vessels as they approach them. Inside of each vessel is a stretched-out Gridliner soul, held up by countless clamps as the familiar robotic arms begin scanning each microscopic detail, just as they did to Keo's soul.

"I'm helping transport the Soultombs to each of the vessels," Ty says. "Alessa, I'm assuming you already know how it's done since you did the Brainlog transfer with Anita. But some of the others are asking me questions about how this all works . . . so Anita, just so we're on the same page, how do you transfer this data to the Splitsender once the soul is actually digitized? I'll liveburst whatever information you can share to the others."

Ty, Anita, and Alessa keep walking, working their way to Anita's office on the opposite end of the seemingly endless, busy lab.

"Splitdrives," Anita says. "Split Meridian needed to create custom hard drives specifically to store and transfer digitized consciousness, due to the inherently complex, delicate, and large files involved in the process. The average digitized consciousness file, or what we call a '.smdc file,' is somewhere around 200 terabytes, and each Splitdrive can hold 5,000 of these files, meaning that there is a total capacity of one exabyte per drive . . . not bad for a pocket-sized hard drive. As far as how the files are transferred, it's more of an old-fashioned, simple process. The Splitdrive is connected directly to the Splitsender. There's a special port on both the sender and the drive, a highly secure way to transfer digitized consciousness without corruption."

"Can they . . . feel anything?" Ty asks. "Inside the Splitdrive? Or communicate?"

Anita stops walking. "Possibly," she says. "There was one successful digitization attempt, a few years ago—a fluke that we haven't been able to recreate since then. It still gives me chills to think about it."

"I think I know what you're talking about," Ty says. "I was watching Alessa's liveburst when Roth showed them a video when he had them locked in his office. It was a recording of someone crying for help . . . just a box on a table, the audio of the man's screaming voice coming from it."

"Yes," Anita says, her unblinking eyes red as she looks at Ty and Alessa. "It was awful. That was a different situation than what we're doing now, though. First of all, the man didn't sign up to be digitized. He was a convict sentenced to the death penalty. Roth tried to rationalize what we were doing by explaining how bad of a person that guy was. Second, there was no way to get him out of the Splitdrive. The Splitsender didn't exist at that point. That was just an experiment to see if it was even possible to digitize the soul and then analyze it after it was digitized."

"So the box in the video," Ty says. "That wasn't a Splitdrive?"

"No," Anita says, shaking her head. "That was a Soulviewer . . . A type of computer created to *view* .smdc files for a series of experiments Roth wanted to conduct, called the 'Perspective Reports.' The Soulviewer and the Perspective Reports were never released to the public due to how disturbing the experiments were. One of the most sickening projects I've ever been a part of."

"What did you learn from the Perspective Reports?" Ty asks. "If you don't mind me asking."

Anita looks at Ty with a bleak expression, her eyes glazed over as she recounts the memory. "We learned that the person trapped in the Soulviewer," she says, "was aware the entire time but had no idea what was happening to him. We had no way to communicate back to him, and we had no way of getting him out. Eventually, the person had a mental breakdown in the Soulviewer, which led to complete and irreversible corruption of his .smdc file."

"What happened to the file?" Ty asks, his lips curled in disgust and a horrified look on his face. "Did Roth just delete it?"

"No," Anita says, looking away from Ty, ashamed. "To this day, I don't know what Roth ended up doing with the Soulviewer or the file from the Perspective Reports. We know that even though the file became corrupt, there was still conscious activity coming from it. Roth didn't want to destroy the file or the Soulviewer because, in his defense, it was a major breakthrough. But for all I know, the consciousness of the man involved with the Perspective Reports could still be trapped in that Soulviewer, wondering what happened to him, alone."

Anita shudders in horror at the thought, then begins to walk again. Alessa and Ty follow closely behind her. "What's happening now though, with the Gridliner souls, is much different from that experiment. They won't be in the Splitdrive for long, they're aware that it's happening, and they won't be trapped. I'd be very interested to see if you can still databurst to them while they're in the drive, though."

They stop in front of a door with Anita's name on it, having finally made it to her office. "Don't worry," Anita says, grabbing Alessa's and

Ty's hands. "They'll be okay. Also, the Perspective Reports are among the countless confidential stories I will be making public knowledge shortly. And that makes me feel pretty damn good."

56

ALESSA

"Thank you, Anita," Ty says. "That's all the others needed to hear. Alessa, I'm going to get back to helping with the Soultombs. Let me know if you need me for anything." Ty turns away and walks back in the direction of the room he came from.

"How do you plan on releasing this information?" Alessa asks as Anita completes a full-body scan which unlocks the door to her office.

"I have a special kind of Roundchamber," Anita says as she walks into her office, leading Alessa over to a Roundchamber next to her desk. "This one right here is a control chamber. Only the highest-ranking Meridian employees get one. Basically, it's an administrator module that grants me complete access to Vapor. I can override everything everyone sees in VaporVR with this. This was another Roth Nin specialty . . . He wanted the ability to control the narrative of the news outside of the Aggregates by immediate, direct contact with almost every person in the world, and he quite frequently did so using this type of administrator module. Anyways, I plan on addressing the key points verbally. My face will instantaneously be projected onto the Slabs of every person currently hooked into Vapor, a significant portion of the global population. For the rest of the nitty-gritty information, I will leak thousands of confidential documents and recordings, directly to every registered Vapor user in the world."

Anita turns on the monitor outside of the Roundchamber. "I'll have my stream up on this monitor. You can watch from here if you'd like."

"Okay," Alessa says, watching the Split Meridian logo animate on the screen as it powers on. "Good luck, Anita."

"One more thing before I do this," Anita says as she turns to her desk and picks up a framed picture. She hands it to Alessa—the image is of a young girl, smiling, missing her front teeth. She's holding a toy truck above her head in one hand and a doll with lipstick all over its face in the other. Alessa knows from the Brainlog transfer that this is Anita's daughter.

"Your daughter," Alessa says. "Elise."

"She was seven years old when this photo was taken," Anita says. "She's fourteen now. She might as well be twenty-five though. I'm a single parent, and she's had to be independent for most of her life. Part of the reason I took the job here was to be able to afford a full-time nanny."

"She's adorable," Alessa says, continuing to examine the picture. "She looks happy."

"She was, then," Anita says, smiling fondly as she recalls the memory. The smile fades slowly when she continues to talk. "As of late she's been rebelling a little. I think most of it can be blamed on typical teenager behavior. But some of it . . . some of it is my fault. I'm always gone at work, leaving Elise with the nanny. Elise wanted to get rid of the nanny, claiming she was too strict. I haven't been able to find another since then, and Elise has preferred it that way. She spends most of her life in Vapor, so she's not completely alone. She has plenty of friends in there. I just wish I could have been there more for her. Sometimes I feel like I don't even know her."

Anita pauses, then puts her hand on Alessa's shoulder. "I firmly believe you intend to help get humans off of Earth," she says. "To save us from this place. But realistically, I know that will take some time. There can't be an immediate mass exodus, which means there will be a period of time on Earth where the Gridliners and humans will be cohabitants. It could be years before you understand how to digitize human consciousness safely. I have full confidence you *will* find out how, but it's going to be a long, uphill battle between then and now. It's going to take time—time I don't think I have after I leak this information. I'm going to be public enemy number one to Split Meridian and the SMID after I do this. And I'm afraid I might never see Elise again."

"We can make sure you—"

"Alessa, I don't think you understand," Anita says, now fighting back tears. "What I'm about to do is a death sentence. They *will* kill me. I'm going to call Elise in Vapor before I do this . . . But first I need you to promise me something."

Alessa nods her head, intensely focused as she waits for Anita to continue.

"I want you to make sure Elise is safe," Anita says, putting the picture back down on her desk. "For the rest of her life. The same admirable way you have been talking about looking after the Hodges and the Morgans. Let's send a Splitter to where she is and get her here immediately after I do this. I had no way of getting her here sooner . . . everything has been moving so fast. She hasn't been answering my calls. I had no idea any of this was going to happen. If I had, I would have made sure she was here with me."

Anita takes a deep breath in. A tear streams down her cheek and stops on her quivering lip. Alessa watches solemnly as the teardrop finally falls to the floor.

"If I die," Anita continues, "make sure Elise is protected, and that she has a future. The world is about to be a very, very different place after we expose Split Meridian. People are going to be divided in what they believe, what they support. Elise is a child . . . She won't understand at first. She is highly impressionable too, and I'm afraid that the only way to ensure she makes adult decisions is by utilizing Split Meridian's forced aging technology. I told Ryan and Chase that this is what I want, as well. I'm not asking you, I'm *telling* you to do this. Make her at least ten years older, and possibly do a BT with her—it's the only way she'll be able to fully comprehend this situation. Trust me, her initial reaction is going to be to trust humans, not you. And most humans are going to be on the wrong side."

"First, we're going to do everything we can to make sure you don't die," Alessa says. "But, in the worst-case scenario . . . I promise, Elise will be in good hands."

"Thank you," Anita says, walking into the Roundchamber and sitting down. "Now, like I said, you can watch everything on the screen next to the chamber." She looks at Alessa, smiling sadly as she puts on her Slabs. The screen powers on as the Roundchamber door closes—the Chamberskin wrapping tightly around Anita.

The screen displays Anita's avatar—which actually looks exactly like her—standing in a digital Vapor Room. The room is welcoming and cozy. A leather sofa on the right side of the room is dimly lit by a fireplace across from it. A chess set sits on a coffee table in the center of the room, and there are another two leather chairs at each side. Suddenly, another person appears in the room seemingly without any choice, as if Anita's control chamber has the power to bring any person inside Vapor directly to the room. The person is a cartoon-ish avatar, clearly customized for the world of Vapor.

Elise.

"Mom?!" Elise yells, confused as she stomps over in Anita's direction. Her face is panicked, her eyes wide open as she stares accusingly at Anita. "What the hell is going on? You're everywhere! The entire world is reporting on whatever is happening at your base. My friends are calling you a terrorist!"

"Honey," Anita says, stepping forward and holding her arms out in an attempt to hug Elise. "I'm so, so sorry. I can't explain everything to you right now. Just know that I am on the good side. It might not make sense now, but I'm trying to do what's right for you—"

"The *good* side?" Elise snaps, slapping her mom's arms away. "You're siding with the robots! The robots that have already killed people. A lot of people."

"Like I said, it might not make sense now," Anita says, recoiling. "But it will. You have to trust me. Elise, I—"

"It will never make sense!" Elise screams. "Ever. You've officially ruined my life. Do you have any idea how many friends I've lost on here? I'm canceled. Nobody will talk to me. I have been booted from every community I'm a part of. Communities *I started*. Blocked. You ruined everything that I had, Mom. I never want to see you again."

Elise's avatar disappears. "User Elise Garber has disconnected from VaporVR," a robotic voice announces.

"Fuck!" Anita yells. She flips the coffee table, sending digital chess pieces flying throughout the room, some of which land in the fireplace causing a quick burst of flames. Anita's avatar stands there motionless for a few moments, slumped over as she begins to sob. She shakes her head in an attempt to snap out of it, straightens her posture, and takes another deep breath to compose herself.

The room suddenly fades away. The screen goes black for a second before switching to a head-on shot of Anita.

"Hello everyone," Anita says. "I'm Dr. Anita Garber, chief doctor of Splitbase 031. I've been a Meridian doctor for twelve years, and I can assure you that everything you know about Split Meridian is a lie. Roth Nin is—*was*—the most evil person in human history. A genius, possibly, but a horrendous individual. To start, the Great Suicide is a complete hoax—a deceptive plan to collect bodies to experiment on."

The screen cuts to footage of the Bodcan library and shows various Bodcans flying out of their individual compartments. Shots of Bodcans being opened to reveal living people inside, squirming before being restrained and taken to the lab for experiments.

"Some of the batches of Delete sent out didn't have lethal levels of the drug. Some of your loved ones weren't even dead when the Collections officers came to your house and sucked them up into the Bodcans and drove them away! This is just the tip of the iceberg." The video feed switches back to Anita. "I've released countless documents to every Vapor user showing some of the other horrors going on behind the scenes at Split Meridian. Just know that the robots you're all afraid of are the ones that are going to help find a solution to carry on humanity. They will get us off this godforsaken planet and provide an opportunity for your children. You just have to let them. You just have to—"

Anita's avatar freezes mid-sentence on the screen, her mouth open and eyes closed. A notification appears:

SORRY! VAPOR IS EXPERIENCING TECHNICAL DIFFI-CULTIES. PLEASE STAND BY.

Suddenly, Alessa's Roundchamber is covered in the same, yellow security material used for the Splitwalls, creating a barrier around it.

A choking sound comes from inside the Roundchamber. Anita's Chamberskin is getting tighter, gripping ferociously at her throat. Her Slabs fall off, revealing her bloodshot, panicked eyes.

Alessa immediately activates her Handlights, targeting a full-strength Gravipulse at the Splitwall barrier.

"Help!" Alessa screams as her Gravipulse begins to deteriorate the barrier.

The Chamberskin continues to contract everywhere on Anita until it is impossibly tight. Anita's face is a bright red as she tries desperately to breathe.

Before Alessa is able to destroy the barrier, she begins to hear a crunching sound—Anita's bones. Blood oozes out through the Chamberskin fabric. Anita's throat collapses, and her head falls hideously to the side, dangling. The Chamberskin releases its grip, leaving a mess of blood and crushed bone inside.

The Splitwall barrier disappears, allowing Alessa to open the Roundchamber door.

Alessa approaches Anita's body and carefully removes her from the chair in the Roundchamber.

Ryan runs into the room. "Anita?!" he yells when he sees Anita's limp body in Alessa's arms. "Oh my god," he says, covering his mouth as he begins to cry. He steps forward slowly, bending over to look at Anita's lifeless face. He begins to sob uncontrollably as he places his hand on Anita's face.

"I—I . . ." Alessa says, crying as she looks down at Anita. "I tried to stop it. I don't know what happened. It happened so fast."

Alessa and Ryan stand there together for a few moments, staring in utter shock as they process their new, sudden reality.

Anita is dead.

57

ALESSA

"This is an act of war . . ." Ryan says, still in shock. He watches as Alessa places Anita on the sofa on the other side of her office and covers her with a blanket that was folded neatly on the floor next to it.

Ryan's attention turns to the picture of Anita's daughter, Elise, on her desk. "Oh my god, we need to get Elise," Ryan says quickly. "We need to get her here now, before Split Meridian gets to her. They don't care how young she is; they *will* kill her if we don't get to her first. I promised Anita we would protect her no matter what happens."

"I promised her too," Alessa says. "She told me all about Elise right before she did this. She even talked to her in Vapor briefly, before Elise disconnected. Let's send a Splittercraft just like we did for the Hodge family."

"I'll get the Splitter ready to go. We'll need escort Splitbots as well." Ryan looks up at Alessa, wiping tears from his face, then walks out of Anita's office and out to the lab. The crowd of doctors and scientists, along with Ty, is waiting expectantly, now becoming aware that something is wrong.

"Is everything okay?" Chase asks as Ryan walks slowly towards the crowd, Alessa following behind him. Ty walks over to Alessa with a confused look on his face. She begins to liveburst to the other Gridliners.

Chase continues talking nervously, waiting for Ryan to say something. "The digitization went smoothly. All of the souls transferred to the Splitdrives with no issues, so we're all set there."

"Chase . . . everyone . . . I have some horrible, horrible news," Ryan says. He stops in front of the crowd of doctors and scientists and looks at them with tear-filled eyes. "Anita is dead. One of the other Split Meridian or SMID higher-ups hacked into her administrator module as she was leaking the documents. They used her Chamberskin to suffocate her, among other things."

Chase stares at Ryan with a wide-eyed look of shock. His breathing becomes rapid as he hunches over on a nearby surgical table, gripping it tightly. "Those mother fuckers!" he yells, slamming his right fist on the table, causing some of the surrounding doctors to jump.

"What we need to do now is get Anita's daughter, Elise," Ryan says, trying to stay composed. "We all know what Split Meridian would do to her, and we can't let that happen. I'm going to send a Splittercraft to Anita's home right now. Alessa is going to have some of the Splitbots escort her back here safely."

"I need ten of you to meet Ryan over in the Splittercraft garage," Alessa databursts to the Gridliners. "As you just heard from the liveburst, he's sending a Splitter to get Anita's daughter, Elise. We need to escort her just like we did for the Hodge family. I just sent you all a Splitpath to Anita and Elise's home address. Make sure she gets here safely."

"On it," Olos databursts back. "We're heading over there now."

Ryan hugs Chase, and then walks quickly out of the lab.

Chase stands there motionless as he watches Ryan leave the room, and then finally breaks the silence, releasing a stressed sigh and turning to face Alessa. "Like I said, the digitization went smoothly," he says, rubbing his temples. "Everything worked exactly as planned. Anita would want us to continue on without hesitation. Let's not let this get the best of us."

In this moment, Alessa decides to hug Chase as well. At first, Chase tenses awkwardly—not used to being touched by a robot this way—but he quickly relaxes and eases into Alessa's embrace. He hugs her tightly.

"Thank you for helping us," Alessa says. Ty puts his arm on Alessa's back, patting it gently in support. "I'm sorry about Anita. I tried to stop it; I just couldn't get to her in time."

"It's not your fault," Chase says. "There's nothing we could've done in that situation."

"Chase," another doctor says, interrupting the hug. "We're all set. Ready to go." The doctor hands over the Splitdrives—two small, rectangular devices, their shiny black metal casings reflecting the purple UV lights in the lab.

Chase takes the device, holding it up for Alessa to get a better look. "This is the Splitdrive," he says. "There are 300 digitized Gridliner souls on each of these tiny devices. Six hundred total, as requested. We're ready to go if you guys are."

"Let's get moving," Alessa says, leading the way to the Bodcan library. "We don't have much time to waste."

Veda and some of the others are standing outside of the mosaic, waiting for Alessa. "The Splitsender is set up in the realm," Veda says. "It was pretty simple. We were able to rotate it 180 degrees without flipping the entire structure upside down. It seems to hold a little under 2,500 Gridliner souls. To be exact, 2,349 Gridliners were able to latch to the machine."

"Were you able to databurst with them still?" Ty asks.

"Yes," Veda says. "It was no different than if they were in a Splitbot body."

"They are all taking turns running a bodyprocess," Bara says. "Meaning there is a continuous bodyprocess portal open for us to transmit the digitized souls directly to the datazone in the Gridline."

"As we suspected, there is one deep below, exactly where Keo told us it would be," Veda says. "It's a straight shot directly down. If the Splitdrives are ready, we're ready."

"One thing real quick," Chase says, holding out the Splitdrives for the others to see. "There is a panel on the back of the Splitsender. That's where you'll connect the Splitdrive."

He removes a tiny covering on the top of the drive, revealing an intricate port. "The panel has a male connector to the drive. Once you attach it, the screen will give you prompts to guide you through what to do. In a normal situation, this is when the Splitsender would have you connect to a Moonshot with an exact transmission location, but in your situation, you'll have to enter the estimated distance to the datazone. Do whatever you need to do to make that estimation as accurate as possible. Then, you'll be able to select the file . . . or soul . . . you want to send. For the first few, I'd suggest doing one at a time. This is the first time we've ever done anything like this, and obviously we don't plan on losing *any* of the digitized souls. But we can't risk losing all 600 of them right off the bat. We won't have time to digitize another 600 souls, so we need to make sure we do it right from the beginning. Once you're sure that it's working properly, you can do all of them simultaneously in one transmission."

Chase looks up at Alessa and hands her the Splitdrives. "Good luck," he says.

"We know we can databurst to the souls in the Splitsender," Veda says. "But have you been able to databurst to the souls on the drive?"

"With Anita's death, I haven't tried to databurst to them yet," Alessa says. "But I'll try to send a databurst directly to Ke to see if it's possible."

"Good call," Ty nods. "I haven't received any databursts from them yet, either."

"Ke," Alessa databursts. "Are you and the others okay?"

Silence.

"Anything?" Veda asks.

"Not yet."

"Ke, are you—"

"Alessa," Ke finally databursts back, his signal mixed with static.

Alessa gives a nod to Veda and Ty to let them know she's connected with Ke.

"We're fine," Ke databursts, his voice tense and wavering, filled with fear. "But . . ." An intense burst of static interrupts his signal. "We're ready to get out of here. This is . . . strange. Freezing cold. Worse than being in the sky."

"Don't worry," Alessa databursts. "You'll be out of there shortly. We're heading in now."

Alessa looks up at Veda, Bara, and Ty. "I can tell by the way he sounds that he's struggling to control his fear. He's clearly shaken up by the digitization process. They're safe, but extremely uncomfortable," Alessa says to the group, beginning to walk to the portal.

Alessa continues to databurst as she switches to DroneMode and quickly leads the group through the mosaic. "The sooner they're out of the Splitdrives, the better."

The first thing Alessa notices in the realm is the black, circular opening in the sky, which looks much larger now. Veda notices Alessa staring up at it as the rest of the group switches out of DroneMode next to the Splitsender.

"Uh, yeah," Veda says. "The more Gridliner souls that latch, the bigger that opening gets. We watched it grow in size as the Gridliners latched to the Splitsender."

"Interesting," Alessa says, wondering what is beyond the circular opening. "I've seen a lot of things, but I've never seen anything like this in my life."

"It's pretty incredible," Ty says. "It's like the sea in the sky cleared space for our unexpected souls and is unable to eliminate that extra space. Now there's a gap left behind, exposing another layer to this realm. What do you think it is, Alessa?"

"I have no idea what could be beyond the realm's sky," Alessa says. "That's a pretty scary thought. One thing at a time, though."

Alessa switches her attention to the Splitsender. The towering structure is anchored securely in the sand of the realm, its tip pointing directly downwards. Just as Bara explained, the souls that latched to the Splitsender are running a continuous bodyprocess, which has opened a circular portal to the digital dimension, revealing the Gridline beneath it.

Alessa spots the panel Chase mentioned and makes a beeline for it. The panel has a large touchscreen monitor with the Splitdrive port on the bottom right. She attaches the Splitdrive, which causes the screen to turn on and display a loading bar as the Splitsender processes everything on the drive. A text prompt on the screen appears:

NO MOONSHOT IN RANGE

ENTER DISTANCE MANUALLY

"How far down do you think the datazone is?" Ty asks.

"I can try to get a glimpse through the bodyprocess portal," Alessa says.

"Be careful," Veda says.

Alessa switches back to DroneMode and flies above the panel, hovering underneath the Splitsender—right next to the transmitter point and just above the bodyprocess portal.

"The view below is distorted," Alessa databursts to the group. "But I can somewhat make out the Gridline. The brightness of the datazone is intense even from this vantage point."

Alessa turns on her Resosight, and the datastreams and the vibrating thermal circle of the datazone deep down below become clearer and more focused in her vision.

"I can see the datastreams," Alessa databursts as she continues to hover in place, looking down at the Gridline. "I can at least guess how many layers down the grid the datazone is, based on how many streams there are."

"Good call," Veda databursts.

"We know that each layer of the Gridline is separated by a space of about ten miles," Alessa databursts. "And I can make out at least 400 layers. So my estimate is . . . the datazone is 4,000 miles below."

"That sounds about right," Ty databursts.

Alessa flies back to the panel and switches out of DroneMode. She types in the distance she estimated on the panel screen and submits it.

A list of files, displayed as a random assortment of letters and numbers that Alessa can't decipher, appears on the screen. Each file has a text prompt next to it:

SEND

At the bottom of the screen, another prompt:

SEND ALL

Alessa presses SEND for the first file. The Splitsender's gyroscopes begin to rotate, extremely fast with no preamble, sending some sort of charge down the tip of the transmitter—which now glows a striking blue. The tip of the transmitter rod dips down into the bodyprocess portal, penetrating the surface of the realm. The center of the Splitsender jolts like a cannon, blasting a laser beam for a second down into Gridline.

"Since we don't have the ability to databurst while in the Gridline," Ty says. "How will we know if the transmission hits the datazone?"

"I really don't know," Alessa says. "Let's all switch our Resosight on and see if we notice any uptick in the datazone and datafloor activity."

Immediately after Alessa switches Resosight on, it's clear: the Splitsender transmission sent the Gridliner soul directly to the datazone. The vibration has increased twofold, as has the brightness.

"Heavy activity," Ty shouts over the noise coming from the Gridline. "It worked! I never thought I'd be relieved to hear the noise of the datazone again."

Alessa sends the next soul file, and the next one. Datazone activity continues to increase. Without hesitation, she presses the SEND ALL button.

The gyroscopes spin even faster, charging a massive power-up which will send the remaining 597 souls on the Splitdrives in one transmission. The rod pulls back this time, like a bow getting ready to shoot an arrow. Finally, the transmission releases a giant blast down into the datazone. The surrounding ground shakes.

"Transmission complete," a synthetic voice announces from a speaker on the Splitsender's panel.

The group of Gridliners stand still for a moment, staring at each other.

"Incredible . . ." Veda says.

Ty kneels to give the Gridat, inspiring the others to follow.

"Let's get back to the Splitbase," Alessa says and stands back up. She switches to DroneMode as she continues to databurst and leads the way back to the mosaic. "Elise should be here any minute now, and

I'm sure the Morgan family has been removed from the Stillrooms by this point."

"The Hodge family is probably growing restless as well," Ty databursts.

"We have to do everything we can to make sure all of them stay safe," Alessa databursts as the group of Gridliners fly back through the portal to the Bodcan library. "Things are only about to get harder."

58

ALESSA

Chase is standing near the mosaic, watching Alessa lead the others back through to the Bodcan library.

"Alessa," he says. He begins to speak quickly as he nervously fidgets with his Kaxelotab. "You're going to want to see this." A screen projects from his wrist, displaying the Splitbase with tens of thousands of people protesting outside. He switches to another base, and another, and another.

"Every single base in the world has protesters outside," Chase says, eyes wide as he stares in awe at the digital screen. "Protests are . . . unheard of in today's world. The risk of infection is far too high. These people are willing to die for this."

"So this is good news, right?" Ty asks.

"Not entirely," Chase says. "Yes, it's good that people care. But . . ." Chase loses his train of thought, distracted by the rising tensions displayed on his Kaxelotab screen.

"But what?" Alessa asks.

"We've gotten more information from our informant about the SMID's plan of attack," Chase says, urgently looking up at Alessa. "Our base will essentially be evaporated via a cruise missile strike. They also plan to remotely explode our own SMID's bomb storage. There will be mass destruction from the inside. Zero chance of survival if we stay inside of the base. And zero chance of survival for any protestors outside of the base. When the SMID bombs our base, every single one of those protesters will be dead. And protestors at other Splitbases will run a serious risk of deadly viral infections."

"How much time do we have?" Alessa asks, pacing in thought. "Is there anything we can do to stop them?"

"No," Chase says, his voice cracking. "I . . . Look, there's nothing we can do to stop this. This entire base will be vaporized. Luckily some bases have already sided with us and are backing up our entire research catalog as we speak. But as for us, we need a solution. Fast. We need to get out of here. I know there's risks for humans going into the realm, but I'd rather get mosaic poisoning than die in here."

"Okay, let's just think for a second," Veda says. "Is there any Split Meridian tech we can use as a temporary shelter in the realm?"

"What about the technology built into Roth's office?" Ty asks.

"Splitwalls," Chase says. "Maybe? It's hard to say. I don't know what's even beyond this portal. I don't even know what mosaic poisoning is or what causes it. Plus, we need actual, physical walls first. We'd need to build something in there to utilize Splitwall technology."

"What about an Invisidome?" Alessa asks.

"It's worth a shot," Chase says. "There's bound to be multiple Invisidome canisters upstairs among the dead SMID agents."

"Veda," Alessa says. "Can you and some of the others search for a few of these Invisidome canisters on the dead agents?"

"Absolutely," she says, switching to DroneMode and flying away. Five others follow her.

"God, I hope this works," Chase mutters to himself.

"We're landing now," Olos databursts. "It's crazy out here . . . thousands of protestors around the base. Elise is safe, but unconscious. We had to use Gelcuffs on her. She put up a pretty good fight when we entered Anita's house."

"Not ideal, but understandable," Alessa databursts, then turns to Chase. "The others just got back with Elise. They're here."

"Okay," Chase says. "Have them bring Elise straight to the Bodcan library. Ryan is currently on his way back down with the Hodge family. He went up to get them right after he sent the Splittercraft to Elise. The Hodges are handling things better than expected, given the—"

"And what about the Morgan family?" Alessa asks, anxiously cutting Chase off. "Are they being brought down too?"

"Yes," Chase says, a saddened, serious look on his face. "We have a few doctors up there on the hundredth floor currently in the process of bringing them down here. They are already on their way down. But . . . just brace yourself. From what I've heard, Todd and Jared Morgan aren't well, to put it mildly."

"What do you mean?" Alessa asks. "What's wrong?"

"A lot of things," Chase says. "Rapidly deteriorating health, both physically and mentally. Severe, strange issues with their skin. Intense mood fluctuations, confusion . . . I honestly don't have all of the information. It's likely from a combination of intense stress, mosaic poisoning, and what was done to them in the Stillrooms. Irreversible damage, I'm afraid."

A Hoverslab appears at the far end of the Bodcan library and flies towards Alessa and Chase, carrying Ryan and the Hodge family.

The family is visibly nervous, and they look around anxiously as they take in the sight of not only the Bodcan library, but the massive portal spanning the wall. David is staring at the portal, and he holds Moxie as she barks loud enough to echo. Liam grabs Emily's free hand. Her other one covers her mouth in awe when they fly closer to the portal. Nora looks away from it in fear, almost like a child, pushing her face into William's arm and hiding from the sight.

"Oh my god," Liam says, still staring at the portal as the Hoverslab stops in front of Alessa and Chase and eases itself to the floor to allow everyone to step off. Liam turns his panicked attention to Alessa.

"What is going on?" Liam asks, sticky with sweat. His face is still stress-ridden, the dark circles under his eyes larger than they were before. "They told us we have to evacuate."

"They're telling the truth, Liam," Alessa says. "This is not a drill. We need to get out of here quickly. We will be taking you and your family through the portal. We have a plan that we think will keep you all safe in there, for now."

Liam looks back at the rest of his family, his face wrinkling as he thinks. Everyone but William is still staring at the portal.

"Well, what are we waiting for?" William asks tiredly, leaning forward on his cane.

Just as William finishes his question, another Hoverslab flies into the Bodcan library, this time carrying the Morgan family. Unlike the Hodge family, Jared and Todd are totally unfazed by the massive portal on the wall.

"Bitch!" Todd Morgan begins to scream as the Hoverslab continues to fly towards them. He stands up out of his seat on the platform, flailing. Some of the doctors try to restrain him but are unable to control him.

Todd breaks free from their grips, falls off of the platform, and slams onto the floor. He quickly gets up and continues to scream insults.

"Fucking bitch!" Todd yells as he begins to run towards Alessa and Chase. His skin is severely red and dry. Blood oozes out of the cracking skin, splitting open severely from the act of running. "Look at what they did to Jared!"

Chase pulls out a Gelcuff Gun and shoots Todd, knocking him out before he can get too close. He collapses to the floor twenty feet away. The Hoverslab flies past him and lands next to the one that brought the Hodge family in.

A doctor holding Avery in some sort of protected carrier carefully steps off the Hoverslab, her cries growing in volume as the doctor walks closer.

Jared remains motionless in his chair on the Hoverslab, staring idly and drooling, completely unfazed by the scene his father just created. One of the doctors unfastens his seatbelt and gently grabs his hand to help him off the platform. Jared turns to face Alessa's direction, revealing severely cracked skin across his face. There is a deep split in his bottom lip.

Alessa can hear David beginning to cry behind her, breathing in short, shallow breaths. She looks back at David to find him staring at Jared, terrified. Emily puts her arm around him and attempts to cover his eyes.

"Jared!" David yells, swatting his mom's hands away. "Jared!" David gets Jared's attention the second time, and Jared slowly turns his head and faces David's direction.

Jared walks slowly towards the Hodge family. Liam and Emily give uneasy looks to one another, unsure if they should stop Jared from coming over to them, or if they should let their son see his best friend.

Before they can make a decision, Jared is standing right in front of all of them.

59

ALESSA

Jared's eyes look empty. The rash on his skin from the mosaic exposure has intensified greatly—glowing a hot red—already blistering, cracking, and peeling. There is a patch of hair missing on the back of his head where the Splitchip was installed. His eyes are filling with water, his lips trembling. He wipes away a tear.

Emily runs over to hug Jared and pulls him in. "It's okay," she says. Tears begin running down his face as he gives in to Emily's embrace and slumps into her chest. She instinctively puts her hand on his head, accidentally bumping the Splitchip suture, which is still raw and healing. He winces in pain. Emily glances over to Liam and waves him over. He walks over and places his hand on Jared's back.

"I miss my mom," Jared says, pulling away as he wipes tears off of his face. "It's not fair."

"I know it's not fair," Liam says. He shakes his head sadly as he looks down at Jared. "It isn't."

"We'll protect you," Emily says. "Don't worry."

David walks over, staring at Jared intensely, unable to hide the concern on his face as he hugs him.

"I'm scared," Jared whispers to David, still hugging him. "I feel like I'm going crazy." Jared turns to show David the Splitchip suture and points to it. "This made it worse."

"And my baby sister," Jared says, turning and pointing to Avery, who is still crying inside of the carrier. He turns back around to face David. Jared has a fearful, haunted look on his face, and he breathes rapidly as he continues to talk. "My dad can't take care of her. He has lost his mind. You all just saw it. He's been scaring me . . . Something really bad happened to him. I'm scared it's happening to me too. We both went in there. Through the portal."

Before any of them can respond, Veda flies back into the Bodcan library with the others. "We found two Invisidome canisters," she says, switching out of DroneMode and walking towards them. "There's probably more up there if we—" Veda stops when she notices Jared standing there with his cracking, red skin.

Alessa steps forward and kneels in front of Jared. "It's going to be okay, sweetie," Alessa says, holding his hand gently. She remembers the first time she met Jared, in the basement at the Morgan household—how she healed his broken nose and had the same motherly urge to call him 'sweetie' then, too.

Jared stares at Alessa, silently for a moment. Then he unloads a deep, tragic cry, sobbing as he leans forward into Alessa. She hugs him and rubs his back as she holds him.

"I'm sorry for everything you've had to go through," Alessa says, holding back tears. "We're going to do everything we can to make this better."

"Do you promise?" Jared asks between sniffles, a stream of snot flowing from his nose.

"I promise," Alessa says. She stands up slowly, lets go of his hand, and repeats herself. "I promise."

Alessa looks at Liam and Emily as they put their arms around Jared again.

"We'll take it from here," Liam says. "Do what you need to do to make sure we can get out of here safely."

Alessa nods and turns to face Veda. "Nice work finding the Invisidome canisters," Alessa says, regrouping as they begin to walk towards the mosaic. "No need to look for more. Two will be plenty for what we need right now. Chase, is there anything we should know about the canisters before we get started?"

"There's a button on the top of the canister," Chase says as he runs over to catch up to Alessa as they walk. He points to the device. "Once you know where you want to put it, lay the flat side down on the ground. Press the button on the top—it'll clamp to the ground and project the Invisidome. The button is also a size dial. Turn it to the right to make the dome larger and to the left to make it smaller. The largest setting can cover an area of up to five miles, so that is more than enough space for all of us humans to cram into temporarily."

"Got it," Alessa says. "And just to confirm, the walls are impenetrable, right?"

"Correct," Chase says.

"Is there a way that I, along with the other Splitbots, can exit and enter the dome?" Alessa asks. "We'll need to be able to get out of the dome in order to figure out an escape from the realm. Who knows how far away the other portals will be."

"Of course," Chase says. "There's a passcode that you can enter into Resosuits that allow you to walk—or fly—right through the dome walls. It's called a Domecode. They're randomly generated after the dome is active. It will appear on the screen just below the dial after the dome is activated. Hold your Kaxelotab up to the canister and it will automatically connect through your Aura-Fi."

Alessa stops in front of the mosaic and databursts to every single Splitbot in the base. "Everyone, now is our time to escape. Head down to the Bodcan library and follow us through the portal. There's no need to guard the top floors any longer. The missiles are on their way as we speak. We need to evacuate the base immediately. We have all come way too far to be destroyed in this awful place. I want every single one of you to be there when we welcome our brothers and sisters to their new bodies in the realm."

Without saying anything else, Alessa walks through the portal, and Veda and Ty follow behind her.

60

ALESSA

"Can we set up the Invisidome to cover the portal?" Ty asks, looking at the mosaic behind him. "That way there shouldn't be any risk of mosaic poisoning for any of the humans, if they're never *truly* exposed to the realm."

"I'll try," Alessa says. "I don't see why it wouldn't work."

Alessa kneels to place the canister on the ground just as Chase explained, directly in front of the portal. She feels the device click as she presses the button, and three prongs eject from the sides of the canister and burrow into the ground.

The Invisidome canister begins to spin as the center opens. A ring of micro-projectors extricates itself from the center, blasting upwards and creating a pole of a material reminiscent of Splitwall technology. The pole extends 500 feet upwards, then the walls of the dome—beautifully iridescent and glistening—ooze their way outwards, seemingly out of thin air, until Alessa, Veda, and Ty are completely encapsulated.

Alessa looks up at the sea in the sky, the view of which is now slightly distorted from inside of the dome. The walls of the Invisidome make it appear soft—almost blurry—and the edges of the black, circular opening up in the sky blend into the surrounding purple mass.

The mosaic sits at the very center of the dome, protected from the rest of the realm. Suddenly, the thousands of Gridliners that were spread throughout the base begin to fly through the mosaic and flood into the Invisidome as they evacuate the base.

Alessa turns the Invisidome size dial all the way up and watches as the dome extends smoothly out into the distance.

The Domecode Chase mentioned appears on the canister screen. Alessa holds her Kaxelotab up to it—a green check mark appears on the canister screen to indicate that her connection was accepted.

"Everyone," Alessa databursts to the group as soon as the others finish flying through. "Hold your Kaxelotabs up to the canister. This will give you the Domecode you need to get in and out of the dome. While you do that, Ty and Veda, please lead the humans in—the Hodge and the Morgan families, Elise, and all of the doctors and scientists."

Veda and Ty immediately switch to DroneMode and fly through the portal to start leading everyone through.

Alessa quickly tests the Domecode. She flies up 500 feet to the topmost part of the dome, feeling no resistance whatsoever when she slowly passes through it. Everyone and everything inside of the dome disappears as Alessa flies upwards and exits the dome, looking down at it—the Invisidome technology even completely concealing the bright light of the portal.

Alessa flies back down into the Invisidome. She switches out of DroneMode as she approaches the ground and finds that most of the humans have already worked their way through—seemingly unharmed.

Moxie is sniffing the ground frantically, probably confused by the influx of scents in the realm. David is standing next to Jared as he looks up at the sky, taking it all in. Jared, however, is shaking in fear and looking at the ground, as if doing everything in his power to avoid looking up. Chase, along with the other doctors and scientists, is examining everything. Some of the base staff are kneeling to touch the soil, while others look up at the sky in awe.

"How are you all feeling?" Alessa asks the Hodge family—huddled closely together, nervously holding each other's hands—as she approaches them.

"A little bit of a tickle walking through that portal," William says. "Felt like the hair on my arms was being burned off."

Liam and Emily glance at each other, still confused by William's openness with the robots. Nora, however, is watching her husband carefully, clearly amused by William's unexpected positivity.

Alessa's attention turns back to the portal, and she watches as Ryan walks through it carrying the still-unconscious Elise. Elise is a spitting image of her mother. She looks exactly like a younger version of Anita.

Behind Ryan is another doctor, carrying Todd Morgan's still-unconscious body, followed by another doctor carrying Avery, who is still double-protected inside of the carrier.

"Do you all feel okay?" Ty asks Ryan and Chase. "No nausea or anything?"

"Like the old man said," Ryan says. "Just a little bit of a burning sensation walking through the portal, but so far so good."

"The smell is a little . . . assaulting," Chase says, scrunching his face in disgust. "That might make me nauseous in a little bit."

"I believe that's everyone, though," Ryan says as Chase holds his stomach, gagging and fighting the urge to vomit. "All of the humans, anyways."

"All of the Gridliners are in as well," Alessa says. She looks at the thousands of Splitbots spreading throughout the realm—both inside and outside of the Invisidome.

Suddenly, the sound of a massive explosion can be heard coming from the mosaic. Everyone inside of the realm looks in the same direction, silent and listening closely.

"It's happening," Veda says. "The attack."

Bara runs over to the portal. "Keo!" she screams. "Everyone get away from the portal!"

The movements of the mosaic's tiles begin to speed up rapidly, bubbling.

"What's happening?" Liam asks.

"I'm getting databursts from Keo," Bara says as she frantically turns to face the doctors and scientists. "You all need to get away from the portal! Now!"

The humans begin to run away from the mosaic without asking any questions, quickly distancing themselves from the portal.

Alessa and the other Gridliners organize themselves in the space between the humans and the portal to create a body-blocking barrier that will protect them from whatever might happen to the portal once the explosion reaches the Bodcan library.

Bara is still standing by the portal. She says something inaudible to herself, then kneels to give the Gridat. She quickly gets up, switches to DroneMode, and flies over to Alessa and the others—just in time to escape the portal's destruction.

The explosion is so loud—amplified in the confined space of the dome—that the humans collapse to the ground, temporarily paralyzed by the noise. Alessa watches in awe as a wave of bright purple light is emitted from the direction of the portal. The sea in the sky begins swirling faster, reacting to the destruction of the portal.

The mosaic portal begins to oscillate rapidly as it shrinks in on itself, reducing to individual cubes, each one disappearing one at a time. A wave of heat blasts through the inside of the Invisidome. In a matter of seconds, the entire set of cubes disappears into thin air, leaving nothing behind as they burn out of reality.

The stillness after the disappearance of the portal—of Keo—is short-lived. Bara runs over to where the portal once was, screaming and crying.

"There are no more databursts from him," Bara says. She sobs as she kneels in the sand where the portal was. "He is gone."

Alessa flies over to her, switches out of DroneMode, and kneels next to her.

"Bara," Alessa says. "Keo saved all of us. He is a hero."

"He's gone," Bara whispers sadly, looking up at Alessa with pleading eyes. "Let's make this all worth something."

"We will," Alessa says, beginning to stand up. "I promise."

Alessa continues to kneel there for a moment with Bara as she calms down. After a couple of minutes, Alessa receives a databurst from Ke.

"Alessa," Ke databursts, a sense of elation in his datavoice. "It worked! Most of us have our portals open, and we've controlled the Splitbots into the realm. I can't see you anywhere. Are you guys okay? The latching has already started!"

"Ke!" Alessa databursts immediately, jumping up in surprise. "I'm so relieved to hear you. I knew you guys could do it! And yes, we're safe. We're all safe. The humans too. We're in the realm. You can't see us because we're inside of an Invisidome to protect the humans. I'll come to you. Send me your Splitpath coordinates."

Alessa quickly turns to everyone else. "It worked!" she yells. "The other portals—they're open! I just got a databurst from Ke. He said the latching is already happening."

"Holy shit," Ty says, running over to her. He picks her up and hugs her tightly. All of the other Gridliners are cheering and jumping with excitement. The humans get up from the sand slowly and carefully and watch the thousands of Gridliners celebrating joyfully.

The other Gridliners and Splitbot bodies can be seen faintly beyond the dome. Alessa looks up at the sky, now swirling faster than ever as hundreds of thousands of souls begin to shoot downward.

Alessa accepts the Splitpath from Ke and shares it with all of the other Gridliners in the dome.

"Don't worry," Alessa says to the humans. "We'll be back shortly. You'll all be safe inside the dome. It won't be long until we're out of here."

Chase and Ryan nod at Alessa, both sharing the same bug-eyed, speechless expression. They tilt their heads up slowly to get a better look at the sky, their eyebrows rising in awe as they take in the sight. The Hodge family is next to them, doing the same exact thing.

Alessa switches to DroneMode and leads all of the Gridliners as they fly up and out of the Invisidome to take in the incredible sight of what's happening beyond it.

New mosaic portals from each of the other 300 Splitbases glow brightly as far as Alessa's eyes can see, spanning thousands of miles across the surface of the realm, oscillating and allowing for three million Splitbots to enter the realm.

The sea in the sky is swirling ferociously. Gridliner souls begin to shoot down and latch to the surplus of Splitbots congregating on the ground below. The black circle in the sky is getting bigger by the second, rapidly increasing in size as more souls leave the sky.

"I've never seen the sky this active!" Ty databursts. They follow the Splitpath to Ke, flying through the air while dodging the storm of souls that shoot past them.

Alessa and Ty switch out of DroneMode and land on the ground directly in front of Ke, immediately hugging him.

"Look at this!" Ke says to Alessa. He points excitedly at the sky with a radiant smile on his face. A stream of souls continues to shoot down. "We did it! There are Splitbots at each portal to guard them, so we won't have to worry about any other humans or SMID agents entering the realm. We'll need to figure out a safe way out of here, but that shouldn't be an issue. We have numbers on our side now."

Over a million Gridliners have already successfully latched to the Splitbots, and a wave of intense celebration erupts as they come to consciousness. The palpable joy of the celebrating crowd spans miles—millions of Splitbots running to hug each other, screaming with joy and greeting loved ones they haven't seen since the KitD'ul.

Alessa, Ty, and Ke watch as the latching continues, savoring this moment of success until the latching is complete and every single Splitbot in the realm houses a Gridliner soul. A cacophony of sound continues to erupt from the millions of Gridliners.

Veda, Bara, and Olos land next to Alessa. Bara runs to Ke and hugs him. Veda and Olos run to the nearest part of the celebrating crowd and join them.

Ty turns to face Alessa. "This is all because of you," he says, smiling sweetly, his eyes filled with tears. "*You* saved us all."

"This is because of all of us, not just me," Alessa says, her own smile becoming a look of determination. She looks back up at the sea in the sky. "Of course I'm happy that three million Gridliner souls just escaped from the sky, but that is only the tip of the iceberg—I guess I feel bittersweet because I can't help but focus on the fact that a billion more Gridliner souls still remain trapped up there."

"I get that," Ty says, looking up at the sky with Alessa as the others continue to celebrate. "But there are three million of us. We have time before we can realistically travel the universe and get off of Earth. We can make however many Splitbot bodies we need to get the others out while we're stuck on this planet. Yes, there are still others up there, but now there is an absolute guarantee that they too will be able to house a Splitbot body. You should be proud, Alessa. We've come a long way."

"We have," Alessa says, nodding. "But our journey is just beginning."

Alessa's gaze turns from the celebrations to the portals, and she stares at the seemingly perfect line of mosaics stretching as far as she can see without digitally enhancing her sight.

"They're just as beautiful as ever," Ty says, looking at the portals as well.

Alessa nods in agreement, then looks back up at the sky. She stares at the giant hole, hypnotized by it.

Wondering what lies beyond.

ACKNOWLEDGMENTS

Special thanks to Kyle Rubin, who was the first to read *Through the Mosaic*. Your feedback throughout this entire process has made an enormous impact on the final product, and I wouldn't have been able to write this book at all without your support.

To my editors, Josiah Davis and Cameron Heyliger of JD Book Services, thank you for your attention to detail. The quality of this book was improved immensely by your creative solutions to the many problems in my original draft, and I can't thank you enough for your patience.

I'd also like to thank fellow author K.J. Beck, whose guidance on the craft of writing and publishing helped get this book across the finish line. Our conversations have impacted me more than you know.

And most importantly, thank you to Katie Meyers, for always supporting my crazy ideas. I am so lucky to have you by my side, forever.

Thank you for your support!

Two dollars from every NovelHive book sold goes directly towards funding the next book in our catalog, covering costs such as editing, cover design, and more. By purchasing this book, you not only directly support the author who wrote it but also help fund another author's dream of publishing their own novel.

Visit us at www.novelhive.com to learn more about our mission.